Warning to the Crocodiles

António Lobo Antunes

WARNING TO
THE CROCODILES

Translated from the Portuguese by
Karen C. Sherwood Sotelino

DALKEY ARCHIVE PRESS

Dallas / Dublin

Originally published in Portuguese by Publicações Dom Quixote as *Exortação aos Crocodilos* in 1999

Copyright © 1999 by António Lobo Antunes

Translation copyright © 2021 by Karen C. Sherwood Sotelino

First Dalkey Archive edition, 2021

Print ISBN: 9781943150137
ebook ISBN: 9781628973679
Library of Congress Control Number: 2021936351

www.dalkeyarchive.com
Dallas / Dublin

Printed on permanent/durable acid-free paper

Contents

Introduction

READERS FAMILIAR WITH António Lobo Antunes's novels will recognize in *Warning to the Crocodiles* the detailed access to characters' acute sensitivity, which requires no suspension of disbelief. On the contrary, the characters' inner lives are so well developed that we may occasionally long for distance from these troubled individuals. They inhabit various neighborhoods in Lisbon in the years following the 1974 Carnation Revolution, although specifying precise location runs contrary to the author's purposeful distortion of surroundings through characters' impressionistic memories.

Published in the original in 1999, *Warning to the Crocodiles* is Lobo Antunes's fifteenth novel, among nearly forty to date. The author is a practicing psychiatrist, and served as a medical officer in the Portuguese army in Angola. Several of his earlier works, including *The Land at the End of the World*, *Fado Alexandrino*, *Knowledge of Hell*, *The Inquisitors' Manual*, and *The Return of the Caravels* deal directly or indirectly with the material and psychological effects of Portugal's colonial wars (1961-1974) and the forty-two years of authoritarian rule under the Estado Novo.[1] In his characteristic style, disclosure of narrative events occurs through flashback. In *Warning to the Crocodiles*, the memories are clouded by each protagonist's tendency to justify as they recall. The characters are among those whose lives have been upended during Portugal's transition from authoritarian to democratic rule. Struggling to readjust, they resort to a series of violent crimes revealed as they are juxtaposed with each character's childhood memories.

Four female voices describe the attempts of their frustrated lovers and

---

[1] The dictatorial regime was introduced by António Salazar (1932-1968) and continued under Marcelo Caetano (1968-1974), who was forced to resign as a result of the 1974 Carnation Revolution, a coup led by the Portuguese army.

partners to regain political power; meanwhile, the men's actions shape and distort the women's worlds. In a manner similar to *The Inquisitors' Manual*, these narrative voices unravel trivial problems and observations, eventually woven back together exposing the cruel, grotesque subversive acts the women either deduce or take part in. The central characters are Mimi, a nearly deaf woman, married to a wealthy man, presumably in business; Fátima, a high-strung woman who has left her husband for her godfather, a bishop; Celina, a self-indulgent, beautiful woman involved with Mimi's husband; and Simone, a poor, overweight young woman who lives in Mimi's garage with the family driver, who is a mechanic. Each of these four women's lives, their families, schooling, jobs and relationships are explored through stream-of-consciousness memories. What they notice and recall, what they feel, what irritates and pleases them are offered gradually. Mimi repeatedly summons the brandy smell of her grandmother's braid. Celina is obsessed with her stuffed Mickey Mouse, her box of silkworms, and being tossed playfully in the air as a child. Fátima despises the men in her life for loving her and cannot restrain herself from deriding their smallest mannerisms. Simone, a dull outsider, reminisces longingly for the familiar disdain she experienced in her childhood. Rewardingly, the continuous blending of these observations, memories and obsessions culminates in the apprehension of the women's identities, how they either married or became involved with their men, and the extent to which they understand, approve, disapprove or even care about their crimes.

Through the women's voices the pieces of a dangerous, incendiary puzzle come together. Their husbands and lovers have persisted in a fragmentary plot to take back the country after the 1974 Carnation revolution. These secondary male characters, seen mainly through the women's memories, with occasional intrusions in their own words, are unwaveringly committed to old Portugal, when they were powerful and important. Their blindness to the futility of their endeavor is a result of this ingrained nostalgia. Holdovers from the Estado Novo period, they style themselves as saviors who would return Portugal to the patriarchal, Catholic, inward-looking state in which they had thrived, economically and psychologically. Indeed, the stunning image of Mercês Church and the long shadow it casts over the neighborhood permeates the narrative, "the shadow of Mercês Church, crawling along the plaza, devouring neighbors, grocery crates [...]; no sooner would we turn out the light than Mercês Church would loom over us heavily, darkly." Another religious motif, auditory, comes through Fátima's bishop, whose comment during the counter-revolutionary gatherings is restricted to, "This is a holy war, my friends, a holy war," underscoring the stark irony that these immoral, lawless individuals view their loss of power not only as an injustice, but as an affront to God Himself.

Throughout his fictional, non-linear narrative Lobo Antunes alludes to certain historical personages and events, including the aforementioned 1974 Carnation Revolution. A timeframe is suggested in the first chapter where Mimi recalls in bits and pieces the bombing of an airplane that killed "a minister" at Camarate airport, resembling the actual 1980 Camarate airplane crash that killed then prime-minister Francisco de Sá Carneiro and his minister of defense Adelino Amaro da Costa. The cause of the 1980 crash is controversial to this day. In the novel, Mimi's husband, the wealthy businessman, is a possible generic stand-in for oligarchic interests, while the monocle-wearing general in one the most violent scenes evokes the faction of the military who opposed political change. The fictional mechanic, Simone's partner, is reminiscent of the real-life men who confessed to the Camarate bombing, claiming the CIA had been involved. The cameo appearance of the unnamed U.S. Ambassador is consistent with U.S. foreign policy toward the post-revolutionary government in Portugal.

Over and above the network of allusions, Lobo Antunes's narrative concerns itself fundamentally with the ability of literature to express the human experience. Existential traumas and joys are depicted through brilliant use of metaphor and imagery, with Portugal as the enduring backdrop: "[...] *where at least they'd let me walk in the parks, Campo de Santana or Jardim do Torel, with Lisbon below, navigating its way riverward, sailing along by way of billowing shirts hung out to dry.*" Visual and auditory personification, tree shadows mingling with moon beams, and jays blending into human voices conjure the depths of each character's experience, such as the lonely Simone dropped into an unfamiliar world:

> at night the tree branches rest on the surface of the water mingled with moon beams, the southern breeze shuffles the domino series of canopies where I guess jays have made their nests since the shadows have transformed into jeers that know about the café in Espinho and don't believe it, I hear them urging me . . .

Impressionistic imagery and personification frame the visual and emotional mental flashes, which are seemingly fragmentary, yet suggest broader circumstances the reader must fill in. The profusion of extraordinary sights and sounds put forth by the four voices evokes a mesmerizing narrative world:

> cedars shadows scraping the floorboards, flailing like people drowning in a river, waving good-bye, my husband's driver [...] carrying boxes to the little room in back, I don't really notice the explosions, but the newspapers explain it all, I see the burning buildings, the dead [...] and my husband heading toward me pointing his gun at me

Here the conflated timeframe, a flashback and a flash forward, replicates Mimi's anguish. She sees boxes, burning buildings, her husband pointing a gun at her, and she simultaneously reads about the explosions in the newspaper after the fact—explosions she somehow didn't notice, in spite of her own description. The layering of imagery, "flailing people, cedar shadows," foreshadows drownings, while the shadows' "scraping on the floorboards" engages the depths of the imagination by rousing the sensory discomfort of fear.

Lobo Antunes's metaphoric rendering of sounds, images and emotions is among the great literary pleasures, by virtue of his expressing the ineffable. Sensations and images that usually begin and end with a vague veil of discomfort are suddenly put into words, made palpable: "last week I called my mother and no one answered, the ringing was choking in the empty apartment, you could tell by the echo there wasn't any furniture, the army took it all [...] memories following one after the other tumbling onto the floor, lightness like disoriented dead butterflies, lunches salty with underlying grief and withered years."

The author's malleable use of language extends to wordplay. Below, Celina's recollection of childhood fishing excursions with her father during which the bait—*worms* in the original and *minnows* in the translation—is the refractory nexus to the memory of both her father and her lover:

> the waves dragged up a beret, the body of a rooster, a wicker basket, nothing the slightest bit interesting, boring, taking so long[...] I kneeled down near the can of floundering minnows
>   — *Wee little minnow wee little minnow*

my husband's business partner would call me
— Come here little minnow Mimi is deaf and can't hear
my father, kicking me
— Be quiet

The straightforward image of the bait at once suggests the childhood fishing excursion on banks of the Tagus and the boudoir of the lovers—at least a decade separating the two experiences. "The beret, the dead rooster, nothing the slightest bit interesting" —such images, in juxtaposition with the mention of the lover could make up an entire narrative. Instead of recalling her affair through a whiff of perfume, a taste of wine, or a view of moonbeams over the Tagus, it is her father's berating her, her boredom and desolate surroundings that call her lover to mind.

The same use of imagery, time conflation and personification is used for the all-essential inclusion of humor in a narrative so permeated with sorrow and violence. Mimi and her grandmother undertaking experiments to come up with the recipe for Coca-Cola to make their fortune, Fátima's father trying to regain his singing voice by practicing with a canary, Celina's written notes to her maid involving meticulous negotiations over minutes worked and the placement of bric-a-brac are hilarious, in spite of their pathos. Among the women, Simone's impressions, recollections of her school days and attempt to fit into the world of these people so much wealthier and worldlier than she is, provide the most comic relief. She struggles to answer questions at school: "catechism open at the first page, the teacher swarming over us with her questioning pointer—Who is God? I, enormous in the back row, taking up two spots on the desk bench, could never manage to sharpen a pencil without snapping the point, finish a dictation without knocking over the inkwell." And when God isn't confounding her, it is the Motherland: "the teacher suddenly soared over the classroom holding her pointer—What is the Motherland?" Simone finally decides the Motherland is found precisely where she goes on Sundays, the only girl without a suitor. It is the "marble boxes with scraps of cloak, skulls, and dead things, after the Motherland we'd have tangerine-flavored soft drinks on the river esplanade." Simone has finally discovered the Motherland: the UNESCO World Heritage site, the Jerónimos Monastery on the banks of the Tagus in Lisbon, containing the tombs of renowned Portuguese authors Fernando Pessoa, Almeida Garrett and Alexandre Herculano. The poor girl later is pressed into domestic service when the conspirators come to dine. Unfamiliar with the protocol, of course she spills, "my boyfriend's boss, looking at me as if he were going to kill me, dunked his napkin in the water glass and crawled over, pushing the secretary out of the way, who was at a total loss, agitated as a hen jumping up and down in a loft, asking for stain remover, like a drowning man asking for a beret."

In expressing the full range of human emotion, childhood joy and fear; the hesitant, naïve delving into adulthood and the tangled consequences of each step taken along the way, *Warning to the Crocodiles* is a tour de force. The considerable engagement on the part of both reader and translator to complete the mosaic of memories leads our imaginations into an odyssey. While the reader gathers information at a subconscious level, as translator I had to be steadily aware of tense, voice, and point of view and tread carefully because of the narrative slippage in both time and space. New narratives are embedded when least expected, such as when mid-memory of a childhood outing with her father and uncle, Celina hears the voice of her aesthetician in a phrase she recalls repeatedly, "Don't worry Dona Celina they're expression lines." Each character has recurrent phrases or lesser events that sporadically interrupt their stream-of-conscious and, of course, these must be replicated in translation. This reenactment of the memory at work, the terrified memory struggling to reconcile itself to trauma, is so engaging that the line between what we have read and what we have lived becomes indistinguishable, our perception of our universe has been expanded through fiction. This Lisbon quartet of female voices sheds light on a specific time in contemporary Portuguese history, but the light is brighter on literature itself.

Karen C. Sherwood Sotelino
August, 2020

Warning to the Crocodiles

1

I'D DREAMT OF my grandmother, just before dawn I walked toward the window, avoiding the furniture, floating above the floorboards as if I were still asleep

(my body was the shadow of my body moving weightlessly in my slippers because my real body was still in bed, in this bed or the bed in Coimbra so many years ago, near the tall willows, the grown-up me observing the little me or the little me observing the grown-up me, I don't know)

as I got to the window the bakery's neon sign on the plaza, missing letters, half immersed in my sleepiness and half out, pale against the pale sky and tree branches, blinked above the awning the words mortar shells, then looked at me, realized its mistake and blushing embarrassedly quickly switched to mother's biscuits, and just then I became aware of the smell of brandy, part of my dream

not exactly a dream but the way things used to be in Coimbra, my family's restaurant on the ground floor, the rooms above, my grandmother

Mama Alicia

who didn't speak Portuguese, spoke Galician, and took over the business and household after my grandfather died. Since she couldn't move, on account of her rheumatism, two servant girls bathed her, dressed her, dampened her hair in a basin of brandy and braided it, set her in the chair at the top of the stairs from where she decided on the menus, settled arguments, berated her children, and went over the accounts in a little school notebook every night, my grandmother, authoritarian and crippled, beckoning me with her terrifying finger

— Mimi

shooing away grandchildren and cats, I remember the hens cackling in the yard along with the crackling willow branches, hens and willows relentlessly pecking rubble, I, climbing the staircase fearfully in the hope the stairs would go on forever, thinking

— She's going to hit me

the neon sign suddenly went dark, it was daytime, any minute now they'd raise the goldsmith's roller blinds, any minute now my husband would wake up

— What are you doing come here

the movement under the blankets like a confused stirring animal, awakening slowly, turning into legs and arms, the parts connecting till becoming a man

(when the Tagus grows calm the moon blends the scattered waters)

my grandmother, instead of hitting me, told the servant girls to close the door, wrapped me up in the smell of brandy, leaned into my right ear while, on my left, the hens and willows were quietly respectful, as if the world fell silent upon her wishes, and whispered

— Don't tell anyone I'm going tell you a secret

she knew everything, read magazines in Spanish, recognized the stars

Aldebaran

she offered advice on wills and childbirth, fired cooks, foretold lightning, swore that in Galicia it rains constantly and roses sprout from the ocean, ever since her husband died she always wore white like an old fashioned bride, insisting they bring her wedding orange blossoms in a brushed glass dome that she would set on her lap and no one had the nerve to say anything, the platters would slip by silently, my uncle with the bad lungs would unplug the telephone, my father perched at the cash register would then straighten his tie

Aldebaran

a secret from someone who reads the stars and governs the world, I, making my way again around the furniture, floating over the floorboards and lying down in bed, the confused animal snorted into the pillow, mortar shells, the minister's airplane, the car on the side of the road, my husband's business partner, missing half his head, sliding to the ground, people coming in and out, milling around the garage, vilifying sentences aimlessly suspended, a glare in my direction, I, moving further and further down the hallway carrying the knitting basket, my husband's sleeve, like a bird's wing, sweeping away apprehension

— Say whatever you want Bishop she's deaf can't hear a thing

Aldebaran, Galicia where it rains constantly, roses sprout from the ocean, I bought her a special telephone with a little blinking light, if you pick up the receiver and listen, Bishop, Excellency, you won't hear a thing, just squeaking and more squeaking, distorted squeals, tell me another one about the communist priest, I, with my expressionless deaf smile, my grandmother perched on her throne mixed soda water, coffee and sugar with mysterious artifice, she couldn't let go of the fear a conspiring relative, or even her own children might bribe a kitchen maid, I haven't forgotten the smell of the brandy soaked braid

Mama Alicia

I wake up with it in my dreams, find it on the pillow, in the sheets, in the trees on the plaza

I swear

— Don't tell anyone I taught you the Coca-Cola recipe

it's the Americans' advantage, makes them win wars and get rich, I was going to be so rich

— You're going to be very rich Mimi you'll marry a count

the queen of New York, owned every movie theater in Galicia and Portugal, twenty buildings in Coimbra, Ford motors, my grandmother and I, grave conspirators, the roller blinds down, sipping our concoction, goose bumps at the thought of our future riches, dirty clothes baskets brimming with currency, drawers sagging under the weight of coins, a gardener and butler, when months later they took her away, skin and bones, breathing through but a tiny corner of her lungs, to die in hospital

the car on the side of the road and my husband's business partner, missing half his head, sliding to the ground

she ordered the firemen carrying the stretcher to stop, warning me, she was nervous the family or the Americans would discover the recipe or that I would cross paths with the men with the machine guns on my way home from school, my grandmother's tongue dragging each word up to her mouth like a bucket of stones

— Don't tell anyone

I didn't tell anyone, Grandma, and I don't own movie theaters, I'm not rich, didn't marry a count

— I bought her a special telephone with a blinking light say whatever you want bishop she's deaf can't hear a thing

I remember the braid swaying on the stretcher as it was carried down the stairs, the

smell of brandy embalming the house, the ambulance jolting down the alley, that smell of brandy, perfume of saints, incense and lilies, I remember being afraid the nurses or doctors would use a pair of scissors to cut her braids, Galicia must still be the same, the constant rain, the mist over the waves, the hungry pigeons, roses sprouting from the ocean, my husband

— When we were courting she had this song and dance she was going to be a millionaire because she knew the formula for Coca-Cola the deaf are strange different than you and me they live on another planet

Aldebaran

just do like me don't pay any attention to her figure out a way to deal with the problem of the priest give me a few days let me talk to the boys

my husband was no count Grandma, I didn't marry a count, he would wait for me outside the Institute, wearing expensive clothes, a medallion on a chain around his neck, his cigarette lighter in a satin case, restaurants where the chickens and willows were kept out of the dining room, unlike Coimbra, where they blended right in with the geranium dust and peacocks in heat, unmended tablecloths, unbent forks, clean silverware, an absence of sport pendants, calendars, my mother not in the kitchen, if I leaned over to look I wouldn't see her stuck between stoves, rubbing ice over her forehead

— Your heart won't last dona Rosário

warning me

— How should I know what he's after or maybe I do they all want the same thing how do you think I got pregnant with you and I'm not deaf I can hear a mile away

— Mother

— We took her to the doctor and the doctor you understand, sir, stuck some little funnels in her and looked inside with a flashlight turns out she's not stupid she's sick

I was so embarrassed

— Don't say that Mother

— Just look how funny listen here be quiet Mimi I'm trying to figure out your future because if the gentleman insists on marriage it's up to him I warned him

so I'd dreamt of my grandmother, just before dawn I walked toward
the window avoiding the furniture, floating above the floor as if I were
still asleep in a body that was the shadow of my body, moving weightlessly in my slippers, because my real body was still in bed watching me,
grown-up me watching little me or little me watching grown-up me,
or little and grown-up me in my husband's office the day the minister's
airplane, the two men I didn't recognize hesitating, my husband, not
irritated with me

— So?

just like that

— So?

which I could tell not by the sound of his voice, but by the reflection
in the window of his moving eyebrows and lips, made larger by a distortion in the glass and amplifying his words

— So?

the two men looked like they worked at the airport, their uniforms too
big, staring at me, staring at him, staring at me again, not understanding
my wife lives in a glass bell of silence, nods her head pretending, smiles
pretending, agrees pretending

— Of course

the two idiots, as if I had all the time in the world to hear about the
bomb, as if they didn't need to get across the border, cool down in Spain

where roses sprout from the ocean my grandma said

that's to say, I'm not going to argue over this, where roses sprout from
the ocean and old ladies in braids make Coca-Cola with soda water, sugar
and coffee, my wife not facing me, but the window over the plaza like
on happy mornings

happy, imagine that

when she dreamt of Coimbra and a miserable brick tavern, with more chickens than clients, fish and rice casserole, pork steaks, bread casseroles, her paradise, a pauper's paradise, obvious from the upstairs rooms where the five or six of them slept, the ragged blankets, doorless closets, wobbly chairs in the living room where I never risked sitting down, the little sofa patched up with masking tape, ceramic doves with broken beaks and beyond all this, permeating the whole place, occupying the whole place, the smell of the dead old woman's brandy soaked braid, the holder of the secret Coca-Cola formula that was to make them rich, buy plaster pineapples to decorate their entryway and send their sick uncle for the sanatorium cure he needed, mortar shells, my husband's eyebrows and lips in his office window, distorted by the uneven glass, the gigantic buildings surrounding the plaza

— Did they at least deliver the order in good condition?

the bishop kissing the crucifix

— this is a holy war this is a holy war
the minister's airplane on a rooftop near the airport in the Camarate neighborhood, airport workers waiting for the van in back, neighbors looking out their windows stunned at the wings, the smoke, what they called dead bodies but were nothing but dark blots, stones, bricks, parts connecting till there's a man, the Tagus growing calm, the moon blending the scattered waters, my husband under the glaring phosphorus of the sheets

— What are you doing come here

I don't hear people, or the telephone, or the doorbell, but nonetheless I hear mundane sounds, the oven, clocks, crackling wood, rattling pipes, anxiety-ridden plants languishing on the veranda, the house's distress and suffering, an extension of my own distress and suffering, a different skin covering my skin with its own incomprehensible innards and nervous vibrations, what was left of the airplane wavering on the rooftop, the airport workers jogging to the van, hidden under their caps, eyebrows and lips thickened in the window reflection, orderly, mute, tucked away in Spain, no phone calls, no letters, just like they told me

— Leave this place

whenever the bishop, or his business partner sliding through the weeds on the roadside, or the general would arrive, the business partner's widow attentive in the entry hall, nary a sign of disgust, protest, teardrops, her makeup intact, not a hair out of place, her eyebrows and mouth to me

— Leave this place

and I understood, just like my father talking to the workers in the restaurant in Coimbra, he'd straighten himself, run his hands through his gelled hair and the workers would lift the platters, the widow wandering through the living room with my husband didn't greet me the same as my mother didn't greet me, didn't speak, didn't see the servant girls, wandering through the living room, talking to the commander and driver who'd ambushed the dead man, they'd stopped his car, shattered the windshield with their machine guns, watched carefully as he shook and kept shaking round after round, and now they got up, set down their glasses and buttoned their jackets to greet me, and then I understood

you didn't understand for the love of God, you didn't understand a thing, it had nothing to do with my partner's wife, what stupidity, not in your wildest imagination, it had nothing to do with revenge, it was to save the Country from the leftists, from what those same leftists insisted on calling colonies, killing thousands of Portuguese in Africa taking the very clothes off the backs of those who managed to escape death, to take back the country starting at the Spanish border, Franco on our side, the Spanish Civil Guard, the Portuguese National Republican Guard on our side the North on our side, the Church on our side, half the army, because in spite of everything we still had an army, on our side

I approached, scared

— You're going to beat me

— *I'm not going to beat you why in God's name would I beat you shut up* movement under the blanket like a confused stirring animal, awakening slowly, turning into legs, fingers, arms, the neon light over the plaza café, missing letters, half immersed inside my sleepiness and half out, pale against the pale sky and tree branches, any minute now they'd raise the goldsmith's roller blinds, any minute now school and the factory chimney

—What are you doing come here

hot and humid, rushing roosters, my father's hand fixing his gelled hair, the servants lifting the platters, moving through the restaurant among the feathers, my husband

— Get undressed

— *You're going to hurt me you're going to beat me*

— Nonsense be quiet stop with your foolishness undress open the bedside table drawer and get the pistol

— *But what pistol but what pistol undress*

I, missing half my head, sliding off the bed I

or a stone, a brick, or a burnt branch

covered with part of a bag at the airport near Camarate, a woman's shoe among the ashes, the remains of a shawl and my hair was still burning, my nail polish was still burning and I know I was dreaming because of the smell of brandy, the throne at the top of the staircase, my grandmother looking up from the accounts in the school notebook

— Wake up Mimi wake up

filled with messy numbers on parcels, lopsided and torn from the pressure of the pencil, my husband

— Wake up

— *She'd never wake up in the morning must be cause she's deaf my mother-in-law warned me that the deaf*

I wanted to wake up so I wouldn't die, to keep the former secret police from setting the house on fire like they did the schools, parliamentarians' houses, party headquarters

my mother-in-law told me the deaf are different from us, self-centered, insensitive, she was the only one who didn't shed a tear when her grandmother died, the family in mourning at the burial and she, her ringlets styled with her father's hair gel and wearing her new dress, getting herself dirty kneeling at the washtub, surrounded by curious little chicks, with a bottle of soda water, a pot of coffee and a canister of sugar, ignoring the guests, the funeral procession, the mass, the urn being carried away, the condolences, making some strange mixture and drinking it, talking to herself

— *No, it's not right*

kneeling near the washtub as if she planned on blending into the dirt or as if she were part of it which I sometimes think she is, no more than an umbrella stand, a clothes hanger, a piece of furniture, anything, an inert thing that never answers and doesn't seem to see, feels nothing, doesn't get excited, never touches the scarves and rings I give her, wears the same smocks as the restaurant servant girls, the workers in Coimbra, without understanding what I did or caring about what I did, I'd wake up and find her staring down at the plaza, I'd touch her shoulder and my wife would push me away as if I were holding a shotgun when all I wanted was to calm her

— *Don't shoot*

tiny, in a corner of the bed her knees tucked under her chin

— *Don't shoot*

my husband

— *Undress*

and me protecting myself with the pillow, sheets, bedspread

— Don't shoot

the bakery sign in the mirror mortar shells mortar shells mortar shells looking at me, realizing its mistake blushing embarrassedly quickly switching to mother's biscuits so I stopped trying to get away

— *She saw something in the mirror who knows what let go of the pillow the sheets the bedspread her eyes changed she calmed down stopped trying to get away from me*

the plaza trees entered the room one by one, the wind off the river, not the Mondego river, but the Tagus, dispelling the smell of brandy, the firemen carrying the braid jolting down the staircase

good-bye grandma

I hope the nurses and doctors didn't cut off her braid at the hospital, since there was no money to pay for a decent funeral, a casket covered with Galician roses sprouted from the ocean, when they told me she'd died I hid by the washtub, to make the Coca-Cola so I could pay for the funeral she deserved, a woman who sat on a throne and decided on menus, settled arguments, did the accounting in a little school notebook amid the cackling hens and leaves and I still couldn't hit on the right amounts of coffee and sugar, I tasted and tried again, pouring from the bottle

— No, that's not right

till my family got back from the cemetery, noticed the stains on my dress and beat me, their eyebrows and lips moving soundlessly and yelling at me, the quiet wind in the willows, Lorde galloping every which way shuddering mute barks, a year later they sold the restaurant, I found my grandma's chair with no brandy smell, no damask, no springs, no trinkets hanging from the back like a gypsy camp, then I understood that she was dead and I started to cry

— She saw something in the mirror who knows what let go of the pillow the sheets the bedspread stopped trying to get away from me her eyes changed and she started to cry for no reason not like a woman but like a grieving child and as she cried she wiped her face with her nightgown trimming, it had to be today just when the bishop's coming for dinner, my partner's widow and another guest whose name excuse me but the less said about certain topics the better it's best to remain silent I took her by the elbow and she stared at me from the depths of her sleep and I said

— Wake up

as the school bell made the curtains vibrate, they lifted the goldsmith's roller shade, the factory chimney whitened the plaza a few years ago we had some problems with some guy who denounced us in court when we managed to catch him that's how he acted, that winter we took him to the sand dunes at the beach in Guincho, tears and more tears, no remorse, tears the raging waves and the fellow in tears, the commander told him

— *Wake up*

· *like me to Mimi*

— *Wake up*

and the man was shaking, we didn't do anything to him, left him in the bushes under the thundering north wind, later I found out that the next day the train dragged him along the coast from Cascais to Estoril, my mother-in-law swore over a thousand times the deaf

so I was in bed next to my husband, the brandy smell evaporating, I was gradually recognizing the room, the lamps, the vanity, realizing I'm not poor, don't always have to wear the same blouse, same skirt, same pair of shoes, and they didn't sell my earrings so we could eat

my mother-in-law swore it was typical of the deaf, strange, they'd confound anyone with their unexpected reactions, she told me over a thousand times

— *Be careful sir*

better not marry her, just live with her and help us out a bit

— *Life is tough for us here in the provinces you understand?*

above all, don't marry her

with that, the sun sliding across the floorboards leaped on top of the wool blanket, lighting up a rectangular patch of green and blue, the bottle of soda water disappeared, Coimbra disappeared, they didn't beat me, they didn't scold me, my husband took me by the elbow, one of his pajama buttons was missing and his hair needed combing

— *Run along next time no more nonsense she stopped crying and smiled at me*

and I woke up.

2

I'M AWAKE UP but don't speak to me till eleven cause I'm a surly cat. I meander around the house, my eyes still shut, bumping into furniture, battling the sun and cursing the world, the sun, of course, pretends it's on its way out and comes right back like some stubborn beast, ingratiating, unbearable, friendly, I don't need friends so I shake it off

— Leave me alone

or I point to the window

— Get out

and the house darkens, I turn on the faucet, splash water on my face and it hurts my skin, I switch on the kitchen light and acid brightness fills my eyelids, I turn on the stove burner and gas spits rancid heat up my nose, the sun doesn't give up, spills over the dishwasher, rubbing up against me, I scrub it with the scouring pad and the darned thing escapes me runs to the fridge laughing, it shines on the jar sitting on the place-mat, licks my chin, hides in the peaches in the fruit bowl, reappears on the floor tiles, full of itself, so I lift my foot slowly, cautiously, disguising my intention to squish it, but the sun gets away, rolls itself up in the living room curtains, sulking

— Good riddance

I just want to sleep, to go back to the warm, hollow, pleasant place that is me, back to my ideal sleep, in color

(never to happen again, naturally)

where, with a little leap, I'd fly from the ground floor down to the cellar, flying over the stairs like a fluttering plane leaf, the slightest draft elevating me with grace I'd never had, I hovered, stretched, brushed against the ceiling, did somersaults without messing up my hair, the sun, having forgotten its sulking, wavered on the kitchen door knob, I was cutting open the milk carton, unable to open my eyes and swat it, I felt like strangling the electric alarm clock, getting rid of that horrible bell for once and for all, just pulling the plug and turning it off, watching the numbers fade, plead

— Don't kill us

I squeezed the milk carton by accident and a trickle of foam ran down my knee like a worm, I moved my hand without letting go of the scissors

(from the corner of my eye I espied the sun, on the tip of the scissors, obviously)

and I poked myself

turn off the alarm clock, turn off the world, peace and quiet, lie down, the trees in Campo de Santana park, black all year round were having the time of their lives at my expense, imitating the geese and swans on the lake, one of these days I swear I'm going to put cockroach poison in their breadcrumbs, I sensed my godfather's bathrobe coming into the kitchen, the sun on his lapel, I blindly grabbed the first pot within reach to chase away the sun, the terrified trees and birds bowed and that was the end of them, the sniveling, shrunken bathrobe

— Fátima

the skittish sun, afraid of me, climbed inside the toaster, I tried lifting my left eyelid a teensy bit groping for the universe and came across the dinner dishes announcing in their whiny little voice

—We're dirty

piles of dust, eggshells scattered on the floor, the entire planet complaining, I dropped the pot and headed toward the sun porch

— Don't any of you say anything to me

don't say anything because till 11:00 I'm a surly cat, from over by the laundry basin the plastic tub filled with soaking clothes blamed me, the bottle of detergent begged me to do the washing, the stepladder leaning against the wall looked my way

I'm absolutely sure

with melancholy resignation, hurt because I hadn't put it away, the apartment was weeping because I don't like it, I let the potatoes sprout, don't paint the closet, don't replace the broken roof tiles, allow the bills to pile up on the olive-oil-stained counter, my godfather's bathrobe hung up, solemnly

(I don't need to lift an eyelid, I know him inside out)

as he always did, pausing theatrically, on the verge of joining the apartment's chorus, I plugged my ears to block them all out

— For the love of God would you all stop

precisely when my head was about to burst, the sun pursuing me relentlessly, the telephone in the den started writhing in one of those aneurysmal fits, flaming wires burning our brains out, my cold bed, my dream of flying lost, my eyes open, the bathrobe with imbecile amiability

— Good morning

like my husband used to do

— Good morning

not realizing what a stupid thing that is to say, not realizing I didn't want to be kissed, didn't want any attention or tenderness, I didn't want to hear a single word, I wanted to be left alone to sip coffee and smoke cigarettes till Campo de Santana park calmed down, till the house calmed down, till the universe finally calmed down, my godfather exchanging his bathrobe for his cassock, his cross, bishop's ring, the sugary syrup at the bottom of the coffee cup covered in ashes till I, bundled up in my bath towel, wearing my hand towel turban, was able to smile at myself in the mirror, dissolve my surly mood into surly bitterness, get dressed, put on my makeup, quiet down the apartment by putting on my rubber gloves and cleaning the kitchen, raising the blinds, and putting away sandals and stockings upstairs, no longer such a mysterious place, no more taking flight, the numbers on the alarm clock would change in metallic flips, the room where my husband, bless his soul, didn't exist nor did I have to blend my mess with his, put up with someone who squeezed the toothpaste in the middle and wrote in childish capital letters on the steamy mirror

— I love you

an

— I love you

I couldn't get rid of, barely out of the shower dripping on the mat I'd run into four or five

— I love you

enormous, all over the mirror, the

— I love you

of a child begging to sit on someone's lap, should I take the new job not take the new job, buy a new car not buy a new car, pave the driveway not pave the driveway, he didn't take the job, we didn't get a new car, we did not pave the driveway we paved

I mean, did not pave

the deaf woman's husband, prudent

— *Now see here, Bishop, Excellency, we're talking about a priest and my godfather*

— *Has nothing to do with it, this is a holy war*

had a bomb placed in the priest's car and I don't know and I don't care, I'd rather not know who set it off, I covered my ears so I wouldn't hear the blast, or the apartment, telephone, pigeons, or the whiff of gas, because before eleven in the morning I'm a surly cat, don't tell me anything, don't chat with me, don't talk, don't threaten me with sunshine because I'll beat it out with the broom, I want to go back to bed, I want my dream about flying, spreading my arms and taking my little leap and see you later, miniature buildings, miniature city, a little strip of the Tagus

we, or rather I, put the apartment up for sale when we separated, the mirror with the

I love you

messy, like nasty graffiti, my angry face, his shocked face

— Don't you like me anymore Fátima?

covering the letters, the diocese Toyota outside waiting, my suitcase on the landing, a forgotten hair clip on the bedside table, my husband twisting the clip over and over again, a clip which, at that point, was entirely me

hoping the clip would answer, would say yes

— I do

or would calm down and, as he pleaded with the hair clip, I went down the stairs dragging the corpse inside the suitcase

the priest's body in the suitcase, the deaf woman's husband showing us the newspaper, a photograph of a woman, a photograph of a man

— *At the very least, a communist, Bishop, Excellency*

*not one body but two bodies in the suitcase, those shocked eyes you see in
photographs of dead people*

*(giving the impression the photographs have just received news of their
own deaths and don't believe it)*

if I could just get away, fly over Campo de Santana park for a while as
if I were swimming, flying on my back around the statue of the spiritual
healer, surrounded by little candles and the prayers of the faithful, street
vendors selling rosaries, paper flowers, clay busts, wax limbs

*— See here Bishop, Excellency, it's not just the courts on the loose the
church is also teeming with revolutionaries one thing there's no lack of at
mass are traitors*

dragging the bodies in the suitcase downstairs step by step, the diocese
driver dumped the bodies in the trunk without suspecting a thing, my
husband writing

I love you

to a hair clip reflected in the windowpane of the empty apartment,
blowing more steam, then writing again, pulling our door bell at four in
the morning, in a sour mist of beer

— I want Fátima back, Bishop, Excellency

standing there on the doormat wringing his hands, each finger with
a life of its own, friskily escaping him and he, unable to regain control,
the faithful spiritualists making their reverence on the plaza, thanking
the mystical curate for healing their gall bladders and cancer

in unlatching the suitcase with the bodies of the priest and the woman

(miracle-working statue)

*they'd been transformed into clothes, brushes, perfume samples, I should
add a candle to the dozens at the dais, my godfather at a loss*

— *What's going on dear?*

*I, somewhat suspicious, rummaging through the blouses to make sure,
shuffling through my cotton sweaters for any stray bones, with a sigh of relief*

— *Nothing*

*what was left of the car not on the road but scattered over the sloping corn
field, were fragments of iron, charred chunks, pieces of tubes I know nothing
about I prefer not to know*

*it's not true, I do know, I used to see him at the meetings here at the house
along with the general, the commander that lived near the Spanish border
recruiting soldiers, guardsmen, former fighters from Guinea, ex-policemen,
poor souls back from Mozambique and Angola ready to invade Portugal, get
rid of the Communists, free Africa from the Russians in the name of what
they call the Homeland, navigators and bearded princes in monastery crypts
under enormous stone vaults, the deaf woman's husband*

— *Now see here, Bishop, Excellency, a priest*

my godfather twisting his ring around his finger

— *This is a holy war my friends holy war*

*the commander with the lever and wires hidden for hours on end behind
a row of walnut trees, waiting for the priest's car to round the bend toward
the bomb placed on the asphalt, buried under twigs*

*the wind among the shrubs, as if the wind were singing its little voiceless
song*

*not planning the death of a friend but something undertaken casually, as
if simply getting a job done, a nearly white rabbit disappeared in a ditch, an
egret dropped suddenly in a whirl of wings, the commander wrapped up in
an old blanket, a bottle of madrone brandy on his lap*

*I'd rather not know, I don't care, don't tell me, don't talk to me till eleven
in the morning I'm a surly cat, stumbling through the apartment bumping*

into furniture, driving the sun away and cursing the world

*wrapped up in an old blanket his tongue freezing, he'd definitely fallen
asleep because his neck was stiff and he woke up at the sound of the first
engine, his tendons were numb, his shoulders felt odd, he wrapped his hand
around the lever, following the truck there was a gypsy wagon with a donkey
tied to the shaft, a group of wild ducks in V formation looking for the river,
insects buzzing around as if the universe were made up of vibrating antennae
and wings, bicycle riding farmers, sparrows, a tractor, oxen pulling a plough
along a trail of mulberries, the hand-cranked telephone they stole from the
army, the wild ducks in V formation had found the river since their loud
quacking could be heard*

*the commander who lived near the Spanish border recruiting soldiers,
guardsmen, former fighters from Guinea, ex-policemen, poor fellows back
from Mozambique and Angola ready to invade Portugal, get rid of the
Communists, free Africa from the Russians, the commander never smiled, he
would bow as he greeted me*

Madam

*he agreed with my husband, excuse me, my godfather when he talked
about the atheists, traitors, about the holy war being the reason for the fires,
bombs, grenades, machine guns, and the dead people on TV, the radio, in
the newspapers*

*— Shut up, I'm not listening don't you see I'm covering my ears with my
fists shut up*

I'm not awake yet, I get things mixed up, I feel like flying, I'm sleepy,
my husband gripping his hands to keep them from dropping off onto
the floor, wringing them unintentionally

— I want Fátima back Bishop, Excellency

bold with drink, ready to steam up the mirror above the umbrella
stand to write

I love you

to write in his childish capital letters

I love you

on silver trays, on the coffee pots, aluminum spoons, the porcelain Chinese figurines, my husband, thinner, his nose longer, standing on the doormat at four in the morning

the telephone stolen from the army hadn't been used in ages, the commander tried out the crank and there was only hissing, the sound of something simmering, voices or honking from a distant city, the Spanish brigade chief not picking up, sitting in a van near the church, he might have left, gotten fed up, given up, a second flock of wild ducks in V formation in search of water, a second gypsy wagon piled with people, the ever-present donkey, his wounds treated with grease or grey paint, tied to the shaft with a piece of rope, his neck in pain, a butterfly caught between his skin and his collar, we'd have been so much better off if we'd handled the press better, if the officers had been on their game and if, during the coup, in spite of all those peo-

— *Don't talk to me, don't say anything before eleven I'm a surly cat*

my husband, writing on the windows

I love you

chasing after his own hands

— I want Fátima back Bishop, Excellency

finding his hands as if by chance, not realizing they were his, I'd swear he'd brought the hair clip in his pocket and I'm not sure if I liked him then or if I was feeling guilty, but the smell of the beer in the entryway made me feel so sorry for him, my godfather unfolding his handkerchief as if it were going to protect him, figuring out how many steps to his bedroom, where he could hide, both of them afraid of each other, ashamed of each other, if I were to lie down in bed and close my eyes, I'd leap up in a flash and fly, and I'd call out to my godfather and husband, all set to write

I love you

on the window panes, don't anyone talk to me, don't anyone say a word till eleven in the morning because I'm a surly cat, I used to fly, everything was so tiny and unimportant below me, just like it was for the ducks in V formation

looking for the river, endless rain clouds and in the middle of all this, the field telephone, cricket shrieks, crackles, sighs, the chief of the brigade warning the commander about something not quite clear

not true, it was clear

that wasn't very clear drowned out by interference, musical clips, foreign words, the chief of the brigade submerged, reemerged, the commander

— How?

the commander

— Repeat

the commander

— What?

he understood the hyacinth leaves in the churchyard, understood the murmuring palm trees, but not the chief of the brigade

it's not true, he understood, he was telling him to not to push the button, to hold back, wait till tomorrow because

— See how I fly I don't hear a thing and I fly

since they're other people in the priest's car and we can't afford to

I cover my ears and I fly, I don't recall a single night in my childhood that I didn't fly over my rooftop with my gold-plated bracelet, my little tortoiseshell ring and patent leather shoes with the pretty bow I fell in love with in the store window as soon as I saw them

we can't afford to alienate people, the commander

—How?

more bicycles, the car on the highway, a herd of sheep crossing the road, five or six crows in a eucalyptus grove, on account of the din in the trees, maybe partridges and weasels reeling, the commander interrupting

— What?

shattering the telephone against the rock, the chief of the brigade quiet, everything transformed into screws, coils, lead plates, the commander feeling his aching neck worried about the rain clouds, just as the car came slowly around the bend, he asked for the last time

— What?

talking to the broken telephone, his hand on the lever

— I can't hear

and he pushed the button

I can't hear, I promise I can't hear, even if I tried I couldn't hear since I'm so busy, cursing the world, chasing the sun out to the porch with my broom, cleaning it with the scouring pad, wiping it off the dishwasher, the placemats and fruit bowl, I'm so busy turning off the alarm clock, unplugging everything, so busy lifting my arms taking a little leap, to fly.

3

FLY, CELINA, FLY, they'd grab me by the waist, throw me up to the ceiling, catch me before I fell to the floor, I'd laugh because I was afraid and I loved that fear, for a second I'd be tossed loose way up there, my nose brushing the ceiling light with the ruffled shade, then down I'd come into my uncle's lap, giggling, panicked and happy

— Fly Celina

for a second I'd glimpse the huge bulging Christmas presents on top of the armoires, covered in starry wrapping paper and ribbons

— I want my present

— What present?

I'd be even taller than the grown-ups, taller than the furniture, my uncle smelled like cologne and my father, like tobacco, when they made me fly, everything was off in the distance, the smell, my mother and grandmother, both happy, my father, very serious sitting in the corner of the sofa, his eyes on his newspaper, I'd call him

— Father

I'd wave good-bye to him and he'd stay behind his newspaper, completely absorbed, he was going bald, seemed sad, I forgot about the Christmas presents

— Father

my uncle would wink at my mother and my grandmother's expression would change, if I'd wanted I could have unscrewed the light bulb and no one would have been able to see in the dark or I'd have fixed the rod on the pleated lampshade the painter had damaged, but as soon as I thought of that, as soon as I was all set to create darkness

(I can make darkness I can make daylight)

— No don't touch the light

they'd set me back down, everything around me spinning, I'd take a second to get used to walking on the floor, crooked at first, then straight, the rug was the rug once again, the house went back to being the house, I didn't feel like laughing, didn't feel like having anyone talk to me, I sat under the lunch table surrounded by the tablecloth and everyone's legs

— Come on Celina, ea-

my uncle's hand on my mother's knee and my mother's knee got goose bumps, her hand must have dropped her fork because it then took my uncle's hand, put it back on his knee and patted him in some sort of scolding or irritated way before disappearing again in search of her fork, my grandmother leaned back, her long finger-nailed hands massaging her shin, my father's legs remained parallel, one of his sagging socks revealing some skin, my uncle's shoe, far more shined than mine or my father's

— Come on Celina, eat

stepped on the tip of my mother's shoe, the high heel of her other shoe, the one missing the rubber tip, started to rub my uncle's ankle, back and forth, his hand moved back onto her knee, made its way up her thigh and, with this, my mother did not move his hand away, this time her high heel kept rubbing his ankle, a nail must have pricked him, since my uncle's backside gave a little jump, my grandmother's worried voice, coming from her invisible top half

— Did you find a fishbone Joaquim?

my mother's hand, the one with the wedding band and the fake diamond ring that hid it

(I tried it on once when she was in the shower and had left it in her bedroom, it was even loose on my thumb)

caressed my uncle's slacks to make him feel better, his hand squeezing hers, their fingers intertwined, every other finger, thicker thinner, thicker thinner, thicker thinner except for their thumbs, which were playing at some sort of war, the thick one winding around the thin one and the thin one trying to escape, my father's napkin slipping and falling, the hands quickly evaporating, shoes all lined up, two by two, like they taught me to do before going to bed, except these shoes were filled with people, my uncle's ankle had a red stripe, his voice, as the pitcher of water clinked against the glass

— I swallowed a big bone

my mother, in a strange tone of voice that gave me a tingling feeling in my tummy

— How awful

not really a strange tone of voice, but a tone of voice that made me giddy for no reason, made me want to beg her

— Say that again

and lie down on the carpet to feel the rough wool or whatever was in my bladder, dance, stretch out right and left, the rug scratching me but it didn't hurt, my father's hand darker, with more hair, reached for the dropped napkin, opening and closing blindly, not finding it, reaching out further, bumping into my mother's foot, her foot escaping, annoyed

— Don't be silly what's going on?

making me giddy all over again and wanting to scratch against the rug to feel whatever it was the scratching did and I knew what it was without knowing, like sweet fury, urging, fainting

— Fly Celina fly

my nose touching the light fixture and the ruffled shade, the smell of
cologne coming and going, I loved that fear, my father's hand found my
skirt and snatched it thinking it was the napkin

— Father

another

— Father

just like

— How awful

from my mother, dark fingers, hairy, his sagging sock covering his
shoe, his face under the tablecloth against mine the whiskers on his chin,
on his cheeks, the strained white of his eyes, a little vein on his forehead
sticking out

— Come on Celina, eat

the pillow on the chair so I could reach my plate, my grandmother
tying the strings of my bib, too tight

— I don't need that I'm a big girl

now my mother from the waist up only, which made it seem like I had
two mothers, the one with the head sipping her soup with spectacular
manners and the one with the legs without any manners at all, rubbing
her high heel on his ankle, and the one with the manners eyed my spoon
impatiently

— Don't spill it and be quiet

I wanted them to put me on their lap, to give me those presents from
the top of the armoire, I wanted to go to sleep and wake up right away
and be their age

(no, older)

and boss them around

— I'm older than you take this bib off me immediately and give me a tricycle with a bell

by the way my mother looked every once in a while, still and staring blankly, as if she were in prayer, I understood my uncle was stepping on her foot again and they were having a thumb war on their knees, my father delved into his plate as if it were his newspaper, my grandmother, furious or anxious or maybe both

— Manuela

fiddling with her napkin ring and setting it down, watching my father, signaling toward me with her mouth while nudging my uncle's elbow with her elbow

— Joaquim

who had stopped chewing, by then also praying, either on the verge of an attack or preparing to fly out the open window, they looked for each other out in the hallway, their mouths coming together quickly, my mother slapping him, breathlessly

— But Joaquim, you're crazy

in a strange tone of voice that made me want to beg her

— Say that again

as the rough wool was scratching my back, not hurting me, momentarily tossing me loose way up high, my nose touching the light, afraid and loving that fear

— Fly Celina fly

higher than the grown-ups, higher than the furniture, happy fear, everything spinning, unlearning how to walk, as he moved his mouth away from hers, my uncle tripped on me, leaned up against the wall, spoke to my mother out of the corner of his mouth

(I could see the drops of fatigue on his forehead, with no running and with no exercise)

— And what if the little girl tells?

the bib and the pillow on the chair made me mad, their insisting I was a child when I was more adult than they were, my shelf filled with dolls should be filled with perfume bottles, I mean I would lose

Catarina Mariana Luísa

I'd keep the dolls and the perfume bottles too, just like, for example, I could ride my tricycle in high heels, anyone can, my uncle, still worried about me being a child, taking his handkerchief from his pocket to dry the little drops

— And what if the little girl tells?

my mother in the sharp tone of voice she would use with my father, also when she spoke to street market vendors, her nose in the air, show-ing her distaste

— Are you afraid?

all that was missing was her coin purse and her shopping basket, all that was missing was her without makeup, wearing flat shoes, at night she'd lock herself in the bathroom then come out in rollers with cold cream on her cheeks, she never let me try it

— Let go of that tube Celina

so I have wrinkles that the beautician swears are expression lines

— They're expression lines dona Celina

expression lines my ass, I keep my face entirely still and there they are, I smile and they're still there, more pronounced than my smile lines

(hundreds)

I pucker up just to make sure and it's the same thing, I raise my eyebrows and see the beautician in the mirror

— Expression lines my ass Elisabeth

thirty-odd years, ten years younger than I am, no cellulite, no varicose veins, firm buttocks, impeccable neck, gaining on me with far less money, a drunken husband, a dog's life, no use crying

— Why do I bother coming every morning?

the other customers are silent, old women like me, meaning they're not yet old enough to not consider themselves old, they're as angry as I am at the passing of time, but not so far gone as to have stopped feeling sorry themselves, a steamy atmosphere, a tepid sense of peace, the pedicurist lining up her instruments, massages, wraps, exercises, the promising falsehood of eternal youth they'll never fulfill, I was just under the table, just now my uncle

— Fly Celina fly

and my mother

(and what if the little girl tells?)

heading down the hallway, shaken with disgust

— Coward

the disdain of the high heels on the wood floor, military timing, the heel with the rubber tip softer, the one with the nail louder, the runner was getting caught, the nail catching on the rug, creating folds, my mother oblivious, my grandmother terrified

—Have you seen Manuela?

opening her glasses case

(I really wanted glasses, I really wanted a brassiere, I'd wear my glasses gain some respect from my family, I'd yawn without covering my mouth, read the newspaper, not have to put up with school)

my grandmother wearing her glasses, examining the tear, using her sewing kit to try to hide the nail holes, turning the runner over and sewing from underneath

— Yes indeed Manuela well done

looking at my mother, looking at my uncle, shaking her head, my uncle was sitting on the sofa next to my father, apprehensive and obliging, their smells of cologne and tobacco blending, and also the smell of fear and the lined face, the sagging sock revealing bones, and my uncle with forced enthusiasm

— How about going fishing on Sunday Fernando?

the two of them on the riverbank wall and I, bored to death on a little canvas stool, I dressed and undressed Mariana a thousand times, and ended up yanking one of her arms out of the socket and forgetting about her, I couldn't lean over

— Don't lean over Celina you'll fall in the Tagus

I couldn't make any noise or I'd scare the fish, couldn't take off my straw hat because I'd get sunstroke, couldn't hop on one foot, just stepping on the black stones, because it irritated my father, I counted the packet boats, but since they weren't all lined up I lost count, started counting again and got bored by the time I reached seventeen, the sun was sowing handfuls of sparkles in the water, the gulls were walking on the beach in a slanted line, staring at me like my grandmother stared at my mother, sewage was floating down the Tagus caught in straw and planks, a man was collecting pieces of broken bottles, putting them into a bag, the waves dragged up a beret, the body of a rooster, a wicker basket, nothing the slightest bit interesting, boring, taking so long, there were abandoned buildings behind us, the windows boarded up, gardens with dried bushes and ghosts, I bet, before the ghosts could hurt me I kneeled down near the can of floundering minnows

— *Wee little minnow wee little minnow*

my husband's business partner would call me

— *Come here little minnow Mimi is deaf and can't hear*

my father, kicking me

— Be quiet

a trawler heaved its trail of diesel, rousing the gulls that stopped staring at me

— So many wrinkles Celina so many wrinkles

and rose from the beach, wailing, pecking at black shreds mixed into the foam, from time to time the fishing pole would arc, the catch would twist and turn but it wasn't bass, it was lead weights, slime, empty hooks, parentheses and commas drawn in the water, expanding around the fishing line like the wrinkles around my eyebrows

— Don't worry dona Celina they're expression lines

and the mirror to me, not distracted, attentive, studying my features

— You're going to die

I, listening numbly because, as I was taking off my rings at my vanity the day before they shattered my husband's windshield, making him stop, the ex-policemen aiming their machine guns at him, his body shaking in the car seat and slipping to the ground, I'd started sobbing at the mirror and my husband, never suspecting a thing, was busy undoing his necktie and putting his cuff links in the dish

— Aren't you feeling well Celina is something bothering you?

— *It has to be tomorrow little minnow don't tell me that's not what you want don't tell me you'd rather we denounced everyone*

Mimi

I'm certain, no matter how deaf she is, she knew about us and she kept quiet like my grandmother kept quiet

— *Her grandmother's better than yours Celina she invented Coca-Cola in Galicia*

the deaf woman, who'd wake up and stare at the neon light in the plaza, used a telephone with a blinking light and no bell, my husband's business partner put the receiver to my ear, echoes of distorted words like the throat of God announcing the Great Flood, the bishop's goddaughter, gingerly handling the receiver in disbelief, afraid of getting an electric shock

— *Heaven forbid*

my unsuspecting husband busy undoing his necktie and putting his cuff links in the dish

— Aren't you feeling well Celina is something bothering you?

a widower my father's age, equally serious, equally taciturn, equally buried in the newspaper except with freckles and red hair on the back of his hands, we met when the second hotel closed and I worked as a clerk at an insurance company, seldom a day without a delivery of hyacinths

not roses, not camellias, hyacinths, his business partner

— *I think the old fellow's fallen for you Miss Celina*

would smile at me, invite me to the movies secretly, out to lunch secretly, lay his hand on my knee like my uncle used to do to my mother

— *We're partners in everything little minnow but he doesn't need to know about this*

if the four of us had dinner his bottom half would nudge my shoe while his top half filled the deaf woman with wide-eyed explanations as she rolled a little piece of bread into a ball never ceasing to size me up, as if I were hearing

— *Don't worry I'll never make a scene the deaf are different didn't you know?*

because she understood things like animals understand, she'd run her eyes over the tablecloth and perceive knees and legs, I'd venture to say she didn't even hate me, as if when she looked at us she were looking beyond us, like this morning when I looked at myself in the mirror

(so ridiculous to get angry over aging, over wrinkles)

the riverbank wall emerged right above my eyes, the sparkles, the two fishing rods, the deserted buildings, gardens overrun with dried bush and no doubt snakes, rats, ghosts haunting empty rooms, Mariana missing her arm and suddenly my father to my uncle

— You bastard

tossing the can of minnows and the picnic into the waves, the picnic coming unwrapped in the water, chicken, potatoes, bread, the gulls abandoning the diesel to squabble with each other, squealing women and children in the background

— *Remember Mimi's deaf, my wee little minnow, don't worry don't stop now*

battling with their claws, wings, their bristling breasts, an albatross shooed them away in a commotion of feathers, snatched a piece of cauliflower and left, scaling the sky towards Malveira, my father's hands just like the gulls

— Do you think I'm an idiot you bastard?

the little canvas stool tossed into the waves, my uncle squishing Mariana with his shoe, the cracked plastic, the mechanism shaking

—Peep peep

it was nothing more than a tiny cloth bellows, no mystery, with a spring like a cuckoo clock, Mariana wasn't breathing, it was that thing, the throbbing little bellows, separated from the doll, the doll dead on the ground and the tiny bellows still alive

— Peep peep

I hate Mariana, I hate everyone in the world, liars, once I get back home to Anjos I'm grabbing a hammer, cracking them all open and throwing them in the trash, they don't need to pretend, make scenes, beg

—Peep peep

argue

— Don't worry Dona Celina they're expression lines

prone plastic irises, a boy riding a bicycle stopped a few meters from my father, using the pedal to rest his bicycle on the promenade

— Hey, buddy

the gulls, suspended in the air, hoping my uncle would fall off the wall so they could tear him apart too, fighting with their claws, wings, their bristling breasts, my uncle, pressing his handkerchief to his mouth

— I'll report you to the police Fernando

the sun was turning transparent and purple, the caves of abandoned buildings were dissolving into shadows, the gulls, gradually giving up, hesitating between us and the diesel, the boy on the bicycle, who didn't smell like tobacco or cologne, who smelled like boat canvas, stuck my father and uncle in the car

—Take it easy

tossed me into the back seat, handed me what was left of Mariana, her amputated arm, the tiny cloth bellows, my uncle started the car, a mangy dog, smaller than his barks, crossed the road, dejected and sad, my father and my uncle, a pair of quiet necks hating each other, my uncle's hands on the steering wheel and my father's hand in the air less furious than before

— You bastard

at the same time the little cloth bellows begged

— Peep peep

abandoned on my lap, I rolled down the window and threw it into the darkness like I threw out her arm

— Liar

then I must have fallen asleep with the swaying because I don't remember anything else, getting back to Lisbon, being undressed, being put to bed, I remember dreaming we were arriving in Lisbon, they undressed me, put me to bed, my father hounding my uncle till my bedroom door was shut, my grandmother

— Boys

my mother shrugging her shoulders in the kitchen

I remember dreaming every night my husband knew he was going to die and blamed me

— *Why didn't you say anything Celina?*

remember taking my rings off as they were approaching him and breaking the windshield, while

— *You bastard*

while the shotguns, while the body slipped, while I wiped off my makeup with no blood on the cotton, no teardrops

I must have fallen asleep since it was Sunday, the alarm clock showing nine o'clock, my parents weren't home, my grandmother had gone to church, my uncle in his pajamas, not smelling of cologne, having his breakfast in the kitchen, his suitcase nearby, didn't speak to me, didn't tug my braids, didn't smile

— Little missy

took forever chewing in silence without grabbing me by the waist, tossing me up towards the ceiling and catching me before I fell to the ground

— Fly Celina fly

and me let loose way up there, my nose brushing against the light and the ruffled shade, making sure the Christmas presents were on top of the armoire waiting for December when the clay Baby Jesus, always scrupulous about the date, would leave the crèche and lay them out on my bed.

4

BEDTIME, WHEN THEY'D SAY

— It's past nine o'clock, bedtime

I'd make them leave the kitchen light on and I'd keep my eyes open, panicked that they'd switch it off

and when they switched it off they'd cover me with a lid, kill me, since death means being alone in the dark but still alive except no one knows, we move and no one notices, they get us dressed as we protest, comb our hair, put on our shoes, lay us down on the bedspread our wrists handcuffed in a rosary, and we call out

— I haven't died

and instead of helping they brush the flies off our face, passing plates of cookies and glasses of liqueur with the hand not holding the teary handkerchief, they leave, caressing our cheeks and we

— No

we're pale, how could we not be pale from all the flowers and candles, tired of calling out explaining, telling them no, they, leaning over us, even more disgusting

— Oh look she's smiling poor thing

till they screw down the lid, we can still hear them out there, where it's daytime, they're hugging each other, talking, shifting chairs around, we can still hear them before we hear the priest and the dirt on top of the box, and then nothing, except for cramped space, silence, our lack of air, I'd keep my eyes open, panicked they would switch off the light, my mother dark against the light doorway

— Aren't you asleep Simone?

creatures in the living room I can't see, I know they're there but I can't see

— If you don't turn out the light she won't wake up tomorrow

I don't say anything because my tongue's stuck, my lips are stuck, the muscles in my throat are still, it's possible I'm already dead, I want to let them know

— Wait

and I'm unable, to prevent

— No

and fumbling for words

— If you don't turn out the light it's such a trial getting her to school

my mother dark against the light through the doorway, the kitchen tiles, stove, checkered dishcloths hanging from nails, a little smiling copper bear decorating the refrigerator, her finger on the light switch, the world suspended, almost cut loose, my heart, a trembling drop on a stem

fall don't fall don't fall

the dark kitchen, dark door, screaming

— Please

till I realized I was lying in my boyfriend's boss's garage, the daylight coming through the little window, a bird on the oak branch swaying in timid hesitation

— *You've put on a lot of weight Simone, pretty soon you won't fit into anything*

with the bird's bye-bye the branch quickly recovered its position, relieved

— *Some women gain weight when they're pregnant are you sure you're not pregnant Simone?*

it smelled like rubber, leather, smoke, gasoline, my boyfriend in the airport worker's uniform he and the ex-policeman wore to put it

— *That's all I need, you pregnant*

in the cabinet minister's airplane, and then five months in Spain

till things cool down, son, take it easy rest no phone calls no postcards just imagine a long vacation reading magazines watching television playing cards you can take your girls if you want

his boss's wife, the deaf woman, wandering around, arranging flowers in vases, oblivious, as if she were flying, my boyfriend's boss to the bishop, the bishop's goddaughter, his partner's widow

dona Celina

— *It's just like living with a child or a dog none of you understand anything*

while the deaf woman smiled, friendly and shy

dona Mimi

when she thought she should smile, agree, she'd try to read our lips, we'd know when she was alone because the television would be turned up so loud we'd hear it in the garage like a megaphone at county fair, news, music, advertisements

and after the cabinet minister's airplane and the five months in Spain, back to the garage, following the general's instructions, some afternoons when my boyfriend wasn't busy with tubes and wires he'd take me to the beach, and I, too shy to get undressed, kneeling, writing my name with a stick in the sand, digging up broken seashells, crab shells, tins, I tried not to eat but it wasn't the food, it was nerves, some day my boyfriend might make a mistake with a connection and the garage, busted into bits and pieces up in the sky, blazing fire, the entire world running and the deaf woman in her chair, still knitting, unaware of the blast, nodding in agreement

— But of course

calm and collected, surrounded by wreckage, chunks of wall, burnt wood, flames, I'd try not to eat but it wasn't the food

— Of all things you're pregnant

once we were supposed to set off a small bomb somewhere down south, in Altentejo, in effect, nothing more than carnival fireworks, a one or two hundred grams, to scare the councilman who'd told the Judiciary about hideouts, meeting places, warehouses, my boyfriend was heavy-handed with the proportions and, besides the councilman, he took out the pillory and the police station, we were waiting over five hundred meters away, our car pointing toward Lisbon, sheep, barren fields, hills, roadside workers patching the road, then all of a sudden little pieces of doorframes right next to us, my ears buzzing, my boyfriend didn't want to belie-

— It's not possible

his hand clapped over his mouth

— It's not possible

so I'm overweight because of my nerves, I even had to have my ring made bigger, the ring my mother left me, I can't find one dress to fit me, the only things I have left from when I was a girl are the ring and the little copper bear that used to jazz up the refrigerator, my father's debts took away everything else, the creditors didn't even leave me with the wire hangers, the little enamel jars, my mother and I in the empty sitting room, the picture of the little clown snatched off the nail, out of pity they lent us a mattress, a table and chairs, I offered them plates of cookies and glasses of liqueur, but I didn't feel like crying or hugging anyone, if anyone had unscrewed the lid my father would be waiting there, near the kitchen light switch, fighting sleep

— If you don't turn out the light she won't wake up tomorrow

on account of the little bomb the general and the bishop got my boyfriend's boss in trouble, my boyfriend's boss got my boyfriend in trouble, my boyfriend's boss's wife would smile, serving whiskey

(everyone called her dona Mimi, yelling, but I think it should be Emilia)

my boyfriend, afraid of the fancy curtains, chests and Chinese porcelain, made excuses for the quality of the Brazilian gunpowder, on afternoons when he wasn't dealing with tubes and wires he'd take me to the beach, changing cabins, tents, sail boats, the train passing through empty stops along the dunes, when I was little, we'd barely make it through the old train station on the way home from school and the notary's uncle would unbutton his raincoat and show us

— Girls

something we couldn't really see, shirt tails, hairy and naked, a trembling knee disappearing in the wild cane field, on Sundays we'd run into him on the plaza, extremely sensible, very serious, buying cigarettes, holding his grandson by the hand, president of the folklore club, member of the fire department committee, treasurer of the library, he'd greet my mother with a tip of his hat and the next morning or two or three mornings after that, as we walked through the old train station, the notary's uncle, suddenly unbuttoning his raincoat

— Girls

he didn't follow us, he wasn't going to touch us, it was nothing more than shriveled wrinkles, shirt tails, white hair hovering over that thing, his struggling little jaunt, tripping over stones to get away from us, we'd see him from the station sitting on a slope as if he didn't remember, I didn't feel sorry for him, but his old raincoat made me sad, I never called him names like the other girls, I didn't throw dirt clods at him

they'd hit his elbows and the back of his neck and he paid no attention

I remember the butterflies, the sound of the reeds and toads, the damp throbbing and those muddy colored stonechats that love lakes and swamps, the train station bench, carved with names, made me feel just as sorry as I felt for the raincoat, the propane tank delivery truck ran over the notary's uncle without giving him time to greet it with the tip of his hat, his glasses were left behind on the sidewalk, also, a little spot of blood and the sad raincoat the taxi carried away, I still see it when I write my name with a stick, smooth out the sand, start again

Simone

my boyfriend, lying face down on the towel, hands me the suntan lotion for his back, so I write

Simone

shoulder blades protruding and the old man in my thoughts, the shirt tails, the hairy nakedness, the dirt clods hitting his spine, his butt, I rub the lotion on his back like dirt clods, on his butt, the stonechats that love lakes and swamps emerge in the wild cane fields in angry little flocks, it's past nine, bed, oh look she's smiling poor thing, if you don't turn out her light it's a trial getting her to school, I'd find broken seashells, crab shells, tins if I could undress like the others, wade in the waves

— *You're not pregnant by any chance Simone?*

instead of fighting socialism, the atheists, the foreigners that stole Africa from us, my boyfriend with me writing Simone and Simone and Simone on his skin

— Who cares about politics it's a way for us to make money in three years at the most we'll be done with it and open a café in Espinho you always liked Espinho

the kitchen light left on would keep me from dying, as long as my eyes are open they can't kill me, at night in Espinho listening for the headlights, the fog rolling over the window, icy slivers, at one in the morning I hide the money in the kitchen, we should have shutters to keep the thieves out, I go up to the first floor, the first floor is all mine, the picture of the clown, the little copper bear on the refrigerator, proper rugs, a leather sofa, curtains, not a garage smelling like gasoline and rubber, a real house, lots of treasures, to sit down in all the chairs laughing at him, at myself, to get up, and sit down again primping my hair, inviting him to sit too, isn't it comfortable, love

— Isn't it comfortable love?

turn the stove on and off, try out the faucets, tie bunches of lavender for the dresser drawers, three more years at most and three years from now, as soon as I'm happy, I'll get thin, stop writing my name in the sand, I'll have my sign, my copper lamps, my trunks in the Espinho fog, no lid will close down on me because no one will make me go to bed

— It's past nine o'clock bedtime

or turn out the light unless I want to, or comb my hair, put my shoes on, lay me down on the bedspread my wrists handcuffed in a rosary, like dona Celina in the chapel

while we were waiting for the boss's partner's car I was paying attention to the quail cries in the olive trees, a dozen quails and a burrow with baby quails since the male was coming and going tirelessly, uneasy with us, I sensed his unease by his tiny blank pupil, tense, his throat moving faster than any pulse, a female trotted out peeping near the guns, another female showed her beak and left, smelling like urine, the clay and straw of the nest, my mother used to roast quails on the grill in the backyard, we'd soak up the bloody, greasy sauce with bread, the aroma of the lemon verbena, of the cumin and the linden that reminded me of winter, golden teas to fight off melancholy and colds, we'd steep the leaves in a mug, with two egg yolks and a spoonful of honey, next to the holy images

Saint Monica Saint Angelica, Saint Vincent, Saint Stephen the martyr murdered by the Romans while taking communion to prisoners

the quails ended up getting used to us same way as with the scarecrows, if we'd had crumbs and a bag it would have been perfect, we'd have given them to my mother who'd put them in the coop, separate from the hens so they couldn't go after them and ruin their flavor

just three more years and I'll stop squatting in the sand ashamed of myself, I'll undress, play ring toss, jump the waves, look for limpets in the rocks, climb any set of stairs without getting tired

quails, turtledoves and angular locusts, we're not here because of my boyfriend's boss, we're here because dona Celina paid, the halo of wind, heavy with droplets and wet branches, eucalyptus or cherry-tree fibers softening voices, the partner's widow shaking her fan without messing up one strand of hair, I've never seen hands so

the light left on all night long, not over fear of dying, of the lid closing over me and killing me, but so I could see the kitchen, microwave, washing machine and counter, imagine how proud my parents would be, guided tours, neighbors' visits, my mother showing off the electric meat slicer, shelves filled with smoked sausage, a metal counter, the alarm system, the chocolates in the window display

not just her hands, all her elegance, her figure, those dangling earrings, like a princess or an actress, brushing against her blouse as if they brushed against me, if I could ever be a woman like her, the deaf woman distracted

— *But of course*

knowing everything pretending not to know, excusing or not even excusing, just waiting

— *But of course*

of course light, never darkness, I'd wake up in the middle of the night and the light promised me I was still alive

I'm alive, my mother's alive, the world's alive, when my father got sick he'd look around and I'd wonder which of our faces he would take with him and how, which image, which sound and how these faces, recollections and sounds would keep echoing in some tunnel or cave of his mind, who can promise me the dead don't

so, when the nurse said

— You all have to leave now

and hid the body behind the screen, I thought mother or me or both of us had gone with him and it was as if they had covered us with a lid, we stopped seeing the same way he stopped seeing, from the other side, we didn't make it to that day, the hugs, the conversations, the minister, the dirt on top of the box, cramped space, silence, our lack of air, while the indifferent little copper bear was cheering up the house and, in Espinho, my boyfriend was watching the fog rolling over the window, icy slivers.

5

I DON'T UNDERSTAND what people say and they don't understand what I understand: I hear words different than what they hear, like my grandmother understood her children through smiles, prattle, through

— Yes mother

— Whatever you'd like mother

— Right away mother

all the while wishing her dead, imagining taking over the restaurant and what they'd do later with the money, my sick uncle, his transistor radio to his ear, my aunt in Canada writing us expectant postcards with more stamps than greetings

— Is the doctor still worried about dona Rosário's heart?

a sister-in-law coming over to our house with a little bag of candied almonds to prod along my grandmother's diabetes, handing it to my grandmother behind my family's back

— A little something from a friend Mama Alicia

anxiously waiting for her to open the package, suck the sugar and fall over

(spasmodic arms and cockroach legs in her demise)

meanwhile, the lawyers divvying up the pots and pans, would cobble together the nothings of the poor into even smaller nothings, my grandmother, majestic at the top of the stairs, commanding her employees solely with the look in her eyes, would bury the little bag of candied almonds in one of her pockets among the jingling keys and change

—I'll taste them later Carmélia

enormous rusty keys to furniture, drawers long gone, armoires from when she lived in a seaside basement in Galicia near the ocean where roses sprout from the ocean beneath constant rain, likened to wax teardrops running down little girls' cheeks, the keys to my great grandparents' house, devoured by zinnias and raging cats, where most likely not even a wall remained in a country remaining only in her memory

— Ah Galicia Mimi

and a shoebox under her mattress giving off a smell of an empty perfume bottle, a purple atmosphere, a vague memory of bicycles, birthday mornings and happy Sundays, stuffed with treasures my grandmother would show me in slow ecstasy, porcelain doorknobs, a pink velvet choker, dried pansies in an envelope where time

or her fingers

had erased any dates from memory, cracked, torn photographs, signed in careful handwriting

Xexus Franco

of a mustached gentleman with a pocket watch chain, a stern lady taller than him, her hair parted down the middle and a slip of a girl with ringlets, clinging to a doggy in stubborn wonder, the three of them against a background of plants and painted pheasants

(the pheasants looking like the number 2, asking me,

— And now what?)

and my grandmother's proud fingernail pointing at the little girl's nose

— Me

but it couldn't be her, how silly, because my grandmother was old, her braid smelling like brandy, the idea of a grandmother my age, facing me from a yellowed, extinct world scared me because it mixed strange parallel worlds with my notion of the world, if I'd have been born seventy years ago we'd be friends, we'd play together and, while we played, I'd know whether to address her casually or like a grandmother, whether or not I'd mind her if she told me to brush my teeth, eat my fruit and stop keeping grasshoppers in my bedroom, my grandmother the same age as me and her little pointing finger

— I don't want to find any grasshoppers in your room Mimi

maybe we'd sleep together, go to school together, I might know my times tables better and the surprised teacher would scold her

— Your granddaughter leaves you in the dust aren't you ashamed Alicia?

although when my grandmother pointed at the little girl with the doggy and boots laced up to her knees

— Me

I believed her without believing, I compared her white braid with those dark ringlets as Mama Alicia bundled her treasures inside a sheet, after opening and closing a copper locket without letting me look inside

— Ah Galicia Mimi

I looked for it later, after she died, nothing more than a lock of blond hair who knows whose, a boyfriend, a child, tied in elastic, completely crumbled to dust, my grandmother, in her bridal gown, her glass domed tiara on her lap, allowing herself one last indulgence

— Ah Mimi

before they set her up at the top of the staircase to preside over the restaurant and the family, to decide on menus, keep the books, control the planet, a slip of a girl with ringlets perched on an enormous chair, to whom my aunt in Canada would send expectant postcards hoping for a heart attack, half in English, half in Portuguese

— Is the doctor still worried about dona Rosário's heart?

and whose inheritance by means of some skewed system the sister-in-law thought she was entitled

(I never understood inheritance or rights, since all we ever got were mortgages and debts, and my father tearing his hair out and my mother in desperation

— And now what?

my sick uncle, his transistor radio to his ear and a bottle of cherry liqueur at his lips, losing weight and fading away, seated at his dominos)

and for whom she bought stupid little bags of candied almonds, hoping to prod along her diabetes

— A little something to nibble on Mama Alicia

my grandmother burying the almonds in one of her skirt pockets as roses

if it's true the roses exist, if it's true Galicia exists

cried wax tears in Vigo, if I lived there I'd spend all year at the window watching the rain over the ocean, I might come across a cracked torn photograph of myself in an old shoebox, underneath porcelain doorknobs and pink velvet chokers, a slip of a girl holding a doggy in stubborn wonder, serving whiskey in the living room, agreeing with my husband, with my husband's business partner, with the bishop

— But of course

without understanding what they're talking about

(— There's no problem gentlemen she's deaf)

and without the others understanding what I understand, hearing them, as they move their lips, saying sentences different than what people hear, the bishop's goddaughter suspicious of me

— Who knows whether or not she hears

the cedars shadows scraping the floorboards, flailing like people drowning in a river, waving good-bye, my husband's driver, with the help of the fat girl he lived with, carrying boxes to the little room in back, I don't really notice the explosions, but the newspapers explain it all, I see the burning buildings, the dead and an airplane wing on a rooftop, my husband heading toward me pointing his gun at me

— Mimi

I, curled up in fear, waiting

turning the gun on himself, setting off a little blue flame and it wasn't a gun, it was his cigarette lighter, reaching toward Celina, who leaned in with her cigarette holder, brushing her leg against his legs and putting her hand over his hand, which I doubt her husband didn't see

— Thank you

the bishop's niece saw, the general saw, the commander saw and the bishop pretended not to see, legs against legs, hand over hand, I, smiling

— But of course

just like I kept smiling when I found her talking to that fat girl and the driver in the garage, the oak branch at the little window warning me

— Look

warning

— Look out

Celina, when she saw me, waving toward the car, screaming

— Don't get in

my husband's driver nervous, I couldn't tell whether or not the
fat girl was too under all those rolls, she on her tiptoes yelling and I
understanding

— Kill him wait for him at the bend near the hotel and kill him

the shattered windshield, the machine guns, the body sliding to the ground

— *At the bend near the hotel then kill him*

*beetles for sure, badgers, turtledoves, it was turtledove season, my father
would take me along when he went hunting and the flocks would emerge from
the orchard flying, the stagnant eyes of dead animals that my mother would
pile into a pan, stray feathers left here and there in the shed, like detached
silver stamens, at the bend near the hotel, she told them, kill him*

the oak tree branches shaking, warning me, I, pretending I didn't
understand with my deaf smile that made the bishop's goddaughter suspicious and kept her on her guard, I, agreeing

— The driver is excellent he'll handle it

the beautiful daisies in the flower bed, the beautiful nards, the driver
in the garage choosing his repair tools, lining them up on a cloth, screwdrivers transformed into rifles, magazines, pistols, the bishop and my
husband talking about holy wars as usual, what was needed for the glory
of Christ and the salvation of the Motherland, the bishop's goddaughter
watching me constantly, increasingly worried, jerking her head towards
me reminding them to speak quietly

— Who knows whether or not she hears

watching my every move, my facial expression, gestures, I, adjusting

the geraniums in the vase, passing out leather coasters, serving juice, ice,
tea

— Who knows whether or not she hears

*those detached silver stamens, I'd take two or three steps for each of his,
his head, or rather his hat with its jay feather, nearly reaching the branches,
the eastern winds ruffling the leaves, as if nighttime were suddenly upon us,
the sun on one side and the moon on the other were spying on me*

— *Mimi*

*to tell my grandmother I'd tortured butterflies, or thrown rocks at the
chickens, spent four or five hours getting my hands dirty, scratching my ankles
through cornfields, vines and March streams, walking to a deserted orchard,
just off the road, where my father would go hunting, rotting cherry trees
surrounded by thickets, insect-ridden lemon trees, languishing fig trees, their
boundless roots searching for water throughout the rocky earth, in our yard,
for example, they'd set the washtub off kilter and lift the chicken coop with
their craggy muscles, there were the ruins of the leper colony, jennets braying,
I swear if my father hadn't been with me, hairy beasts that don't dare come
out when grown-ups were around, would jump and devour me, I held his
hand to make sure they knew I was his daughter, that would show them,
and they'd leave me alone, they could just lie in wait for one of my catechism
classmates or some lost gypsy girl, a hundred meters before the orchard we'd
start hearing the turtledoves, the fluttering, soft fluster, females with bloated
necks singing out to the light, my father his broken jay feather*

*(he looked terrible in that hat, whenever she got the chance, my mother
would hide it and my father, furious, would point to his head*

— *Rosário)*

*he looked for a low wall between the orchard and the road where there
were dozens of cartridges, a mule pulling a plow off in the distance, as shiny
and miniature as a wooden toy*

(when my father got angry

— *Rosário*

my mother, grudgingly, would get the hat from the pantry where she'd stuck it in with the potatoes and onions, the grains, she'd pat it to straighten out the rim and get the dust off

— *I don't like you in this hat Arthur*

oozing distaste as my father would put the hat on, checking out his reflection in profile, as soon as he got it back on he'd become measured, grave, noble, eyeing the servants' bottoms with firm resolve, allowing himself whispers, chuckles, promises, invitations, my mother horrified

— *For the love of God*

my grandmother on her throne, in her bridal outfit, orange blossoms on her lap like a scepter

— *Arthur)*

the two of us feeling the easterly winds, on the wall between the orchard and the road, waiting for the male's signal when the whole flock would fly out towards the hospital, there must have been snakes and frogs hovering, maybe even hyenas, who was to guarantee there were no lions or tigers, escaped from the circus, starving, sleeping lazily right nearby, suddenly pouncing on our backs and I, with no whip or tall boots to protect myself, half an hour, an hour, thankfully no hyenas, the lions and tigers off devouring little girls in the neighboring village, if we were to keep walking ten seconds we'd come up to the trail where cars, herds and their cowbells, wagons, workers on their scooters all come down from the city, my husband's partner back from the hotel, the beautiful daisies in the flowerbed, the nards reflected in the swimming pool tiles, Celina in the garage, leaning over amid whispers toward my husband's driver and that fat girl, no, Celina in the garage leaning over amid whispers towards my father and me

— *Finish him off*

I wanted to answer her

— *No*

holding onto my father's arm

— *No*

oppose her, forbid him, get angry

— *No*

my husband's partner running into us, the white and grey male, leader of the group, beak wide open, my father looking at the orchard, the trail, trying to decide

— *Mimi*

my father or the driver, no, the driver calls me

— *Dona Mimi*

my father, with his ridiculous jay feather in his ridiculous sort of hat

— *Mimi*

the beautiful daisies and nards, I bought limestone statues to decorate the boxwoods, porcelain gnomes, theological virtues, I don't know how much Celina paid him, what promises she made, which arguments

— *Finish him off*

I don't really understand what they say but I understand their moving lips, even if they hide them behind their hands

— *Finish him off*

I understand the limestone statues, the porcelain gnomes, the theological virtues, the whispering daisies and nards

— *Finish him off*

the flock of turtledoves heading toward the hospital just as my husband's partner is approaching the curve, all that's left of the ruined leper colony is an arch and a fragment of the cloister, the slate tombs, my father resting his shotgun on top of the low wall and aiming at the road, my grandmother encouraging him

— Arthur

the automobile heading down the slope with one of its wheels spinning in the air, my husband's partner looking for his gun in the glove compartment, reaching for the stock and losing his glasses, my father rushing

— Shoot

tucking the shotgun into my chest, putting my finger on the trigger

— Shoot

the body slipping slowly to the ground, one shoe on, one shoe off, daisies, nards, the oak branch warning

— Aim carefully look

me, weightless, floating like detached silver stamens escaping in airy little bursts if we try to catch them, the automobile with the broken windshield, the thighs that kept sliding off the car seat, that old man and his sciatic nerve pain, so polite and thoughtful, full of formalities, he'd offer me little gifts at Christmas and Easter, he'd call out, his chest bursting with effort to come out with a solid

— Merry Christmas dona Mimi

while the woman was talking in the garage with the driver and the fat girl, without me understanding what they were talking about but comprehending what they said, the bishop's niece watching me straighten the hyacinths in the vase, passing out leather coasters, offering juice, ice, tea

— Who knows whether or not she hears

watching my behavior, my facial expression, my gestures

— Who knows whether or not she hears

my husband interrupting the bishop's speech about the holy wars and how soldiers had entered his church without removing their caps or even making the sign of the cross

— The entire building could fall down and Mimi wouldn't notice

speaking to me, fiddling with her napkin ring on her baby finger

— Isn't that so Mimi?

I, distractedly widening my smile

— But of course

as my husband opened his arms in a victorious gesture, as if my deafness added to his prestige

— And there you have it

taking the gun out of his pocket again to commit suicide with a shot in the throat, everyone silent, panicked and the cigarette finally lit

— And there you have it

if they ask him, and not a day goes by without someone asking him why he married me, he answers that ever since he was a child he'd known that what a man needs in life is a good maid or housekeeper, cross-eyed or crippled, makes no difference, sadly his own father, for example, never

just like my grandmother when she'd finish making the Coca-Cola

— And there you have it Mimi

the two of us in the room, immersed in the smell of brandy, with a bottle of soda water, coffee and sugar, tasting in secret, getting nervous if we heard anyone coming, and laughing, not a child and a crippled old lady thinking about Galicia where it rains all year long and roses sprout from the ocean, wax teardrops running down cheeks, but me and a slip of a girl with ringlets, clinging to a doggy in surprised defiance standing in front of a screen painting of plants and pheasants, the photographer's name in careful handwriting

Xesus Franco

not me and that old girl, between the mustached man with the pocket watch, a stern lady taller than him, her hair parted down the middle, but two girls the same age, absorbed in the purple halo of an empty perfume bottle, vague memories of bicycles, birthday mornings and happy Sundays, Mama Alicia and I on our way to Vigo

— Take me to Vigo Mimi

looking for my great-grandparents' house, devoured by zinnias and raging cats, somewhere we could play for as long as we wanted, with no shots, no shotguns, no dead people, no grown-ups with that grown-up obsession of always getting us in trouble.

6

WHEN THE SUN finally stopped teasing me, the gas started having fun at my expense. Seriously, the terrible attitude of objects is beyond me: I'm not even talking about mirrors, always at the ready to find fault, I'm just talking about pen tops rolling off to God only knows where, coin purses never found where we left them, slippers, we can only find the right one feeling around with our feet, the front door keys simply taking off on their own, forcing us to empty out all of our pockets and purses on top of the table, not to mention all the furniture corners out to leave us crippled, glasses dropping from our hands while we're washing them, leaving shards the brooms don't notice then the emergency-room nurse spending hours trying to extract them with a pin, finding a speck far smaller than the pain it caused, not to mention jammed zippers, mysterious stains on our blouses, the toothbrush leaving the odd strands of hair in our mouth that elude our tongue, seems like we're about to get them, but no, there's always that tiny opening in the gums too small for our fingernails where they hide and laugh and from where they never emerge till they get stuck in our throat after a coughing fit. Sometimes I think things like to suffer: if the television goes blank we bang it and the picture comes back, if a lamp goes out, two smacks on the shade will turn it back on, the vacuum cleaner just waits for a good kick and then it will get back to work. The treachery of things confounds me: they're all there, surrounding us innocently, all lined up, expensive, with their false air of submission and competence, their pretense of being useful, their plugs, their buttons and chrome, their foreign logos, their leaflets in four languages

with diagrams and arrows

that instruct us in thoroughgoing detail how to work them, and all they manage to do is triple our electric bill and force us to pay technicians for incomprehensible parts

(normally they need new resisters, as if they didn't have enough resistance to give us a nervous breakdown and wreak havoc with our lives)

or, in the best of circumstances, electrocute us for once and for all, releasing us, with a requiem mass, from their satanic assistance. But to get back to the point, I was saying the sun had just stopped teasing me, first shining on the dishwasher, then the fridge, then the floor tiles, then it was the gas's turn to have fun at my expense. I should have seen that coming, except for my tendency to forget every cruelty, making me the ideal victim for these objects, searching all over the house for the glasses I'm already holding in my hands or pleading with the toothpick dispenser, forgetting the simple fact that it will either deny me a single toothpick or else it will dump them out all over the plate, forcing me to fish for them in the swamp of sauce, patiently defeated, and this of course happens mainly when we have guests who in turn feel obliged to help and end up knocking the cruet set all over the sweet egg pudding that took me hours of work, and all the while my godfather will be reassuring them, sparing them their embarrassment, removing the little sticks from the disgrace

— It's nothing at all, not to worry nothing at all

and me dying to escape to Campos de Santana park and beyond where I can at least find some peace, trees and vast expanses instead of crucifixes and martyrs, to station myself with a little candle opposite the bronze spiritualist praying for all the objects to go away and leave me alone, to sit down in the Torel Gardens among the beggars and the poor souls from the mental hospital in the hopes my husband will take me away with him

— I've come to get Fátima, Bishop, Excellency

swaying on the landing, emboldened, with his beer breath, heading down the tear-soaked staircase, heading for the nearest tavern, lingering till daylight amid tearful ditties, and I, hoping my husband will take me away with him, away from the holy wars and the bombs, and also before the deaf woman, with that little smile grating on my nerves, tells the police what she pretends not to know and the police drag us away in the middle of the night to interrogation chambers, prison or

with a little luck

the insane asylum five hundred meters above here, where at least they'd let me walk in the parks, Campo de Santana or Jardim do Torel, with Lisbon below, navigating its way riverward, sailing along by way of billowing shirts hung out to dry. Sometimes I ask myself why I stay here starching incense-smoke-saturated cassocks, in this apartment where piles of linen swallow the echoes and an old man envelops me with his gaze the same way bulls gaze

(I put up with his heavy kidneys when he's not touching me, he breathes down my neck when he's nowhere near, coughs into my hair when he's in his office dealing with the Bible, he chokes out requests and yet remains silent)

the slow hooves, stiff hindquarters, gelatinous tenderness blurred by his glasses, enveloping me with his gaze the same way bulls gaze

— Fatinha

huge nostrils, heavy neck

— Fatinha

— *Kiss your godfather's hand Fátima*

the other hand on my head, fruit candies stuck with paper

— *Such a good little girl goo-*

I didn't dare spit out the pieces of wrapper, just like I didn't dare pick at the host stuck in my gums, afraid of offending Jesus, I'd swallow without chewing

— *You're not supposed to chew*

and I didn't know how to do anything, terribly afraid I'd swear, disobey, sin, if we sin, the host bleeds, the catechism teacher said a woman took communion in a state of sin and Christ's blood gushed from her mouth, the woman died writhing in pain and the Devil gobbled her up down in hell, another woman stored a host away in a chest and that same night her house burned down, she went blind and a priest had to fetch the undamaged host from the flames and ashes and, although three firemen who never went to mass ended up screaming at the hospital, not one strand of the priest's hair burned, the idea of sin, blood and fire wrought by sin terrified me just like the dozens of etchings of torments all over the sacristy terrified me, gallows, cauldrons, whips, forks, tongs, howling creatures with pointed ears, funny-looking devils engaging in cruel acts, much happier than the saints, who were always so dramatic, some of them bearing wounds and sharp arrows and looking so unpleasant, not to mention their hearts covered in thorns, and always keep in mind the Virgin Mary hates you to touch each other so no, I asked

— What touching?

and the catechism teacher

— Naughty girl, go wash your mouth out with soap and just hope God wasn't listening

(seems as if at times God got distracted)

if you were to die right this minute you'd suffer forever

I was also supposed to practice charity and generosity, charity

that was easy

just be nice to the poor but I don't know about the generosity, once my mother caught me with my window open handing out some of her old clothes, blouses, dresses, skirts, trying to be generous it was a miracle she didn't end up strangling me to death

— Kiss your godfather's hand Fátima

the other hand on my head, fruit candies stuck with paper, yellow lemon flavored, red strawberry flavored, orange pineapple flavored I was afraid of breaking them, just in case there might be some fragment of Jesus lurking

— *Good gir-*

if he absolved me I would go straight to heaven, filled with sad, virtuous souls, a huge hollow room, no floor no ceiling

(hell was more humane, there were even verandas with little devils peeking out, the big devils' children, not yet allowed to play at burning us up)

with little lonely creatures, praying, busying themselves here and there with pointless virtuous tasks, and equally solemn angels, their wings spread, hovering over plaster clouds, possibly sounding like ravens' dirty feather overcoats, no one touches each other, no one kisses each other, no one gets mad, everyone speaks quietly during mass, everyone careful with their new shoes, making sure no one noticed them, silently disapproving, we'd confess through wire mesh to a vague sniffling form, a sort of ailing marine monster moving around in there mumbling blessings, meanwhile the church verger wearing his dustcoat, receiving neither bows nor respect, would vacuum the sanctuary, sweep the altars, polish the saints, open the alms box for the souls in purgatory, dump the coins into his pocket, and I'd always thought the angels collected them, although I'd never really grasped how money fit in with celestial dealings

— *Kiss your godfather's hand Fátima*

the gas having fun at my expense, as the bath water got colder and colder, I turned the cold faucet all the way off and burned myself, I turned it back on slightly and was drenched in polar ice, I turned them both off, pulled the curtain, which seized the opportunity to fall off the rings, I got out, drenched in shampoo, slipping on the tiles, holding the towel in one hand and the curtain in the other, the light blinking on and off made me appear and disappear, hidden inside the islands of steam, among tubes and jars there was a different woman, not me

I never thought I looked like myself, I never really recognize my own face, my hands, how this chin can be my chin, this mouth my mouth, why I'm called Fátima, people think I'm me, get me mixed up with this stranger, what would happen if I appeared before them like I really am, a different face, different hands, a different chin, mouth, voice

a woman different from me, staring at me angrily, disappearing into
the kitchen, down the furniture-lined corridor, heavy furniture with
metal handles and tureens, candlesticks on doilies, and besides all this,
the window overlooking Campo de Santana park, rooftops, chimneys, tall
trees, beggars, the retired men playing dominoes near the lake, everything
coming to life, coming undone then coming back to life, like bubbles on
the surface of water, rust stains on the pipes, now enormous, the warped
window frames in the sunroom, cracked stucco, the missing piece of tile
so blatant the other tiles aren't noticeable, what is noticeable, though,
is a column of ants heading for a dead beetle, a crust of bread, crumbs,
I could just open the door to the street, go down the stairs, leave, and
a week or two later the deaf woman's husband's driver standing right in
front of me, the drive to Cabo Ruivo seaplane airport, a strangely vibrating halo over some village, Barreiro or maybe Alcochete, they kicked me
out of the car, pushed me out to the end of the bridge over the water, the
smell of wind coming off the water, stagnant petroleum, leftover stuff that
would never laugh at me again, and I was guessing, almost having fun

— You all think I went to the police, but I didn't

worrying, sensing their rush, their hesitation

— You all think I told the police everything, but I didn't

imagining my godfather

— And now what?

his enormous nostrils, heavy neck, one hand offering me candies, the
other hand on top of my head

— Good girl good gi-

a length of wire around my ankles, a length of wire around my wrists,
two balls of lead to weigh me down, won't take more than a few months
and I'll be nothing but a bundle of rattling bones caught in the algae,
how many months will it take for some part of me

liver, spleen, a spongy lung

to float to the surface, much to the joy of the gulls, I am the Resurrection and Life, he that believeth in Me, though he were dead, yet shall he live, everything is so simple, so easy, I thought I was afraid and, after all is said and done, that's all there is, the sound of train wheels on a bridge, waves of mud, my godfather explaining to the general and commander, who'd arrived from the Spanish border with some gloomy Spaniards

— This is a holy war my friends a holy war

slowly flickering lights, Barreiro or maybe Alcochete, Barreiro probably, based on the distance, islands and jetties, bays, tree tufts visible in the low tide, the lead balls came loose and they refastened them, Barreiro or Alcochete, Alcochete, we were wandering around some neighborhood strolling, down a block, buildings, stores, a pharmacy, cafés and all of a sudden the river Tagus appeared as if half the village were under water, as they threw me from the bridge, a spiral of shacks faded away, then there was nothing or what's called nothing, that hollow space with people praying, angels, their wings spread, hovering over plaster clouds, possibly sounding like ravens' dirty feather overcoats, my father, my mother, the catechism teacher and her book of threats, with God on the cover sitting in a chair made of lightning and below Him hundreds of creatures in ecstasy, I tried to explain

— I don't understand

the driver and the ex-policeman moved away, down the bridge, the deaf woman's distracted smile, just like when she'd adjust the hyacinths in the vases

— But of course,

staring me down, ordering daisies and nards to decorate the room

— *if they ask me, and not a day goes by without someone asking me why I married her, I answer that ever since I was a child I'd known that what a man needs in life is a good maid or housekeeper, cross-eyed or crippled, but serviceable, as long as she doesn't bother me, sadly for my own father, my mother nev-*

setting the visitors' condolence book and the tray for calling cards at the entryway, swatting away the flies with a fan, receiving guests, accompanying them to the door, sending them on their way, perfuming the room, turning on the fish tank light in the garden, the fish attacking like knives

— if they ask me, and not a day goes by without someone asking me

applying my makeup with her own kit so than no one would figure out that I had died by drowning, instead they'd think I'd drowned myself, go to the beach at Guincho, walk straight out into the ocean, when the dizziness started three weeks earlier, I'd wake up in the morning feeling strangely weak, as if my bones weren't there, without so much as a pharmacy test

— For a friend

or an appointment with some doctor I didn't know, I just gripped the counter when the world started spinning around me, my godfather at my heels

— Kiss your godfather's hand Fátima

I fought the walls encircling me, calling out to me, the hands on the clock, first closing in, then far away, I wanted to put my hand under my nightgown and yank myself from my self, the catechism teacher pointed at me with her nail-less finger

— I told you not to touch yourself Fátima, let's just hope the Virgin Mary has no idea

the catechism devils in high hilarity, the verger in the duster offered to divide the purgatory alms

— Midwives are very expensive Fátima

the invisible monsters in the confessional mumbling in Latin, the walls stopped spinning, the trees in Campo de Santana park were still, the world now corniced and gabled, the morgue, Jardim do Torel gardens, the flowerbeds, I tried to take a step, balancing on the wheels I now had on my feet, my godfather

— Fatinha

while I was walking on Guincho beach toward the room, the unmade bed escaped me but I managed to grab a corner of the bedspread, I crept on my knees, reaching the pillow which was trying to displace me onto the wood-floor carousel, music, children's screams asking for

— Yes

I bought a kit at a pharmacy far from home, the salesman and the other customers couldn't stop staring at me, the passengers on the metro were all talking about me, they could all see the package hidden in my purse and the people in the plaza looked down on me, I closed the door like a thief, bounded up the stairs quietly, I could tell all the neighbors knew by the sound of their cutlery, I locked myself inside the bathroom, feeling like they were watching, just like God was watching, I prayed the color in the tube wouldn't change and it did change

pregnant pregnant

the commander and the ex-policemen in the office with my godfather, along with the crosses and picture of the Pope, talking about the deaf woman's husband, and they stopped when I walked in, waiting for me to leave to start up again

— What's the problem we'll kill him

— *Maid or housekeeper cross-eyed or crippled, but serviceable*

because he'd never leave her, tell her goodbye, replace her with me, who'd adjust the hyacinths for him, you could see a little bit of Paço da Rainha palace, it was always obscured behind the boxwoods, I'd never seen the veranda open, so I imagined furniture shrouded in sheets, closets left wide open, dusty and deserted, deathly, my grandfather went to bed fully clothed, wearing his cap, everything was normal, his coloring, the expression on his face, his appetite, the doctor listened to his chest, tapped him, took his temperature and told my parents

— He's in good shape

and my parents to my grandfather

— You're in good shape

and my grandfather asked for some soup and the next morning he died, his cap not having moved one millimeter, when the curtains were open, the palace appeared between the plane trees and the buses around Mitelo Plaza, my godfather to me

— What?

the candy wrapper bothered me, it's a sin to spit out the host, whoever does will go blind, whoever hides a host in their truck will see their house burned to the ground that very same night, if my godfather approached me I'd grab the kitchen knife and cut him open just like a fish, then toss out the guts, those grey eggs

— What's the problem we'll kill her

on the Cabo Ruivo bridge beyond the cargo ships, my wrists tied with wire, two lead balls, the street lights of Alcochete village reflected in the mud, my color altered by the make-up, it was impossible for the commander and the ex-policemen not to know, for the entire world not to know, even my godfather, his pupils gazing at me the same way bulls gaze

— Fatinha

October clouds above the palace, the hand on my head, the commander

— Kill whom, dona Fátima?

the walls slightly spinning, the desk, bookcase and crucifix, the picture of the Pope, a diploma in Latin, everything dead, grey, but I don't tell them who has to be killed, I don't tell them whose routine needs to be verified, their routes, their timing, the boarding-house room where we'd meet, the nails without pictures, the bathroom, the vase, the tiny window onto a garbage alley, the owner, in front of the key cubbies writing down made-up names, I ask the ex-policemen to wait for me outside in the street as I climb the stairs under the burnt-out wall lights, door numbers painted on ceramic, a huntress Diana figurine and a clay donkey on a little table, pull the latch, push open the door, the vertical square patch of the window, the horizontal square area of the bed, the bench on which he placed his clothes, the raincoat on a hook

(it was never raincoat, it was an overcoat)

two or three steps at most to reach the mattress, puffing out his chest, his shiny ring, something like a smile

— Hi there Fátima

open my purse, get the gun out, look at him without seeing him, his body now sitting down, his arms attempting to flee and everything happening without me noticing his body falling in the mirror, not in the room, I think it was in the mirror because after the shot I'd shut the door and run downstairs outside into the street.

7

AFTER MY UNCLE left, no one ever came to my room to tell me good night. They'd turn out the lights, close the door and I'd be alone with the dolls on the shelf above my bed, the bears, turtles, a stuffed Mickey Mouse missing an ear, with a vest button replacing its left eye, a torn arm my grandmother had mended, stuffing the wound with sawdust and stitching it back up, Mickey Mouse on her lap, not crying or anything in spite of the needle and thread, if they called me to trim my fingernails I'd hide my hands behind my back because the scissors hurt

— I don't want to

watching my mother get them out of her sewing basket impressed me, she promised to give me a sewing basket just like hers on my birthday, with compartments for pins, snaps, spools, ribbons but she didn't, she'd put on her glasses, hold my fingers under the lamp even though it was daytime, and, as usual, when I was scared the house seemed to be screaming, my mother threatening, getting ready to take her shoe off

— Do you want me to hit you Celina?

the house would fall silent, immediately calm down, I would pull all kinds of faces, on the verge of tears

— Let me go

my mother could wear big earrings and I couldn't, she could wear lipstick and I couldn't, she could go out without saying where she was going and I couldn't, all I could have were my bears, my turtles, my Mickey

Mouse missing an ear, and a soup bowl with an elephant in suspenders at the bottom, as soon as the elephant appeared I'd clench my jaw

— All done

my grandmother would lean over the table and look inside my bowl

— There are three more spoonfuls here

there was the bowl with the elephant wearing suspenders and a cup with little blue and lilac stars that made the lemonade taste better, my father would hang his coat on the back of the chair and lean the newspaper up against a bottle without speaking to anyone, a minibus plunged off a bridge in France on the television, ten dead, the fireman lined up the stretchers amid a tangle of broken metal, they'd come back to me in my sleep, covered in bandages running out onto the road, waving good-bye

— Let's get out of here, even though we're dead

first the smell of cologne and afterwards my uncle sitting on the edge of my bed holding a cardboard box filled with silkworms signaling to me that we shouldn't tell anyone

— Good night

waking up the dolls on the shelf, rubbing my one-eyed Mickey Mouse's snout against my nose, judging by the sound of the pots and cutlery my grandmother was in the kitchen washing the dishes, my mother and father were arguing, slamming closet doors, the upstairs neighbor, banging their floor with a broom in protest, my uncle would hide behind Mickey Mouse, then Mickey Mouse would talk to me, not him, my husband, surprised at not seeing anyone in the room

— Who were you talking to Celina?

just as he'd be surprised at my disappointed expression when there was no elephant in suspenders emerging through the potatoes when I ate quickly, I'd stare forever, telling the maid to wait, the elephant wasn't there anymore, I was furious they'd tricked me

— Where'd he go?

my husband getting up to study the plate

— Where did who go?

the two of them leaning over and scrutinizing the porcelain manufacturer marks, covered with expression lines, Elisabeth, those horrible ropes of skin running between my chin and my shoulders, me sitting in a tub of mud up to my neck, peddling bicycles desperately, dying my hair, adding more wires to my bra, fighting my cellulite with Burmese seaweed

— Stop worrying about getting old, dona Celina, most people would say you're twenty if you're a day

Elizabeth, Mariana, Liliana, Alda getting the better of me, snacking at some counter instead of having a proper lunch and getting the better of me, taking camping vacations and getting the better of me, my husband would sit back down, his cheeks trembling, telling the maid to clear away the dishes, and me sitting there wishing she'd break them all, I have no liking for plates without elephants in suspenders to let a person know whether or not they're all done, my uncle, his finger over his lips, conniving

— This is our secret Celina

(and it still is)

would put the bears and turtles back up on the shelf, rubbing Mickey's snout into my face

(the vest button eye was easier to see than the other one)

he'd set him on the pillow next to me so I could get through the night, for example when I had those dreams we were being chased by a thief, everyone gets away, we try to run but the soles of our shoes get stuck to the ground, or when a stranger robs our house and our parents look on without defending us or doing anything about it, sometimes I'd wake up for no reason at all headlights lighting up the ceiling, the bedspread and dresser top would show, the car would fade away at the intersection, and the bedspread and dresser would evaporate, before the thieves got there, I'd reach out to hug Mickey Mouse, rub my nose into his little snout, my husband, pushing me away sleepily

— Let go of me

he didn't smell of felt and sawdust, didn't peer at me through a moth-er-of-pearl vest-button eye, he'd gather himself to the opposite side of the bed, grumbling, batting me away with his fingers, like a duck shaking off water, complaining fitfully in a whiny snore

— I've already taken the pill, damn it

me turning on the light, warding off sleep on account of the thieves, surprised my uncle wasn't there, nor my dolls on the shelf, surprised I was grown up, with painted fingernails, getting up and finding expression lines on the child's face in the bathroom mirror, and not understand-ing the forty years that have suddenly settled in on me in an avalanche of diopters and varicose veins, whatever happened to my waistline, my youthful hips, my thick eyebrows now nothing more than two curved pencil lines, I tried to ask my uncle for help and my uncle, wherever he is, was having breakfast in the kitchen, didn't help me fly, left with his suitcase without saying good-bye

— See you soon Celina

a letter or a postcard

Dear niece

an address jotted down in my school notebook, if I could turn time inside out as if it were a sock, I took out an advertisement in the news-paper, with my telephone number and home address, I waited for weeks and no one answered, I went to the newspaper offices countless times, the woman working there, shuffling through the pigeon holes just to clear her own conscience, a look of pity, wanting even more than I did to come across an envelope addressed to me

— Nothing for you

she wore two widow's wedding bands, I could tell she wanted to answer my ad herself, she invited me to drink herbal tea at a nearby bakery, told me she lived alone with a crippled basset hound and was constantly at the veterinarian's on account of his bad liver, she'd call herself on the phone leaving messages from a made-up friend inviting her to the movies then she'd be almost happy for almost two minutes, imagining going to the movies with a friend, but she wore a really strange fringed Indian scarf with little jingling bells and an enormous, ugly ring with sculpted Brahmins, which made me feel ashamed of her, then I'd feel ashamed for feeling ashamed, but she'd have already gotten into the taxi, I couldn't gather the courage to look her up, the little bells and the ring terrified me, to share the dramas of her basset hound's digestive system in an office ripe with the stench of shearing, nor to visit her in what I imagined would be her tiny apartment, with pillows on the floorboards gnawed by the failing basset, incense infesting the entire place with moribund sweetness and altars with Oriental gods, their multiplying arms and smiles in the forefront of piles of dirty clothes heaped in a corner, ten-year-old magazines and ratty carpeting, while my uncle most certainly was rubbing another Mickey Mouse's little snout in another girl's nose at night making her fly up to the plaster ceiling

— Fly, Berta, fly

(or Adelaide or Madalena or Ester)

where she'd probably discover the Christmas presents on top of the armoire, unscrew the lightbulb and turn off the world, my grandmother had died years before, my father had stopped reading the newspaper after his stroke and, although he couldn't move, stuck to the fabric without taking up any space, like a dinosaur's footprint in stone, my mother was always bumping into him

— Clod

facing off with those increasingly frail Jurassic bones, the shadow of a knee, the indentation of his hipbone dissolving into the velvet, he died in April by which time we could barely see him, he'd become part of the house itself, falling apart along with it, my mother disheveled, her ankles swollen, so different than before

(— Expression lines, dona Celina, expression lines)

shuffling over to herself, insulting the photograph

— Get this idiot out of my sight, Celina

nonetheless barely had I put the photo in my purse, planning to get it out of the apartment with the jammed Persian blinds that were missing slats, where it was strange to think I'd ever lived, tiny, barren, humble in colors I only now realized didn't match, in materials I only now realized were cheap and my mother, outraged as she opened my purse to put the framed photograph back on the television

— Leave your father in peace, Celina

six months younger than her husband and so similar to the house, tiny, barren, humble, the vase of flowers on the veranda, in need of spraying, just like her hair, my husband greeting her, greeting my father, waiting for my grandmother to come from the kitchen, drying her hands on her apron, to greet him too, my family noticed his different clothing, different manners, and he pretended not to see, he smelled like my uncle's cologne except it was more French, he didn't put me on his lap, didn't toss me to the ceiling, didn't rub Mickey Mouse's snout in my nose, he crossed his legs and no portion of skin showed between his sock and his slacks, no sagging, like my uncle, except more polished, better manners, and my mother, enchanted

— Senhor Borges

nearly a silhouette of her old self, my grandmother brought cakes and set them on the table, decked out in necklaces and rings borrowed from her cousin, wearing one of my mother's blouses, too big for her, my father curled up, uncomfortably ensconced in his newspaper, which he wasn't reading, obviously, on account of his trembling hands, they showed my husband the album of me as a child with the protective tissue sheets between each page, me as a baby on a pillow, me on the beach with a straw hat catching my braids, me in the finalists' ball at the Industrial Club, me in a capelin hat, along with the bride and groom at my neighbor's wedding, my hair in a bun and wearing gloves, I could have been a fashion model

— Have you noticed her figure, senhor Borges?

or an actress

— Have you noticed her voice?

and instead I was a temporary secretary at an insurance company earning a pittance and a half per month, just think of how unfair, senhor Borges, my husband on the sofa with the loose springs setting my father off kilter, the rest of us sitting around on wooden chairs, my father leaning his newspaper against the bottle of wine, irritated, shrouded in advertisements, a close friend knocking at the door with some fabricated excuse leaning into the living room to catch a glimpse, my proud grandmother, sharing the secret the entire building already knew, drawing the bamboo curtain so the neighbor could take a better look

— My granddaughter's fiancé, dona Edith

if I'd knelt down under the table I'd have found my husband's hand in search of my knee, lingering over my kneecap, his hand sliding slightly up my thigh and suddenly only the bottom half of me existed, I mean my top half was using the knife and fork, drinking wine, cutting my meat, answering questions while my other half was battling my husband without really battling, getting smaller and smaller, frazzled, now miniscule, trying not to notice him not to push him away, not to feel him, if my father were to let his napkin drop, if it weren't for the tablecloth, if dinner were to be over, my husband's partner

— I'm not going to leave Mimi, Celina

talk to the driver and pay him, if I talk to the driver and pay for the café in Espinho, a way to get away from here, the driver and that fat girl

Simone

to go somewhere no one knows him among the fog and gulls, fishing boats, those zinc cabins, more like barns than cabins, the police making their way into their café, and them thinking they're invisible among the beers, fried tidbits, snails

— *We're not here*

my husband's hand in search of my knee and lingering over my knee-cap, my mother indifferent, my grandmother indifferent, my father invisible behind his newspaper, settling into the corner of the sofa as if the rest of us didn't exist, excessive nerves, too many opinions, too many people, too many voices, my mother

— Coward

I, flying up next to the ceiling in thrilled joyfulness

— Father

if I could fly now my husband's hands wouldn't be touching me, his stiff smile wouldn't be getting bigger, his sleeve wouldn't be touching my sleeve

— Don't kiss me, they're looking at us

and I might even have liked him, I don't know, I felt sorry for his sad enthusiasm, his anxious rush to agree with me, moving his sleeve away from mine

— Sorry

holding a bouquet of flowers like a proud child with a lollipop

— Sorry

and me like a dead body in a casket surrounded by tulips, the dead body I come across in the wedding photos in the living room, drowning in organza, my mother and my grandmother supporting me, happy with the mummy, disguised in their rented formal wear and my uncle didn't come to my wedding, nor did the bears and turtles from my shelf, nor did Mickey Mouse, rubbing his snout against my nose

— Hi, Celina, see you tomorrow, Celina

I, like when I couldn't run in my dreams, my shoes glued to the floor, my muscles weak, my movements stuck and, just like in my dreams, my family looking on and not doing anything, my uncle shaking Mickey Mouse right and left, I, pretending I believe Mickey is moving by himself and then really believing it

— Has anyone ever told you you're a very pretty girl, Celina?

with no adult hands shaking him, nor mouth speaking for him, no adult disguising their voice, manipulating him, making him act silly, do pirouettes, somersaults, the cloth arm reaching for my arm under the sheet

— Aren't you going to hold my hand?

to my neck nestled in the pillow

— Can I snuggle with you Celina?

Mickey Mouse, without my uncle's company was dejected, his arms and legs mixed up, as limp as the regrettable lion I never touched, kind of idiotic, losing his colored cotton mane, my mother and my grandmother would come in and Mickey Mouse, all excited, jumping buoyantly out of the dark, roused

— Celina

I never met anyone again who pronounced it the way he did, he made it sound so pretty

I mean it

in falsetto, different than all the other names, original

and Celina was me, it may seem ridiculous but I'm still waiting for someone to call me like that, waiting for that tinny enthusiasm, somersaults and swaying I still understand

— Celina

and my heart leaps with my jump, there were no mashed potatoes, no sandals two sizes too big, or teaspoons full of aspirin dissolved in sugar, only strawberry ice cream and hamsters, just me dressed up like a fairy on a golden throne in the school play, I was never the fairy, always the nanny or the shepherdess, or a star or flower and I had to hold still the entire time, my head poking out from the pieces of pointed green paper around my neck, dying of itchiness while the others accepted the applause, held out their skirts, took their bows and, if a flower off in the corner of the stage were to sob spitefully, the enraged teacher would tell the princes and princesses to stop

— Raquel

as she dried the flower's eyes in threatening fury

— Next year you won't be a flower, or anything else, you'll sit out in the audience you'll see

the flower, sniveling, the princes and princesses starting all over, Mickey Mouse would persuade me that being a flower was the height of success, he himself had spent twenty-eight years just dreaming of being a flower, whenever he saw a play, he had eyes only for the flowers, didn't give a damn about anything else

— I wish I were a flower Celina, if I were a flower, I'd wait, in no time you'd be grown up

(*Elizabeth, victorious, standing at the counter snacking instead of lunch and victorious*

— *Expression lines dona Celina expression lines*)

and I would marry you

it's completely stupid, but nonetheless I want to write Mickey Mouse so badly, I'm already grown up, I'm big, marry me, and write Mickey Mouse on the envelope, that's all, plus the stamp, no address and Mickey Mouse would get it, we'd both be dressed up as flowers, wrapped up in green paper with petals at our temples and Conception, who loved being a bee, would be there in her yellow and black striped costume buzzing around our ears flapping her elbows up and down

— Zzzzz

enthusiastically singing a song out of tune written by the director who compared bees to students and times tables to honey, okay now children, let's learn our times tables like little bees extracting honey, Conception running from flower to flower and now extracting sweet honey in a costume without black and white stripes, serving clients in a ready-to-wear outfit, without any of that energy to flap her elbows up and down, without buzzing, having forgotten the okay now children, let's learn our times tables like little bees extracting honey, with a lot more expression lines than I have, except she doesn't have any Elizabeth to remind her of them nor time even to see them, if I ever run into the princes and princesses from school good Lord how they've changed

Conception Aline Mécia Luísa

given that, away from any mirrors, I'm still me, they offer me a Spanish sweet and a chocolate umbrella which I immediately accept, they challenge me to a one-legged race from here to there and they get a head start but I win, drawers filled with useless, precious treasures, pencil stubs, stickers with photos of actresses, illustrated magazines, secret passions, diaries, a passionate mess, the photo of the best friend who we'd give our life for

— Filomena

I happened to find out she lives in Venezuela, they'd let her pin up pictures of four American singers clipped from magazines, she got her period before me, showed me her pads in secret, hiding in the kitchen nook, she, extremely proud of herself and I, amazed

— So lucky

I never respected anyone as much as I respected her that's why I was thinking of telling Mickey Mouse

— Aren't you going to hold my hand Celina?

but I couldn't, I was terrified he'd lose interest in me and visit Filomena instead, rub his little snout into her nose at night, waddling three buildings away without giving me a thought, my uncle grabbing her by the waist

— Fly Filomena fly

and I, devastated and earthbound, Blessed Mother who stole all that from me, I know for sure I didn't lose it, they stole it, my husband stole me from the insurance company, nothing but manners and caution

— Miss Celina would you do me the honor of allowing me to invite you for lunch?

so that's why I had to seek out the driver in the garage, the oak tree branches at the windowsill murmuring to me what I didn't want to hear, persistent, criticizing me, insistent, the driver screwing and unscrewing a part, I, talking to one of the oak tree branches

— Shut up

if the driver hadn't listened to the branches, changed his mind, apologetically making up some excuse, if a person's never eaten from a bowl with an elephant in suspenders on the bottom then she can't understand, drawers filled with useless, precious treasures, now filled with prescription labels, gas bills, my bears and turtles replaced by melancholy knickknacks, souvenirs encased in glass spheres from holidays in Tangiers, my sinusitis inhaler, ear plugs so I can sleep, a parking ticket written out in childish handwriting, a small package of tissues to dry the tears they also stole from me, that my husband stole from me

— Miss Celina would you do me the honor of allowing me to invite you for lunch? replaced by rusty old drops, slimy streaks, dripping make-up, if my uncle were here to tickle me with the cloth arm, show me Christmas on top of the armoire, I wouldn't be living like this

—If you were a flower I'd wait a minute or two, you'd grow up and I'd marry you

taking sleeping pills to get to sleep and panicked at the thought of sleeping, same reason I didn't go to a doctor to fix my breasts, fear of the anesthesia, I, holding still in bed not daring to make one move, eyes wide open in the dark, with nothing out there in the dark except for darkness and even more darkness, if my husband turns on the bedside table light I'll hold still, my ankles are so far away from me, at the other end of the mattress, my body has grown so much longer than I am it doesn't belong to me, regions in my depths not belonging to me and nevertheless are sometimes painful and Elizabeth paints red with the care of a miniaturist using a tiny brush and cotton balls

— You don't have a single callus on your feet dona Celina, you could frame them

just like rotten trees, with only roots remaining, it wasn't me that rotted, I was rotted by others, my husband rotted me, empty drawers once filled with a passionate mess, beloved precious treasures, stolen, stolen

I knocked at the garage door as the oak branch scraped the window frames, I asked if I could sit down, I, a grown married woman, asking a driver who was unwrapping a piece of cloth folded in three, screwdrivers, a piece of wire, and I was afraid of the oak branch at the little window as if the branch were to tell someone

— It doesn't matter, just forget it

and it wasn't on account of the Motherland or politics, or the communists, or the Russians in Africa, it was because my husband stole from me, how much do you want to finish off a thief, not an honest person, but a thief, without him understanding what he'd stolen and, when he said he didn't understand what he'd stolen I said it didn't matter, since the courts wouldn't understand either, they haven't written laws about stealing what my husband stole from me, I'd pay him nearly half what he needed to buy the café in Espinho if he'd

— *Double it*

the entire café, the transfer, furniture, supplies, an employee to help with deliveries, everything, the oak branch scraping the window and I, worried about the branch's frenzy

— *So?*

and so the day before they killed my husband, after I'd put on my cap, the plastic frilly turban that makes me look like a hardboiled egg, to make it easier to remove my make-up, put on my nightgown, and my wool socks since it was winter, turned out the lights, snuggled in and gotten settled, hearing my parents and my grandmother in the living room, my mother's and grandmother's voices and my father's newspaper, crackling as he straightened the pages, I sensed them opening the door slowly and closing it again, I sensed my uncle's breathing, the effort to not make any noise that makes silence unbearably filled with noises or makes us want noise like we want to throw ourselves off the veranda, Mickey Mouse, his arms and legs jumbled up, as limp as the regrettable lion I never touched, quivering, coming alive, trembling somersaults, rubbing his snout into my nose

— Celina

and then everything was once again in its place, in order, no one would come after me, bother me, hurt me, no one would steal from me ever again and I could sleep.

8

I MAY LIVE with the driver but I'm not one of their servants, I don't have to wear a cap, uniform and gloves and serve at table

(— Take the plates from the right Simone, serve from the tray on the left)

when the general and the secretary come to lunch, the boss, obsequious at one end of the table, the end with the decorative silver bowls and funny little animals from Macau in the background, and the deaf woman smiling at the other end, her detached pleasantness, giving me orders with her eyes, now the fish, now the sauce, now clear everything and bring the cheese, as if only her smile were there and she, freed of her body, were hovering God only knows where, real and invisible, like souls tapping us with their fingers in séances

— Cucu

I, dizzy from the rustling branches, the sound of the faucet in the empty swimming pool and the general's monocle, serving from the right, clearing from the left, getting the order of people I should serve first mixed up, pouring red wine over white wine, dripping the sauce, the general pushed his chair back, his pants stained

— Oh

my boyfriend's boss, looking at me as if he were going to kill me, dunked his napkin in the water glass and crawled over, pushing the secretary out of the way, who was at a total loss, agitated as a hen jumping up and down in a loft, asking for stain remover, like a drowning man asking for a beret

— Excuse me

wiping the general's thigh with the dripping authoritarian napkin, rubbing the stain with both hands, like a washerwoman at the river, the general shook him off with his riding crop, affronted

— You're getting my shoe wet you idiot

the deaf woman's indulgent, kindly smile, like an unflappable crescent moon lurking above us, lifting her fork slowly and politely from the tablecloth to her mouth

I dreamt I'd had a child, that I had a son, the doctor promised me I'm normal, it wasn't my fault I wasn't getting pregnant

— *Cat got your tongue Simone?*

and I, lying quietly on the mattress in the garage, smelling the damp dirt the gardener was watering, the evening breeze, the seeds and roots running through my body, I wanted to ask him and I wasn't able to, I wanted to ask him

a child

my boyfriend's boss trying to dry off the pants by blowing, ignoring the crop tapping his back, the monocle tearing him apart, the jelly on his chin

— Idiot

the decorative silver bowls and the funny little animals from Macau taunting

— Idiot

the secretary on the verge of stabbing me

(— I'm not your maid, not your)

tossing the boss's napkin at the flower vases outside the dining room, shoving him, helping the general stand up

one of his feet walked normally, the other one made a little noise like a swamp

everyone bending over looking at the stain in horror at the sacrilege, the commander, bishop, ex-policemen, the partner's widow who was terrified of the oak branch, everyone except the deaf woman, blissfully peeling an apple, in agreement with the mayhem and telling the world

— But of course

believing she was answering some question or fulfilling a request, my boyfriend, who was guarding the house with a machine gun, was making threatening signs through the window at someone that wasn't me since I wasn't wearing that uniform, those gloves, stopped in the middle of the dining room balancing a platter from which something was dripping

the pudding

falling in huge purple drops splashing onto the wood floor, the commander stepped in one of them

— Damn it, damn it

and stood there forever contemplating the sole of his shoe, just like those aluminum stork garden decorations, rocking back on forth on one ankle, cleaning himself off with his pocket handkerchief, the diamond shaped kind, sticking out of his upper coat pocket the way that made men look so elegant, the secretary was helping the general trot back and forth, his good foot solid, his wet foot clomping along, punishing the universe one stomping foot at a time, I was worried about the flower vases, the Oriental statues, the porcelain greyhound, with stupid eyes staring at leftover stew in hungry expectation, if it were to come by a morsel of lamb I bet it'd yelp with pleasure

— Thank you

the faucet continued complaining in the empty swimming pool, a vexed turtledove, dozens and dozens of hidden, tearful children, begging, calling out, the deaf woman finally noticed there was something strange since the knife stopped on the apple and the smile transformed into a silent question, the partner's widow was wringing her pearls, one of the ex-policemen, not the taller one, the shorter one, helped me steady the platter, the one who helped my boyfriend with

— Is there something wrong with you or what?

who helped my boyfriend with the minister's airplane, I saw them build a little box with cylinders and tubes, get a hold of the mechanics' uniforms at the airport, put on the caps, wait for the van, the taller policeman at the wheel at the back gate, the deaf woman staring at us from the terrace was like a canary on a branch, her neck beating quickly

tic tic tic

and I, alarmed

— She knows

trying to stop them, not let them leave

— She knows

because at that point she wasn't floating or smiling, she just kept combing her hair in long gestures like those life-sized dolls at fairs, playing the violin or marching, monotonous and blind, but able to see inside us with their painted pupils, I tried to hold my boyfriend back so the deaf woman wouldn't kill him like those dolls kill us if we don't get away in time, the men who keep them plugged in

— Don't come near

the dolls, acting as if they're harmless, beating drums, moving their wooden chins, my mother her hands clasped in prayer

— Saint Anthony

at the mercy of a wooden claw, an electric shock, a blow, God's vengeance, who knows, these might be like angels, they might shake frighteningly, might be as cruel, the Bible says they would burn cities with their breath, in three months at most I'll have a café in Espinho and I'll be happy, I don't want my father to appear accusing me like silent dead people do, following us around, I don't want

I dreamt a child came out of me and I couldn't see him clearly, I told my doctor

— I dreamt I had a child

those soft, small feminine doctors' hands, touching without touching, so smooth

— Your husband should take a test ma'am

he brought the test folded up inside an envelope

(it seemed as if I could only feel the paper, I couldn't feel my agenda, or my coin purse, or my keys, nothing except the test inside the envelope, forever present and extremely heavy)

and for two or three days I didn't dare, the oak branch spied on me through the little window, so I'd turn my back, hide among the tools, the engines and, even then, the branch

— Ah ha

one afternoon, when we got back from the beach, I handed him the envelope before he and the ex-policeman shut themselves away in the little back room, where I wasn't allowed inside and from where they always left, quiet and serious, with a package that the commander or the secretary would come pick up, handling it as if it were made of crystal, my boyfriend

— What's this?

turning grey, turning red, then grey again

(the oak branch, jubilant

— Now you're in trouble)

and grabbing a fan belt, pulling off my buttons, throwing me on the floor, the taste of myself in my mouth, my boyfriend's eyes like the life-sized dolls at the fair

— You went and told the doctor I'm no man, you went and told the doct

playing the violin or marching

(near the Indian woman's fortune telling wheel a bug-eyed witch gyrating vulgarly, my mother, hands clasped in prayer

— Saint Anthony)

the fan belt as I was bumping into soft objects, inner tubes, tires, a broken car seat, a calendar glued to the wall with four strips of dressing tape, pliers, screw drivers on a low shelf, a print of a naked woman straddling a motorcycle till some part of my body broke, one of my legs gave out, lying on my back in an archipelago of oil

(a patch of sky through the garage roof and in the patch of sky February swallows, their mud filled bills reaching toward their nest)

my boyfriend grabbing the paper, holding it up to the cigarette lighter and letting the flames fall on me

— Now go tell the doctor if I'm a man or not

a sharp little flame falling off me before I got burned, rolling into ashes, slowly piling up and evaporating into nothing, the trigger clicked as I moved away

— Am I a man or not tell me I'm a man or not

I looked at him without protecting myself, without crying, the trigger clicks, and there was no bullet, clicks again and there still wasn't a bullet, that night as I lay down next to him I thought it would be so easy to kill him, just kill him, seeing the reflection of the oak branch in the swimming pool, the porch light covered in mosquitos, the smell of the damp dirt the gardener had watered, the wind, seeds, daisy stems and my baby in a crib, not his, mine, the three bell chimes that helped him get to sleep, I went down the stairs in Espinho feeling the corners of the stairwell with the tip of the revolver, I found him arranging the chairs, tables, coffee cups, glasses, putting up the partitions, balancing on a beer crate to reach up and turn off the alarm, and with this, the deaf woman on the terrace combing her hair in lengthy empty gestures, I, alarmed

— *She knows*

the dolls at the fair playing the violin or marching, monotonous and blind but seeing something inside us with their painted pupils, I tried to hold back my boyfriend and the ex-policeman, to stop them leaving

— She knows

the gardener wearing his gloves, the blight spray around his neck, clearing the rose garden, pruning branches and leaves, if I found myself alone he'd be up on the step ladder paying me compliments, for example when I took clothes off the clothes line or returned from the grocery store, I'd find him whistling

— Hi there sweetie

men are such children, so weak

(my baby came out of me, just look how perfect he weighs three kilos)

my boyfriend tilted his head towards the terrace, noticing her fingers apparently plaiting her hair

— She doesn't know anything, didn't notice a thing, she's utterly absorbed with her braid a single braid dampened with brandy, the deaf woman told me about how every single morning her grandmother's servants would get her dolled up in some city in Galicia

she swore it

where it's December all year long, hours spent on her braid, dipping it in a basin of alcohol, then setting her paralyzed grandmother on some sort of throne, with saints, to bless the café where the family lived, her mother in the kitchen, her father receiving payments and doing the accounts, the sick uncle going from table to table, the rain steaming up the windows, mixing with the steam from the food, my boyfriend wearing the airport uniform and cap, arranging the package inside the automobile

— She didn't even notice us

the ex-policeman covered it with a blanket, secured it with string, my boyfriend's boss ambled off the porch, not wearing a tie, tapping his watch with his finger

— Half an hour late, half an hour late the general's orders were

walking right past me, ignoring me

— Hurry up

the deaf woman had stopped combing her hair mid-gesture, I could have sworn someone took out her batteries like when the fair is over and they strike the snack stands, stop the music, turn out the lights till there's nothing left but an empty lot and hobos looking for leftovers in the grass, not only had she stopped combing her hair, but she was leaning over the veranda terrace, following us with her painted pupil eyes, I wanted to tell my boyfriend's boss

— She knows

but my boyfriend's boss was still tapping his watch

— Hurry up

going down the road covered in winter potholes, from the gate down the hillside, a blackbird in the neighboring property kept insisting

— Simone

just like my finger

— Simone

in the sand, and when the cars headed off toward Lisbon and I went back through the gate, the gardener had disappeared into the toolshed with the pliers and the rose bush branches and the two of us were there in the garden, the deaf woman on the terrace and I, near the garage, without words, since men don't even realize we talk

— You know, Ma'am

the blackbird coming and going between the canopies, jumping to the ground quickly, stared at me, fled, and she also, without words

— I know

and as she said

— I know

starting back to plaiting her braid, I understood she would never tell anyone, the police, courts, government, not because she was worried about her husband but because her husband didn't exist, just like my boyfriend didn't exist, we existed, waiting

the doctor told me that I can have children, I'm normal, it's not my fault I don't get pregnant

she, there on the terrace, combing her hair, looking at me and the tulip vases, the drizzle and the blackbirds in the pine trees, I approached the tool shed where there were sacks of bulbs, rakes, sickles, ropes and a piece of hose on a hook, it seemed like she was smiling again

— But of course

as if only her smile were there

a pretty, chubby woman

(thought the gardener)

not one bone showing, unlike those skinny women who remind me of gypsies' donkeys, all elbows and knees like blades, I, working in the hyacinths and she, coming out of the garage, in her bathrobe, barefoot, getting the driver's shirts off the clothesline, barely had to get on her tiptoes to reach the clothespins, her shoulder showing through a big tear in the fabric, I'd give up a week's pay for half an hour's chat, I'd set to whistling and she'd be putting the shirts in the tub, she'd pick up the tub and carry the tub off, this went on for a month, two months, three months, I'd show her some signs, but nothing, then five days ago, who'd have ever thought, I was cleaning the disinfectant pump before changing my boots and going home, then a shadow covering my shadow, fabric brushing against fabric

the deaf woman no longer on the terrace but right there

— But of course

looking approvingly, underst

I, rubbing the pump with a rag

(thought the gardener)

the woman closed the door, leaned the shovel against it, pulled up her dress, and I thought

— *This is a lie*

— *This isn't happening*

— The boss's trick so he can have an excuse to fire me or they're both play-ing me to get money, they'll hit me up screaming

— Pay

I defended myself with my arm and hurt myself on a nail, I looked closely to see the blood on my hand, squished the flat of pansies, the flat of dahlias and don't really remember what all else but I am sure I didn't drop the pump, because I was thinking that, although the rusty pump had a jammed piston, it would save me from her, just like I'm sure the woman answered the smile in the garden belonging to someone else with a smile

(thought the gardener)

and aside from smiling it seemed to me she was saying quietly

— But of course

as if she were answering an echo, she put her dress back down, opened the door, rounded the shed towards the garage and I, sitting there in the dahlias studying the nail hole and the blood on my hand, realizing my pants were down, around my knees, one of my boots was off, my collar had come unsewn, hoping my wife wouldn't notice but if I know her, complaints to her friend, suspicions, tears, I stopped by my sister's so she could mend the shirt

— If I get home looking like this Rosalina will give me a sermon, a long, sung mass included

my brother-in-law, an envious fellow who doesn't deserve what he has, walked me out to the motorbike shooing away the gun dogs

— So, how was the gal?

and even if I'd wanted to answer I didn't know because it wasn't the pretty, chubby girl, with not one bone in sight, wearing her bathrobe and reaching up on tiptoes to unclip the clothespins, it was a smile at someone I don't know answering

— But of course

as I was sinking into the bag of bulbs, packages of sulfate, fertilizer, till I realized I couldn't breathe, till I didn't realize, till I didn't

I'm not their maid, I don't have to wear a cap, uniform, gloves and serve at table when they invite the general and secretary to lunch, all I have to do is lie down in bed without answering my boyfriend or anyone else, writing my name in the sand

Simone

in the sheets, erasing and rewriting

Simone

writing again

Simone

in the sheets, waiting for my son, a child, my son, the one I got from the gardener in the tool shed, to caress me, call me, talk with me and, still caressing me and still talking, to come out smilingly, slowly from me.

9

I'M NOT TAKING anything with me: I'm leaving the suitcase, keys, money, the wig they bought me when I got sick, I'll start walking and none of them will catch me. When I get to Coimbra, I'll steer clear of the city in case any of my cousins

— What happened to you Mimi?

run into me by chance, at first distracted then, their expressions changed, the question

(— I'm not sure how I know her, but I do know her)

the doubt

(— She's lived in Lisbon hasn't been here for over fifteen years, so it can't be her)

the certainty

(— It's Mimi)

the question, again

(— I heard she was sick, hospitalized, lost her hair)

the smiles surrounding me, concerned and happy, concerned and happy no, feigning concern and happiness hiding their curiosity, their surprise

(— Some people do survive cancer after all)

and instead of

— You're still alive Mimi?

hugs and kisses, fearful I might be contagious, that they might also
lose their hair

— What happened to you Mimi?

not knowing whether the hair is mine or if the surgeon implanted
it because after all her husband is so rich, and since he's so rich she
started ignoring the family, she's ashamed of us, a deaf woman, a cripple,
ashamed of us, I never understood why

— You're still alive Mimi?

Mama Alicia liked her best, she always called her, she'd get her to bring
sugar, coffee and soda water then the two of them would lock themselves
in the room doing who knows what, Mama Alicia, to us, angrily

— I don't want anyone bothering me now

and always smiling at that idiot, go figure, if at least she were pretty
and smart, but she's neither one nor the other, quiet, skinny, flitting
about off in some corner, if we ever talked to her, she'd smile instead of
answering, we could say whatever we felt like saying, call her names, make
a fool out of her, tease her, pull her leg

— Isn't that right Mimi?

and she'd be as thankful we'd rattled her as if we'd invited her to play,
she was never the matron, always the maid, we of course would be the
housewives, we'd boss her around, make her run errands, tell her to go
fill little bowls with grass, dried insects, little stones and dirt so we could
then cook meals on our little flameless tin stove, we'd move our mouths
as if we were really chewing

— It's delicious dona Clotilda would you like some more?

and Mimi, hungry, sitting on an overturned bucket about three meters away, dying to taste too, but we'd shake our finger

— Since when do maids eat with matrons get out of here

so she'd sit there perched on the bucket watching, unable to taste the grasshoppers or the sand and, as soon as we got sick of eating and turned into teachers and students or doctors and nurses, she'd come over slowly, hoping we wouldn't notice, then, just when she'd be getting ready to take a tiny forgotten grain from the stove, we'd stop being teachers and doctors, run over to her and shake our fingers

— Don't even dream of it

we'd chew up the little grain and go back to our doctor's office, Mimi would perch herself back up on the bucket in silence, she never complained, never cried, didn't tell on anyone, went along with having her appendix removed, being punished, standing next to the cedar for the duration of the class, one night we heard noises out in the yard, we imagined wandering ghosts and beasts, which of course we couldn't identify but which we knew were horrible with hairy, black fur and always hungry to eat little girls that didn't mind their parents, we could sense the footsteps between the washbasin and the outhouse, it was the beasts for sure, so we started trying to figure out which of us had been disobedient that day, we weren't sure whether to huddle together in the bed or to keep our distance because since it was so dark we didn't want the beast to get mixed up about who hadn't minded and eat us unfairly before we could scream

— No it wasn't me it was Julia

begging in vain from inside the hairy stomach where there were already other sobbing little girls, feet or paws dripping with children's blood were getting closer and closer to the creeping vine, it was no good calling our parents because our parents

(who had described the beasts and threatened us with them in the first place) didn't seem to believe us when we swore they were chasing us, they'd think it was just an excuse so we wouldn't have to go to bed and it wasn't, all you had to do was to look down the hallway and there they'd be, bristly, erect and at the ready, you'd have to be blind to miss them, we heard noises out in the yard, this time not near the creeping vine, or between the wash basin and the outhouse, but further away, near the flowerbeds or the henhouse, our hearts stopped beating so fast, our fear subsided a bit, we managed to stay put, not to go out, not to walk through the house to the grown-ups' room, whispering

— Get up and look out the window Clotilde

— You look out

— Scaredy-cat

— I'm not afraid, just being respectful

the restaurant clock with the Roman numerals and the chipped enamel

(life would be so much happier if the Romans hadn't invented those numbers, meaning one thing on the left and meaning the opposite on the right, besides the restaurant clock they were only on the statue in the plaza and on the pharmacy clock

— Go up to the blackboard and write thirty-nine in Roman numerals Palmira)

the clock would swing its brass belly button, imperturbable inside its glass case, mice could be heard scampering near the kitchen table, taunting the mousetraps loaded with rotten cheese, looking for hiding places in the sacks of flour and rice, the wide-eyed dog, his snout right up against the floor tiles waiting to gobble them up as they escaped, if it'd been the black-furred beasts circling the yard, there would have been nothing left of the dog, not even the tiniest bone, we approached the window on tiptoes, paying careful attention to the smallest creaking in the floorboards, the slightest difference in the sound of the clock that when you couldn't sleep would click every once in a while, but it was useless to wait forever for that clicking sound because it'd never happen if you were waiting, just like grown-ups never get undressed in front of us, they must look very strange undressed

horrible beasts with hairy, black fu

and the other houses through the window, chimneys, rooftops with those little shelf-like tiles where pigeons hiss, gutters, verandas, yard walls with pieces of broken glass running along the top shining nastily, sharper and bigger than during the day

(pieces of broken glass in different colors, now uniform, all the same)

the trees were also gigantic, their leaves still and somber, you could count them one by one, when I was seven years old I counted up to six hundred on one canopy, the outhouse, a tiny window cut through the aluminum, the shiny toilet and the freezing geckos, multiplying in the summer and if one ever fell on you, it would make your skin spotty and chapped, the washbasin set atop three cement legs

(the fourth claw broke and its iron shin was exposed)

the plastic basin next to it and the henhouse, a tipped over step ladder serving as a perch, the flowerbeds equally strange, deeper, more somber, a mortuary-like silence, punishing, mysterious voiceless threats and the presence of death, which we didn't understand, they'd say

— Go outside and play

they would put everything under the wreaths of flowers, drink their Port wine, snack on chicken giblets and leave in tears

(when they went to Mama Alicia's funeral, they didn't just cry they also argued, returning from the cemetery screaming and yelling, their tears forgotten

— Why are you arguing over who owns the restaurant daddy?

— Be quiet Julia)

and the black furry beast was Mimi, ignoring the thieves, kneeling near the lower flowerbed, putting grasses, dried insects, little stones and dirt on the tin stove top, keeping her eyes on the flame that wasn't there, pretending to fan it with a piece of paper, radiantly swallowing a make-believe supper, I remember her pajamas, I remember her plaid slippers and so many years later here she is in Coimbra, alone, without her purse, wandering around

— *I'm not wandering around*

her scalp showing beneath her sparse, grey hair

— What happened to you Mimi?

— I've been playing doctors and nurses in Lisbon

tubes up my nose, stuck in my arm, my throat, that folding partition around me, a little bag of cakes waiting to be opened on my bedside table, a juice carton with pictures of pineapples, a vase of pale worn-out carnations, their heads drooping, I ask them to take them away, I don't want to end up like them, dying in water, brittle, skeletal, my name is Maria Emília Baptista Amaral, Mama Alicia always called me Mimi, forty-one years old, married, childless, they give me injections through the tubes, show me X-rays, wear green smock coats, talk amongst themselves, it can't be true, it's not fair, I don't want this, as they gave me anesthesia I put every ounce of energy I had into catching the stretcher-bearer's eye, shutting my right eyelid more than my left, I started repeating, shutting my right eyelid more than my left, shutting my right eyelid more than my left and I started falling, as I fell I passed my cousins sitting in the yard around a little tea service, plates, spoons, cups, drinking nothing, solemnly, pushing me

— Don't even dream of it

I passed my father at the cash register, pompous and full of himself, straightening his tie and counting money, my mother in her cap engulfed in steamy pots, hairy, black-furred monsters trying to bite me and my grandmother on her throne

— Don't forget the Coca-Cola recipe Mimi

my husband talking with Celina in the living room, his arm leaning on the pillow, Celina saw me fall, pointed at me, my husband turned to look at me for a second then continued talking

— Don't worry, she's deaf, doesn't understand

the arm leaning on the pillow tightened around her waist, I was trying to tell Celina about the Coca-Cola recipe, but she was smiling at my husband, a smile that was more than a smile and right after that, little cakes on the bedside table, juice, carnations, everything was so sad, so useless, everything was pale, drooping, dead, one of my legs was asleep, my other leg woke up, but it was as if it were still asleep, I noticed an ankle outside the sheets, just tendons and veins and it took me a while to realize it was mine, there were blue and purple I.V. marks on my wrist, and tiny red marks from needles they'd stuck in me, the surgical tape irritated my skin and it was impossible to scratch myself since my fingernails wouldn't obey me, I looked for Clotilde, Palmira and Julia and none of them were with me, they'd woken up earlier, had already left for school, they were amazed at the insecticide spray equipment in the vegetable garden, my uncle spraying the collard greens and adjusting buttons

— If anyone plays around with this machine they'll end up going straight to the hospital, wheezing and writhing

yelling loudly just to make sure I'd heard

— Did you hear that Mimi?

he was missing teeth, we were all missing teeth for lack of money and the teeth that were left were dark, my mother, for example, was nothing but lips and cheeks, when they gave her false teeth, half her wrinkles disappeared, several summers younger and two centimeters taller, a dainty young lady just like they say in the schoolbooks

(— What does dainty mean mommy?

her mind searching in vain, flipping through words

— Dainty?)

for the entire week my father lost interest in the restaurant servants
and customers, my mother had gotten used to chewing her food with her
gums, so she'd put the false teeth in her apron at mealtime, the lower part
of her face aging tremendously, all the wrinkles back, after coffee she'd
put them back in, move her jaw around to adjust them, her face would
fill out and my father, enthusiastically

— Wow

now I have money and teeth but I'm not carrying any money, I start
walking and no one picks me up, as I approach Coimbra I steer clear of
the city, those girl doctors and nurses removing my appendix sewing my
belly button back up with an index finger

— Hold still

arguing over who was boss, they'd stretch me out on the lawn in the
planter and my pinafore would get damp and cold, Julia would start
cutting into me with her pinky finger scalpel, Clotilde with her sleeves
already rolled up

— Out of my way

all of their hands, including Palmira's, removing meters and meters
of invisible intestines, Palmira would gather them as if she were rolling
yarn, all the way over to the partridge cage, then they'd get scared, fluttering through rubble

warm eggs, cashews, make a little hole with a pen, drink, Julia spiteful

— I'm going to tell Mama Alicia Clotilde

so I let them operate on a second appendix, they dropped me and
ran off to collect daisies, kind of like little scraps of paper doing somersaults by the river, Julia, furious, no one watching her, holding back her
angry tears

— If you don't watch, I'm really telling

the rooster was prancing around them like the pharmacist, deliberate and puffed up

senhor Teles, not wearing his regular tie, instead, a little bow tie

every once in a while, he'd spread his feathers, pounce on one of the hens in an angry fit then, leaving her, he'd shake his hindquarters, recover his dignity, boastfully, alone, grand, his eyes wide open, if I went into the pharmacy with my mother, senhor Teles would grow larger, bristle, change his tone of voice, now deeper, more friendly

— How can I help you dona Rosário?

leaning his chest over the counter, the dark edge at his cuffs and collar in need of detergent, a little ruby-like scab of blood in his hastily shaved whiskers, he'd put his hand inside a jar and come up with half a dozen cough drops tasting like resin, a man with sideburns on the wrapper, he'd let me weigh myself on the scale, moving the large and small cylinders along the numbered cursor, the same man who would kick us out, stomping his feet if we ever showed up there by ourselves

— Scram

now friendly, thinking I'm cute, taking coins from my nostrils, showing me them, putting them back in his pocket, getting more out

— Look what I found dear

I got tired of trying and nothing, not even one of those dirty rusty pennies, my mother wearing a new dress, which still had the price tag on, lingered, revenge for the hours and hours spent in the kitchen, it seemed to me their thumbs were touching at the counter, their mouths blending into a simultaneous prattle, the stuffed kite in the cupboard balancing on a varnished base

— Heh heh

when the pharmacist stomped his feet on the floor the kite would tip over, one of the tacked-on glass pupils would roll away over the floorboards and senhor Teles, crawling around pawing the floor trying to find it

— Scram

minus one pupil, the kite was no more than an inoffensive toy, not a bird, the pharmacist's hands exploring the cracks in the floorboards, he got up, the pupil stuck to his ring finger

— If I die of tetanus you devils will be to blame

the tilted kite no longer scared us and as I got off the scale, thirty-two kilos, the pharmacist was holding my mother's wrist, his fingernails as dirty as his collar and cuffs, and my mother, more spirited than ever, drew back in mock reprimand

— Shocking, senhor Teles

and on those days, she wouldn't lose patience with the kitchen maids, didn't care about the seasonings, styled her hair with extra care, sometimes she sang, the price tag on her skirt fluttering, my father snipping it off

— You're for sale dear

and my mother, confused, beet red, when Mama Alicia got sick they sent me to get cough medicine at senhor Teles's house behind the pharmacy, you had to walk around the store into an unpaved alley, buildings on one side and poplars on the other, I rang the doorbell and only heard trees blowing, if I'd rung the doorbell the previous year I would have been afraid, I was still afraid, but the fact that I now weighed thirty-nine kilos helped, the cursor no longer wavered over thirty-six, I'm big now, I had started to understand why grown-ups never undressed when I was around, it was only one kilo after all, simple, I spent hours thinking about it, senhor Teles lifted a corner of muslin to peek out, came out to the doormat in his bathrobe holding a bag of ice over his stomach, did not offer me cough drops, did not find coins in my nostrils, he was walking over stooped, dragging an ankle

— This won't do young lady

there was not one clean item in the house, moldy dictionaries, a pile of greasy, shiny cold food, more stuffed kites, without all the anger, their bills wide open, one of them was lying out on table covered in ants, you could see an unmade bed with muddy shoes set on top, senhor Teles emerged from smelly alcoves with dripping faucets, wrapped up the cough syrup in newsprint and handed it to me without ever stopping his coughing, spitting stuff into a handkerchief

— This won't do young lady

I think he'd been married and one day his wife, the wind joggling paper orchids in a vase, joggling hangers, joggling open the empty refrigerator, the poplars breaking through the curtains, sweeping through the living room, I felt bad leaving him there with his bag of ice and his ragged bathrobe, the wife moved to Pombal to live with a priest, senhor Teles

people said

would take a bus and hide in a café just to watch her go by, he didn't talk to her, he didn't approach her, didn't bother her, didn't make a scene, he just watched her for a while through the store window, then went back to Coimbra, to feel his clients' wrists on the other side of the counter, knowingly peevish

— How can I help you dona Rosário?

my hair didn't fall out at the hospital, that happened later, with the treatment, my husband, along with his partner's widow, brought me the wig in a box

— A little gift Mimi thank Celina she helped me pick it out

I untied the ribbon, lifted the top and found orange colored hair covering a white plastic head, with traces of colorless features and ruby red lips, my husband held it up to the light to show off the hair color

— Why don't you try it on Mimi?

the widow removed the wig from the plastic head and put it on me, adjusting the elastic, she stood back a little to see how it looked, took her hair brush from her purse and gave me some bangs, opened her make-up bag so I could see myself in the little mirror over the little squares of various ambers with a brush affixed inside a tiny indentation, and what I saw was a pink fingermark and beyond that a person that was not me, with jutting, sharp bones, serious, emaciated, dead, my husband saying to Celina who answered something and started laughing

(a pink fingermark on her teeth also)

till she realized I noticed she was laughing, my husband realized I could tell and lifted my chin with his index finger

his mouth looking happy, but not the rest of him, like in hospital visits when only the mouth looks happy, nothing else, gestures like scarecrows, muddled and abrupt

— It suits you perfectly Mimi

also only with his mouth and nothing else, the driver would bring me gladioli on Thursdays, the bishop came once with his goddaughter and a train of respectful nurses, measured, imposing, he placed his ringed hand on my forehead

— We each have our cross to bear, my dear

and the other patients kissed his stole, the bishop blessed them, distributed medallions, rosaries, religious prints

— *This is a holy war this is a holy war*

— We each have our cross to bear my daughters

and me there in the chair in front of the television, quiet, in my wig, feeling like one of those little circus dogs dressed up like people, balancing unstably up on their rigid hind legs, dripping fear, dripping slobber, their eyes begging to be allowed to go back to being a dog, Celina and my husband hid their smiles behind their hands, the red lips on the plastic head guided me

— Don't pay any attention

their shoulders together, their knees together, their mouths in unison, amused, mockingly

— It suits you perfectly Mimi

the plastic head choosing Clotilde, Júlia, Palmira

they never talked to me, never told me secrets, the three of them would huddle off in a corner talking about dances, having their dresses altered, bows and lace, the nephew of the veterinarian from Águeda whose uncle was going to give him a new American car with dozens of headlights as soon as he was old enough

— I get to sit next to him first

— I said so before you

— No you didn't

— Yes I did

— I'm four months older than you do you think a boy with an American car is going to pay any attention to children

they'd stop talking as soon as I came near, or skip in a circle with me in the middle, with my wig, dressed up like a circus dog

— deaf girl, deaf girl, deaf girl

my husband and the widow on the sofa, my cousins skipping faster and faster circling me

— deaf girl, deaf girl, deaf girl

it wasn't them after all, it was the wind blowing the curtains, I haven't seen them in fifteen years, I guess they've all married, although not to the veterinarian's nephew, who contracted a disease in his esophagus before he was old enough to get the car and the ambulance took him off to a clinic in the mountains, wearing a nightshirt, in a wheelchair, my cousins on tiptoe barely concealing their giggles over his outfit, I, on the other side of the fence with a handkerchief, drying the tears running down my cheeks, of all of us, I was the only one who had never ridden in the front seat of an American car, shy, ugly, sentimental, they'd pull my braids and I never hit anyone, they'd hide my doll and I never said anything, I'd sit on the floor and cut pictures out of magazines, or write with a pencil stub in my school notebook, so they always thought about how unfair it was that I had married into wealth and lived in a nice house in Lisbon, while they

it's not that there's no money, the problem is how tiring it is to be short, separating it all into envelopes, this much for gas, this much for water, this much for electricity, this much for cleaning products, this much for the children's school, this much for transportation, this much for groceries, juggling the money from envelope to envelope, substitute margarine for butter, vegetable oil for olive oil, cut down on meat, convince the appliance store to accept late payments, not turn on the heat throughout the entire winter and now, so unfair, the plastic head suggesting

— Kill them

not getting the revolver from the bedroom and shooting my cousins, but one of those carnival pistols, you pull the trigger and a bouquet of flowers pops out, they, their hands on their heart

— Whew, it was just a game, we didn't die

surprised I hadn't brought anything, I'd left behind my suitcase, keys and the orange wig they'd bought me when I was sick, I start walking toward Galicia and no one picks me up, arriving in Coimbra I keep my distance from the city so I won't have to have my appendix removed, nor stand up against the cedar, if they had at least allowed me to try the little dinner, the herbs, dried insects, stones and dirt, if at least I hadn't had to sneak down to the garden at night, if at least senhor Teles

— How can I help you dona Rosário?

— This won't do Mimi

instead of holding the bag of ice to his stomach, he had given me pine flavored cough drops, taken coins from my nose showing me two that were always the same, even though he'd put them back inside his pocket

— What's this, young lady?

I'll steer clear of Coimbra and in no time at all, I'll reach Vigo, constant rain, Mama Alicia's house among the bushes, boulders, stray cats, thorns, my mother wiping her arms on her apron, complaining

— What a day

and if the house has disappeared, I can always watch the roses over the ocean, sit down on the ruins of a wall, forgotten by all of you, watching the roses over the ocean.

10

MY FATHER WOULD get home at the same time as the pigeons reached
Mercês Church and my mother had put a scarecrow up in the back yard
to frighten them off, just like she would have done in the front yard too,
with huge teeth drawn in charcoal, ready to bite, if she could have been
sure my father would have been frightened by a corncob head rolled up
in a sock, two arms made of cane with newspaper hanging off them, my
father, terrified, on the front doormat defending himself with his briefcase

— What's going on?

my mother, broom in hand, shooing him away just like she did with
the cats that spoiled the onions and the sparrows, the figs

— Go back to your lover you scoundrel

but since my father wasn't afraid of scarecrows, she met him rigid in
front of the kitchen clock hanging over the refrigerator, a fork and spoon
for hands, its face imitating a green enamel pot, the canary tipping over
his water bowl

— Oh Augusto

my father pretending he didn't notice, walking on eggs, turning on
the charm

— Good afternoon

the pigeons on the church façade, their pupils dilated, sleepless, the neighbors would bring their chairs outside chatting against a background of framed firemen and wooden Saint Roch statues, my father as polite as could be, lifted the lid on the pot to see what was for dinner

— Good afternoon

it was obvious he'd re-tied his necktie since he left for work just like there was something in the way he smelled that was mixed with some other smell and wine, my mother, her back to him pointing at the clock, her voice spewing daggers

— You mean good evening

the canary jumping from the lower perch up to the higher perch and from the higher perch back down to the lower perch

— Oh Augusto

the fork keeping the minutes moved ahead in a lurch that shook the world, vibrating as if moving forward excited it, held still till it had permission to jump forward once again, my father's head disappeared in the steam of the stew as he tasted the sauce

— Good evening

innocent, nice, astounded, the same man who on Sundays would walk around all day in his pajamas in confused grumbling, picking up the newspaper, dropping the newspaper, bored with the television, bored with the radio, getting the stamp album from the drawer and not even bothering to open it, contemplating Mercês Church with hatred

— Miserable life

the sort of anger against the church, against the pigeons, that was personal, it's their fault I feel like this, they're the guilty ones, my mother, my cousin and I, all of us making ourselves scarce in the pantry, they'd send me out to spy from the entryway into the living room to assess his mood, awaiting my report in hollow expectation, with bated breath

— Now he's in the kitchen torturing the canary

without his tie, without his smells, without his wine to soften him, one morning he let the canary out of the cage and sunk into his chair

— At least you've been freed

it was awful trying to catch that bird, hiding up in the chandelier among the glass pendants, releasing its strange laughter, we got the step-ladder, my mother and I held it steady and my cousin, stuck on the third step, going neither up nor down, clinging to the steps

— This makes me dizzy

we, with the anxiety of mountain climbers, scoping out the step-ladder cliff, encouraging everyone to stay calm, the canary rattling the light-fixture pendants with its beak, my father having disappeared into his chair, only his hair and his shoes remaining, directing his disdainful lips toward the church

— Miserable life

or dragging himself to the window facing the empty plaza, not one automobile, not one child walking to or from school, no street vendors, no one at all, the sun beating down on the stones, an empty, cloudless sky, the kitchen clock telling the same time, the only things that change, and I don't know why since they're precisely what doesn't need to change, they're my wife getting bigger and my daughter growing taller, my wife whispering

— Go check on your father, Fátima

cautious steps as if I were going to turn around and strangle her, I, who ask for one thing only, peace, just leave me alone, the report mur-mured into a nervous ear

— He's still in his chair not cursing or anything peeling the varnish off the wood with his fingernail my wife, looking for furniture polish since furniture is expensive, cleaning each and every knick-knack, each and every copper eyesore, every little china cup with passionate care, happy with this cramped apartment, this church, these pigeons, these onions in the yard nursed from a watering-can feeding bottle, wearing my hat, transforming this disaster into joy thanks to liver pills and chrome angels, never expecting anything more, except for less tension, my niece balancing on the step-ladder, the canary laughing at her, my daughter who's going to end up in bed with her godfather because I can see clearly how the canon eyes her and to make matters worse

— You mean good evening

now they've come up with some café waitress in Penha da França or a hairdresser in Arroios, the ungrateful canary chiming in

— Oh Augusto

the idiot, instead of disappearing into town went and hung itself on the skeleton of a chandelier my mother-in-law left here, clinking out dim light all winter long, my mother-in-law, my wife and I, entire evenings under the same lamp, in this same house, watching the humidity take over and listening to the mice in the cracks in the floorboards, the women thinking about our marriage and I, thinking

staying

how to get out of there, my wife with a little whisper, entrenched in the kitchen

— Go check on your father Fátima

cautious steps as if I were suddenly going to turn around and strangle her, getting closer, then pausing for a second, drawing away and rather than my daughter I was the one explaining

— He's trying to figure out how to get out of here

the liver pills, chrome angels, and braids of onions hanging from a nail in the sun room, that widowhood of hanging tears, swinging joylessly, lacking the nerve to fall down

— And what if I don't marry Augusto dear God if I end up alone without any help when mother dies?

not out of any love for me but out of fear of the landlord's tyranny, robberies, footsteps out in the yard, my wife pushing furniture up against the door, defending herself with her rosary, asking ghosts

— Who's there?

the hallway is long, with tiny rooms, the doorknobs fall off in our hands, barely enough room in the kitchen for the refrigerator, the trunk that an uncle who worked as a cargo ship machinist brought back from Egypt with some mummies, two-headed falcons and pinchbeck sphinxes, endless evenings with neighbors coughing through every wall and Mercês Church getting bigger and bigger, suffocating us, one Sunday we went down to the churchyard with her mother, and an open umbrella, behind

I don't remember if it was raining but I remember the open umbrella and that my wedding band was bothering me

(shake my finger really hard it'll come off)

we signed our names on the wrong lines in the sacristy, I'd brought my suitcase from the boarding house with one sock hanging out, the clock with the spoon and fork hands was there assuring me the world would go on forever, a constellation of residents, all of them old, with their little shopping bags, paused here and there on the stairs like owls, without the strength to make it up the next flight, I'd go out in the morning and get back at five, taste the stew in the pot, greet my wife politely

— Good afternoon

my wife, offended that I didn't share her love for the mummies and lamps, imagining lovers

— Good afternoon, no, good evening

the canary jumping around ridiculously, pecking at the bone I'd stuck through the cage

— Oh Augusto

and the old people in the same place for weeks on end, leaning on their canes, a skylight, so distant, a bewildered cemetery silence, the shadow of Mercês Church crawling along the plaza, devouring neighbors, grocery crates, what was left of the trees August had beheaded, my daughter who's going to end up in bed with her godfather because I can clearly see how the canon eyes her, my wife having forgotten I died years ago and the three of them remained, still on the stairs, swinging their little shopping bags, a bar of soap, a little bottle of olive oil, a packet of sugar

— Go check on your father, Fátima

cautious steps getting closer, pausing for a second, moving away at an angle, my father

Sorry father, it's me talking now

my father dead for years and in spite of that his place still set for him at the table, mismatched plates, mismatched glasses, flatware greenish with sulfate, the orphaned canary jumping from his perch, his laughter gone, my mother motionless in front of the kitchen clock in the hope of hearing a key in the door, when I got married she refused to visit me

— You've dishonored your father's memory, Fátima

I moved to Campo de Santana to live with my godfather and realized the same pigeons as from Mercês Church flew there, gray and blue, famished, stupid, leaving the statue to circle our veranda in search of crumbs, leftovers, I even found them in the oratory, in the storeroom, on my unmade bed, wandering on top of my pillow and in the sheets, accusing me of I don't know what, like my father would accuse me

— Father

I don't know if I liked him or missed him, my godfather tells me about loving our true superiors and nevertheless no superior has ever seemed true to me, like you for example, what right do you have to get me pregnant, the American ambassador visited us with the commander, general and ex-policemen, my godfather held out his hand, his ring for him to kiss it and the ambassador, not noticing the ring, shook his hand, the secretary kept track of the boats bringing the guns, money and drugs

(my godfather nervous

— Drugs?)

Spanish trawlers their lights signaling along the coast Peniche, Cascais, Tavira, in an engraving above the ambassador the half-naked dead faithful were being resurrected in a landscape of ruins, in another engraving Jesus was walking on water, blessing the olive trees, while dazed bearded disciples beheld Him from some kind of raft, who knows maybe transporting guns, money, explosives, and Saint Stephen wasn't hiding prisoners' sacraments from the Romans in the folds of his tunic but revolvers, mines, grenades, the elderly neighbors' little shopping bags stopped on the stairs, rheumatics patiently hoping the oxide attacking their joints would take pity on them, forged bills, maps, heroin strewn about, after the grocery store closed my mother would ask me to go borrow eggs and sugar, the doorbells seemed to ring within uninhabited caverns stirring clothes moths, the hinges turned like thin cardboard tearing to reveal dark attics, doorless armoires inhabited by greasy coats, troubled eyes looking out at me over their glasses

— Fátima

rummaging in chipped drawers, their wounds shuddering, bandages around their ankles dragging on the floor

dona Mécia dona Mariana senhor Araújo

when they weren't home, cooking on kerosene burners to save on gas, they'd hobble from Mercês Church to the local clinic where their open varicose veins would be brushed with iodine, sometimes I was woken by the invalids' screams

— Rosa

the pigeons would flee the windowsills, grazing trees, chimneys, rooft-
iles, we'd put a blanket on the cage to calm the canary

— Make that bird shut up Fátima

a feather danced over the walls on its way up to the roof, disappearing inside the chimney, reappearing the next day darkened with soot,
the bottom of the cage was a square that slid in and out, cleaned with a
knife, my godfather feeling around in his pockets for candies

— Fatinha

*contrary to what my friend, may he rest in peace, unfairly alleges, not only
did I never look at her in any sort of special way, but I never thought about
living with her, I limited myself, after she got divorced, to taking her into
my home in Campo de Santana because she was like a daughter to me, since
I had supported her, provided her with a religious education, overseen her
studies, presided at her wedding, paid her visits on Sundays out of Christian
charity and in the presence of her husband, I helped them with their rent, left
them an envelope of money at Christmas and Easter, of course my house had
become too big for me, I had a hard time sleeping, missed having someone
with me, I'd kneel to pray in my office and nonetheless her body, her face, her
voice, I'd push them away and they'd come, I didn't ask for their presence, I
didn't want them to come, her knees when she crossed her legs, the tips of her
shoes swishing back and forth, the way she brushed her hair off her face, as I
held her fingers carefully and kissed them I never asked for more than to hold
her fingers and kiss them, when she'd get up to set the table they'd tear her
away from me, it hurt me, I'd think I'm sixty-seven years old dear God, my
heart is broken, I was ordained forty years ago, why now, et ne nos inducas
in tentationem, the first time I went into her room I found her sitting on her
bed reading, saw her clothes folded over the hanger, her sandals, so moving,
set right next to each other, the clock and her ring on the bedside table, she
seemed like a child to me, I wanted to beg her*

— *Do whatever you want with me*

beg

— *Punish me Fátima I deserve it*

and I couldn't talk, I was stunned by the innocence of the lace on her blouse, her neck was so white with the ribbon from her first communion and the medallion of the Virgin, if someone were to take a pair of scissors it would be so simple, if I were to take a pair of scissors unbeknownst to her and her throat I'd be at peace again, requiem aeternam dona eis, Domine, requiem aeternam, and instead I sat on the edge of her bed my broken heart, my kidneys the doctor recommended two liters of tea a day Bishop, Excellency, to dissolve the stones, if I'd brought candies I would have been able to say

— *My dear*

sitting on the edge of the bed with my broken heart, she closed her book her finger marking her place, a beauty spot near her collarbone, another on her wrist, if I get up, if I go back to my room, dear God I don't know if there would still be a God, I don't know if I believe in God, my God, like a mustard seed a man took and it grew in his field, my hand touched the beauty spot on her wrist

— *What are you reading Fatinha?*

perfume bottles, pots of creams, brushes, her index finger marking the page pulled out slightly, not her face, not her body, a canvas chair on the other side of the bed with a stack of fashion magazines and on every single page of those fashion magazines photographs of the three enemies of man, World, Devil, Flesh, models as thin as a rail, obscene, their legs like the lever which they taught me at school could move the Earth if I knew where to stand, if someone were to take a pair of scissors and their throats forever, my God is a jealous God, if someone kept them from reducing my broken heart to ancient dismantled nothingness, models clothed but naked, like my goddaughter's nightgown which she put on taking it off, a young girl's pure lace telling me to tear it, the overly thick stucco the painter applied, the medallion of the Virgin around her neck, her index finger marking the page ordered me

— *Tear me apart*

tear me because I put quilts bordered with fine Egyptian lace on my bed and I perfumed the sheets with myrrh, aloes and cinnamon, the bats around the Jardim de Torel park lanterns could be heard, I made the decision to let the Spanish policemen and the deaf woman's husband take care of the communist priest, in line with the Bible's command to renounce sinners just as I was willing to receive the American ambassador, although he is a Protestant, the arms, money, drugs, fires, bombs, in order to help the suffering of the Golden Calf and to destroy Sodom and Gomorrah, when they told me about the explosion in the minister's airplane, I thought, invoking our Lord, how can one indulge a philistine who forsook his wife and children and who lives in sin with a foreign mistress, between the blood of the Lamb and the blood of men I chose the blood of man, revering the instruments of evil in praise and to the glory of God, I, with my broken heart, faulty gall bladder, kidneys relying on two liters of tea morning and night, my goddaughter, her neck resting on the headboard, her chin on her chest, I kissed the mustard seed beauty spot on her wrist

— What book is it Fatinha?

in the hope that she would do whatever she wanted with me, reject me, send me away, perfume bottles, pots of creams, brushes, her index finger marking the page, the clock and her ring on the bedside table, her sandals set right next to each other, her clothes folded over the hanger, I rested my head, distressed

he laid his head on the pillow next to mine

— Let me rest a little, Fatinha

he didn't hold me, didn't speak to me, didn't come close, I marked my place in the book, set it down on the canvas chair on top of the pile of fashion magazines, I leaned across my godfather to turn out the light, I could sense the trees in Campo de Santana park, the buildings, the monument of the spiritualist and I must have fallen asleep right away because all I remember are the open blinds, the sun on the floor, running up the coat stand and thence to the marble bureau top, and I, throwing my pillow at it to get it out of my bedroom, all I remember is my godfather's absence, the empty half of the mattress to my right, the clock on the bedside table that showed eight twenty-six, no, eight twenty-seven, and wanting to get up

I don't know why

wanting to get up, I don't know why, as quickly as possible.

11

WHY DO THINGS die inside us? Now when he tells me he's not leaving the deaf woman

(and the deaf woman right there in front of us, obsequious, mute, smiling from her distant country, blessing us)

I don't get irritated, don't get angry, don't suffer, I allow my hand to be held, secretively

— Tomorrow after lunch I'll stop by your house

his fingers on my fingers bothered me, my thigh is squashed, instead of exciting me the voice in my ear grates on my nerves, I have to refrain from picking my ear with my little finger, get that out of there, the echo, the damp sensation, I say yes in hopes that he'll let me go, outside, the driver walks by on his way to the garage, the gardener ignores the roses, his eyes on the fat girl who's taking clothes off the clothesline, furniture uglier than mine, lamps I don't like, the ashtray with the bronze sailor, the vase shaped like a newspaper boy hawking dailies, if by any chance I were to marry him, the first thing I'd do is give the sailor and the hawker to the dim cleaning lady, drying her gratitude in her apron

— Dona Celina

carrying those monsters off with sacramental care, my husband's partner shaking Mimi

(such a grotesque nickname, Mimi, I can't get used to it no matter

how many times I repeat Mimi Mimi Mimi just as I can't imagine her as
a child, she's an ageless woman, colorless, faded)

— What are you thinking?

apparently she lived in Spain with her sickly grandmother, her family
owned a restaurant or something, travelled hundreds of kilometers to
find a cripple, so odd, who knows, maybe the lamps, curtains and furniture were her idea, I never heard one full sentence out of her, I've never
been able to imagine what she thinks about, at dinner always smiling,
instructing the maids, her forehead creased

Don't worry dona Celina expression lines

her face suddenly harsh and then absent again like when my mother
used to look at first my father, then my uncle, and who's to tell me the
deaf woman's legs under the table aren't also

I don't believe it

— What are you thinking about?

my uncle disappeared, after that my mother was always harsh, she
stopped getting me in trouble, when I first tried high heels she asked out
the window, the one seeing birds would crash into

— How is this going to end dear Lord?

without telling me to take them off, fully committed to growing old,
filled with hatred, pleased with the warnings about her blood sugar levels,
announcing to the open newspaper in the hope my father was behind it

— I'm not good for anything anymore

waiting for a second before adding if the newspaper moved at all

— You'd all get along beautifully without me

mother

if instead of asking Mimi they'd ask me

— What are you thinking about?

I'd answer I'm happy in the certainty everything's coming to an end tonight, tomorrow there won't be anyone in my house after lunch except for the daily cleaning lady, amazed at the absence of any instructions written on the pad on top of the microwave, rereading the notes from the previous day

Dona Alice please change the sheets pick up the pork tenderloin and ribs I ordered from the butcher the man to fix the washing machine should be here at three o'clock to fix the hose buy a sponge cake at the supermarket we're running out of yogurt if the seamstress telephones say I'll be back at six thank you Celina

writing

Senhora Dona Celina since you didn't tell me anything I did a thorough clean of the living room and left the salt cod to soak the man took the washing machine to his shop because it's not just the hose something burned out I paid for the sponge cake and the yogurts with my own money there was only strawberry I left early because my son is sick see you tomorrow God willing Alice

why do things inside us die, given that it doesn't seem to happen gradually, slowly, instead we notice all of a sudden we're fed up, all we feel is irritation, boredom, the desire to be left alone, far away from him, how could I have told him angrily

— Would you mind taking your shoes off that?

rearranging the rug fringe with little yanks, whisking the cigarette ashes off the pillow wanting to whisk him out of my sight with the same stroke of the brush

— What a mess

the more obvious we are the less they understand, here come the caresses, the kisses, the atrocious tongue

— Love

a body that doesn't embrace me, squeeze me, the sticky breath, idiotic words that used to be so charming

— Pretty little fly

this, from one moment to the next, pretty little fly how idiotic, and they're so insistent, so stupid, if you'd at least fall in love, introduce him to my girlfriends, insist on going out to dinner, having fun, going out at night, wish he'd approach me apprehensively, cowardly, proposing compromises, partial escapes, in the hope of keeping us on the back burner just in case

— Nothing definitive, just a few weeks without you to think things over

the fat girl had disappeared from the clothesline, carrying the basin under her arm, the gardener had gone back to the flowers, clippers filled with longing, the driver was carrying packages out to the van

didn't I say it'd all be over tonight, that's the proof right there that it's all going to come to an end tonight

before he could take my hand and whisper in my ear, creepily, tepid

— Tomorrow after lunch I'll go to your house

my uncle picking me up by my waist

— Fly Celina fly

he took me far away from the bronze sailor and the newspaper boy hawking dailies, from the curtains and furniture uglier than mine, with inlays, exposed polished nails, copper detailing, put my joyful laughter in his lap, smelling like the cologne I love that no one wears anymore, a one-liter bottle with a golden top and a Spanish label, Mirada Sedutora, bearing an extraordinarily dark handsome gentleman, his hair parted down the middle and a carnation in his lapel, I looked everywhere and they could never find it, they'd just keep repeating, mumbling as they searched the shelves

— Mirada Sedutora Mirada Sedutora

reaching way back, blindly searching, bringing a ladder to reach the top shelves, covering the storeroom, asking the manager, an older employee, the old fellow in the warehouse

— Mirada Sedutor senhor Albuquerque, do you know it?

the old fellow stares at me worriedly, riffles through his memory from which the years have torn out entire pages and stained whatever's left with blots darker than the letters

— Mirada Sedutora

the entire shop murmuring in defeat in the slow speech we hear in our sleep

— Mirada Sedutora

and I

— It's a bottle with a gold top and a label in Spanish with a gentle-man, his hair parted down the middle and a carnation in his lapel

long noses, discouraged arms, admissions of defeat

— It seems like we don't carry it, maybe on Rua da Madalena or in the Baixa District

the old fellow stubbornly checking his ragged books, ignored by everyone

— Mirada Sedutora you said Mirada Sedutora?

my uncle lifting me up by the waist

— Fly Celina fly

lifting me again way above the little gossiping voices, the nards, the orange wig we'd picked out for the deaf woman, wavy and crinkling, going from room to room illuminating the walls with little flames, sparkles, the kitchen maids' scorn boiling over

— She's a clown

I bet they cheated her in the accounts, scorched her blouses intentionally, moved clothing from drawer to drawer so she'd spend hours searching the closets, although she never complained of pain sometimes I found her taking pills on the sly, her skin so tight you could see through to her teeth, she'd swallow the pills and after a little while her teeth would shrink back to normal, her features looked peaceful, her fixed smile would reappear, the secretary separating his syllables into elastic grimaces

— Anything wrong dona Mimi?

and I, my uncle tossing me into the air above the cancer, will never die, cats die, turkeys die, the deaf woman's husband

— Tomorrow after lunch I'll go to your house

would lie down next to me in bed and I can't stand it when somebody lies down next to me because the room changes so fast, things that were close are far away, the furniture, the veranda no longer in their regular places, the absence of my own odor on the sheets, a strand of hair, not mine, on the pillow case, the indentation in the mattress too big for me, I couldn't concentrate, couldn't

— Wasn't it good Celina?

push him away, take back my side, see the furniture and the veranda in their normal places, the stationary bicycle between the vanity and the bureau, with the felt gorilla perched on the seat, pedal five kilometers every morning before breakfast

— Pedal five kilometers every morning before breakfast and good-bye cellulite

instead the bicycle seat hurt my bottom and the cellulite spread, my husband's partner adjusted his necktie in the concave mirror meant for plucking eyebrows, searched for a comb messing up all my jars, brushes, pewter knick-knacks, the miniature saint, he even dared open the locker where I store my hairdryer and curlers and studied the hooks, as if he owned everything, familiar, entirely lacking in respect, stepping on the bedspread with his enormous shoes, the manager at the dry cleaners showing me the stain

— Mud dona Celina

he'd move things around, pile them up, drop things, spew hair spray at me

— Isn't there a mirror in this dump Celina?

everything my husband wouldn't dream of doing so I wouldn't get offended, he was always asking permission, if it doesn't bother you, if you don't mind, if you don't find it inconvenient Celina, he never stretched out onto my side, never touched anything, never undressed in front of me, he'd say

— Excuse me

and take his pajamas into the bathroom, I'd hear the sounds of fabric, faucets, the electric toothbrush, the top of the valium vial, the door being unlocked and my husband, tiptoeing, another way of asking permission, his suit folded over his arm and his shoes dangling from two fingers, the socks rolled up inside, everything in its place, leaning over to blow a speck of dust off the pillow, if he happened to knock anything over, like the little saint for example, he'd rush to set it right

— I'm so sorry so sorry

tipping over the Eiffel Tower because he was so nervous, anxious, worried about upsetting me

(if he hadn't stolen my childhood none of this would have happened and we'd still be together)

he'd steady the Eiffel Tower and the Aladdin lamp would teeter, the world, reduced to a constellation of fragile silhouettes, was falling apart piece by piece around him, with the contagious tumbling my husband's fingers multiplied, steadying indecisive picture frames, flickering bulbs, little glass owls falling into each other, the glass of water now with an iron turtle snuff box at the bottom, the gorilla on the bicycle seat seemed as if it were wavering, my husband looking at the paintings on the wall, panicked they too would get knocked down, he reached out vaguely to straighten them, asking for help breathlessly as if he were drowning

— Celina

as if he were keeping the turtle in the water glass company, one side of the curtain got loose and the city lights, up till then calm, invaded the room along with buildings, stores, avenues, plazas, and my husband protecting himself with his collar

— Celina

the river overflowing through the windowsill engulfing the apartment, just as it was flooding the bed my uncle took me by the waist

— Fly Celina fly

my husband lay down on his side, switched off the light and the space was immediately taken up by a mountain of blankets piling up and down, he'd pretend to sleep and never ever slept, he'd wait for me but couldn't admit he was waiting for me, my father hidden behind the newspaper, my mother happy, my grandmother wanting to tell the neighbors

— A perfect gentleman Celina

laying the new tablecloth, new glasses, little bowls of pine nuts, a cake bought at the bakery decorated with his name set between daisies made of marzipan and nuts senhor Borges

never Alberto or Borges, senhor Borges they warned the baker

— For a perfect gentleman

they spent the afternoon sweeping, waxing, polishing, turning the coffee cups on the buffet around so the broken handles wouldn't show, fussing with the tassels on the chair, laying out little doilies under picture frames, my grandmother asked at the funeral parlor for a Saint Sebastian and set it on the buffet, with metal arrows and painted blood, they watched me for hours

— Don't move

they found a pimple on my chin and the world fell apart

— Holy Mother of God

they tried disinfectant, alcohol, iodine, and ended up covering it with ointment

— Make sure you don't scratch now

at eight o'clock the three of us, still primping our hair, waiting for the doorbell thinking we'd heard it when it hadn't rung, they thought I looked like an Italian movie actress whose name I can't remember, they tried to dress me like her, make my bangs the same, squeeze me into a velvet belt, paint my lips dark red, by the end of dinner the actress's mouth was spread all over the napkin and all I had left was a little bit of the movies on my teeth, my mother to my husband, embarrassed in her confusion

— This is the first time this had ever happened senhor Borges

rubbing my gums with a handkerchief and then it started raining and people were rushing, in a black and white whirlwind of streaks like in silent movies, my grandmother brought the coffee pot from the kitchen and the raindrops on the roof smashed down in a clatter of metal on metal, we stopped eating to listen, four forks suspended mid-air four faces following the path of the drops, apprehension turned into relief if the coffee pot echoed, another crack, a second coffee pot, my mother grasping senhor Borges's shirt to keep him from fleeing because we were poor

— Just last February we spent a fortune fixing the roof

we didn't fix anything, not the roof, not the pipes, not the crack in the veranda, not the dishwasher, a bucket underneath it and held together with a rag, we'd get it done in two or three months when senhor Borges pa-

— Don't you think my daughter looks just like an Italian actress

eighteen years old and eyesight not one degree off, not one wrinkle, not one varicose vein, the flood lights kept shining on me, the cameras never stopped rolling, the man on the Mirada Sedutora bottle, so dark and handsome, his hair parted down the middle and a carnation in his lapel was spinning me around the dance floor to all eternity, I wanted to bring Mickey Mouse with me when I moved, my mother who was helping me pack my suitcases came across him hidden amongst my blouses and pulled him out by the leg, wobbly, doddering, bleeding saw dust

— What is this?

one of his eyes replaced with a button, his arms and legs virtually nothing but felt, his nose eaten away by humidity or clothes moths

— Hi there Celina

not even

— Good evening Celina

or

— Till tomorrow Celina

no ruckus, no somersaults, no joy, mute, who knows, maybe offended

I'd married, who knows, maybe he was hoping I wouldn't leave, my mother shaking out the rest of the stuffing

— What is this?

furious I would enter senhor Borges's apartment with its walnut furniture, its study and carved picture frames, carrying that debris, a rag, a stupid toy, senhor Borges would take one look at the thing and send me right back home and the living room ceiling would continue to drip on the coffee pot just like the crack in the veranda would continue to give her a cold in November, everything rotting except for my father, protected by his open newspaper, reduced to a sagging sock rocking back and forth, my mother opened the trash can, I wanted to say

— Hand it to me

but the words stuck in my throat, just like my body was stuck, my husband

— Is something wrong Celina?

a bed that wasn't mine, an enormous bedroom filled with pillows, bureaus, tables, it was one of the animals on the shelf that brought me here or else witches or a werewolf, I noticed the wedding band on my finger and started to cry, my mother clicked the trashcan lid down with Mickey Mouse inside along with the peels, dented food cans, and bottle that was shi-

— Stop sobbing child

-ny and everything went dark, an immense strange hostile room, bureaus suddenly decorated with ridges, knobs, the cameo of a woman in an oval frame

— Who are you?

it didn't smell like mildew or dust, it smelled like wax, polished leather, old lace, the sounds of a vacuum cleaner or murderers

in the room next door, my mother as she closed the buckles on my suitcase and my Mickey Mouse

if at least my father remembered to save him from the garbage truck taking him away dead forever

— Stop sobbing child

but it wasn't my mother there with me nor the shadow of the oval cameo, it was my husband in a violet bathrobe, so different from the Mirada Sedutora man, so disheveled, so ugly, pouring water into a glass and handing the glass to me

— Is something wrong Celina?

and I, explain to me why I sleep with you if all we've ever done is have dinner and go to the movies five or six times if that, I never let you hold my hand, didn't kiss you even once, where did you put my bears, my hippopotamuses, my rabbits, who said you could substitute my pinafores for dresses, my tights for garter belts, my comic books for nothing and now what am I supposed to read to send myself to sleep, give me one good reason why the band on your finger is just like mine, what makes you insist on being good to me, worrying about me, giving me presents, bring me a new Mickey Mouse

— I thought you liked this Celina

because I don't care about any of this it's not mine, take it back to the store, keep your money, there must be plenty of people who'd like it, I paid them to kill you and I'm certain you, sir, know and don't care

I can't stop calling you sir can't you see, no matter how hard I try I'm not going to call you by your first name

all you care about sir is that I like you but I don't, that I talk to you but I don't, smile at you but I don't, behave yourself, don't call me sweetheart, don't insist you adore me, dry those tears, for the love of God dry those tears and if there's another handkerchief dry mine too, not just for Mickey Mouse or my uncle, I think they're for, just imagine

I hate admitting this

for you, not for me although I know everything will end tonight, not for me, I promise I won't push you away any more, I'll pretend you make me happy, I'll try to kiss you, don't pay any attention when I close my eyes when I kiss you, I put my hands on your hips, I talk to you, almost smile

lend me that handkerchief again, bear with me

I smile even with your mother pushing me out, don't get upset if I ask you to put the picture back, you don't have to put it away inside the drawer, just move it over a little, thank you, start over, don't get stressed, don't tremble, look at my fingers carefully, strong, I look like that Italian actress don't I, it's as if we were in the movies isn't it, eighteen years old instead of forty, and not one expression line, no cellulite, not one varicose vein, natural hair, no eyebrow pencil, tell me now you love me, that you're dark and handsome, with your hair parted down the middle and a carnation in your lapel, dance with me

I'm sorry

dance with me, nestle your chin in my bangs, take me

I'm sorry

take me round and round the dance floor endlessly, the cameras behind us, the spotlights, lights, you smelling like Mirada Sedutora my love, you didn't die, right, promise me you didn't die that everything won't end tonight, that they didn't shatter your windshield on your way back to the hotel, there weren't any machine guns, or pistols, or grenades, none of that because I'm smiling, look, I'm smiling, I'm still smiling after we're done staring at the ceiling in this empty house.

12

IF MY BOYFRIEND makes a mistake with the wires and the entire garage blows sky-high, as far as I'm concerned, I swear, I don't care. I'm tired of sleeping on a mattress behind cars, waking up with gas-fumes head-aches, taking sooty clothes from my suitcase, living with a bunch of tires, engines and clutches instead of paintings and furniture, I'm tired of the general and the others coming in and ignoring me, without asking permission, or even a simple hello, of dressing in a rush, putting on my shoes, digging for my comb in a pile of screw drivers, haphazardly fix-ing my hair as jays hop around the oak tree outside, people whispering things I'm not trying to overhear, the gardener skimming the leaves off the pool, my boyfriend, explaining something or other, suddenly stops talking, the secretary or one of the ex-policemen gives me an angry look, addresses me off handedly

— Can't you find something to do outside?

sending me off to the summer house, the talking would start up again precisely when the gardener smiled at me as he put leaves in a bag, at night the tree branches rest on the surface of the water mingled with moon beams, the southern breeze shuffles the domino series of canopies where I guess jays have made their nests since the shadows have trans-formed into jeers that know about the café in Espinho and don't believe it, I hear them urging me

— Stay here

the deaf woman on the terrace observing the flowerbeds, moving around with no feet, just like lights on the ocean, if I told my boyfriend what the jays say

— You're crazy

he'd laugh at me and exhibit the restaurant permit, the open awning, the outdoor tables, seagulls flying between the plaza and the beach, the voices of the general and secretary repeating the same questions, the commander giving a long speech that the murmuring nards drowned out, one of the policemen in the foliage

— Further

they came from Spain every week, bursting through the fog in their furtive automobiles, with orders, counter-orders, crates and uniforms they'd pile up in the garage, my boyfriend would get his wallet out and give me cash

— Go on out to the Baixa district for some shopping

I, who can never find any skirt to fit me, the buttons don't reach the buttonholes, snaps don't snap, pants get stuck at my knees, the general getting irritated with the secretary, pointing out the foreigners meeting with the American ambassador without asking his opinion or even seeing him, just like he never saw me

— I don't obey these people I don't obey anyone

they rummaged through every corner of the garage, waste, batteries, scrap metal, my boyfriend's boss worried the American ambassador would take offense

— They only advise, General, sir, you make the final decisions

they were stepping on my mattress, flipping my pillows over, rummaging through my drawers, which I had lined with newspaper, emptying my suitcase, my entire life spread out all over the floor, the photograph of my parents, the tickets they sent me for vacation camp bundled together inside a rubber band, my green bead necklace from the dinner at the Ateneu, fifteen-, twenty-year-old outfits I can't bring myself to throw away, I'd look at them and see myself in a little pony tail, sitting quietly at my desk where no boy smiled at me, just like I tried to answer but never got it right the teacher, fed up

— Be quiet, Simone

the map of Portugal, each district shown in a different color, bearded kings following bearded kings, a hodgepodge of discoveries, battles, multiplications, copulative clauses, isosceles triangles, catechism open at the first page, the teacher swarming over us with her questioning pointer

— Who is God?

I, enormous in the back row, taking up two spots on the desk bench, could never manage to sharpen a pencil without snapping the point, finish a dictation without knocking over the inkwell, when I'd write the names of the rivers on the blackboard the chalk would squeak and the entire world would cringe, the teacher covering her ears

— Simone

on my way home they'd follow me and pull my ponytail, grab my book bag, and if I tried to catch them I'd trip and fall

— fatty fatty fa-

my mother would complain at school when my hair ribbons were missing, my lunch box, books, my teacher would stick her nose up, putting a stop to the complaints once and for all

— Your daughter is empty-headed dona Esperança she's all body, no brains

if I had been elegant like Benilde, Gisélia, Fernanda, the copulative clauses and the isosceles would have been so easy, I didn't know who God was

(— Laurinda, explain to Simone who God is)

but I knew He didn't like me since if He'd liked me He would have made me elegant and given me some brains, made me able to run, Fernanda would have invited me to play in her father's wine cellar, the sexton's grandson would have sent me messages on pink paper with little star decorations, our heads together, reading out loud below the hatch, at ground level in the vineyard, hundreds and hundreds of wine bottles in metal stands, a lilac vapor that made us lethargic, Fernanda would have cleaned her pocket knife on the hem of her skirt, pricked her finger and my finger and we'd have rubbed our blood together

— From now on we're sisters, sis-

but since I didn't have any brains, all body, it was Benilde or Gisélia that went down into the cellar, secretively, conspiring, happy and I'd stay outside alone, on my hands and knees peaking through the hatch, I could make out a brownish aura, the shiny blade pricking the fingers, a furious face stepping up onto a barrel, level with the windowsill

— Beat it, fatso

just like the policemen would kick me out of the garage

— Outta the way

they didn't call me miss, or by my name, they'd wave me off scornfully with their guns as if I were one of those roadside hussies trying to push themselves on truckers, one look at them and anyone could tell, without any catechism, that God is the omnipotent creator of heaven and earth and my boyfriend, instead of defending me would hand me some cash

— Go on out to the Baixa district for some shopping

the oak tree through the garage window said goodbye to me, the deaf woman on the terrace between the creeper vines and the vases, guys with bazookas on guard at the entry gate, the American ambassador crossed through a beam of light streaming through a glass roof tile

— We'll tell you what needs to be done and you, General, sir will make sure it does get done

the commander terrified, the secretary terrified as the general got smaller all the while talking about communists, Africa, the Motherland, the teacher suddenly soared over the classroom holding her pointer

— What is the Motherland?

the playground was next to a car repair shop beyond a wild cane thicket where the mechanics would hide to spy on us, not on me, of course, on Benilde, Gisélia, Fernanda they'd wait for us so they could invite us to the movies, the circus, Sunday outings to Belém, down by the river where they keep the Motherland in tombs in the monastery, our steps would echo as we walked through the cloister arcade, if the teacher

— What is the Motherland?

asked me now

— What is the Motherland Simone?

I'd say it's marble boxes with scraps of cloak, skulls, and dead things, after the Motherland we'd have tangerine-flavored soft drinks on the river esplanade, Benilda with a companion, Gisélia with a companion, Fernanda with a companion and I, alone, wearing my new dress with the tulle detailing, alone, no one paid my bus fare, my tickets to the movies or dances, damaged steps, a party room with paper lanterns and garlands, the management's warnings, firemen wearing helmets keeping an eye out for fires, an orchestra on a poor imitation of a stage, the vocalist wearing a scarlet jacket tap tapping the microphone, one two three testing, proudly announcing

— A the request of the distinguished crowd the beautiful zarzuela Lola Lolita

balloons, spirals of streamers curled up on the ceiling, as soon as the music started the men, bunched up at the bar, would advance like a pack of calves, slip sliding stinking of beer, each one with their prey spinning around, just the mothers and I sitting it out

(if my boyfriend mixes up the wires and the entire world blows sky high, as far as I'm concerned, I give you my word, I don't care)

the mothers fanning themselves with fans missing ribs and I, entirely
still in my chair till five o'clock in the morning, opening and closing
my purse holding back my tears, I could have gotten a machine gun
and gunned them all down and the smell of beer along with them, if
God is the omnipotent creator of heaven and earth, why me, why not
Gisélia, Benilde, Fernanda, wasn't it enough that they pulled my ponytail,
grabbed my book bag, mixed their blood together, if I'd at least had my
own room to cry in with no one looking, close my eyes and think up a
fellow, any fellow who'd take me

not the money, it wasn't the money that bothered me

on the bus, to the movies, to the dances, if they'd talk to me not
about isosceles triangles, give me their arm in the salon, the men leaning
against the bar, insistent, furtive, spitting lupine bean skins on the floor,
the singer showing her pleasure over the clapping with mischievous gestures, retying her little bow, tap tapping the microphone again, one two
three testing

— The Pasaran tango, respectfully dedicated to all the ladies present
for over a thousand years

one of the balloons on the ceiling turned pale and exploded, the
streamers shook like lazy snakes, fluorescent city employees cleaned the
Estefânia neighborhood sidewalks, sweeping plane leaves into piles, scraps
of newspaper, and the ruins of my disillusionment in the gutter, I want
to sleep wrapped in my tears, with my door locked, those girls and their
dates never dreaming, my mother upset, pacing the hallway with little
mechanical partridge steps

— Simone

I just want to die, my corset suffocates me and doesn't make me any
thinner, my mouth against the torn sheet

— Leave me in peace mother I'll be there in a minute

the only person who worries about me, a stupid old woman, her ankles swollen with arthritis whom I'm ashamed to introduce to anyone no matter who, Benilde my mother, Gisélia my mother, Fernanda my mother a pathetic woman who could barely read insisting nervously, scratching at the door lock like a desperate animal

— What's wrong dear?

seeing doctors for her kidney stones, her wretched knees, bruised eyelids, in the middle of making dinner she'd drop to the stool, her gaze flowing out past the yard in search of who knows what, who, how, my grandmother dead now for so many years, my grandfather in the olive grove trapping thrushes, the vicar drinking lime tea by the trellis, paying attention to her heart racing, a thin strand of grey hair trailing from her nose, into her mouth, reappearing then going back in, her neck grey with veins, the spoon would slip from her apron to the floor, she'd lean against the fruit bowl filled with glass peaches that used to be shiny, the copper greyhound jumping on the placemat, her blind fingers searching for my elbow, and before she could ask me for help before she said

— Simone

I'd stand in front of the fruit bowl and the hound to save them, and set her straight

— Don't think I'm going to help you Ma'am

since it was all her fault if she hadn't given birth to me I'd be thin, normal, I wouldn't spend night after night swallowing insults leaning against posters of starlets in garters and corsets, flashing their sequins, irresistible, blonde, I could feel them breathing down my neck, velvety sticky whispers, the smell of perfume, the fake eye lashes, the ringlets brushing against me, the lips made fuller with lipstick in a sort of surprised anger

— Why don't you dress like us Simone?

fishnet stockings, voile necklines, tin bunches of grapes for earrings, if I could walk down the street looking like that, if I got myself dolled up like that for a waltz or a tango, my mother, thank God without a word, finally decided to move, stand up, pick up the spoon, lean over the stove burner while I, clicking my fingers, screaming silently, making the loudest angry noise I could, put the peaches and the greyhound back in the center of the table, hoping after all that she would say something so I could say

— You leave me alone Ma'am

(— *Leave me alone ma'am my daughter would answer I've seen it all now, my own daughter, the only one I ever had, fooling around with the fruit bowl that's got fruit so perfect you can't tell it from the real or fake, all the same, all the same size, all pretty, with little stems, little blooming buds, I'd play with the little animal my husband got me at the fair when we were courting, giving it to me shyly*

— *You look like a real hound Esperança*

when we first got married he was too shy to unbutton his shirt, I'd have to help him get his belt off, his shoes, pull off his socks, he was all elbows and knees, he'd come shrinking into bed in his long underwear, we spent fifteen nights like that getting ready, lying on our backs with the light out, both of us our eyes shining in the dark so when I stopped expecting anything to happen, one thigh, then the other one, the weight of his hips, breathing like a fish something strange going on down there, not inside me but down there nothing happened inside me the usual silence except my bones simmering, an open wound down there, a cat stretching in the yard I know I heard it and it wasn't a cat after all it was cartilage inside me, a thick paper bellows rising and falling, the wound getting bigger and healing, my husband sliding in waxy sleepiness over to his pillow, not gooey not murky, clear, settling into the mattress, we went back to lying on our backs, the two of us still, quiet, every time I touch the hound I remember buttons wanting unbuttoning, shoes still on his feet, the midwife's basin filled with water, her towel, the nail hole in the wall I'd never noticed, small and dark, at first I thought it was a bug, the pains starting and I thinking about the nail hole

— *We've got to get that fixed I have to remember to get that fixed*

the pain started going away and I stopped thinking about the hole, I only saw it when the pains started up again, I wanted to look away but I kept going back to the nail hole, I asked if they'd get a little caulk and hide it, that little hole made me so tense, I was trying get the midwife to let me go so I could see it better, see how big it was, how deep, what color, then all of sudden a small wrinkled red creature, tiny, dirty, furious at me, bossing me around while they took care of her, slimy with algae, fat and mud, they got her breathing by hitting her feet

— You leave me alone Ma'am

she didn't walk yet, or was just learning, I'd put olive oil-soaked rags on her gums to help bring her teeth in, I calmed her tummy with sulfur dressings and flour paste, broke her fevers by dunking her in milk, lit her Saint Januarius candle against dreams of death and she turns to me, hiding the fruit bowl behind her, hiding the hound

— You leave me alone Ma'am

like the nail hole coming back with the pains making a hole in me, I covered it with a little bit of caulk

— You leave me alone Ma'am

now I don't see it, I don't know, I get up, get the spoon, lean over the burner, turn down the flame, carry on making dinner)

I, night after night swallowing insults leaning against photographs in the party room, starlets in garters and corsets, flashing their sequins, feathers, canes, the smell of perfume

— Why don't you dress like us Simone?

their lipstick smeared mouths made fuller in circles of amazement, more beautiful

how stupid, there's no comparison

than Benilde, Gisélia and Fernanda, on carnival Saturdays the starlets would sing at the club, they'd arrive by taxi, with chilly goose bumps, incredibly pretty, wearing their fur coats and Fernanda, envious of course

— they're fake

with their little transparent umbrellas protecting them from the rain

the cashier with his armband

Management

flushed with pride, he would help them up the stairs bowing and scraping, the same man who, if we talked too loudly, would put his fingers to his mouth scolding us, threatening, terrifying

— Hush!

blinded by the shiny lamé, the face powder, the clipping sound of the high heels that ripped my soul apart and tore it up in wonder

— Right this way mademoiselles, be careful girls with the platform

one of them, the tallest, dropped a cigarette and I kept it in a little glass box for months, I'd take it out in secret with a jeweler's tender care, sit in front of the mirror with my legs crossed, blowing into nothingness pretending I was smoking, the starlets would disappear coughing, not coughing like we do, coughing like starlets, in the president's office, hidden away with a filing cabinet and cockroaches, used for their dressing room in spite of the dampness, they'd get mad there wasn't enough light coming from the broken bulb, they'd burst open the door and call for the cashier in a tone of voice that surprised me coming from ladies like that

— Marçal

Benilde would shudder in sympathy her concern fermenting

— Poor girls

the cashier stuck a candle stub on a saucer, enthroned the candle on top of a dilapidated filing cabinet where a pregnant cat was stretching, yawning, up close they looked different than on the posters, older and shorter, but still pretty, maybe a little less, almost the same, but wrinkles

I hadn't counted on, a missing side tooth, or else chipped and black, I was listening to them speaking a language that sounded more like my mother's than mine, wiping their noses, complaining about some bra fastener, giving each other boarding house recommendations, rented rooms, pawnbrokers, their feathers seemed vaguely sparse, their sequins dull, the blonde hair poorly dyed and mixed with grey, blemished skin, bruises, burns, scars covered up with a pinkish paste, they left the room in muffled bickering, grapes missing from their earrings, lipstick smeared over the mouths from their chins to their noses, but even so once they got on stage by way of a shaking wavering mason's step ladder speckled with paint, they looked like the starlets on the posters again, Fernanda thought they looked messy but not me, Gisélia thought they had no rhythm but not me, Benilde thought they looked crippled not me, their boyfriends all thought they were wheezing but not me, they leaped around the platform in a frenzied rush, waggled their way back down the step ladder massaging their muscles, one of them limping, another one removing her shoe to examine her foot, they were panting, wiping their noses on their sleeves, the cat on the filing cabinet greeted them crankily, with bored patience, the president accompanied them out the door, covering them with gentlemanly raincoats to protect them from the rain, not really rain, but a murky melancholy reminding me of my own, a vague pervasive feeling of wanting to die for no reason except that life made no sense whatsoever, the taxi took them off, breathless, to some other ballroom, the same confetti waving in drafts of wind and the same balloons withering slowing, the orchestra warming up in absent minded apathy, the singer

— *Tell Simone what Motherland means*

and Lurdes solemnly, didactically posed

winking

— *The Motherland is*

at her friends

— *The Mother*

the tap tapping on the microphone to check the sound one two three testing, the men straightening their ties

— *Where we were born*

gathered into a fury of young bulls anticipating their onslaught, on an Estafânia neighborhood patio an old couple supped on shellfish, you could see the little skewer digging through the shells in circular scrapes a pinkie fingernail cleaning an ear, the musicians approached the edge of the stage and the young bulls immediately began to fight each other eyeing Fernanda, Benilde, Gisélia especially Gisélia

(they looked brown to me even so Gisélia swore they were green, she'd lift the lamp right next to her, opening her eyes as wide she could

— What brown they're green tell Simone what color are my eyes Benilde

Benilde, never taking my side

— Green

Gisélia, setting the lamp down triumphantly, basking in her glory

— There might be little brown speckles everyone has little brown speckles but you can tell right off they're green

I don't understand why people with brown eyes always think they're green, mine don't have any speckles except for the little ball in the middle so you can see)

— From the great Paco Rincar the Mariposa Habanera cha-cha-cha for the pleasure of our wonderful members

the accordion, the saxophone, the stampede of young bulls a bustle of pants, shoes, ferocious dancing, spinning ankles, empty chairs, I, alone leaning on the posters of the starlets, on the corsets, the garters, and standing right there, waiting for me, I couldn't believe my eyes, God is the omnipotent creator of heaven and earth, a

not like the others, smaller, thinner, a plain, thin shiny necktie, inherited from his grandfather in the provinces or which some dead relative
had charitably left him, a plain shirt in need of ironing, a vest with all
mismatching buttons, one made of leather, one mother-of-pearl, one
made of bone, nonetheless a man

he was talking to me but I couldn't understand, his mouth like a fish's,
one minute rounded, the next nothing, a strange sensation inside, gratitude, or fear, I still wonder how I was able to stand up

— Me?

his eyes weren't green, they were dark, alarmed, squinting, the round
mouth again, disappearing, reappearing

— Yes

Benilde smiling and one week later, no, nine days later, this happened
on a Saturday, so nine days, we entered his garage with my suitcase tied
up with rope because the latches were broken, and a cardboard box filled
with towels and bedding, the deaf woman quiet on the terrace, the gardener wearing his gloves pruning the roses, my boyfriend brought the
mattress from his room, the blankets needed washing, half a closet, he
made a wall out of sheets of metal and tires, took one of the cars covers
to use as a blanket, the oak branch scraping the little window scared me,
the clouds passed over the glass roof tiles, it was June, swans, dozens of
nests at the viscount's palace, not very hot yet, dim, sudden rains for no
reason, my mother

— Where do you think you're going?

Benilde who lived two houses further down

— Simone

I can still see them standing there in the middle of the street where the
eucalyptus had lifted the tar, there are times, I can't lie, I miss the hound,
not my mother, the hound, maybe my mother just a little bit although
more the hound, maybe both, maybe my mother more than the hound,

maybe only my mother and it might be that's why if my boyfriend gets the wires mixed up and the whole garage blows sky high, as far as I'm concerned, I swear, I don't care, not because I'm tired of sleeping on a mattress behind cars, of waking up with gas-fume headaches, finding my sooty clothes, living with a bunch of tire rims, engines, and screwdrivers instead of paintings and furniture, I'm tired of the general and others coming in and ignoring me, without asking permission, or even a simple hello, without seeing me, but because I miss the clay fruit bowl, the crummy yard where nothing grew except weeds, I miss looking out the window and seeing, through the steam from the simmering stew, the neighborhood rooftops, the little plaza, the dead palm tree sticking up in the planter, stiff and brittle, my mother setting the pan on the tablecloth, serving my plate first, then hers, sitting across from me, smiling tenderly

— You're so pretty and chubby Simone

and something like hope, like joy, like the hint of a future growing up inside me.

13

SOMETIMES I THINK I'm lucky I don't hear. On Fridays when I'm at the hospital getting my infusions, the treatment room is an aquarium of fish lying down blowing little bubbles of words up to the ceiling, green, translucent, no hair, deformed by their skinniness, lying on the sand of the sheets with liquid curing their cancer, dripping down into their arms and their teeth and mouths constantly moving

drinking water spitting water drinking water spitting water drinking wa-

gill ribs heaving in and out, skin sinking around bones, crab nurses checking needles, changing the rate of the drops, they hold us with big tweezers and, so odd, everything's the same outside as if we weren't sick, nursery schools, automobiles, exhausted feverish partitions leaning against the window, my feet like strangers to me, fingers I don't recognize, if I move my wedding band to my middle finger my joint will keep it on, every once in a while they replace one of the fish and the mouths not wanting to ask but asking, scattered fearful bubbles, I can't die I don't want to die I'm not going to die, don't let me die, the crabs' bubbles, they've got their health, what a silly idea to die now actually maybe I'm wrong about not hearing because, if I could hear, I'd believe them and I think I'd prefer to believe them, to calm down, reach for the handkerchief in my pocket except we don't have pockets, we're naked, I've stopped noticing the nudity, women I've only known for two months torsos, elbows, knees, since even torsos have turned into elbows and knees, a bone covered in rough edges, a head bobbing above, lips and teeth on the floor of the aquarium, smiles floating, separated from lips, wash away my cancer, yank it out, get it out of me, the doctor

—If we can reduce the tumor maybe the surgery

I remember the necktie, I don't remember him, I remember the cufflinks, the objects on his desk, the photograph of his wife, a child wearing glasses, elongating his features and not in a good way, pompous, and
another must have been his so-

—If we can decrease the size of the tumor

my husband was talking, the doctor was talking, the doctor in a bigger
chair, my husband's and mine, more modest, matching, the doctor and
my husband agreeing on clinics, appointments, costs, and me because I
had nothing to do with it, I wasn't the sick person or it was me, but not
me, someone unknown, a stranger, I felt like going home, forgetting about
the necktie and the cufflinks holding the little bronze knife, going out
on the terrace and spotting a tiny little Tejo squished between churches,
a gull flying above diseases and with this the little bronze knife started
hurting me like when we've got a cold and curtains or some piece of furniture stings, when I was little, sick with typhus there was a loose corner
of wallpaper, folded over and crooked and, no matter what kind of pain
I was in, I couldn't stop looking at it, if I looked away the sight of the
wallpaper returned like a fingernail returns to a molar cavity, to get back
home like before, sit down in the living room, take my crochet from the
basket, smell the nards out in the garden, my husband telephoning Celina

— Mimi's got can-

perceiving, without listening, that his voice had changed, bubbles and
more bubbles floating up to the ceiling mixed in with the wind's bubbles,
talking outside near the planters and the servants' bubbles

— The deaf woman's got can-

who would have guessed that the cyst in my kidney that didn't jab
me, didn't bother me, that I just happened to notice by chance one time
getting undressed

— Cancer

I'll be honest, it did bother me, my muscles stiffened but I didn't want to find out, I kept thinking I'd wake up the next day and it'd be gone, I'd just barely touch it, not the whole thing, then convince myself it'd gotten smaller, the same way I pretended I'd put on weight even though my clothes were slipping off my waist and my blouses were flapping over my breasts, the little red pointer would go from zero to the line at forty-eight kilos, what a relief, I've gained weight, my lack of appetite must be due to my colitis, my fatigue and troubled breathing to some virus, the general, the commander and the American ambassador standing in front me and I, unable to get up, the little bubbles floating up towards the ceiling, ceremoniously, slowly

— How are you dona Mimi?

I'm like our dog in Coimbra dying in the kitchen, his eyes still alive, but his body, dead, I was certain he was on the verge of asking forgiveness as if it were his fault, explaining himself, explaining but nevertheless no little bubbles, my father put a cartridge in his rifle, wrapped him up in a blanket, took him out to the back of the yard, his eyes still on me, on the verge of speaking, but quiet, I didn't hear the shot, I perceived it because the fig tree vibrated and the turtledoves were frightened, one of them, the general, the commander, the secretary, the ex-policemen is going to lay me on a blanket, dump me next to the wall, aim their rifle at my head, eyes that keep staring on the verge of revealing the truth about things, taking aim, firing

— How are you dona Mimi?

and I, face down on the kitchen tiles, the bowl of water I don't drink, the bowl of food untouched, they brought my grandmother downstairs on her throne, I mean they brought her down step by step from the top of the staircase, her braid swinging at her back, the smell of brandy from right to left, she hadn't been down to the ground floor in over fifteen years, she observed the stoves, the pans, the pantry, knitting her brows in scorn, irritated with us

— Fools

pointing out every single error on the menu, every chipped glass, they brought her over to the jerking dog, shooing chickens, ducks, hens and my grandmother, also irritated with the animal, poked him with her cane, an eighteen-year-old creature who'd dared to die before her eyes

He didn't ask permission, I didn't say so, I didn't give the order

— *Die*

and not only the dog, so shameful, my house is dying the restaurant is dying and now my granddaughter too, the only person I taught the recipe for Coca-Cola so she'd be rich some day, if I could at least call her, forbid her to

— *Don't even think of it*

meanwhile I'm dead wearing my bridal dress with orange blossoms, new shoes my bones shaking in the dirt between the yard and the swamp, one day when they resurrect what's left of m-

the cane poking the dog's back a second time, a third, my mother

— Mommy

and the cane suddenly turns to her, my grandmother releasing fast, offended bubbles, demanding to be taken back to her room

— Fools

one day when they resurrect what's left of me

the smell of brandy faded away, the geese went back to the kitchen

— I'm done with this fool, done with the lot of you

in realizing she was old, forgotten, useless, a ghost with her queenly fierceness deposed and the comical secrets that her children made fun of, the formula for Coca-Cola imagine that, if Mama Alicia asks for sugar, coffee and soda poor thing it doesn't do anyone any harm it's a way for her to keep busy without bothering anyone, if she wants soda, let her have as much of it as she wants, as much coffee as she wants and sugar too, let her have the pitcher and a spoon and let her fool around with her nonsense as long as she leaves us in peace, and my grandmother radiant, drying a tear that wasn't a tear, it was time grinding her down

Mama Alicia

making me mix coffee and sugar, calculate the proportions, add, taste, pass the cup of dark liquid to her for her to taste

— What do you think?

my father wrapped up the dog and took him to the bottom of the yard, the fig tree shaking, the turtledoves fearful, my mother held the bundled blanket with the invisible child that wasn't inside, my father his rifle under his arm, embarrassed, tense

— You all bury him

straight to the bottle on the sideboard, his hand shaking on the cork, half the glass spilling out on his shirt, I thought he was going to cry but he didn't, he just kept pouring out more wine in trembling gestures like marionette doll

— You all bury him

exhausted bubbles like the hospital patients, long, long teeth I'd never seen

— You all bury him

and they weren't his teeth or they were only his when he didn't know what to do, more and more disappearing bubbles

and I, in the treatment aquarium with a tube in my vein

— You all bury her

Celina, generous

— It's been quite a while since she's looked so good you know?

the barrel of the shotgun pointed at me, my grandmother upstairs in her velvet chair, insulted her permission had not been asked for me to die of cancer nor authorization to di-

— I'm done with this fool, done with the lot of you

the ex-policemen with vague greetings and a few days later I read in the newspaper that a communist meeting place had gone up in flames, a Catholic rebellion in the north, weapons stolen from barracks, a bomb at the home of a Deputy in Souzel, I'd ask my husband with my eyes

(I don't have cancer do I, promise me I don't have cancer)

my husband also with his eyes

— What cancer dear God

lying just like the doctors and nurses were lying

(— It's not cancer at all, just a constitutional abnormality that will be cured in no time at all)

the doctor with the X-rays and my husband with the maps, veins underlined in pen and roads highlighted in blue, the same pen that drew circles around my liver encircled a curve on the road, a spatter of houses, a hillside, men kneeling, hiding in thickets, crates of grenades, the van behind the bushes, the field telephone ringing, different names for people, numbers standing for letters, cautious, reticent facial expressions,

— What about her?

the doctor in a guarded tone

— Seven eight months at most it's already in her spine and lungs it's not worth operating

if it's not worth operating I don't know why they don't wrap me up

in a blanket and get it over with, out past the garage, for example in the
gardener's shed, no one will notice the shot, I won't stand up, won't protest, won't escape, just my fish mouth, my gill ribs, my skin sinking into
my bones, my forehead and neck have certainly shrunk because my wig
keeps slipping off, a beret a few sizes too big, a hat slipping off, why move
the red pointer past zero since it always stops at thirty-five or thirty-six,
not fifty-three like when I got married and I had to cut down on sweets
and bread, at first, before my swollen back, fragility, the absence of my
period, a strange lassitude, I thought I was pregnant, I told my husband

— I'm pregnant

and he stood up, panicking, imagining a deaf child

— I don't believe it

but the doctor's necktie, the starched cuffs, the objects on his desk,
the wife's smile and his son in glasses, the didactic bubbles

— If we manage to reduce the size of the tumor maybe the surgery

hunting scenes with captions in English, gentlemen in tall hats chasing foxes, spotted dogs leaping alongside, I recall the paintings, I don't
recall him

— Reduce the tumor

maybe because he didn't exist, my death existed in his voice, the
word death behind the hopeful words, the consoling gestures toward
my husband

— Be patient

as if my husband were the one in need of patience, the one sharing
treatment in the hospital with fishes lying around opening and closing
their mouths in silence, baskets of rejected corpses at low tide, how many
times have I wandered beaches and found not one albatross, only the
January wind through the dunes, stray remnants of a beret, a plastic board
all banged up, broomsticks missing their brush, sticky tar on the soles of

my shoes, the doctor's voice coming from the pictures of the hunt, not the doctor's voice, the hunters' in their tall hats to my husband, friendly, understanding, upset on his behalf, not over me, concerned about his troubles, the expense, the night nurse's salary, the house in disarray, the confusing series of medicines, oxygen, the adjustable bed, all the hustle and bustle, the crying out that ruins his sleep

— Be patient

the exhaustion of picking me up off the floor, wrapping me up in a blanket, carrying me off to a corner of the yard, aiming the shotgun, fire, a quiver, eyes looking without seeing, a bubble that wasn't quite a bubble, evaporating and right after that, flies, ants, insects from the dirt, the general, commander, bishop and secretary

— You're looking well dona Mimi

if I could just be alone in my room, take stock of my cancer, evaluate it, feel it, follow its passage through my bloodstream, my husband poked me with his cane, ordered

— Mimi

the ex-policemen escorted the American ambassador into the room

when God calls me whatever remains of me will rise up from the grave, what will my face look like, my body, how will I show myself to Him, what will leave my throat, what will I respond

like my grandmother's servant brought her down from her throne at the top of the staircase, do not forget the smell of brandy, do not forget the sugar, the coffee, the soda, the Coca-Cola recipe that my cousins don't know, that no one else knows except me, the only one to get rich, owning movie theaters in America, automobile factories, sky scrapers, oil, richer than all the other fish in their mute questioning, their mute suffering, just as green as they are, just as skinny, laid out in the depth of the sheets in a golden wig.

14

GOOD LORD I'VE never seen this house as dark as it is today. The sun reaches the window sills and stops, it doesn't tease me, flowing from the refrigerator to the floor and from the floor to the laundry basin on the porch, doesn't look over my shoulder, challenging me, hoping I'll chase it, instead it stays outdoors sulkily, the trees aren't shaking against the wall, swallowing silver and gold leaf, books, consoles and, depending on the wind, hiding then revealing the large crucifix, the ivory Christ covered in blood, like my husband when he was young with his arms open looking at me wanting something from me

— Fátima

a gesture, a word, my hand seeking his after dinner, I'll stay with you, don't be afraid, I'm not leaving you, my husband with his briefcase, wearing the old worn-out suit and tie he's got to wear at the bank, now shiny at the elbows, which used to move me but doesn't anymore, I, quiet, wishing

— Don't talk to me don't make this more difficult don't talk

sitting across the table from each other, the platter between us, staring at each other without staring, neither one having removed our napkin from the ring because taking the napkin from the ring was like removing our wedding bands, the same names engraved now smoothed out with time, Augusto, Fátima, the day my husband noticed I wasn't wearing my wedding ring I felt naked, I put it away in a drawer where I keep receipts, I without my ring and he wearing his, a single woman in the company of a married man, how awful I felt as shy as if I were undressed, it's hard to explain but I needed a ring to feel dressed again, I went and got the one I'd inherited from my aunt, like someone covering their entire body in modesty, I was watching my hand and my hand with the aquamarine had changed and no longer belonged to me, it moved when I told it to but it wasn't mine, some unknown person's hand holding the fork, scratching my cheek, breaking my bread, smoothing over the tablecloth, being careful not to touch his, which, even though it wasn't moving, seemed to be waiting for me everywhere, ready to grab me, hold me, squeeze me with atrocious tenderness, the huge aquamarine took up the entire table, we ended up freeing our napkins at the same time as if we were each other's reflection, our bodies equally straight, our elbows at identical right angles, I bet our feet were withdrawn equally at the ready to escape our chairs, fearing that our mouths, in opening to swallow, would start a bitter argument don't talk don't make this more difficult please don't talk, my husband hesitated, gathered his courage, leaned over toward me almost into my plate, a cracked fingernail, a writing callus on his middle finger, I was afraid, my stomach leaped, I no longer had a chest or a belly and was left with only my shoulders if you touch me I'll scream and finally he moved away with the bottle of wine, the lamp gave off vague ghostly shapes, the hand with the aquamarine wiped my chin, I quickly put it back in my lap to replace it with the real one I still had, we ate slowly hoping dinner would never end because when dinner was over what would we do who would go through the door first, who would clear the dishes first who would put on the apron and rubber gloves and start washing up, who would choose what to watch on television, the ivory Christ with open arms covered in blood, the nails piercing the tendons, the thorns, the fallen head that the trees were hiding or not, depending on the wind

—Fátima

a Christ now alone with his shiny jacket and tie, squeezing too much detergent onto the sponge, scraping the grease from the pans, settling in to watch television, his wedding band on display, the psychiatrist thinks I should be a nurse, should nurse men instead of marrying them, and he takes one hundred dollars from me every week to repeat that idea, which makes me think that in some way I really am sort of my husband's nurse, also the psychiatrist's, and my godfather's, lurking around me terrified that his God is going to punish him, all the while there's a pigeon observing him from veranda railing first with one eye then with the other, my godfather imagining that it's the Holy Ghost as he locks himself away in his office, on his knees praying for help, to my husband on the cross, open arms, wearing the flower print apron and rubber dish-washing gloves, whenever I see his wedding band it's an accusation, I don't notice his face or his body, I notice only the ring just like he probably notices only my aquamarine because his expression changes and before his voice can blame me, it's not the stuttering, not the scenes, not the anger, it's his sorrow that pains me, that wavering dignity breaking down in tears, the sobs wrapped around his words, my name in long syllables

— Fátima

— Don't speak don't make this harder don't speak

I, who've never seen the apartment as dark as it is today, the sun curdling on the windows, the trees in Campo de Santana park still, neighbors in a different city and not one swan's cry, not one ambulance, not one sparrow on the statue, the domino-playing retired folk have moved along, the spiritualists are gone, I switched on the lights and the darkness was transformed into etchings, sacristy trunks as heavy as the urns I haven't gotten used to yet and I never will, leave but where to since I don't have any money, a boarding house, a rented room, one of those places where nuns take people in for free, tramps, drug addicts, prostitutes, widows kicked out by their landlords, dormitories filled with hospital beds, cheap dolls smiling from the pillows, my godfather, benevolent

— My daughters

riding in the automobile, his shoulder against mine on the curves, I thought it was by accident then, when there were no curves at all, his shoulder still against mine, I noticed the driver's eyes in the rearview mirror

—Fire him

and he barely understood what he was about to say

—Fire him

the respectful eyes, averted, neutral

— I didn't do anything, Miss, I didn't do anything

I switched on the lights and the ivory Christ jumped off the wall smelling like beer, one of his shoelaces untied, blotches of egg yolk on his lapel

— Come home Fátima

come home Fátima because I'll change, I promise I'll change, I'll sleep in the living room, I'll leave you in peace, I won't bother you, we can have dinner at different times if you don't feel like seeing me, I'll leave before you wake up, you won't even notice me I swear, you don't need to wear your wedding band, take care of my clothes, have lunch at my mother's on Sunday

— *Don't speak don't make this harder don't speak I never explained it to you but I couldn't forgive you for*

the ivory Christ jumped off the sidewalk just like he jumped from the wall at me, his arms open, covered in blood, smelling like beer, shellfish, tobacco

my husband never smoked before we separated and now there's a squashed butt stuck to his brown lip with spit I bet he found it on the ground just like a bum, jutting it at passersby without taking it from between his teeth, red water soaking his eyelashes, submerging him entirely

— *Gotta a light*

part of a magazine sticking out of his pocket, an automobile repairman's cap with a metal badge, he must sleep, all my fault, surrounded by cartons and bags in buses parked in the plaza, the psychiatrist, arms open

another Christ, another Christ

— *Such intrigue dona Fátima, such exaggeration, you should really nurse these men instead of marrying them*

the worn-out suit and tie, shiny around the hems, the sleeves, the knees *who's going to starch his clothes, who's going to the supermarket, who's going to take care of him, the psychiatrist, who was missing only the rubber gloves and the excess detergent on the sponge*

a nurse, if only I could nurse you all

yet, it's so funny, it never crossed my mind to nurse my father for example, I watched him wheezing all over the place, answering my mother rudely, opening the canary's cage and instead of feeling sorry for him

— Must be stupid

Christ in the smock prescribing me tranquilizers, sleeping pills, vitamins, medicine costs to justify the cost of the appointment

— And dona Fátima, Ma'am, this obsession with your husband is getting out of control I'll end up having you committed, thinking you're losing your mi-

my husband indifferent to my godfather, to the driver, to the couple at the bus stop, to the tenant on the second floor who grasped her shopping bags to her stomach in horror

— Come home Fátima

without suspecting I'm carrying a child in my belly, what would happen to him if he, my godfather or my psychiatrist even dreamt that or even worse my father if he were alive staring at me, his eyes filled with hatred throughout the long Saturday afternoons, the deserted plaza with Jesus and the church

where he regretted thousands of times that they'd married

over the windowsill, telling my mother to put the photo albums away in the kitchen

— Where I can't see the misery I've caused

behind the pear liqueur, the pots of jam and the bowls of broth where hopefully cockroaches and rats would gnaw at them right down to the spine and metal fasteners

— My miserable life look at yourself Emilia you horrible slob

and the nights were even worse, the mess seemed to increase, the dust, thicker, the chips in the stucco more pronounced, the beaten-up chairs more obvious, you could hear footsteps where the beam was sagging, all the objects on the sideboard cramped next to each other, askew, every once in a while my mother would choose one or two of them, guaya-can wood gazelles, lead soldiers, baby swallows with broken beaks then come back from the pawnbroker's cautiously clutching a few bills, she'd bury them in the fake orchid pot, my father scratching the wound still healing on his ankle

— First the family treasures, now the swallows, before we know it you'll be having our daughter serve customers in a bar

to call this stuff family treasures, a few necklaces and pairs of ear-rings made of imitation gold, imitation silver and imitation pearls with flaking veneer and not strung on nylon but filling an old cough syrup bottle, softly rattling, if my psychiatrist had grown up with me he would understand, as soon as my father got on the bus to go to work, mother would head out to the plaza in the morning to shop on credit, my cousin would open the door to her boyfriend, yet another ivory Christ covered in blood, nails through his hands, arms wide open, doomed, biting his lip

— Hi Fátima

— *See, it's just like I've been saying dona Fátima, not their wives, their nurse you start taking care of them as soon as you see them*

they don't ask permission to come into my life, they jump right in without permission, covered in thorns, too big for the house, too awk-ward, too nervous, when my godfather comes into the kitchen in the morning I have to shrink into myself, I and my bowl of cereal, I have to eat on the porch because there isn't any space for me, my godfather digging through the yogurts

— Am I bothering you Fatinha?

in a sort of bleating that gets on my nerves, convinced I live here because I like him

— Am I bothering you Fatinha?

just like the ex-policemen when my husband emerges from the stairwell to meet me, tripping on a stair and they grab him by the neck, oh, such a dead rabbit dangling and inert

— Has this gentleman been bothering you dona Fátima?

the hare, stinking of beer, drifting aimlessly with the retired folk, their card game interrupted, my husband hanged like the communists in a burning cellar, the building on a farm in Alhandra, broken tiles, a page of newspaper blowing here and there in the apartment, murmuring old news, refugees from Guinea wandering through the bramble, hoping turnip soup and fish filets might start flowing from the leaves, an absence of boats reflected in what must have been the Tagus, hollow, roofless windmills, glowing fish waiting for the tide, Loures or Bucelas or Alverca or Vila Franca sighing, just like those women dozing, soaking in the bathtub, wearing their pearl necklaces, I remember an empty bottle, a soup tureen top shaped like a happy Chinaman, a woman's stocking on a hanger, I looked at the stocking thinking

— One of these days I'm going to die

and my death came to me so clearly

(the casket entering the cemetery, the sound of the dirt on the mahogany, an unfamiliar girl

me?

leaning against a tree trunk disfigured with pity)

I shook my head to push it away, the newspaper hid in an arched window, dried branches were seemingly complaining in the stone planters, a suitcase on the stairs gave me the impression the people who'd disappeared were still there, the way the stocking was looking at me, hostile, scornfully, swelling up on the hanger, it was appalling, the bottle slipped slightly to my left of its own volition, screaming at me

— Get out

and thankfully no one heard, the deaf woman's husband sent the tramps on their way, my godfather tried out the stocking on the tip of his finger

one couldn't tell whether or not that animal would bite

the commander and the Spanish Civil Guard sent the communists down to the cellar where there was a warped ping pong table, a rusty tricycle and a footlocker filled with old carnival masks, fake noses, everything still so alive in spite of the dust, so real, so present, strange faces copied onto the walls like old mirrors, not clear but blurry, a tall lady, a man with a cane, servants carrying trays, a sick person coughing in bed, a ringing telephone, voices, I wanted to explain myself, ask for forgiveness, say

— Excuse me

but as I opened my mouth I saw them disappear in an automobile heading for Brazil in a tumultuous crowd of trailers and barking dogs, with suitcases, bales, baskets on the roof of the car, something fell off as they drove down and they didn't come back to get it, the dogs got it and dragged it off to some box woods and I'm certain the communists, their arms bound with wire, nonetheless, open, ivory with nail and blood marks on their palms, I'm certain the communists, although communists and therefore insensitive, silently understood me, as they listened to the bottle's hatred and the murmur of the newspaper fluttering through the house, as they saw the tall woman and the man with the cane, the servants and the coughing patient inhaling eucalyptus steam, the communists whom the Spanish Civil Guard had dressed up in fake noses and cardboard glasses

— Take that now you can laugh

crouching next to each other on a school bench, the deaf woman's husband hid behind a one-toothed witch mask, the commander in a black mask, cloak and twine wig waving streamers all over the cellar

— Oh joy oh joy

the secretary with Styrofoam lumps under his coat sat down cooing on the prisoners' knees

— Such darling handsome boys

since there was no light in the cellar, just dangling wires and broken bulbs, my godfather set up a lantern on the table, outlining the shadows of the golden flames, hissing as they expanded and spitting out soot, the features of the Christs

— This is a holy war this is a holy war

disappeared behind the fake glasses and noses, pleading with me

— Fátima

if only I could leave, forget about them, if I weren't wearing a fairy mask, if I were dancing in the cellar around the trunk

— Oh joy oh joy

distributing rubber mallets, confetti, exploding cigarettes, if I didn't want to disappear into the yard so badly, where the marble Venus dripped something mossy and yucky, if I'd paid attention to them when they pleaded

— Fátima

— *For the love of God could you stop being a nurse for just one second dona Fátima*

the tank on the corner with the poplars where a toy duck was swimming, gravel alleyways, at one time clean, now messed up from the rain, the pig sty, the shed, Loures or Bucelas or Alverca or Vila Franca I have no idea which spot is sighing, dozing in the bathtub, necklaces, tacky rubies, glass emeralds, dead bodies drifting lazily towards Lisbon, we, defending the people that lived there from murderers, atheists and the bottle or the tricycle, with no consideration whatsoever, mistaking me for a thief

— Get out

like the newspaper I

— Get out

wandering around the floor, I thought I heard the ping-pong ball on the table, the radio on the first floor starting to play a waltz, alternating voices, silverware, and in the silent intervals the same yelling

— Get out

like my father telling my mother or the Mercês Church, simmering in his bitterness

— Get out

walled in by the number of days gone by eating away at his future, envious of the canary's endless instinctive fluttering, like a coil spring, no sooner would we turn out the light than Mercês Church would loom over us heavily, darkly, my mother thirty years previously with her black hair, used to whisk around the rooms giggling happily, my mother now followed her old self enraptured, elbowing us

— Just look

my young father adjusting her dress with adoring tenderness, the fur-niture smelling new, the curtains starched, not a fly in sight, the knick-knacks intact, not one tobacco or moldy stain on the ceiling, my past father showing himself off with a spin to my father in his pajamas

— Just look

sitting on the prisoners' knees

— Such darling handsome boys

three ivory Christs their open blood-stained arms, wearing carnival glasses and noses, streamers over their hair, legs, and laps, the commander dumping confetti over them and setting off firecrackers inside their shirts while my godfather still insisting on the holy war poked the oil lantern that was flickering angrily, the Spanish Civil Guard tied ropes for hanging pigs to the ceiling, my mother, elbowing me radiantly

— Sit down here dear

pointing to the deaf woman's husband in the witch mask who was bucking up the communists by undoing their collar buttons and freeing their necks

— I don't want anyone upset I don't want anyone upset

I, the fairy, kept dancing with my invisible partner, clicking my heels to the rhythm coming from the radio that wasn't there, sorry, there was one upstairs but I was the only one that noticed it, just like I was the only one to notice the tricycle's anger

— Get out

endless waltzes on the shiny waxed floor, not in some dilapidated house, drizzling rain down the cement and a bunch of people in masks attaching ropes to the ceiling, I, wanting to open the door and go out into the yard where the duck would stare at me through its shiny little eye, endless waltzes along with the tall lady, more of a lady than Celina, more elegant, more distinct, and with the man with the cane, just as handsome as the American ambassador, and the coughing patient inhaling eucalyptus steam, who they must have taken off to Brazil zigzagging feverishly, propped up with pillows and disappearing into his scarves, he must have died in the boarding house where he lived by himself before they fled again, the ex-policemen were pouring gasoline on the sofas, the wooden floor, the roof tiles, they set bottles stuffed with cotton and canvas lined packages in the corners of the room, the commander blowing into a little cylinder that rolled in and out squealing

— Oh joy oh joy

he made the ivory Christs stand up without taking off their glasses and noses, one of them almost spoke but didn't, it was the newspaper on the stairs, step by step it was right next to me

— Get out

Carnival Saturday Jesuses how strange, nail marks, thorns, wounds imitating wounds on their ribs, stomachs

if I didn't feel so much like whirling around the cellar tiles, I'd want them to hurry up and set them on the school benches dangling from the ropes, I'd want the Spanish Civil Guard to tighten the pig nooses, the secretary to give them one more chance at the Styrofoam and that my mother now

— How ugly you are Emília, doddering, lazy

my mother from thirty years ago would move the bench from them with her joyous giggle, poking me with her elbow

— Just look

that my father would make me look at the Christs wearing carnival noses and glasses, holding my forehead with the excitement of a harlequin

— Just look

the canary ever faster in the cage, on the perch, then the watering bowl, dumping out his seeds, flapping at the cage, wiggling and opening its beak happily, the radio sped up the waltz rhythm, forcing me to cover my ears beneath my fairy mask

— No

I never thought I could cry while my body kept time with music, while I felt so tired, almost without flesh, dizzy, if my husband were to pull me away from the wall, inviting me

— Let's go home Fátima

I would go, I'd nuzzle into your neck, give you my hand, forget about the Christs who they'd told to be happy to be celebrating carnival in June, hanging like piglets from the beam, I'd stop seeing those awful noses, those glasses, the disjointed bodies in that strange position, one shoulder higher than the other, broken at the waist or else I'd become some kind of something hanging, paper cardboard noses, streamers, wire glasses, without

— Oh joy oh joy

without any joy at all, the ex-policemen finished pouring out the gasoline, putting armfuls of straw in the cellar, setting the matches to the cans, leading us out to the yard

— Hurry up

where the toy duck was following me with its shiny pupil, I don't want my godfather, I don't want Campo de Santana park, I don't want a dark house like this where the sunshine stops at the windows, I don't want the ivory Christ covered in blood with open arms staring at me as the trees withdraw, I want my husband, ask me to go home with you, I promise I will, you don't have to say anything, promise anything, guarantee anything, I'll go, you don't even need to call me

— Fátima

I'll go just so long as there is never a night like this, these flames, the rooftop collapsing in huge slabs of ashes and my mother enraptured, elbowing my father

— Just look

pointing at a fairy mask, crying and wrapped in streamers, heading towards Lisbon, chased by a toy duck that kept screaming get out.

15

JUST LET NIGHT fall quickly to put end to all this, and make sure none of us survive, not even a trace, like when they'd turn out my light and the entire world would cease to exist, I mean, there was something out there but it didn't have anything to do with me, somewhere else, some other time, voices I could barely hear, breathing I imagined, glimpsed light beams, maybe some people, this pain at the back of my mouth the dentist couldn't cure, discouraged he leaned over, his nose at my nose

— If it hurts, raise your arm

and the words

— If it hurts raise your arm

said not by a man, but by a white mask, they increased the pain which spread through my jaw just like my increasing desire for night to fall quickly and for none of us to survive, not even a trace, and for the entire world to cease exist and if there's anything out there, somewhere else, some other time

voices, breathing, people, vague fragments in the dark

for those to cease to exist too, the deaf woman's husband's driver

Manuel João Pedro?

would not accept my check, he lit a match and burned it because I'd written his name on it, brushed the ashes off his hands, the ex-policeman watching us from inside the garage, working at a board filled with tools, using a jeweler's eyeglass and, with pincers, carefully placing wires into the mechanism inside an alarm clock that had been taken apart

— You wanna seem me in jail dona Celina?

as he lifted his glasses over his eyebrows, his face lost its look of swank competence, just like the dentist would suddenly become common and powerless once he finished working on me, a sort of God transformed, so disappointing, a little man who couldn't harm me and to whom, instead of raising my arm in panic, I extended it with no hesitation whatsoever as I left, so free, so light, just a simple arm

— Shall I pay the receptionist or you?

the insignificant creature who'd been leaning his smock into my submissive knee forgotten, my vulnerable mouth open, terrorized over his power to erase half my head with one shot of Novocain, my gums, tongue, the corner of my mouth, all of them waxy, he ordered

— Rinse your mouth out

into the tiny sink, a stream of water flowing around the inside rim, a little pink spurt sluiced down the drain, my crooked lip wanted to go along with it, leave me, the nurse put a little chrome hook in my mouth with swift indifference

— Keep still

a tray of nickel instruments of incomprehensible purpose threatened me ferociously from a gauze towel, the bib around my neck sabotaged my peace of mind, since the doctor's knee was the only thing reminding me I was alive, I leaned into it hoping he'd take pity, a cardboard poster on the wall demonstrated the advantages of a certain cavity-fighting elixir through a series of drawings, the last of which showed a girl and a boy with dazzling cuspids walking out to face the World, which gave off rays of sunshine, thanks to gargling three times per day with the product the grey haired lady, exuding equally good health, brandished trium- phantly in the face of my unforgivable carelessness, I tried to memorize

the name of the medicine to escape my inevitable suffering but the spot-
light blinded me, condemning me to bad breath, rottenness and the drill

— Keep your little mouth open dona Celina come now this little
mouth open

marble dust floated between us

— Spit

you lean over the little sink to spit but nothing comes out, the liquid
slides toward my ear dragging my lipstick and face cream along with it
in long dark streaks, my tongue discovering loose, scratchy particles, a
bandage dropped in lazy disregard, my uncle would give me twenty-five
cents for each one of my baby teeth, rather at nighttime Mickey Mouse
would ask me to show it to him, shaking happily, he'd put it between his
felt paws carefully, like a treasure

— Is it a tooth Celina?

he was in charge of telling my uncle in the morning and my uncle

(not my father, it was never my father, my father, forgetting his toast
on the other side of the universe, lost in his newspaper)

searching through his coat when I was about to leave for school, finding a coin among toothpicks, schedules and tram tickets

— Mickey Mouse told me about your tooth, here you go

during the winter the windows and lamps would stagnate in splashes
of rain, I'd mess up the puddles with the tip of my boot, my socks would
get wet and the windows and lights would shatter, at nighttime, as soon
as they were turned out and disappeared, day would linger in the trees,
everything was black, yet the branches were still visible to the last leaf,
the neighborhood solemn and still in the absence of wind, the table set
before anyone had gotten home, mismatched plates, three brown and
two green why in God's name we can't get a full set of dishes is beyond
me, when I turned five and my grandfather died, we didn't move him

into the burial vault, we buried him in a hole and I never ever had a
grandfather again as if I'd never had one, my mother came home, my
uncle supporting her, I gave Mickey Mouse a really good tooth, one of
my front teeth, and he ignored it, foolish on the shelf with the rest of
my animals, I held my lip up so my uncle could see and my uncle didn't
even sit me on his lap, didn't fuss with my hair, my mother dabbing her
lids with her handkerchief

— Be quiet

I felt like hitting her but I couldn't, like sending her away, but I
couldn't do that either, I kneeled underneath the table with my silkworms
and no shoe stepped on any other shoe, the nail from the high heel
scratching the floorboards was the only thing left, as my grandmother
sniffed, one of the silkworms was striped blue, the downstairs tenant's
relentless rheumatic rattle, when he crossed the street the cars would stop
and he, moving along one millimeter at a time, would wave his cane in
thanks, in order to turn his head, no matter where he was looking, he'd
shift his entire body is a succession of spastic gestures, his illness had
locked up his joints and thrown away the key, his overcoat no longer fit
him, it drooped from his shoulders, his cane drawing a vague arabesque

— Thank you

next, a steep sidewalk, taller than a wall, and he'd wait there for it
to flatten, I'd find him groping his way up the stairs of the building, lit
only by a skylight, the woman would open the door and a four-legged
animal with curly fur would scurry down the stairs jubilantly, the old
man would try to hit it with the tip of his cane, cut it off, put an end to
its joyous frenzy but his movements were so slow, so predictable, so like
the final seconds of a wind-up toy, the animal would escape with a silly
leap, only to return seconds later, I'd hit it with my ruler in vengeance
for the sick man, the four-legged creature would escape to the trash cans
yelping, the woman would complain to my mother who'd then take off
her shoe, at the ready my uncle

— Come here Celina

so in order for the night to come quickly and for none of us to remain, at most an old Mickey Mouse holding a tooth between his felt paws, I handed the driver the money under the oak tree, where flowers in need of pruning would grow haphazardly along with reeds and grasses, and my expression lines disappeared, the men on the slope, the machine gun barrels smashing the windshield, my husband slipping from the car seat, his eyes on the first page of the newspaper not bothering me and knowing, not accusing me, not angry at me, calling me with his usual shyness

— Celina

sawdust flowing from his body like from the dolls I don't have any more, my rabbit, my monkey, my seal with spread fins balancing a ball on the end of its nose, not long after we married I spent an entire afternoon in the stores downtown, I got home with dozens of stuffed animals that made me feel good, smiling giraffes, penguins, dolphins, squirrels, pandas, whales, leopards, I started putting them on bookshelves, sofas, on top of the refrigerator, the stove, on our bed, the decorator outraged, ordering me to take them back, not letting me fly

— What's this?

endless rooms filled with porcelain vases and Japanese trunks that weren't mine, rejecting me, not one seized-up faucet, not one loose floorboard, closets where I don't find my dresses, I find new dresses my size, bracelets I don't recognize, but that fit me, a photograph of a couple arm in arm in a park

arbors

my husband and I pretending to be other people because I don't smile like that, the decorator piled up the dolls into a box, holding them with her fingertips an expression of nausea on her face, my school mornings disappeared, my uncle disappeared, if I lose a tooth, who will I show it to, someone I can still see, someone who's happy with me

— Swish

someone who visits me in my room when the rifles, when the bombs, when I hide under my pillow to silence the shots and, since I've silenced

the shots, my husband is still alive till tonight, when this is all over and
there isn't anything left of any of us except for sawdust, a section of wall,
distant ruins

— Swish

if the doctor tells me to open my mouth I'll hide under the table and
I won't let him hurt me, on my birthday in May, my uncle rented two
bicycles in Campo Grande park, he'd give me the one with the bigger
light and bell and a metal basket on the handles and we'd ride around
the lake, I, ringing the bell making a funny little noise and he, coveting

— I'm envious

we'd race to the boats and back, the prize was a vanilla ice cream and
I always won, my uncle would finally get there, exhausted kilometers
behind me, feigning to wipe his sweat with an imaginary handkerchief

— I can't go on

off balance, stressed, a leg on each side of the bicycle and suddenly
his fatigue would vanish, he'd lean the bicycles against a tree, my fender
was white with chrome and a reflector, he'd give me a piggy-back ride to
the water, jumping, imitating galloping hooves and I

— Faster

— Swish and rinse

and he

— As you like, Ma'am

we'd lie down in the grass looking for grasshoppers, potato beetles,
ladybugs and my uncle, who knows why, wouldn't let me yank off their
legs or step on them, if there were girls nearby he'd get his comb and a
little mirror out of his pants pocket, fix his hair, moisten his finger and
go over his eyebrows, hold in his stomach with the help of his fists and
start smiling at them

— I killed her

my uncle for whom I had stopped living, cruel and indifferent, would approach the girls, his stomach held in so tightly his pants dropped to his hips

— Now you just wait here a little while Celina

the girls would fluff up their hair, arch their feet, breathe in deeply to increase their cleavage, I hopped on my bike, certain my uncle would soon tire of them, especially the heavier one, a brunette who was bossing her friends around, who held out her hand so he could read her fortune, I'd beat her any day easily, five, ten, twenty races in row, she was probably afraid of geckos and spiders and at that time I wasn't, I bet she couldn't chew sealing wax or imitate the sound of a cork popping with her fingers, which my uncle loved, he'd show me off to his friends full of pride, pinching my cheek

— Wait up, don't go yet, don't you want to hear my niece imitate a bottle opening?

my uncle, not caring at all about corks, taking the brunette's hand in his left hand and moving it to his right hand, his thumb making a tickling motion

— It's written here that I'm the young lady's type of guy

the jealous girls offering him their hands as well, their fingernails polished and mine bitten, their bra straps showing, cut-bead earrings, plastic cigarette cases with golden clasps

— Would you like one?

older girls, maybe twenty-one or twenty-two, accountants, interns, typists and I, by their age, was going to be a doctor or engineer or architect and the brunette, respectful, not lying down in the grass expanding her bosom, standing at attention with a tablet and pencil

— Yes, Madam doctor engineer architect

I was going to be a general with enormous soldiers and I'd arrest them for wearing brassieres or order them to leave the lake

— Beat it

for now I'd go ahead and arrest my uncle, I didn't speak to him at dinner, made a face at him if he winked at me, wiped off the kiss he gave me on my forehead, even Mickey Mouse's

the perfect gentleman, incapable of exchanging phone numbers with strangers, making matinee dates, promising outings to the fishing village Sesimbra in the car he didn't own

coming into my room playing ambassador to intercede on his own behalf and even then, with my quivering jaw, I kept quiet, kept still as long as I could, not moving one muscle, not answering questions, wishing I were twenty, had a job, and black straps more than I'd ever wished for anything else in the world, to sit with my girlfriends around the lake at Campo Grande park and wait for someone to come to me, smiling, tickling my palm and reading my future, till my mother appeared, a silhouette in the rectangle light of the open door

— If you don't cut this out the child won't go to sleep

whispers, sighs, something resembling a struggle, a little giggle like the girls wearing the emerald earrings, I could hear my father's newspaper pages, my grandmother's exaggerated bronchial coughing as if in warning, I don't know who or why, Mickey Mouse climbed back on the shelf, limp with despair, my mother's silhouette and another one, the same shape and size as my uncle, disappeared down the hall, one high heel with the nail and the other one without, clicking on the floorboards alternately, as if it were the echo of someone limping along in a hurry, my grandmother's cough was suddenly cured in great relief with a single clearing of her throat, after the sound of a newspaper folding, my father walked through the apartment towards the pantry, shifting around jars of sweets, I suspected my grandmother, while I was asleep, would grumble quietly, suspecting she was hearing those jars moving about

— Don't you know how to behave yourselves?

but still, maybe none of that was true, it might have been one of those dreams larger than life, distorted, I remember hearing my father's bedsprings angrily squeaking when he went to bed, a triangle of light that disappeared from the wall, coming and going unexpectedly, all the lights went on, plastic sheets replaced the curtains, a hook in my mouth suctioning saliva, I thought I saw the neighbor with his cane but it was a woman in a smock holding a tray of molds, the dazzling couple made their way out into the World thanks to their cavity elixir, false teeth broke out in screams

— Swish don't swallow swish and rinse

and my room changed into the dentist's office, electrical things, the shelf filled with instruments, the stream of water circling the rim of the sink, nobody was riding a bicycle in Campo Grande park, no one took me piggy-back riding down to the boats on the dirty cement platform, covered in leaves where a man was aligning cork buoys, the dentist's office, the chair I was sitting in, grabbing onto the arms without realizing how tightly I was holding on, my mouth wide open and a napkin around my neck, the knee digging into my hip, an aching lump at the back of my throat and suddenly a freezing drop into my scalp

raise your arm, raise your arm, the drill taking over my entire body and my arm unable to lift, as dead as the dead half of my head, the one where my stuffed animals would hide, I couldn't see them but they were there, still, steady, the decorator

— What's this?

porcelain vases, antique landscapes, silver trays, huge furniture with brass handles, my husband

looked older when he wasn't wearing his tie

divided between his respect for the decorator and fear of upsetting me

(I might have been able to like you had you understood all I needed was twenty-five cents to

I mean it would have been enough if you'd visit me at night, this night, when everything comes to an end, when nothing remains of any of us)

raise my arm quickly and explain

— I can't stand living in this house

my throat released some sort of sound, it must have been my throat that released some sort of sound, the dentist broke open two vials

— I'm going to give you a little more Novocain Dona Celina

my mouth, shrunk, the little freezing drop stopped, the left side of my skull was even deader, tonight the deaf woman's husband's driver will only have to worry about a part of me, not all of me, just a part, the one lying on the towel with the silkworms in sulky anger, the easier part, more vulnerable, more secretive

— Get back to your place right now Celina what sort of behavior is this?

and I, to myself as if I didn't hear

— Swish

clinging the box of cocoons to my chest

— I'm crawling into my bedroom I'm locking the door, running away to Spain

except I couldn't run away and be happy and beat everyone in all the bicycle races from here to wherever you want, you choose, I couldn't escape because I gave them the money and the general and the secretary and the bishop and the bishop's goddaughter and the deaf woman's husband all saw, not the deaf woman outside smiling on the terrace, I think she's the only one who noticed the driver putting the packages in the storeroom, in the cellar, in the columns below the living room, the only one to notice the electrical wires running from the garden to the pine forest facing the house and the detonator lever in the pine needles and, instead of telling on me, calling them, pointing at me

— It was Celina

she just stayed there in her orange wig, nearly content, nearly approving, approving, I'm sure she was agreeing with me, spending all afternoon smiling at the nards so I had nothing to worry about, everything was at peace, everything was fine, everything was going to work out, nothing hurt, I didn't feel anything, I leaned over into the little sink, then back into the chair, put my head back, opened my mouth and the dentist's eyes approached me just in time to see me pedaling towards the lake ahead of my exhausted uncle

— I can't go on Celina

who, defeated, leaned his bicycle up against a tree.

16

WHENEVER MY BOYFRIEND finished a job I'd be afraid of him. The boss, the secretary, the commander or all three at the same time would come at night to pick up the box, wrapped in newspaper inside a larger box lined with cotton, they'd carry it to the van and put it inside, protected by old pillows and strips of rubber, the oak tree branches would push the moon away so all that could be seen were layers of shadows, the dark glow of the swimming pool, I'd bet the deaf woman was on her veranda, talking with her roses, the ex-policemen were opening the entry gate, since the street lights suddenly appeared as the gate hinges squeaked, random portions of the wall growing large and pale, more cars outside, one of the shadows was yelling at them in Spanish, the van was heading down the hill, its engine turned off, the sections of wall and the street lights narrowed and disappeared when the gate was closed, one last shadow, mixed in with the nards, turned the key in the lock before also disappearing, there was a halo of headlights moving down toward the river and we were left alone in the garage, my boyfriend and me, not counting the deaf woman, but she didn't count, she was less important than the oak tree and less alive than a corpse, with her orange wig and fake smile, if she thought we weren't looking at her, there was no wig or smile, just sharp bones, making up a face overtaken by a terrified expression, one time I walked in on her in her bedroom to refill her water pitcher and I found her sitting on the rug, her legs crossed like a child's, mixing sugar, soda and coffee in a glass and explaining to the photograph on her dresser

— The Coca-Cola recipe Mama Alicia

as if the Coca-Cola recipe would garner forgiveness from the creature in the photograph, an old-fashioned bride sitting in an enormous arm chair with an endless braid and regal eyebrows, staring at the deaf woman lifting the glass up to the level of the dresser

— The Coca-Cola recipe Mama Alicia

seeking approval she wasn't going to get, she stopped what she was doing when she sensed I was there, like animals sense us, a sort of tropism, a sensory reaction, a change in the atmosphere, turning to face me with her tattered grey hair, her kindness dissipating into tea

— Simone

cancer, I've got cancer you wouldn't mind holding me, helping me wrench the disease out of me

the girl's knees crossed shyly, her thumbs fiddling with the edges of the pinafore she no longer wore, a girl from Coimbra, just a kid, moving her lip up and down quickly

hold my lip, tight, keep it firm, don't let the driver's girlfriend see

(my husband forbade me to be friendly with the help, get too close and they'll take advantage of you in no time at all)

that I'm so afraid, I shouldn't tell you but I'm so afraid

when I re-filled the pitchers and asked the fake hair, the orange flaming on her forehead, if there was anything else, the glass of soda, sugar and coffee evaporated on the chair, didn't wear a pinafore, or sandals, or scabby knees, but even so I got the impression she was kissing the photograph and quickly adjusting it, the creature with the endless braid and the regal eyebrows

— I don't need anything else you may leave

I don't need anything I just need

I'm so ashamed to say

If you weren't a servant oh my God I'd like to

the room smelled like medicine in spite of her perfume, like somewhere bodies have been after they're taken away, the depressions of the
body and the shoes in the bedspread, drops of wax, the remaining dirt
from the chrysanthemums, vigil crumbs, a sort of dense stagnation, I
realized the gardener was watching me from his step-ladder, his clippers
like a stork in heat, all eyelashes, whistles and pluck

— Bye gorgeous

so I wouldn't have to listen to him, I went back to the garage by way
of the vegetable garden, where the cats were tearing at the lettuce and
the ex-policemen, guarding the house, were sitting on a tiled bench with
their rifles, when I reached the little back room I found my boyfriend
organizing pliers, hammers, bottles and tubes and, like always whenever
he finished a job and had to wait two or three weeks for the commander's visit, he'd lie on the mattress in the garage without saying a word,
following the eastern clouds through gaps in the roof tiles, I was afraid
of him: I'd make his dinner and he wouldn't eat, no matter what I asked
him, all I got back was a strange absent silence, his blind-man's-cane eyes
touched me and immediately switched direction, not interested, feeling
their way along a route beyond me, when I turned off the lamp, the trees,
leaves and the outline of the grate would close in through the previously
dark window, my boyfriend, opening trunks, rummaging through piles,
talking to himself, making the sign of the cross in front of the saint with
rosemary decorating his feet

— If you help down the airplane I'll treat you to a heart-of-palm tidbit

an image at the open market reminded me of Celina, the same smooth
cheeks, the same eyebrows, the same delicate gestures, there were thirty-five of them, all identical, the price tag hanging from the stomach,
between the jeweler's stand and the chicken coop, thirty-five Celinas
with a price tag on their bellybutton visiting us Sundays, the cook would
call me to help her with the platters as if I were a servant and I'm not, I
own a café in Espinho on the plaza near the beach, I'm the one giving
the orders, shooing people away, clapping my hands, the mist and the
gulls and the waves on the esplanade, thirty-five saints at table and I, as

thin as they are, also wearing real gold rings, also a wedding band, also rich, handling the lever of the beer on tap behind the counter instead of serving the bishop and the commander and the other plaster nobodies, the deaf woman's hair nodding

— Of course

I wanted to buy a chimney sweep in a top hat carrying a broom for the tool bench in the garage but we needed a saint to get rid of the communists, help down airplanes and keep my boyfriend from grabbing a pair of pliers and killing me, when my mother didn't manage to kill the writhing little lambs hanging in the patio, my father would come running from the shop with a pair of pliers and tighten the pliers around their necks, we could hear something like hollow cane snapping, not bones, and squealing, that must have been their souls letting go on their way to heaven

— *If you don't keep still and behave mind my words Simone your father will bring the pliers*

my mother would skin the animals till they looked like skeletons covered in pinkish tendons, she'd slit their stomach to remove their intestines, running down over their lashes, she'd make me cut out their eyes with the tip of a knife, I, lying in my bed, don't know if then or now, I think now I'm in the garage because of the smell of cylinders and oil, my boyfriend suffocating me with the pliers

— You didn't keep still and you didn't behave Simone I saw you in the seed house with the gardener

I'd look at him from the bed without seeing him, afraid he was afraid of the deaf woman's husband, the secretary, the general would enter the garage with the Spanish military men in a helter-skelter of oak stumps, revolvers, machine guns and rifles

— The plane didn't crash

just like how in July we entered the ex-policeman's boarding house, bounding up the narrow stairs, shoving aside the manager, who collapsed on the counter

— I have an incurable disease gentlemen an incurable disease

leaving the registry book half open and the telephone ringing, women flurried around tripping in their high heels looking something like the women at the dances except without sequins or garters, very nervous men peeking at them while buttoning their shirts, a mulatto man stretched out on the stairs waving a card

— I'm Portuguese don't kick me out

the first thing I remember is the closed door, then the door wide open, the blast of the hinges broke, but I still don't remember the door opening, I recall a child on the veranda facing the building shooting a plastic cap gun, the ex-policeman flattened inside the closet where a felt bathrobe was dancing on a hanger, I remember seeing him look for his comb aiming to spruce himself up for the general, secretary and commander, the empty bathrobe sleeve patting him on the shoulder and telling us

— Take pity on him

and we did, we took all the pity in the world on him, but for no reason at all, the bedside table was knocked over backwards, a little aquarium with two fish flipped over, pebbles and plants, a bottle shattered, we really did take all the pity in the world on him

— I didn't give out any names I didn't expose anyone

but really, without any adult in charge it was impossible to convince the child to stop leaping around the veranda, stop twisting his wrist trying for better aim, stop shooting off his plastic gun in our direction

a few meters away from the child, a woman, paying us no attention, was stoking her oven flames with a wicker fan, as the flames got bigger the enamel pots reflected the general, the secretary, the commander, the Spanish military men and my boyfriend, the two aquarium fish breathing on the floor, one of the starlets peeping from the hallway hesitating in her high heels, it was impossible to get the child's attention, explain

— That's not nice

just as it was impossible for the woman to hear us, preoccupied with her oven charcoal going out, if any one of us had been rude enough to tell her

— Your grandson

she'd have gotten distracted if she'd tried to hear what we were saying, might have gone out onto the veranda to be polite and in leaving the oven unattended, the flame could have gone out, ruining dinner, the ex-policeman raised his arm to say goodbye, I think it was to say goodbye since we'd all worked together for months upon months in the fight for the Motherland and some ties always remain

— I didn't give out any names I didn't expose anyone

and of course we agreed, accepted his statement, believed him, the commander even smiled at him, the oven coals caught fire, the fish finally decided to give up forever, the secretary, who was very well informed, extended his hand in forgiveness

— You're right brother let's not give it another thought

and of course it wasn't any of us, it wouldn't ever have been one of us because as far as we were concerned the misunderstanding was over and done with, it was the child, poor thing, who pulled his plastic trigger, just for fun, not being mean, an innocent game, the child dropped his pistol and started backing into the kitchen, having understood by the fall, the blood and the bathrobe in the closet dangling with no shoulder to pat, that he'd hit one of our friends, a faithful ally who didn't give out any names and didn't expose anyone, the child was clinging to his grandmother's knees in panic as the ex-policeman slid down slowly and carefully, moving his mouth describing I don't know what

— I didn't give out any names

with the thought that I don't know what would back up his words, make them truer, as if that were necessary, more sincere, more believable, till he stretched out on the damp floorboards, paused staring at us peacefully, fainted face down on the shards, the bathrobe left the hanger, maternally cozying up to him, the entire world at peace having made up with us, not angry with us, calm, the commander and secretary put their revolvers back in their pockets, it didn't smell like gun powder, it didn't smell like death, it didn't smell like anything except the starlets' perfume and the woman's roast, she'd closed the oven door, put the child on her lap, taken his toy gun away, studying it and shaking her head in distaste, she stuck it in her apron mumbling disgruntled words we couldn't hear, came toward us as she locked the veranda door, through the blinds I noticed she was talking to a girl, showing her the body and the gun while a man nearby, wearing glasses, was sitting reading his newspaper, as he interrupted his reading to clean his glasses, then started again, I wanted to show my boyfriend

— Look

that it looked like a nice family, like we could be

— Look

the secretary adjusted the bathrobe carefully around the ex-policeman, blaming the veranda with a melancholy gripe

— Careless youth

the Spanish military men set the bedside table upright, straightened out the room, planted the fish, pebbles and leaves back into what was left of the aquarium, the child with a napkin tied around his neck, having forgotten what he'd done, was banging on his milk cup with his spoon, the man wearing glasses sighed, raising his eyebrows to the ceiling, the woman took the spoon and brought a bowl of soup from the counter, a family, what a family should be, what I wish we were, as we left the room heading towards the stairs, after turning out the lights so as not to bother the ex-policeman

— Sweet dreams

and the commander still irritated as he put his pistol back in the leather holster

— They should be brought up more carefully a pistol how crazy

the patriotic mulatto wasn't on the stairs anymore, when the star-
let saw us she broke out in a steady wail as if we were about, horror of
horrors, to strangle her, we who'd watched the toy gunshots powerlessly

— I didn't do anything I didn't do anything

scorching hot out on the July sidewalk, people sitting in their front
yards, bell pepper salads, everything I didn't have and wanted, stuck in
a disgusting garage, with moldy sheets and tin-blotched floors, the deaf
woman's husband arrived with the ambassador and bishop

— Thank God the plane blew up

so the following Sunday we were able to go back to the open air market where we bought the saint, the tents, wickers, piglets, little wooden
trinkets, seven or eight stands along the street, a bridge where a cork oak
was crucifying the sun, a church tower, a windmill missing a few blades,
we were nearing the end of the geography lesson, the maps were already
folded up except for the one of the digestive system with captions in
English, when the school caretaker came in to tell the teacher his wife
had perched herself up on top of the farm windmill after recess, we were
gathered below, the teacher took one step up, looked back at us and
gave up, till that day I'd never noticed the nail hole tear in his pants, and
now, whenever I remember that nail I feel like crying and I don't know
why, maybe it makes me think about how lonely everyone is, back then
I didn't like the teacher and now I feel strange when I think about him,
we, down below, his tiny wife way up high, like springtime in her straw
wallflower trimmed hat, the caretaker

— Come down dona Isidora

the springtime wife at school with her husband, she didn't wear
grown-up clothes, she dressed like we did, ribbons and bows, after we
left they must have pushed back the desk and set up a bed underneath
the digestive track that started with a mouth and no other features, just
the word mouth, and ending in a funnel with no buttocks with the word
rectum, people would point and whisper she's crazy when she ran errands

and would avoid stepping on the black limestone, sometimes with tiny steps, then great big ones, with a very serious expression and a little satisfied giggle through her nose, we'd wanted her to jump so we'd be let out of school, spoilsport caretaker

— Come down dona Isidora

and dona Isidora, her hat blowing in the wind, looking out over factory chimneys, houses and streets like in pirate movies

— I see Madagascar

Madagascar, she was calling a circle of streets, buildings, convents, storks flying over hobo tents as patched up

(— A café, I'm going to be the proprietor of a café)

as we were, I think it must have been the teacher who called the firemen since the caretaker never left the windmill in the illusion she'd catch her if she fell

— Come down dona Isidora

it must have been the teacher who called because in no time at all the fire truck arrived honking, swirling lights, a swarm of helmets and a pitiful chief, moving the caretaker out of the way, brought the teacher's wife down from the windmill, she didn't commit suicide, didn't protest, didn't put up a fight, she came down on one of their backs adjusting the elastic band under her chin, making sure the flowers were in place, ignoring the crying caretaker, our teacher, us, the neighbors' amazement, walking towards the infirmary supported by a male nurse, vainly holding her head high, skipping over the black limestone with tiny or huge steps, and you can bet your buttons that beyond the factory chimneys, houses and streets, in her eyes you could spot a place with snow covered mountains and palaces and dragons and ladies-in-waiting and princesses whose name no one knows but what must be Madagascar, it's probably Madagascar and I'd bet anyone whatever they want, even my café in Espinho, that it's Madagascar, for sure.

17

EVEN IF THEY stand right in front of me moving their mouths, silently urging me along with huge scarecrow gestures

— Mimi Mimi

Why in devil's name do they call you Mimi?

I don't know they've always called me Mimi I didn't like it before because it didn't seem to be me but now I don't care I don't care about most things now

I'm not getting up from this chair till tonight, feeling the wind through the pansies, thinking about the sea while my husband and the maid are packing our suitcases so we can get away to Spain before they arrest us, I saw the maid open my little jewelry box, take a ring out and try it on, her eyes met mine and she turned white, she hid her hand quickly, my husband was waiting, wading among shoes, scarves, jackets

— How long are you going to take Aurora?

the ring must have gotten stuck because she was making faces and squirming trying to get if off and, with that, a little shiny thing rolled over the carpet, her eyes narrowed, my maid to my husband, back to emptying drawers and trampling my raw silk dress

— Sorry sir

my nightgowns, my neck scarves bought on airplanes, the antelope coat I used to love when I was still healthy, if I ever felt sad or homesick

I'd walk around wrapped in that delicious softness as if I were being carried on someone's lap and I'd feel better, even now, when I'm in so much pain, I ask the cook to bring me the coat, and she, not understanding

— It's not cold

and death seems so far away, smaller, distant, as if seen from the street, a silhouette through a lit window in a house not our own, watercolors, bookcases, people and death just like everything else, not with us, with others, familiar, bringing dishes, removing them, helping with supper, sitting in one of the three places on the sofa, friendly, smiling, nice, studying them leisurely and choosing one without their knowing, when I look at a group photograph I know death is that smiling creature at the back, somewhat faded, looking like a long lost friend whose age and name we can't recall, a relative who's been amongst us the entire time for years on end, staring out at us from the photo album, who only introduces herself when she comes to get us, discreet, gentle, I'd go so far as to say regretful, death is a stranger bearing a little box of cakes greeting us fleetingly on the stairwell or holding open the elevator door, asking which floor, saying goodbye with a nod of her head as she continues upwards, if we were to pause and look back carefully instead of searching our purse for our keys, we'd realize the elevator doesn't stop as expected, no one enters any apartment because she doesn't live there, has merely stopped in for a visit, remembered us and

we think

maybe she'll forget us for months, maybe when I put on my antelope coat and I look different, it'll throw her off, even as thin as I am, when I have on make-up and shoes, do my hair, wear my earrings, the mirror believes I'm healthy, my husband thinks I've put on weight, and I think I'm a scarecrow under an orange wig not scaring anyone, stuck in this chair feeling the chill of the wind among the pansies and thinking about the ocean, watching the driver moving around mysteriously, circling the house with packages and wires, watching Celina, who no longer speaks to my husband, doesn't call, doesn't visit, barely talks to us, peering at the packages from the gate while I'm thinking about the ocean, he left one in the cellar, one in a pot in the shed, a third next to the veranda off the office, he dragged the wires slowly toward the pine woods, the wires asking

— Why do they call you Mimi?

instead of answering

— I don't know they've always called me Mimi I didn't like it before because it didn't seem to be me but now I don't care I don't care about most things now

death is what they mistake me for when I put on make-up, shoes, do my hair, wear earrings, I'm not like that, my cheeks aren't overly red, my eyebrows too thick, my lipstick too dark

I thought that night, unless they arrest us during the meeting and if they do hopefully they won't take off my wig and won't see my grey tufts and sores, we'd arrive in Galicia where it rains constantly and roses sprout from the waves, unless, sitting in my chair I declare

— I'm not going

and stay here by myself till the walls disappear and darkness covers everything and takes me away and then when God proclaims

— Resurrect

only the orange wisps will rise, spiky and dull among the radiant bodies singing His praises, feeling sorry for the maid in her misery, I was inclined to tell her just to take the ring and wear it, the driver's girlfriend was piling bags inside the garage as if they too were going to leave and I saw the detonator, the explosive, Celina near the gate, something in her manner like the day they ambushed her husband, the same furtive serenity, the same relief, she looked at the pictures in the newspaper of the bishop consoling her, blessing her and caressing her hands, the bishop who'd bless us and caress our hands endlessly when his goddaughter wasn't nearby, Celina, just like the maid, looked at me pleading

— Please don't tell

addressing me casually, but not genuinely casual, without a single word that would give us away

— Please don't tell

don't tell that I was with the Spaniards and the policemen, I paid them, watched as a flock of egrets was scared off by the shots, fled the olive trees, flying from canopy to canopy towards the beach, I couldn't like my husband on account of the fact he took from me the little I had, my childhood, my dolls, don't think I didn't try, I promise I tried but I couldn't, I, reassuring her, agreeing with her

— But of course

to keep her quiet, not indignant, not angry, and far away, I was feeling my body giving up and me giving up along with it, on the road to Lisbon there's a wasteland of broken-down cars decaying in the sun, no windows, no tires, spread out over weeds and rains, crusts just like us in the hospital treatment room, the afternoon they came to inform my parents we had to give up the restaurant in Coimbra I told the doctor

— I don't want to be cured I'm not coming back

the rest of the patients opened and closed their fish mouths searching for water that wasn't there in the sheets of sand, the afternoon they came to inform my parents we had to give up the restaurant I went out into the garden and made lunch from insects and leaves on top of the little toy stove, not one of my cousins interfering, I paid more attention than ever to the stones and trees, the rabbit hutch, missing a beam and off kilter, the mended portion of the metal chicken wire a lighter color than the rest, I served the plates of sticks, pebbles and ants, setting them between the cutlery like my mother would do, the doctor carrying a stack of test results

— I can't take responsibility if you refuse to come back dona Mimi

I filled the little glasses in the washbasin, set everything on the torn sheet tablecloth, taking my time straightening the knives and forks, I saw my mother crying in the kitchen, my uncles arguing with the court clerk, Mama Alicia's empty chair upstairs, it didn't smell like brandy, it smelled like dampness and rats, the doctor catching the male nurse's eye, he in turn squeezing my elbow

— Now now dona Mimi what's all this about us not wanting to get better?

when I went back to Coimbra with my husband, the first time we went for weapons, the restaurant had become a barber's shop and a tax collection agency, my parents had moved again because they hadn't paid their rent, although they swore they had, they lived in a hovel way out on the other side of the city, their sink and refrigerator in the living room along with a looped rope dangling from the light such that, if pulled, it would make the light smash onto the floor, and they, threatening to kill themselves till my husband took out his wallet asking

— How much?

my father standing up on a stool to untie the rope and handing it over in exchange for the money, if we ever showed up unexpectedly it would take them a while to open the door

— Just a minute

they'd rush to get something, anything, a piece of tape, string, elastic to tie anything up high, a windowsill, curtain, pipe, they'd roll the wine bottle under the mattress, and greet us, their poverty in disarray, my mother worn out from her arthritis, my father still holding his forgotten glass, mumbling so I couldn't understand, filthy walls, filthy sheets, clogged faucets, leftover stew, as soon as the male nurse started dragging me, I expected my husband to help me but he remained motionless, more and more stretchers, people, endless swinging doors along the hospital hallway between us, drip bags, needles, excessive brightness blocking out gestures, nearly everything meaningless except for this aquarium, this moaning, these fish, death holding the elevator waiting for me, greeting me, stepping aside for me to get in first, asking me which floor, emerging from the slightly pale corner of a photograph smiling along with us, a friend, a cousin, the cousin's colleague, no one or else a glance out of the corner of our eyes as we passed each other years ago out walking, in

October, under a brisk umbrella, the reflection of a shadow in a store window, a forgotten overcoat like the thousands of others I'm remembering only now, catching a cab, addressing me so timidly, sorrowful, embarrassed, fulfilling her obligation so unwillingly, I cannot hate her

— I hope you'll accept this I hope you'll understand

my mother would store the bills away in a coffee can, she'd lifted a floorboard and buried it amongst the junk, my grandmother's headless ivory crucifix they'd once pawned for a pittance, tiny gold tacks, actually not gold but painted copper and worthless

— We'll send you a money order as soon as we get our pension we've never owed anyone ever not one penny

lit by a single weak bulb in the hopes of keeping the electricity bill down, so weak it was hard to see them among the all the junk, two tiny childish images in relief trapped in a room by all the useless stuff old people collect out of some sort of strange greed, a dented unpainted mailbox, tissue-paper stars, plastic carnations, a broken candlestick, palindromic bus tickets, posters, an iron lock to drive away thieves, too heavy for either of them, all of a sudden I was certain they went out begging on Sundays at the neighboring church, she in a man's beret, exaggerating her ailments, he offering amulets, nail clippers, religious prints, the commander coming in through the back

— Excuse me

took his revolver from his pocket and killed them, the childish images in relief disappeared into the junk, my mother's fingers reached out to the bottle uselessly, my father, using his shirt tails to wipe the top of a camphor chest

— Please sit down

my mother offered a little spoonful of jam from a topless jar, the two of them framed in the window watching us leave, I could have reached out for them and set them in their frame in our library or over the fireplace, shown them to the bishop, his goddaughter, the commander, the general, Celina, above all, to Celina

— What do you think of my parents?

supported by the cigarette, her hands didn't fall off, gnawing on doubt, her mouth knows I knew about her husband, about my husband, about the driver hiding the wires in the pine woods, her smoke, not her lips, asking me

— Are you going to tell them?

the silhouette of death off in the distance, as if seen from the street by chance inside a building where we don't live, watercolors, people, an invisible porcelain woman laughing hysterically, shattering onto the floor, I greeted the ambassador as I answered the smoke

— Why?

Celina let go of her cigarette, spoke to the bishop who blessed her, enveloping his hands around hers, at that point you couldn't see any packages, or the detonator in the pine woods, all that remained were our suitcases in the entry hall and the maid wearing my ring and my antelope coat bringing the tea tray, and my husband

— Aurora

the ring and the antelope coat faded away immediately, the general, secretary, bishop, commander and Celina pretending to eat little cakes like my cousins and me in the backyard, grabbing me by the elbow, annoyed, what's all this about us not wanting to get better dona Mimi, plane trees, laurels, aloe, my father at the cash register having forgotten to smooth his hair, furious with them

— You're all muddy you should be ashamed just look at your pinafores

the general, secretary, bishop, commander and Celina all squatting in the big basin where my aunts were pouring buckets of hot water, they were combing my hair with a damp comb whose teeth indented parallel grooves in my hair, in August they'd take us to the beach on the bus,

riding under towels, umbrellas, picnic baskets, there were always soldiers
or office workers who'd switch places so they could chat with my aunts,
as soon as the doctor found out I'd agreed to the infirmary

— Of course we all want to get better dona Mimi

he adjusted the drip and left, the fish were still there, earthbound,
ever skinnier, looking around to see who was missing, the usual trees out
in the park, the elderly lady with her rosary whispering her Hail Marys,
interrupting her prayers screaming

— No

the rosary dropped on her pillow, they moved the screen around her

— It's nothing

and they took her away, a seventeen- or eighteen-year-old girl, who'd
started treatment before me, started sobbing, the wooden steps from the
beach café echoed like seashells, a tamed weasel roamed the counter getting fatter and fatter, the thunder of the ocean covering and uncovering
the rocks, dressing and undressing them

(limpets and moss dripping dark beards)

drowned out the patients' voices, the lifeguard ship slid down a tarpaulin ramp into the water, the woman with the rosary passed by us
covered in a cloth, her left ankle bobbing on the stretcher, her microscopic fingernails reflecting the neon ceiling light, the male nurse to the
seventeen- or eighteen-year-old girl who'd had her knee operated on and
who looked as if below her skin she had only successive knees, each artic-
ulating against the other with no musculature whatsoever

— A slight setback we'll bring her back in no time at all be quiet

death wearing a panama hat went by, pretending not to see us, heading toward the weasel café, holding her shoes in one hand and a child
begging for ice cream in the other, a man in dark glasses called out to her,
something I couldn't hear over the sound of the waves, nearby there was

a violin player, holding a tin a mug for coins, dancing along to his own playing like a daddy longlegs, when I looked at him, he bowed respectfully drawing ovals in the air with his bow

— Young lady

I stuck my fingers in my mouth and clung tightly to my mother who shook me off

— Always so clingy let go

just like a calf's ears flicking away insects, the same sudden, irritated movement, the violinist bowed in a second greeting so I covered my face with my hands making him disappear, as I looked cautiously through my fingers he was putting his instrument back inside the case and dumping the coins from his mug into his pocket, a rickety goat following along a thicket leading down to the lagoon, where sewage was vomiting murky tumbling globs, two assistants changed the elderly lady's bedsheets tossing the pillowcases and blankets onto the floor and it seemed to me as if the pillowcases and blankets were still her, her rosary Hail Marys interrupted as she protested

— No

Why do they call you Mimi?

I don't know they've always called me Mimi si-

like a theater actress dressed all in white carrying a white parasol, her chin held high, defying the invisible audience silently applauding her, the ocean thundering in the background, she stopped waving her fan in a perfumed sigh, the morning too was still and the violinist, weasel, time, my cousins throwing sand, laughing and bickering, the male nurse returned to the treatment room to check the tired hanging drips, the seventeen- or eighteen-year-old girl was filling her lungs, holding her breath with a terrified expression on her face, the hot chocolate the general was serving the bishop spiraled from the pot into the cup, five or six plastic seagulls were perched on the café railing, a drop from my drip bag plunged into my hollow body like a stone crashing into an empty bucket, my insides, my guts crumpled and changed color, the secretary came to perk me up with a box of bonbons and a book of engravings of landscapes and castles, I leafed through the landscapes wanting to tear them apart, the elderly woman's voice made my own deeper

— No

and it must have been right then that the whale got stuck between the lagoon and the rocks, either the whale or a gigantic octopus, the ocean was rising as if in alarm, the rocks donning the limpets and moss ever more quickly, actually it could have been a mixture of whale and octopus since it had arms and two adjacent sockets not looking out at anyone, in the sharp glow of oil lamps just before going dark, the waves pulled back like a towel, leaving dozens of glimmering dots that the next wave would make iridescent, the goat backing away in fear, trembling at the corpse, the violinist, the actress, my mother, my aunts and I, and death, her shoes in one hand and a child in the other, all walked down the sand as the city's remains spread out into the mud in a message, an opinion, an impression, I leaned over in the hope of hearing something, the seventeen- or eighteen-year-old girl smiled at me, almost happy between her sobs, her father, a man from the countryside constantly repeating

— Beg pardon

even if when there wasn't anyone nearby, he'd take her in a wheelchair out to his car, the fenders attached with rope, a missing headlight, he'd settle her into the back seat awkwardly, embarrassed, and cover her with a blanket, the car, taking forever to start would go chugging down the hospital ramp, father and daughter disjointed inside, their two heads blending into a halo of brake lights till the next treatment when the car would come back, chugging along and the father, begging pardon right and left, would help her out to the wheelchair, death, now wearing her shoes and without any child, there among the patients in the waiting room, waiting for us there eternally, a crochet basket on her lap, just as modest as everyone else, so pale, so humble, if I were to tell my husband, if I were to make a complaint to one of the ex-policemen, explain to the commander, if I were to show the driver, they'd touch her arm, whisper in her ear, make her stand up without anyone noticing, the crochet basket would be left alone on the bench, just by looking at it, I could imagine her house, the copper alarm clock, the unpaid telephone bill, photographs of her wedding, of her chubby grandchildren, a lamp made out of a hunting horn, I could imagine the lack of courage even to work up anger when they made her get out of the van, take a few steps into the pine woods, lean against the tree, her shawl stuck to the resin, shoelaces untied, the coin purse empty except for the Virgin Mary medallion and a tram ticket, a fresh handkerchief, her eyes questioning the machine guns in troubled vulnerability, when she went to the hospital she'd hide the key in the geranium vase to make sure the man from the gas company couldn't check the meter, each photograph had a different frame but they were all gold metal, the alarm clock didn't ring or else it went off at four o'clock in the morning, startling the clothes moths, after the bullets she was still leaning against the tree for the longest time, the silence interrupted only by the north wind carrying along a blackbird, and the enormous pounding of wristwatches, the blackbird exchanged the wind for a little branch and only then did the woman fall over sideways entirely, her legs giving way like rigid objects

(I didn't see blood, I didn't see broken bones I didn't see any holes in her blouse)

her little metal bow-shaped hairclip, the cheap kind that come as a prize with toothpaste or soap, ended up in the pine needles an inch or two away from her face, the secretary shoved her with his shoe, the pine woods canopies yawned and the woman flipped over onto her back in obedient inertia, revealing a patch of skin between her shirt and skirt, greenish oxidized Saint Philomenas were pinned to the edge of her cotton jacket, one of the ex-policemen suggested throwing the body into the river, now who would turn off the alarm clock at four in the morning, the picture frames suddenly strange in the sitting room, in the broom corner, a wash basin with slips waiting for soap, a lonely sock, a nightgown, a little locket, and some change in a tin cup, an envelope with polaroid photos of a mustached man wrinkled at the edges, the ex-policeman kept saying the body should be dumped in the river, the blackbird seemed to be singing or maybe it was just the shifting wind, the commander putting the weapons away in the van where there was more space without the presence of death answered

— What difference does it make?

with a curious expression seeing the actress, violinist, my mother, my
aunts and I walking out over the sand toward the octopus, the goat was
leaving the lagoon trying to hug the grasses, having lost its thickets, the
gargling sewage, gushing birch leaves and a house gable beating up against
the beast repeating decisive words I couldn't understand, a message, warning, advice, seemingly speaking to me but I couldn't hear it, no matter
how hard I tried I couldn't hear it although I supposed it was saying

— No

and kept on saying

— No

but it must have been too late since the thundering waves covered me
entirely, before closing my eyes once and for all I could just barely make
out the violinist perched up on a fish, bowing to me in an attitude of
blessing, comical on account of his lapels, an attitude of blessing or an
attitude, even funnier, of forgiveness.

18

IF MY FATHER, poor fellow, only knew, I can't even imagine, I only agreed to move into his room because I felt sorry for him, so I replaced his crucifix with my hair dryer and perfume bottles and I said yes, the window didn't look out onto the Campo de Santana statue like on my side, all I had to do was glance out my window and I'd see the swans and the spiritualists out praying, instead it looked out onto a garden where retirees would play cards, and beyond the grating the entire nest of Lisbon below, rooftops jumped out at me wagging their chimney tails, trying to lick my chin with their smoky tongues, if they didn't get their way, jealous bus engines would immediately start grumbling, if I latched the shades they'd bark their honking in protest, at night, even with the blinds closed, I could sense the damp eyes of little windows seeking me out like Christ's eyes from the wall

— If your father poor fellow had any idea

— Leave me alone

and then those smells from the church, Our Lady in a dusty little cloud of clay, a corner chipped off, no sooner did I turn around than my mother's voice would come screaming at me

— Seriously Fátima

the diploma in Latin with the Pope's blessing, the retirees, each with his own aureole of sparrows, playing their trumps under the cedar, the one wearing a sergeant's cap kept his cigarette butts behind his ear, the one-handed tinsmith used his chin to indicate his move, an eager fist with knotty fingers would reach out for the card, the tinsmith grumbling

— Not that one you idiot the other one

a second knotty-fingered fist would exchange the queen who'd been putting on airs like me for a worthless six, as the breeze came in from the east, the wisteria aroma cancelled out the smells from the church, blue petals fluttered around windowsills, the tinsmith, an accordion of pawn tickets pinned to his jacket, demanded they start the game over since they'd seen his cards, in the afternoon, accompanied by the sergeant decked out in his medals, he'd come to the café esplanade to brag about his millions and show his stump

— I ended up like this because I saved two kids from dying in a fire in Abrantes

a sigh behind me frightening the wisteria, a plea, not from a person, but from something old, moaning from a camphor chest, beach house pipes complaining, the friction of curtains in empty lofts, the eager fist drawing the queen across the table, the knotty fingers attempting to caress my neck

— Fatinha

you're all wrong, don't pound the table, don't try to tell me it's a worthless six, the letters of the Pope's blessing had gotten bigger, the vowels were swallowing me up with their rounded mouths, the Christs were watching the whist game under the cedar, cigarette butts tucked behind their ears, each of them with their own aureole of sparrows, thirty-year-old vests, smart neckties, pockets lumpy with crusts for the pigeons, tram tickets folded around the bejeweled ring covering their wedding bands, by mid-afternoon they'd leave together, polishing their apples on their sleeves, in the rustle of pages they wouldn't read, instead tucked into their shirts to keep the cold away, heading off to visit friends in nearby hospitals where they'd sneak them brandy in small cough syrup bottles, brushing against each other, a toothless bunch of grapes, the whist chairs now alone in the park in a silence I always found frightening, when I got home before my parents and there wasn't anyone there, the stiff, silent furniture would terrify me, the harvest plate from Alentejo, hung up behind the sofa with three clips, would warn me

— Be careful

as the chests crept in on me, the carpet runner slipped under my feet, preventing me from getting to the kitchen where maybe the canary would protect me, I'd drop my school books, umbrella, my little purse, listening to the clock and the bird jumping from perch to perch till my parents or my cousin inserted their key in the door, quieting the harvest plate, moving the furniture back in place, I, picking up my books, umbrella, purse, an adult wearing an overcoat staring at me suspiciously, the outside lights and chill permeating their gestures

— Did something happen Fátima?

picking up an ashtray or knick-knack I'd have broken, tossing the pieces into the trash, checking to make sure I hadn't gotten into the cookie tin in the pantry, flipping through the pages of the Bible, making sure all the money was still there, hanging up the outside lights and chill along with their overcoat, laying their hand on my forehead along with the last traces of the city

— You're not sick are you?

thinking about the medicine from the pharmacy, the doctor's fee, the curtains would have to be washed before he came from the hospital to administer the shots, we couldn't let him think we were poor, the elongated diamond-shaped Mercês Church, one tip pointing toward the Tagus, skipped through the windowsill and put out the harvest plate, the furniture, most importantly, the chest, they'd threaten

— Just you wait

if they thought my mother was watching they'd stop immediately, faking it, since the doctor was fat he'd wheeze his words instead of speaking them, recommending fresh country air for me and suppositories for my father's bronchitis

— I really don't like the sound of this cough

and after he left it would seem as if he were still there because everyone still moved about formally, careful with our grammar, all the defects
in the house stood out, one sofa pillow more worn out than the other
one, the weft showing through the design in the fabric, little dust balls
in the corners, a sewing needle shining between floorboards, my mother's broom and slippers peeking out from the little bed, we'd look at the
rooms through the doctor's eyes and the people who lived there weren't
very neat, certainly below our status, it was a good thing he hadn't noticed
the bed, or the tiles the plumber had taken off the kitchen wall, two
columns of ants, one going up, the other coming down, marching along
the grout, greeting each other hastily with their antennae before going
on their way, Mercês Church brought with it nightfall, pouring it over
the plaza, my father lit the lamp and settled into the worn sofa pillow,
complaining to my mother

— I don't need suppositories for my bronchitis what I need is peace
and quiet

my mother answered something unintelligible from the kitchen, the
doctor faded away and the house's defects abated, after all, the ivory rhinoceros attacked by a tiger that I don't know who inherited from some
other I don't know who

(a businessman, a trainman, a soldier?)

who in turn had brought it back from Mozambique or Colombia,
would fit in just fine in a rich person's house, if we got the dent fixed,
polished it, and our pride, my grandmother's conch teapot, with a pineapple pattern design and wooden handle we knew was magnolia

(such a beautiful handle, and so old, just one dent, it had to be
magnolia)

enthroned in the middle of the living room set on a damask table
cloth I was forbidden to touch was the reason we had installed grating on
our windows, it amazed our neighbors who'd be on the verge of crossing
themselves whenever they saw it, even my father at his most discouraged
and furious would lower his voice if he happened to be near the relic, the
doctor, entirely oblivious, set his stethoscope on the cloth and the world

came to a standstill for the duration of his visit, scandalized, covering its mouth with its hand just like my father

— I can't even fathom

if my father had ever even dreamed I'd said yes because I felt sorry for him, I moved into his room, took over his drawers, replaced the crucifix with my hair dryer and perfume bottles and said yes immediately as the wisteria petals fluttered in the windowsill, on a corner down São Bento avenue there used to be a home for odd children, who couldn't walk, talk or feed themselves without help, they'd put them outside on the patio to play with rubber rings, tooth-marked balls, old shoes, even with their own hands, which they would look at in amazement turning them over again and again slowly, boneless

some of

tied to chairs with torn sheets, crying all day long in desperation making no more sense than wild peacocks, my mother, driven to her wits end by the crying, would stuff cracks with rags and towels, complaining to the teapot

— I can't take it anymore

my cousin, who writes me occasionally to complain about her health and ask for money, emerged from the room next to mine, separated by a partition so thin I could hear her talking in her sleep

— Auntie

the house's defects, old age, negligence, once again came to life and gave me the chills like certain kinds of laughter, certain broken faience, the defects of the old house, among old lopsided buildings supported by scaffolding canes, where my mother's grandparents used to live

(there was a likeness of them in our living room near the rhinoceros and the tiger, which my father would insult by way of insulting my mother, a woman in flowing skirts with a bitter look, a man balancing on a stool whose boots didn't reach the floor) a woman and man among the used furniture surrounding us, with whom my mother lived when she was little, bringing back happy memories since later, whenever they came up, her embalmed teary smile looked like a dried flower preserved between two sheets of glass, looking out tenderly from the wall, friendly ghosts who'd take her on Saturday outings in May to the beach at Montijo, our house reminded my mother of those miraculous Saturdays filled with mossy buildings adrift on the river, for my father, prisoner to the sofa, the house was a source of anger and for me it was the humid cubicle I avoided showing my school friends, I'd say goodbye three of four blocks away and walk convincingly in the opposite direction, straight towards a street with big houses, and granite vases filled with lilies till one morning they asked me if my parents were rich peoples' servants, so I started walking home from school alone, banging on street lights with my ruler since each of them was one of my mean schoolmates, houses so different from this apartment in the Campo de Santa neighborhood with two rattling elevators in the building and a central button to call both

(if the one on the right comes first what I want to happen will happen, if the one on the left comes first then I'll have some sort of terrible problem this year, sometimes I'd miss one for some silly reason, by a second at most, the two arriving at almost exactly together, and mine, what bad luck, as lazy as can be, would announce with its big square mirrored mouth

— I swear you're going to have major problems

I'd ward off the bad luck and tell myself

— It didn't count this time

after a half an hour I'd finally reach the landing

— Now it's for real

trying to see where the elevators were, watching the cables, feeling guilty, same thing regarding the color of the next oncoming car

— If there's no red one while I count to fifty I'll fall in love this month regarding even numbered license plates, and the number of the next bus)

the apartment in the Campo de Santana neighborhood where, from every nook and cranny, God would condemn me just like the communists' corpses would condemn us before we threw them down the ravine, they'd lose some of their clothes in the fall and we'd rush to dress them so they wouldn't arrive in hell naked, I remember a nail clipper attached to a key ring, the top to a pen, a rectangle with a woman on one side and little girl, resembling the woman, on the other, I recall being surprised they had locks and families and their lives at least in some ways were exactly like ours, coincidentally, living in houses somewhat like my parents' with the same rickety side tables, the same worthless treasures, rhinoceroses, tigers, and teapots, they might greet me out walking

— Good day

offer me their seat on the tram, become afraid as they pushed the elevator button that the mirror we didn't want would show us our face, the corpse on the end, the only one wearing a necktie, wore wired rimmed glasses

(an engineer, office worker, teacher?)

and since I couldn't stand his indifference, his lack of accusations, I helped the driver drag him by the arms

(a small bracelet with a name I didn't want to read)

and throw him down the stony ravine where he ended up impaled on a box tree, the fact that he'd lost his glasses transformed him into a sort of live creature waiting for us to call him, lying on the precipice, as I was leaning over a broom bush I sensed someone breathing heavily, fearfully at my side till I realized it was me, it was my breathing and my fear increased, the teapot came into my memory and disappeared, the ivory tiger was tearing at my neck, I wanted to escape the cough

— I really don't like the sound of this cough

the ants greeting each other on the wall, the mixture of smells, sorrow and dust, my father threw up blood five years ago, the secretary kept me from falling down the ravine

— Are you dizzy dona Fátima?

even so, what I remember most isn't him, it's the iron set on top of the ironing board, the cover stained with round scorches, the sound of the whistling teapot over the flames making the windows tremble, music or news coming from a radio in the building next door, my mother with a rag and a bottle of bleach telling my father

— Don't move

the canary still on his perch, in compensation the kitchen clock

(I remember thinking as I was looking at the clock

— What does God want from us?

reeds shivering on the edge of the road during the night as trains carried away the ghost of sleep far off into the distance

— What does God want from us?

and the possibility there was an answer scared me)

the minute hands of the kitchen clock, number by number, not caring how much time was left, getting closer and closer to what I never wanted to happen, ever, I visited my father in the hospital with a little package of strawberries, stairs, waiting rooms, workers, visitors, a child crawling around looking for something under bedside tables, a tennis ball, the strawberries started bleeding a pinkish paste from which undecipherable sentences emerged, requests for help, at four o'clock a bell would shake arrows on sign boards

Radiology Urgent Administration

the secretary guided me away from the ravine

—Are you dizzy dona Fátima?

after they threw a gasoline-soaked blanket on the communists, who'd painted walls with insults, the flames clung to the stove and went out, we saw them paint insults on government housing, we smiled as if we agreed with them, the ex-policemen shot their pistols from inside their coats, the paint spilled all over the ground, my mother got very upset, scrubbing the mud with dish-washing detergent

— I bet this is never coming out

as sure as my name is Fátima, just as I was about to show the rhinoceros and the dented teapot to everyone, just as I was about to tell her in an angry whisper

— Be quiet mother

the one in the wire-rimmed glasses looked at us holding his paintbrush and in the next instant his lens shattered, his pupil disappeared, the man

his pupil had been the mechanism keeping him alive

fell down, as helpless as a parrot falling through stagnant air, dropping the rectangle with the photographs, if my mother could hide it under the sofa so the doctor wouldn't notice, along with the plate of cooling potatoes and the newspaper my father left open, disasters murmuring on the floorboards, if my mother were to clean up the dead bodies at the bottom of the ravine till no one could see them, if she were to take them from this room out to the retirees' garden and the wisteria petals, the bodies every blessed night

— Fatinha

in my godfather's voice like something behind a jammed window, if my mother were to bring her mop and wipe away my godfather like she wiped away the blood stains, wipe away my entire life, my habit of counting objects, the number of bottles of chocolate in the candy store window, packages of diapers at the supermarket, medallions on wallpaper, steps from the notions store to the entryway of my building, my mother next to the bed, wringing a cloth over a basin, soaking it in soapy water and checking the results of her efforts

— If your father poor fellow even imagined I don't

and finally standing up

— Fine

relieving her aching shoulders, the stain, at one time blood, at one time a person, now reduced to a vanishing mark on the floor, soon to fade away entirely I'd be just like the communist in the wire-rimmed glasses, next to a gasoline-soaked blanket, flames dying out in a coagulation of ashes, sometimes I'd wish the ex-policemen would fire at me, one of the bodies was an old man whose chin was so split it slipped to the back of his mouth like a puddle, and then I'd change my position as I slept, I thought about the trees in Campo de Santana park, their canopies heavier just before dawn, fattened with pigeons, I thought about Lisbon and the rooftops leaping over chimney tails to the park gates, Mercês Church strangling us, in my mother's fear my father would dream I

— Your poor father

would think I was such a wretch that I'd close my eyes again, my godfather touching me gently

— Fatinha

would think I was such a wretch that they'd talk to me or hold me, if they'd at least whisper my name I might be born from myself, start everything all over again, I might be able to find an excuse, a motive, some reason why, the patio's brighter now, the convent ruins are just barely appearing, the signs in the pale sky have faded, the neon, although turned off, still shining for a little while like the extinguishing glittering constellations lending the Tagus and the boats a certain hue, my perfume bottles, my clothes in the drawers helped me, a wisteria branch, thank God, kept me company at the windowsill, and I said yes, brushing against someone's neck, maybe the communist in glasses, my father, my godfather, someone at any rate impossible to see since I hadn't opened my eyes, I heard

— Dear

Fatinha

— I can't even fathom

and to this day I don't know who was talking to me since after they threw me down the ravine they covered my body in a burning gasoline-soaked blanket.

19

Or else we'd go to the circus, my mother, my uncle and I, where instead of ushers the performers, the clowns, the lady with the intelligent dogs, the Cossacks galloping from horse to horse, not yet in their costumes

(for example the clowns wouldn't have their jackets or guitars and the trapeze girl wouldn't have her make-up on yet, she'd wrap her robe over her silver bikini)

would lead us to the seats surrounding the stage, my uncle would lean back between the two of us, put his right arm around my mother's shoulder and his left arm around mine, holding us tightly

— My girls

my mother would be smaller, more liable to feel the cold, more fragile, she'd make a tender little sound in her throat that my father never deserved, she'd rest her head on my uncle's shoulder and I wouldn't care since one of the clowns, who had a big red mouth covering his real one, said goodbye to me, smiling with his real mouth while the big red one remained the same, the owner of the circus, accompanied by another man, also in a robe, the one who'd go inside the lions' cage with his whip, forcing them to jump through rings of fire, was counting the attendees from the orchestra stage, where there weren't any musicians, the gypsy spreading her arms in front of the target, riddled with knife dents from the dagger thrower, went from row to row selling little bags of peanuts and cheese tarts, you could hear the circus dogs' jabbing barks, walking on their back legs wearing hats, it smelled like the contortionist's face powder, animal urine, and a couple's screaming toddler's diaper that they were changing, through a big tear in the canvas you could see the caravans, stables, lit trees, a bear being led on long leash, children who the guard was trying to keep from peaking inside, brandishing his stick at them, the couple trying to distract the toddler showing it the ceiling lights, most of which were broken, blinking in agony

— Look at the lights Fausto

shaking a rattle filled with stones or bones, the exhausted musicians mounted the stage slowly, one of them warming up on his saxophone out of boredom, a pained note instantly resounding

(as soon as the sound stopped the toddler started wailing again)

without moving her head or opening her eyes, my mother put her hand around my uncle's waist, her fingers touched mine, touched them again, then started assessing, realizing it was me she sat straight up in her chair, drowsily startled, feigning a sleepy voice, drowsily startled

— I fell asleep how odd

latecomers moving along like an Egyptian frieze kept me from smiling back at the clown, making me lose a friend and bumping into my knees

— Excuse me

into my knees, jackets and overcoats kept brushing my face, the tip of a crutch attached to a very old seemingly sexless person, wobbling at the other end, hurt my ankle with big lead shoes before crashing into the seat so clumsily that the entire circus shook and, as if they were waiting for that shake to start the matinee, the circus owner and the lion tamer disappeared behind a curtain on the other side of which there seemed to be

in some kind of atrium the magician, perched on top of a vat swinging his legs, was eating a banana

seals wheezing their damp colds, the orchestra struck up a march and a bird fluttered from a distressed clarinet, attempting escape, beating B-flats against the walls of the music, the performers circled the stage greeting us in their tattered cloaks lined with Saturns, the creature with the cane was turning into a doomed cone, five or six balloons had been released, twirling toward the ceiling, disappearing through a crack in the dome into the invisible sky, the couple with the toddler who waved his little arm emulating joy none of them felt

— Say hi to the circus Fausto

the music stopped, the performers slipped off the stage, trotting through the curtain behind the orchestra

(a cotton flake was dancing by itself with a questioning air as if waiting to be told what to do)

the squealing seals entered, waddling their obesity, led by the circus owner, now sporting a general's uniform and offering them sardines, the toddler's pacifier popped out, as relieved as a cork, tumbling down onto the stage, pausing to take courage on the edge of every step, the father crawling under the chairs, the cranky old sexless person resuscitated sufficiently in order to complain

— Geez

from a stony place, carved out from white fur which then closed back up like a healing scar, then she died again, shrinking inside the outfit till there was nothing left but a collar with several chins above, the seals smelled like the smell of the Tagus at low tide, a length of mud where living things rot, the toddler's father brought the pacifier back lifting it like a trophy, workers hastily set up the lion cages, my mother, her thumb and forefinger like tweezers

— Hang on

she'd found a strand of red hair on my uncle's lapel, studied it in disgust, she was no longer small, liable to feel the cold, fragile, sleepy from leaning on people and making tender little sounds in her throat, instead she pursed her lips, sharp and splintered, shaking the strand, creasing her brows like she did with my father

— Whose is this?

(with me and my silkworms listening to her in silence under the table, surrounded by legs, her high-heeled shoes entwining and untwining in furious knots, the entire world, Greece, India immobilized in wait, the soup steam took on another meaning, my grandmother's orthopedic sandals shuttled back and forth trying to fix the disaster with an adhesive plea

— For the love of God

when, if the sandals had been mine all I'd have had to do was to set down my spoon, raise my arm and give the order

— Quiet down)

the lions, limping exhaustedly, were perched around the stage yawning in absent-minded obedience, the toddler with the pacifier was kicking and screaming, wanting one of the dome lights, every time a draft blew open the curtain to the atrium the magician was exposed, sitting on the vat, peeling a different banana, the Tagus dew from the seals brought back the memory of a cousin who drowned and the night of the vigil, one of the guests, a blind man, dipping biscuits into his wine, my uncle leaned over to examine the strand of hair and, by the way he looked at it, with exaggerated attention, without seeing, it was obvious he was searching for some sort of lie, rejecting them one by one for being too idiotic, the blind man's crumbs stained his shirt, one of the lions, leaning against the cage bars, refused to abandon the arena, the clown who'd smiled at me was tempting him with a chicken drumstick, the knife thrower prodded his haunches painfully and the lion turned his head toward him, winking his sandy eyelids with no bitterness, the blind man's wife, even as she stood right next to the urn, asked my grandmother to guess how much her patent leather bag had cost, she'd bought it that very afternoon and with all the upheaval of the death hadn't had time to remove the wads of tissue paper, my grandmother interrupted her grief to feel the bag, taking a guess, the drowned cousin, although laid out in the coffin, wearing plaid socks, had a damp aura about him, looking frogish or else like a submerged hazel tree leaf the candlelight rising from behind the furniture seemed to accentuate, although he was short and chinless I was two years three months older than he was, nope, I'm lying, April, May, June, July, four months, and he'd had kidney troubles since birth, his sister sitting on the floor

(— You're feeling sad aren't you Cacilda come and tell dona Adélia all about it)

was cutting out princesses from an illustrated magazine, the fact she was cutting out the princesses, besides giving everyone something to look at, also suspended time, not one single thing happened except they'd put more cookies into the blind man's hand and the woman to my grand-mother's left was asking to hold the patent leather bag so she could try out the clasp, precisely when my grandmother, wanting to go back to her grief, was about to throw out a random number, the lion left the stage wiggling his haunches, accompanied by the knife thrower's rod, the man with the whip thanked shuddering pools of sporadic applause, the crea-ture with the crutch emerged from her collar to point out regretfully that the Country was in such a sorry state that there weren't even any more wild animals able to swallow an entire audience in one gulp, snow leop-ards, boars, leopards, gorillas, my uncle whose excuses had abandoned him, removed the strand of hair with an evasive flourish, and gave my ear a little tug in the delusion he was making himself more believable

— A nothing little strand of hair how would I know it must be Celina's I don't know

the woman on my grandmother's left gave the purse back to the blind man's wife, risked a guess and adjusted it twofold, at the hospital build-ing a man was hanging a picture and another man was gesticulating in contortions trying to get him to straighten it out, the drowned cousin's sister opened a drawer, took out a box of colored pencils and turned the princesses green, the blind man's wife, caressing her new bag with her little finger, rejoiced at the guess

— Come on

as she kept her husband from eating more cookies by removing the tray, the blind man's fingers groped in vain endlessly and ended up meeting unhappily

with his vest buttons, I thought about helping him, guiding his arm to the sideboard and discreetly moving the tray towards him, my cousin had drowned when he was walking on the river-wall and what they pulled out of the mud wasn't him, but a princess cut out of an illustrated magazine, the clown who'd smiled at me, the one in charge of filling in the intervals between acts whenever they had to change the scenery, entered somersaulting with a group of performers, very sad exclamations and laughter, mistreating a dwarf clown who, at one point, tired of being picked on, took his cap gun out of his pocket and killed them all, the circus workers dragged them off the stage in wheel barrows, the man hanging the picture joined his colleague to study the painting, I started crying because of my friend, carried off jolting and jerking to the cemetery, and my mother to my uncle, ignoring the orthopedic sandals under the table, still holding the strand of red hair between her thumb and her forefinger, with a shout that frightened the old person with the crutch, who released a breakwater sob, trembling owls

— Don't you dare bring my daughter into this you scoundrel

a breakwater sob, trembling owls, an old convent or abandoned farm, a little bamboo sofa in the shed, covered with vines, where the commander was waiting with his machine gun for sure, sheltered behind that wagon wheel, the little broken handrail, blotches of sunshine on the grass, the rustle of geese on the reservoir, the apple tree on the road that made my husband stop, the commander didn't want me to approach the automobile

— Don't get my daughter involved in this

where the radio still played softly till one of the Spanish military men turned off the engine, the clown, my uncle, my husband lying on his back on the slope, my mother

(to which of them?)

her face covered with her hands, without noticing the trapeze performers

— Let go of me

devastated, not even angry or unhappy or bitter anymore, looking
at me, so sure, even after so many years, that I was the burden preventing her from living, she never kissed me, only ever allowed me brush
her cheek with my lips, it's true she wasn't demanding, may never have
asked much

— God knows I don't ask for much

little pleasures here and there, a movie, out to dinner on Sundays, to
be able to hand her coat for someone to hang up, to hold the back of her
chair as she took her seat, to serve her, to ask her

— How are you enjoying your little dinner Madame?

eight days in Aljeciras in summer with some man, other than my
father, who would think about her every once in a while, find her amus-
ing, compliment her hairstyle or perfume, laugh when she read the newspaper over his shoulder instead of whisking the page away as if he'd been
accosted, take her hand at table

(— You'd have liked for them to take your hand at table mother?)

a little bottle of perfume tucked into a napkin, anything with meaning, trivial, reinforcing her illusion that they were thinking about her,
noticed how she wore her dress, the belt she'd chosen for Christmastime,
her black stockings, different nail polish color, listened to her tell the same
old story all the way through, how she went to her doctors' appointments,
sat in the waiting room, reading illustrated divorces

— So?

the chagrin of the drive home, the furniture chosen and now despised,
looking around like a stranger in search of excuses to leave, the fashion
magazines she liked to read stored in the basket, reminding her of her
own basket, the vase just like the vase she'd inherited from her parents,
mended in the same place and with the same chip on the edge, her photo
there, her pack of cigarettes and, even if it all belonged to her, a certain

malaise, melancholy, oppression

— How many more years?

what am I doing here what am I doing here what am I doing here, the silent car radio made the death more real, larger, the owls' demise, a hare dashing low to the ground from raft to raft, the hillside walls pale under clouds all the way west to Cabo da Roca where everything, houses, crags, the lighthouse, tourists, bends in the great wind, the commander helped me into one of the cars, hidden off the narrow gravel road beyond which there were cucumber patches and a dozen goats grazing weeping willows, the couple were making the toddler clap for the trapeze act made up of three young men and a girl, who looked like siblings, my uncle to my mother, patting her consolingly, watching the trapeze girl out of the corner of his eye

— There there

the patent leather bag was getting passed around, no one able to guess the right price, nightfall and the warmth of the lilies made my cousin's skin more fluid, his features more adult but thoughtful, someone counting their own heartbeats, if I hadn't known, I'd never have suspected he had kidney disease, the blind man ended up finding the tray of cookies and went back to dipping them in his glass, his wife entirely absorbed in determining the price of the purse, restricted herself to brushing crumbs off his shirt every once in a while, my cousin's step-father took some sort of document from his pocket, unfolded it and showed it around in worried indignation

— Now what?

and now my mother, moving away from my uncle

— Don't touch me

— Relax I won't touch you fine

and now gravel was pinging off automobile fenders, cars heading toward Lisbon, the ocean at Cascais, same color as the sky, blending into the horizon, cloud shadows alone laid the tiniest of dark patches on the water, the clowns, alive after all, were torturing the dwarf with cleaning brushes and brooms, my mother, who was digging unsuccessfully into her purse where keys were jangling ended up accepting the handkerchief my uncle handed her, dabbing her face, grimacing, the circus owner came to the dwarf's rescue and fled carrying him off, the furious clowns hard on their heels, their brooms at the ready, stumbling on account of their huge shoes, there was a drum roll to announce the act with the intelligent dogs, who were dressed like bullfighters, with the benign fat lady introducing them, lifting them up to the sky and kissing them after every trick, her appetite so voracious it gave me the same shivers I'd get from nails on a blackboard, my mother finished wiping her face, folded the handkerchief slowly and carefully, as if that little piece of cloth were what she really liked, handed it back to my uncle who held her hand, their fingers entwining and holding each other till my mother, once again fragile and small, sighed dreamily, her voice coming from a place of happy floating memories

— Careful the little one might be watching

the lady with the dogs held a sugar cube between her lips and one of the bullfighters steadied himself then leaped with a frantic yelp, grabbing it from her, the lady opened her arms to the audience asking for applause as the animals danced, whirling on their unsteady paws with their idiotic snouts, one morning the retired accountant who lived upstairs from us set her mattress on fire and started dancing on the landing, oblivious of the flames, till the police took her away, for days afterwards the door to her apartment, where the charred wreckage still cooled, was left open with a plant in a can on the windowsill at the back, my breathing whistled against the old wood, someone had taken me out of the drawer and was turning me green with a colored pencil, the magician assisted by the trapeze girl, who'd changed her name and was now called Miss Suzy, was turning rabbits into Turkish flags, unfurling them mysteriously, helpers brought out a coffin and Miss Suzy climbed inside, her neck and feet sticking out either end, the magician sawed her in half, separated the two portions and my uncle let go of my mother's hand, nearly getting to his feet in distress, the two portions were reunited, the magician opened the coffin, Miss Suzy landed in a pirouette and my uncle calmed down, our building landlord, who paid virtually no attention to the tenants and considered my parents a pair of tramps, ended up changing the lock on the accountant's door, worried about gypsies and, from his superior attitude, it was pretty clear he meant us, the plant in the can on the windowsill died slowly, when I walk around the other side of the building I noticed it wasn't there anymore, only pigeons on the crossbeam and a cat hanged in an empty shed, the orchestra broke into the same march that had introduced the show, the bird from the clarinet once again beat its wings against the walls of music, the performers came back out on stage greeting the audience in their Saturn-bedizened cloaks, the lights dimmed and everything seemed less grand, more cramped, more like our own home when we'd feel overwhelmed at how pointless everything is, the lions stared at us wearily from their cages, covered in flies as if they were dead, the dwarf, a pipe clenched in his teeth, passed by wearing a smock, carrying a paint bucket and brush, one of the trapeze artists, now grounded, was frying fish on a gas burner, the intelligent-dogs lady, her dress bursting at the hips, was arguing with the circus owner over the lack of money to buy food for the animals, the blind cookie man, napping in a pile of crumbs, was resting his head on the urn, my uncle was looking for Miss Suzy in the seal tank, in the ticket booth, in the buses that had brought spectators from some distant village, a grasshopper fluttered in the grass, my frightened mother put her hand on my neck, and we were the same age, ten years old, the two of us afraid of the lions and clowns, missing our house, if we'd been home the dolls would be talking with us and helping us, we'd recognize all the sounds, the pipes, mulberry trees and wind through the blinds so no one could come threaten us at night, when we don't know what is there, we only know it moves, talks and chases us, my mother's hand, so womanly in my uncle's hand, was now just like mine, if I were to dress like her, people would get us mixed up, Miss Suzy barefoot, was washing clothes in a basin and didn't even look up to see us, a hamster was pedaling in its cage, running away from itself without managing to escape, when my grandmother washed the dishes, I'd sit on a stool watching and everything seemed to make sense, I'd wish it would go on forever, the dishes moving from the sink to the dish rack, she didn't need help from any stuffed mouse with its squeaky chatter, my father and uncle weren't there, didn't interrupt the clarity with their silences, their orders, odors, huge bodies that would catch cold and get even bigger, taking up even more space in the world, not a clean ashtray in sight, my mother took her little mirror from her purse in the tram, redoing her eyeliner, which the swerves constantly messed up, my uncle's arm, slipping down the back of the seat just happened to land on her neck, my mother met my eyes and moved away from him, the arm returned to the seat back so quickly it caught my attention, my husband

— Celina

and I, quiet, pretending not to feel his feet feeling for mine under the blanket, obstinately marching like insects

— They're going to trample over me how awful

my hair was falling behind my ears and I felt naked, a corpse in the morgue, a nametag tied to its foot, my mattress transformed into a slab of marble, my husband was cutting me up, dictating to an invisible typist the weight and color of each of my viscera, when he finished he piled everything back inside my torso, turned off the fluorescent ceiling light, hung his rubber gloves from a hook, two people's footsteps could be heard off in the distance, his and the typist's, chatting away as they receded further and further down the hallway, a door closed with a turn of the key and I was sleeping in cold silence, dripping faucets in the background, till I realized it was the clock ticking and I woke up shrieking surprised to be still alive, I switched on the light, and vases, lamps, a man's shirt on the chair, a necktie still stuck in the collar, if I were to call for my mother the high-heel nail coming to find me would hurt me, the next Sunday we went back to the circus my uncle and I, and instead of the caravans we found filthy rags, rubbish and a very old man

old man pleases me

who was on the neighboring esplanade looking at his gaiters, my uncle was rummaging through the rags with the tip of his shoe in the hope that Miss Suzy would joyfully emerge with a pirouette, as I was thinking about what my father would rummage through and who he'd hope to find, the old man on the esplanade wasn't interested in knowing where the circus had gone

— Bunch of gypsies

so we walked along the river, ignoring the flow, there were some kids

torturing a seabird, breaking its wings, they'd left their bicycles at the
Campo Grande gardens, ducks sleeping on a ramp, boats attached to
the breakwater, no one was waiting for him on the lawn near the lake to
make a date, the morgue door was opened, the fluorescent tube lighting
went back on, I realized they were unlocking a closet where there were
more corpses laid out and they were putting me in there, I thought I
heard Mickey's voice greeting my happily

— Hi there Celina

my mother kissed me distractedly, my father brushed his cheek against
mine, my grandmother said goodbye as usual, meaning see you tomorrow

— Don't forget to brush your teeth

I had to turn away lest I cry, to look at the waves for quite a while as
the waves moved off into the distance, the commander referring to my
husband

— There was nothing more we could do dona Celina

but the care I was taking in putting toothpaste on my toothbrush kept
me from hearing him, although I could hear the driver's footsteps as he
set the detonator in the pine woods and the rook in the tree canopies,
my grandmother grabbed a cloth to wipe my mouth, get the lather off
my chin, and my sleeve

— Oh this little girl, this little girl

which was her way of saying

—I love you

the dolls were lined up on my bedroom shelf, the chimpanzee, elephant, bears, three different-sized pandas, Mickey Mouse, my grandmother lifted the blanket so I'd get in bed, tucked me in, and instead of

— There was nothing more we could do dona Celina

she threatened

— Now just make sure you get up

her way of saying

— Sweet dreams

and of course so as not to upset her I didn't say anything about the explosion, how much I'd paid so that a few hours from now I wouldn't remember a thing, I simply let her leave, till she was no more than the shadow of her apron and, as I was falling asleep I had the idea I was out walking with my uncle by the Tagus, looking at discarded city refuse like my husband and the deaf woman and, I, with my cellulite and expression lines, abandoning my hairdresser

— There's nothing more we can do for you dona Celina

turning away as much as I could so I wouldn't cry.

20

GOD WILLING BY this time tomorrow we'll be in Espinho, not at my café yet, of course, but in some room at a boarding house away from the beach so I won't wake up scared in the middle of the night because of the sound of the waves, thinking they've come to get us, machineguns, uniforms, my boyfriend thrown against the coat stand, the water jug and vase of fake flowers on the floor, a glaring light in my face

— I had no idea the woman was so fat

behind the light, confusing shapes, someone opening our suitcase, turning it over and spreading our clothes all over the bed, gigantic details, a long fingernail, the wire for fastening the daisies, my hair ribbon on the pillow, a shiny silver tooth getting closer, so I want a room far away from the ocean where they won't upset my vases or call me fat, we wear glasses, speak with a foreign accent, I do my hair differently, we write different names on the registration form, but even so we wake up in the middle of the night either surprised at the silence or else surprised at the interruption of the silence, a bat or a cat

or a drunkard

in cardboard boxes out on the street, thinking I'm hearing jeep brakes and doors below, orders, counter orders, the telephone ringing twice, then stopping, the nervous whisper of the lady that gave us the key without looking up from her magazine, a parakeet pecking her earring in skewed passion

— Here

and right after that, machineguns, uniforms, my boyfriend thrown against the coat stand, the water jug and vase of fake flowers on the floor, a glaring light in my face, their surprise

— I had no idea the woman was so fat

having forgotten they'd come to arrest us, surprised by me, the lady who owned the boarding house peeking out between the soldiers, the parakeet, bothered by its callused feet, dropped the earring so it could whistle in surprise, my boyfriend, in handcuffs, watching, also shaking his head, therefore by this time tomorrow once we've gotten to Espinho I want a boarding house room far from the beach or else close to it, I don't really care, and a pill that will keep me asleep for a long time, one of those red capsules the deaf lady takes for her disease, her pain, we take her a glass on a tray and ten minutes later she starts apologizing, smiling, meanwhile we'd see the little vein on her neck, her dry cracked mouth, her foot moving up and down discreetly denting the carpet according to the rhythm of her blood or of the gardener's clippers, surrounded by leaves, piling them up, we'd put the package of capsules away again and when we looked back through the arch separating the hallway from the living room, we'd see her there by herself, her back to us, unwrapping a package of tissues, using one, her shoulders shaking like a child trying get rid of a secret fear, her foot was still, the willows

I mean

the refracted surface of the swimming pool rippled over the window's skin, the porcelain vases, encouraged by the late sun, came up with a meaningless question that instantly faded away, the same kind of question as the oak branches scraping the little garage window, my boyfriend was hiding timers, wire and tubes in a bag, God willing by this time tomorrow we'll be in a boarding house room in Espinho and even kilometers away from the beach we'll hear waves, how many times in August after dinner did I lie on the wall and feel them, every once in a while a scale would glimmer and then vanish, what was I talking about, I've never had anyone I could talk to about myself, explain who I am, when I walked my breath was always walking ahead of me, it would stop and look back at me, then escape me again, reach out to grab my lungs, the doctor told me it's no wonder I got tired, you're overweight Ma'am, the bishop to his goddaughter, if she keeps on like this one of these days she'll burst, and the goddaughter worried I'd notice, she's pitiful, just shut up, at school I didn't run like my classmates, I'd rest on a bench or by the swings, envying them, whoever won would yell from a distance

— Tell them who got there first Simone

and I'd be twiddling my hair around my finger, at the carnival none of the photographer's costumes fit me, not Snow White, no duchess crown to console me, they'd end up putting a washerwoman's scarf around my head and a bundle of washing on my lap

— Just be quiet

my mother collected photographs in an album, out of focus on account of the teardrops fallen on the ankle boots, stepping on each other resentfully, I tore all the pages out of the album and burned them on the patio, thirty or forty washerwomen catching fire, first scarlet, then black, then grey and finally spreading into dusty butterflies, my mother chasing the butterflies desperately

— Simone

there were mirrors at the fair that made me thin, I didn't care about the roller coaster, ghost house, death pool, carousel, or the life sized woman, named Madame Dolores, you could feed a coin into her belly button and she'd eject a card printed with your future, all the futures were the same, a serious but curable illness, marriage to a kind gentleman, a boat trip, an unexpected inheritance, and the woman would actually get it right since most futures are the same, although maybe apart from the marriage, the trip, if I happen to run into my school friends they've got a lot to complain about, overdue bills, the entire world closing in on them, overflowing with installment payments and colds, so I'd stay in the tent with the mirrors and the sign, just laugh, static chuckles coming through speakers, long thin face, my body like a ribbon, skeletal arms and legs, the employee, one long cap wearing miniature shoes, would touch my shoulders, the size of his voice not matching the size of his body

— We're closing

I'd alternate between looking at him and the reflection, confused by two different people reeling off orders from only one of them, a little sparrow foot was losing its patience in the mirror, human fingers squeezing my bones outside the mirror, both surrounded by

just laugh

tuneless chuckling since the needle was skipping, creating various zigzagging hissing sounds, the two people started protesting in unison in a speech the recording drowned out, the light went out and I disappeared, it went back on and I came back to life, apparently with the approval of the record, now joyous, skipping enthusiastically then suddenly falling silent when an older man came in along with the employee and soon became a tiny insignificant tyrant outraging angrily

— Out

everything had been shut down, and also the roller coaster, haunted castle and death pool, a hunchback was chaining up the carousel, the restaurant cooks, behind closed doors, elongated in their chefs' hats, were eating chicken shish kebabs, dripping into the coals in a glow of rings and little white bones, the mirrors were gone, all that was left was me and my endless shadow on the ground, mixed in with newspapers and rinds, with no chuckling applause, a woman was unscrewing a stomach, which turned out to be a safe after all, Madame Dolores, and was dumping coins into a can, she'd open the top of Madame Dolores's head to replace the batteries for the printed futures, the signs of the Zodiac whirled sparks, skipping over defective Capricorn, glass stars sparkled, the fortune teller's eye melted into a sigh and, maybe because of her blindness, authoritative predictions shot out one after the other, marriages, trips, serious but curable illness, unexpected inheritances, a record player chortle lost in the silence ordered

— Out

the first thing I'm going to do as soon as we get the café is install a mirror just like that for my bedroom, my sad mother stirring the photographs with a little stick

— Why did you burn the photographs Simone?

the fair, with no people or music, seemed like a planet of ghosts, a burnt city of scarecrows and iron scaffolding where little sailboats were dancing, stirring ashes in the hope of a daughter, a scarf on her head, carrying a bundle of clothes, the employee and the older man were looking me over in the tent suspiciously, my mother found the top of one of the photographs, a piece of cloth and some hair, I swatted her fingers, no, I mean I thought of swatting her fingers, decided not to hit her fingers but I still hit her fingers and the photograph fell, I still remember the expression on her face, a weak old lady afraid that I'd kill her, or maybe not afraid, it was just her sticking her arm out to pick me up in the kitchen like when I was a child

(the stove was different, the tiles were different, there were clay pots with parsley and cumin, back then the house still hadn't had time to shrink, there was always a dog peeking out from the doorstep)

and I wished she'd pick me up and that scared me, just the same as liking her smell and also being afraid of it, if I got too close I wouldn't exist anymore, I'd dissolve into her blouse, a stain along with the egg yolk stains, a nothing presence and later I'd be sure I'd found my father in her body, a sort of beard, indifference and grumbling, the bicycle leaning against the wall, my father sitting down to eat, pushing potatoes with a piece of bread, and the two of us standing, he never touched me, never touched anyone, I remember pants drying on the cloths line, chasing cats from the vineyard, the top of the ladder disappearing into the chestnut tree, all I'd notice were the boots and the burrs on the ground, if they were to say

— Choose a name

I'd never choose Simone, I'd choose Cynthia, all the dolls I ever had were named Cynthia, the next day I didn't see the top of the photograph on the patio, I found it hidden between the doily and the radio, I showed it to my mother along with a lit match

— You are stubborn Ma'am

the film in flames rose towards the ceiling light and disappeared into
the glow where flies were napping, my father swatted his hand against his
ear to get rid of an insect, looked at his hand, never looked at me, never
looked at anyone, but we still smelled him, if they gave me a piece of
soap I'd scrub myself as long as it took till my own smell would return,
I, my hands behind my back at the table

— Why didn't you name me Cynthia?

my father, without seeing me, pushing fish bones to the edge of his
plate with a piece of bread

— What?

my boyfriend and three Spaniards came back to the automobile, settling into the back seat, the commander pushed up his sleeve from his
wrist to check his watch

— Five minutes

billboards, posters and flags at the bullring, a man on the platform
interrupted by songs and hymns, sometimes the sound would disappear
and another man would come out and adjust the microphone, screwing
in plates till the sound came back on, as they fixed the sound equipment,
the man giving the speech would step back somewhat deflated, his papers
slipped from his hands, a girl approached him screaming, pronouncing
each syllable like a little toy bear shaking a tambourine, a few other voices
started joining in, the working microphone let out a panicked squeal,
the man with the papers gradually puffed up his chest, went back to his
speech, which spilled out all the way to the trees at the train station, to
the turtledoves out in the fields, to us piled into the automobile, waiting, the commander, whose pistol was uncomfortable against my chest
pushed up his sleeve again

— Thirty seconds

an orange grove filled with wasps, the cargo train crossing the Roman
viaduct, a group of houses tucked into a fold of earth, the world so
perfect, so clear, it didn't seem alive to me, it seemed like a drawing,

everything in color, everything in its place, I'd find a nice frame, maybe imitation silver, just perfect for my café in Espinho, if the clients ever irritated me I'd glare at them, I was remembering peaceful things, resting, as far away as a shepherd with his sheep, as far away as smoke flowing from chimneys, as far as ten seconds, as far as tiny stepladders between the bridge and the road, there are stores and notions stores

your Home deserves the Best

with identical pictures in the windows that were more expensive than the armoires, plywood bars and chairs, with a picture like that on the wall

— Now

hours go by in a minute and you don't feel it's winter, there were also lambs, sketched very carefully, hooves, tails, bells, first there was a small explos-, as I was saying carefully sketched lambs, every last curl, the holes in their snouts, the car window prevented us from ruining the artwork with our fingers, smearing the paint, when I put it up on the wall in the café I won't let anyone get near, if we ever go away on vacation I'll put it down in the cellar or I'll ask a neighbor I can trust to take care of it, first there was the small explosion, on the other side of the road, just as the commander turned to my boyfriend and the pistol, now pointing at us, stopped bothering my chest

— Five seconds late what's your excuse this time you idiots?

the shepherd was still there with the sheep, the train still on the viaduct, the houses tucked into the fold in the earth, the colors didn't change, a small explosion on the other side of the road, on the fence there was such a stink it would even stick to a person's body

(all he was missing was an arm to push the fish bones to the side of the plate with a piece of bread)

that came from the wooden stakes where they'd keep the bulls before the fight, the songs and hymns stopped, the man giving the speech was suddenly still, gurgling perplexed, if you paid closer attention you could see our car kind of covered in clouds in one corner of the painting, the shape of people in the seats, my boyfriend shrunken at the steering wheel

— We did everything you told us to Commander sir be careful that gun could go off

first there were one or two small explosions, then, almost without a pause, part of the bleachers and the boxes caught fire as fast as the photographs in the album, a voice in the microphone

— What's going on?

collapsing steps, advertising signs coming unglued, torn flags, yelling, an explosion on the platform where a boy, his hands cupped to his mouth, was promising

— It's nothing

and he kept promising

— It's nothing

till the floorboards gave way, in the restaurant where we have dinner on Sundays there was a print next to the bathrooms of a brush fire in Africa, baobabs, deer, hippopotamuses, and thatched huts floating, galloping towards us, chased by Africans with feathers and spears, my spoon would sag limply into the tureen in amazement, the electric wires buzzed, slashes of sparks, the generator blew up huge green petals, to me it seemed like half the plaza had been slaughtered in the arena but my boyfriend's breathing fogged up the window, if my father still hadn't had too much to drink he'd tell me to be still

— Look

he'd light a match, put the match inside his mouth, close his mouth, my mother

Hélder

he'd open his mouth again and take out the lit match, if he'd already had a lot to drink, he'd hand me the match with a strange chuckle

— Try it

and I'd hold it without daring to swallow

— Hélder

the dark tip of the match would get narrower and drop onto the floor, the other half of the bullring, like the match, shook spasmodically, the planks separated and were also slaughtered, the commander staring at my boyfriend in a way that seemed to me to be fearful

or maybe nauseated

put his pistol in his pocket, as the train moved along the picture disappeared little by little, I couldn't see the train or the bridge or the houses any more, I ended up with nothing to brighten up my café, looking out the back window, tiny people were fleeing the plaza where explosions were still going off, a van near the fence caught fire, all that was left of a banner were fluttering rags, the church bell was spitting a mayhem of insomniac bats, a blue flame went up suddenly reaching us, the commander to my boyfriend who hadn't said anything

— Be quiet

if his eyes had stayed like they are now, tiny and blind, I'd feel like yelling at him like the commander had in the car

— Be quiet

no

— Shut up

as he'd say to us and the communists who were apologizing, or sobbing, or quiet trying to guess who we were and getting it when the general entered, opening the door, and my boyfriend's boss gnarled

— Stand up

or when the Spaniards spoke unawares, using a burning stick to prod memories, I never thought feet could bend so much or scratch the cement floor like that, shoes missing heels, soles, broken fingers, the bishop looking down at his ring, nothing else in the world, not even his goddaughter, just the ring, if I were Cynthia people would respect me, how are you dona Cynthia, your health dona Cynthia, you've got a package from the post office dona Cynthia, they've saved the rump steak for you dona Cynthia, see you soon give my best to your husband dona Cynthia, at each moan the commander

— Shut up

whereas with my boyfriend he was the communist, the one asking forgiveness, sobbing, trying to guess, hiding everything in a nervous command

— Be quiet

unable to tell him to shut up just like he'd never say that to the people he took orders from, the general, and bishop, the American ambassador, he'd wave maps and straighten his posture

— Whatever you decide sir is the right choice

to my boyfriend's boss it was

— Shut up

to my boyfriend, who obeyed the boss, wanting to get away from him in a panic he was trying to hide, afraid of going home to his own house burning down, the walls collapsing one after the other in flaming explosions, a flame rising suddenly devouring the peacocks

— Be quiet

the ex-policemen were waiting for us under the oak tree outside the garage with the widow of the boss's partner, who treated me worse than the others, never answering when I said hello, talking to me in the same way as she did to the servants, I could tell by her face she was making fun of me and the oak tree right next to all of us all scandalized

— Burn her

so I did, just like I burned the photographs in the album, the woman went red, then grey, and a pile of ashes gathered at my feet, every time I dreamed I was dying I'd wake up afraid and my mother, instead of Cynthia

— What happened Simone?

holding sea bream from lunch, burn the fish, burn my mother, no one to torment me when I wake up, opening the blinds on purpose and moving the curtains, vegetable sellers, buckets of mollusks, pointless agitation, colors and sounds that made me hide under my covers looking for the night that wasn't there anymore

— Leave me alone

the sea bream recoiled, scared, the commander recoiled scared, in the boarding house in Espinho, machine guns, the water bottle and the little vase of fake flowers on the floor, the bench where I'd put my clothes tipped over, the flashlight searching through the blankets, stopping at me, the telephone ringing twice and stopping

—I had no idea the woman was so fat

when I'd bring the tray in with the lunch, I could feel the bishop's glasses travel over me, travel up my ankles slowly, and I'd suddenly feel naked there on the carpet, I tried to cover myself with the tray and it fell, the secretary

— What are you doing?

if I went into the lunch room I'd find the bishop in the lunch room, if they told me to go get a bottle of wine, there he'd be

— Come a little closer sweetie

he'd put the lit match inside his mouth, close it and open it again and the flame would still be lit, he'd hand it to me with a strange chuckle

— Try it

he'd look around and there was nothing there, just spider webs, bottlenecks, little patches of moss, the humidity of the stone, something breaking and dragging over the floor, the secretary positive the democrats had invaded the house and were about to bound upstairs with knives and daggers

— What's happening?

the commander staring at us afraid, sort of nauseated or scared, cross out nauseated, scared, he called my boyfriend's boss as the deaf woman was serving the pitcher of soda, mixing the sugar and coffee with a helpful spoon

— Get rid of them as soon as possible

my mother trying to hug me as if I were elegant

— No

I felt like telling her to fix her hair, wash up, take those awful medallions off the string, stop making me ashamed to introduce her to strangers, I helped my boyfriend set off the detonator in the pine woods, the murmuring trees and insects in the background, the wind all talking about me, but just as it got dark we'd put a stop to such rudeness by setting off the detonator,

— Serves you right

cousins I didn't even know talking, boldly invading our house, shaking my father's hand, kissing my mother, kissing me, settling into our chairs, shocked our stove had no enamel finish, one table leg propped up, photographs of equally puny uncles wearing coats too big for them

— Get the port Simone

not Cynthia, a decent name, Simone

we had only three glasses so we also had to use water glasses and one or two jam jars, so they'd really understand, exchanging glances

(— Why insist on demeaning us Mother why show them who we are?)

over how we actually lived

— We're out of Port run over to the grocery store and ask for more Simone

not buy, ask, one more sheet of paper marking our debt in pencil stuck on the nail full of other penciled debts, cigarettes beans potatoes bleach my cousins, jam jars in hand, curious

— The girl's gotten so fat is she sick?

strange children rummaging through my drawers, fooling around with my perfume samples, rubbing them on their neck, then showing their parents

— Look father

when they found my shells, they put them up to their ears, disappointed,

— You can't hear anything

forgetting where to put things back, putting everything in the wrong order which got me really upset because when I tried to put everything back in place it never worked out, move the shell forward just a bit, shift the clay frog in a school uniform slightly sideways, no, that's not right, not right, I'd get a bad feeling, a kind of discomfort that's hard to describe, the out-of-place frog upset my life, no matter how many times I move it, I can't get it right, and later I'm sure things are missing, I thought I wasn't worried about them but if they're not on my dresser I feel like I'm suffocating, my elephant hair bracelet, my comb missing a few teeth, only now do I realize why I kept it, every day I'd come back to my room and promise myself

— I'm going to throw that in the trash basket

and I'd leave it there, where's my comb, go through their pockets, demand they give it back, hit them, things I hadn't even noticed suddenly so important, a broken ashtray, a pack of cigarettes where there'd been three and now there were only two, the little vase with the wilted orchid they'd tilted without asking my permission, I can't sleep, calm down, I get up fixing everything, sit down, get up again trying to fix things, asking about their health be quiet and let me fix my own life, as I straighten the orchid one of the petals falls off and once one of the petals falls everything's changed permanently and I'm done for, always oblivious to my world falling apart my cousins were drinking port in jam jars, my mother was feeding herself toast and old stories, baptisms, funerals, picnics, birthday dinners in Santarém, that train ride to Gouveia I don't even know where that is, I hate Gouveia, I help my boyfriend set off the detonator and goodbye Gouveia, goodbye mother

— Your girl's gotten so fat is it some problem with her blood or is she sick?

trying not to touch where I was touching, shooing the kids away from me, I help my boyfriend set off the detonator and goodbye baptisms, funerals, picnics, birthday dinners in Santarém, the first small explosion in the kitchen, a second explosion in the hall, the walls in my parents' bedroom in flames, the leather sofa in flames, the lamp in flames, the dresses in flames, the question disappearing in a spiral of ashes

— Your girl's gotten so fat is it some problem with her blood or is she sick?

I, alone in the mirror tent at the fair, beautiful, elegant, peaceful, not paying any attention to the chuckling from the speakers or to the worker touching my back

— We're closing

since Madame Dolores, who knows the future, promised me a kind-hearted husband, a boat trip and an unexpected inheritance.

21

SOME DAYS I feel so happy I think I must be in Coimbra, after mass on Sunday when my mother would change out of her new clothes into her cooking smock and apron, the servants would prepare partridges, lambs and goats whose bodies we couldn't really see, I'd notice their eyes looking like grown-ups' eyes when they listened to piano or gazed out at the ocean, till they become the piano and ocean themselves, I'd sense the sounds through their postures, my uncle would set the tables furthest away from the window with the oldest cutlery, the cat would curl up on the windowsill where its surprising mouth would emerge from a ball of yarn in a fat yawn, my father would wait for me in the yard, listening for bells, the quail net in his knapsack, my brother died at birth when I was three and I remember only the bells, to this day the only thing bells make me think of is an empty crib, after a few months they put the crib away in the attic and the skylight shone on the dirty sheets, as I approached to shake them off, a prickly mouse threatened me from the pillow, every time the bells rang the first thing my father would do was turn his head toward the tower, his face would change, grow smaller, then return to normal and the two of us would walk toward the eucalyptuses, he looking for nests and I, proud in my lace collar and patent leather shoes, trying to fit both my dress and the crib into my thoughts, I was sure it rocked during the night to help the dead baby get to sleep, the eucalyptus woods drowned us in murmurs, silencing the bell and my brother, partridge-filled branches emerged from the balsa tree, my father would crouch down to set up the net, his back rounded, his fingers attaching the reeds, a little piece of soap in his beard made him seem vulnerable, softened me, I noticed his first strands of white hair and tendons starting to show on the back of his neck, when we beat the bushes the partridges fled too quickly and escaped the net, one of them, a male on a branch acting as lookout, stared at us, his wattle vibrating, I must be in Coimbra because someone's perfuming a braid, soaking it in brandy, a mouse is threatening me from the pillow but it's not a mouse after all, it's the doctor letting go of my wrist, adjusting the drip, asking my husband

— How do you expect her to travel to Spain in the state she's in sir?

my father knelt down to throw a rock at the partridge, a second flock flew screaming by us in the direction of the swamp, the gusting wind tolls in our direction, I'd wave them to be silent, the crib and dusty sheets would blow toward me with the tolling gusts, I tried to hide my baldness with the wig, I stretched out my arm, the bedside table was gone and the doctor and my husband, the two of them so tall their heads touched the ceiling

— She must be thirsty poor thing give her some water

we moved the net over to the shrubbery, withering in the sun filled with shaking wings, the miller's boat wasn't painted, just keel ribs, a dead hare, covered in wasps, seemingly believing it was protecting itself by showing its incisors, my husband tipped the cup to my tongue, spilling the water on my blouse, the doctor warned him

— Slowly

there was gurgling beyond the trembling wings, speckled eggs, a broody swollen animal, one of the partridges got caught in the dropped net, another one disappeared into the hedge, I went into their room after going down endless meters of dark hallway, hiding my eyes in my arm

— I can't sleep

my mother got up, half her bosom exposed

— What's going on?

fastening her blouse, my father

hurry up hurry up

trying to find the right belt hole, first too tight then too loose, my mother still trying to get her brassiere back on, still exposed

— I knew this was going to happen

another time I woke up with the clock pendulum disturbing my sleep but, contrary to I what I'd thought, it wasn't the pendulum, it was their bed against the wall, I opened the door

it was February and the oranges were piled up in the yard in the rain

and I came across several bare feet right next to me, my mother's face on a neck that wasn't hers, half the feet shrunk and the rest turned into my father, who'd forgotten that his pajama pants were gathered at his ankles

— Don't you have any consideration for the girl?

the smell of the wild roses in the blinds, lambs for tomorrow's lunch were protesting fearfully, my father pulled up his pajamas over in the corner were there wasn't any light, where the chest with the baby's clothes was simmering lavender, in the place where the bed was banging, under the crucifix with the little blue ribbon, there were marks in the wood veneer, it seemed like I could hear the crib's moaning mattress in the attic, the doctor, now visible more clearly against the terrace vases, was advising my husband to hire a nurse

— If your wife lasts a week it'll be a miracle it won't be that expensive

a small bird

not a partridge

a bee killer or something like it got crucified in the netting, my father, furious because the netting had torn, untangled it, the servants were braiding Mama Alicia's hair, she was already seated on her throne upstairs since the smell of the brandy was keeping me awake, my husband emerged contradicting the doctor and their silhouettes blended into the stucco

— Be realistic doctor I hire a nurse and two hours later we'll have the army here arresting us

men in oilcloth aprons were slitting lambs' throats, the blood spurting in angry bubbles into the jug as the secretary tried to escape, looking for a crack in the wall, showing us a photograph of his granddaughter as if she could save him, he'd kiss the medallion around his neck as he looked at us and, on his knees, kept kissing it after the third blast, one of the ex-policemen took the medallion off the cord and stuffed it into his mouth so he could take it with him when they threw him into the Tagus, the bell had just rung when I heard a child crying in the attic, a child crying or maybe it was the furniture my mother accumulated up there that in the winter months would squawk and crackle, begging for someone to arrange it back in the living room from where it had been banished, every time I went upstairs it tried to get out from under the blankets, looking at me, offended, the doctor leaned my kidneys up against the pillow explaining to my husband

— They always get agitated as they go into a coma

my grandmother called me from her throne as the servants took the basin of brandy down to the main floor

— Mimi

telling me about Galicia where roses sprout beneath the rain, the doctor, we can never tell if they're aware of us when they're in a coma, my husband, you can say whatever you like, she's deaf, you can't all leave me here alone because as soon as it gets dark the driver in the pine woods, you've got to get me dressed, put on my wig, settle me in the seat between pillows and blankets, the secretary when the Spanish military men handcuffed him

— You've got to be kidding

baffled, to the commander, the bishop, my husband, and the driver who was taking his wallet out of his pocket and handing it over to one of the ex-policemen, an agenda, tickets, his granddaughter in her school uniform, an envelope in the coat lining, the gardener's clippers stopped,

the bishop was getting his glasses out of his cassock, my husband's business partner's widow kept sparking her cigarette lighter, the American
ambassador's oblivious fingernail removed a spot of dust from his shoe,
they were scooping the leaves out of the swimming pool with a pole, say
whatever you like, she's deaf, the commander took the envelope from
the bishop

— Just a minute

the cigarette lighter kept on sparking and going out, the ambassador
was leafing through an album of old paintings, descents from the cross,
miracles, Pharisees, the commander gave the envelope to the general, I
kept on serving tea, sugar, milk, hot water, handing out little spoons, if
at least the cups were empty and they'd ask me for more, as I approached
the secretary my husband took the teapot from my hands and threw it
out on the veranda, the general was reading and rereading

— I don't believe it

one of the ex-policemen showed him something in the agenda, the
general handed the envelope back to the commander and pointed to one
of the pages in the agenda with his little finger

— Here too

my father put the partridge net away in the kitchen, my cousins in
their Sunday dresses, meaning their hair was combed, and wearing stockings, were chasing chickens in the yard, a felt moose watching from a
rock, you'd pull a string and a mechanism in its stomach would reel the
string back in till the moose fell silent, the secretary's stomach mechanism was whining

— Just let me explain General sir

the string reeled back in and he too fell silent, one of my uncles set
up a swing on the fig tree in the yard, made from a board and two ropes,
if you closed your eyes you couldn't see the house or the crib in the attic
or my mother calling from the kitchen window

— Don't get dirty Mimi

or the hospital treatment or the wig or the cigarette lighter flame or the dead lambs or the bishop, anxious over the agenda

— My God

not even the ex-policemen who were carrying the secretary over to the garage, the stomach mechanism again

— Just let me explain General sir

the string reeling back in, silence, go out into the garden to get the broken teapot, even though it's useless, ask them to send him away and serve them tea, Celina and I and no one else in the living room except for the pendulum behind the glass of the old clock, the confusion of the Roman numerals, problems with washbasins, faucets, trains, station A and station B are one hundred kilometers apart, if the train leaves station A and travels eighty kilometers per hour and the train departing station B, seventy kilometers per hour, calculate at what distance from station A, Celina put down her lighter, pulled up her chair, adjusting her skirt, advising me

— Don't stay in this house

and I, smiling, passing her the sugar as if I hadn't understood

— But of course

thinking about the trains, the stops, the travelers, the ground sliding backwards, to this day I could swear it's not the train moving, but the land going backwards, we stay still and the hillsides run past the window, girls turning toward me

— Tell Mimi where the trains meet Edith

a little myopic voice emerging in front of me, answering with adult capability, not noticing the bridges, the olive trees, the triangle of ocean between the dunes shining for just an instant staying with me for years, every time the doctor

— It's not worth operating

I'd think about it to dispel my fear, how much time does a boat take, at sixteen knots, leaving from the intersection of the horizon, with the dune on the right, if the observer is located such that all three form a twenty-seven-degree angle, a small angle, a triangle that if you wish

although the fact wasn't relevant to the answer in the slightest

you can fill with stars and suns and imagine it squeezed between hillsides of tulips, dahlias, daisies, just like I'd withstand the hospital treatment knowing the drip bag containing five hundred cubic centimeters released sixty drips per minute and knowing that each drip contained four millimeters of liquid, I'd calculate how much time, just like when my husband got home late I'd think of our house as point A, coming from his partner's house at point B, at a speed of fifty kilometers per hour, taking into account that he'd left at three-thirty in the morning and that house A and house B were seventeen kilometers six-hundred meters apart, tell me at what time, hours minutes seconds, hurry up with the calculation before Edith lifts her adult glasses and her little arm with a pencil at the end, all the faces turned toward me, the teacher

— Tell Mimi Edith

Edith got run over and died on the last day of school, after she'd received her bouquet of flowers and her red and green sash for being the top student because she forgot, for the first time in twelve years, that the six o'clock bus left corner C, where store S was located, heading down slope R, a three percent incline, at a steady pace of twenty centimeters per second, hitting her at location L, ninety-three millimeters off the sidewalk, as she ran at five kilometers per hour toward her parents, her bouquet blocking her vision, at precisely the moment, and according to the elementary rules of optics, when vehicle V with a gross weight of two metric tons

(very important: keep in mind the eyeball is a simple lens, therefore subject to the law of incidence reflection and the image formed is inverted in the occipital lobe from where it is sent to the nobler structures of the brain)

Edith, who had no time to explain to anyone, not even the inspector who'd promised her a future position in the ministry to the glory and honor of Pubic School 26, how many rib fractures, or how many cubic centimeters of internal hemorrhage she suffered on the way to the hospital, on arrival of the corpse, or how many people attended her funeral taking into account that the sum total of her closest relatives was thirty-one and each of them had four close friends, or the amount of time taken by the funeral mass with a priest expending on average fourteen Latin words per minute, or how many shovels of earth, each containing three kilos and three hundred grams, were needed to fill a grave one meter eight centimeters long by sixty-two centimeters wide and one meter sixty-four centimeters deep for a total volume of fifty-nine liters of casket including adornments, iron crucifix with inlaid screws, stainless steel identification plaque, bronze handles, the top covered with the best student sash and the salvaged nards, some of them slightly trampled, others intact although blackened with April mud, the teacher, who weighed forty-seven kilos

(barefoot on an empty stomach)

came to the funeral relieved of two kilos six hundred and sixty grams

(on an empty stomach)

of her Pekinese that went everywhere with her, although the total weight of her clothing, umbrella and prayer book amounted to three kilos five hundred and seventy-five grams, which, in practice, meant a relatively insignificant decrease in the effort expended by her muscles, respiratory system, and her peripheral and cardiac arterial system, to the sum of ninety-one grams, which, according to current charts, resulted in an expenditure not exceeding twenty point eleven calories, easily replenished with three quarters of a cup of low fat milk, the ex-policemen carried the secretary from the bench to the garage, Celina and I, in the living room with no one else except for the pendulum of the old clock

whose weight I have no idea

moving hands on the face with the Roman numbers decorated with designs I didn't bother to convert into numbers, maybe ten to two, four-twenty, six twenty-seven it doesn't matter, Celina put her lighter, shaped like Aladdin's lamp, on the table, its flame releasing the promise of a turbaned genie, arms crossed and deep-voiced, with the power to make three wishes come true, and she pulled up her chair, adjusting her skirt, advising me

— Don't stay in this house

and I, smiling and passing her the sugar as if I hadn't understood

— But of course

Celina, pointing to the garden, the floor, making hand signals toward the road, drawing a roof and a diamond shape with her hands, removing them quickly as if the roof and the diamond shape had disappeared into thin air, pointing to the floor again, making more signs toward the road, sitting down with an exhausted whisper

— Don't stay in this house

with me at my school desk trying to solve the problem of five dyna-mite bombs each weighing seven kilos, placed in the cellar, ground floor, and first and second floors of a house, that is, four floors, each approxi-mately one hundred and seventy square meters in area, made of cement, bricks, stone and wood, a bomb that a manual command set off from a distance of sixty meters, in pine woods where it so happens I'm not feel-ing the wind right now, nor does it look as if there are any skylarks, one or two foxes in the gorse, one or two badgers in the space between the trees, maybe a woman walking with a bundle of wood to the government housing, bombs that a manual command would set off forcing them to explode simultaneously or at intervals no greater than zero point six sec-onds, well aware that inside the said house are a general, a commander, a bishop, the goddaughter of said bishop, a terminal cancer patient, whom doctors have given up on, with generalized metastasis, weighing thirty-three kilos, equivalent to just over the weight of her skeleton, the husband of the former, ex-policemen, who are supporters of the regime overthrown by the revolution, and Spanish officers, who are supporters of the regime not yet overthrown by the revolution, calculate what will remain of these creatures once the explosion occurs, with me trying to solve the problem and understanding that nothing remains, so I lifted my little arm with a pencil at the end hoping the teacher at the dais would call on me

— Tell Celina Mimi

and I, in a victorious little voice under my orange wig, my make-up masking the sores on my neck and forehead, so happy I think I must be in Coimbra on Sunday when my mother used to change out of her new clothes into her cooking smock and apron, the rabbits, lambs and goats looked at me as if they were listening to a piano or the ocean, and I, understanding by the sound, by the way they held still as they listened, I, fixing my wig and smiling steadily

— It's precisely because nothing will remain that I'm staying here because absolutely nothing of us will remain is the reason I'm not leaving.

22

TODAY EVERYTHING SEEMS different but I don't know why: the trees, the
retirees, the lake where leaves make black patches of what's left of the
sun, the people on the esplanade and around the statue, even the shadows of the houses as they tell me goodbye, martyrs' gestures blessing me
in silence, some kind of sign in all of this, of separation, of a farewell I
don't understand, even in the kitchen all of a sudden there's a lack of intimacy between me and everything, I'm moving among strange objects, I
hesitate, try to remember, this stove could be mine, this dishwasher, this
clothes washer, the harlequin perched on top of the fan is encouraging
me, I open the cutlery drawer and find napkins, I look for cups in the
cupboard and the cruet set jumps out at me, two smiling countrywomen
whose hats are the stoppers and whose arms, carrying a little basket,
are the handle, you can always tell which one's the olive oil because her
apron's cracked, everything's so different today, I can't figure out why, but
I feel like spreading my fingers apart and letting the cruet set drop, let it
break into pieces, there'll be nothing left of the happy countrywomen,
afternoon begins over by the Tagus, the retirees' cards dissolve in the
dusk and all that remains are their caps above the lethargic swans, at the
start of the afternoon at my parents' house Mercês Church, drowning us
under the weight of its stone, would also drown my mother's anxiety and
my father's anger in the living room, when they got married he was high
tenor in the choir, but time and his job warped his voice, my mother got
the canary to help him get back in tune, my father would place himself
in front of the animal unbuttoning his collar to expel sounds from his
chest, my mother would try to help, rocking back and forth, when she
fed me soup she'd open and close her mouth as she gave me the spoon

— Let's eat

so I'd keep my teeth clenched thinking it wasn't my job to swallow, the canary drank water, changed poles, would wring out a note accompanied by the pot on the stove, my father's silhouette would stretch toward the ceiling, his features

eyes eyebrows forehead nose

transformed into lips, my mother would stretch out along with him, a pair of abandoned mongrels on a deserted farm howling at death, insect-ridden cherry trees, weeds, the pulley missing its rope at the pond, maybe a roofless house off in the distance with a couple of blinds banging in the wind and a tipped-over bucket on a tiled patio, the canary, sensing it was being watched, pondered for a few minutes in artistic meditation, dumped a few seeds from his metal dish, repeated the note one octave higher, my mother, cousin, Mercês Church and I would be on the verge of happiness as my father's Adam's apple dunked into his necktie bearing the beginnings of an aria with it, the pot on the stove crackling out bub-bles, the cries of the ambulatory knife sharpener's barrel organ climbing up and down the scale, my cousin taking a deep breath in tense expecta-tion, each muscle at the ready to accompany the opera

— Uncle

my father rose a little in his shoes, his organ tube of a neck elongated to perfect the singing, his sleeves spasmodically flapping like wings, about to flee the nest, fly, to disappear above the roof tiles in a bassoon trail, to circle Mercês Church and get lost among the sparrows on their way to the docks, his pants pulled up over his polka-dotted socks but, in spite of it all, there he stayed, earthbound, along with the furiously spattering pot, spitting out drops of saliva burning with hate, his neck having returned to normal, his Adam's apple having returned to above his collar, his face having reacquainted itself with his eyelashes and ears, my disillusioned mother wringing her dress

— And?

to the high tenor releasing a sorrowful little gasp, the knife sharpener's harmonica climbing the scale, at first two or three steps, now endless, leading to the center of the earth inhabited by roots and dead bodies,

my mother's grandparents who'd take her on boat rides in Montijo village, during that happy past, her memories taking her back to her youth,
surprising little dimples, and then, back to the roots, hellish catechism,
those caldrons of oil in rusty lighting, what my godfather thinks about
first thing when the morning scales open up the bedroom crucifixes,
accentuating God's angry gauntness, and I hear him reciting prayers in
Latin begging for help

— Fatinha

so different from the young man who'd give me candies at my parents'
house, or the other more important one who'd lecture the communists
about Jesus before the ex-policemen pushed them over the Peniche cliffs,
little white flowers, goats in the gorse, the roar of the lighthouse, the
wind blinding me and blocking off my hearing so that, by the time we
left, nothing had happened, at most there were fewer footsteps over the
pebbles, as if we'd been abandoned without warning, when the lighthouse
beam lit us it made our features red, more like rag dolls than faces stirring
those little rocks, my father would sit back down in his chair weighed
down by the catastrophe

— I can't

the canary on the little cane pole was triumphant in the kitchen,
the bubbling fat spitting sarcasm all over the linoleum, my mother and
cousin busied themselves with lunch, having accepted the high tenor
was not to fly off with the sparrows in a bassoon trail, if at least he'd take
them on Sunday boat rides in Montijo where they'd see windmills and
swampland as they went along, if at least my godfather would let me sleep
in peace, carry his Latin and his guilt off to his office, following a path
of saintly oil lamps instead of lurking around me in sobbing humility

— Fatinha

afraid of waking me up and wanting to wake me up, reminding me
there in his bathrobe, without the dignity of his cassock and ring, of a
two-man pantomime cow at the fair, when my father lifted me up above
the audience's heads, the back half of the animal would shake slowly and
sink softly to the ground, the front half would pause and turn around

wondering what had happened, wrinkle, twist, unbutton itself with great effort, one arm, then the other, a knee, a whole man investigating

— Arménio

feeling back to the part of the cow that wasn't him, who knows, maybe a relative, a friend, a trained animal, rummaging through the hindquarters till a numbed head emerged, a gold chain, little dangling fingers, whatever would the ex-policemen write from one of the buildings opposite, separated from our building by poplars and puddles, what would they tell the general, and commander, and the American ambassador, what could they really figure out from behind closed blinds, curtains, with the lights out, maybe they also noticed the way we left the house, how things in the closets had been moved around, doors I was afraid to open, scared of what I might find, furniture playing dead so we wouldn't notice it, if they'd have shown me the report, I bet I'd have read

and it's not true

that it was my fault the two men in the pantomime cow ended up by themselves on the plaza where the fair had been, the general calling my mother to read the report to her out loud

— Listen to this

my mother embarrassed in her Sunday dress, the shoes she'd been keeping for centuries next to the closet, saving to wear in her coffin, looking through her purse for her glasses, struggling over

(I know her so well)

words she didn't understand and rushing through the reading in the hope they wouldn't understand what she didn't understand, handing back the report, trying to defend me

— It's not possible, sir

so terrified, so shaken, so proud of her dead woman's shoes and I, wondering if there'd be money to buy some new ones so she wouldn't have to arrive in Paradise with worn soles, my mother who'd wear perfume to go to the doctor's, a drop or two from the tiny sample tubes they'd give me at the cosmetics store, which I'd give to her out of charity, she'd choose her least worn purse, put on slight blush of lipstick and end up forgotten in the waiting room from seven in the morning till the end of the day, never complaining, the nurse having changed out of her smock and, locking up the clinic, already wearing her coat and noticing the poor woman sitting on a little corner of a bench

— You're still here?

I'd take her on an outing to Montijo village far from Mercês Church, from Campo de Santana park, from my godfather with his prayer voice

— Fatinha

far from the silence of things taking leave, motionless in some kind of farewell I don't understand, stroll through the village hearing the drowning people in the river, bewildered grandparents studying me, intrigued, asking her who I am

— Who's this girl?

searching for their features in my features, similarities, affinities, they hold up my chin the better to see me, in the same way my godfather held the communists' chins to explain to them about mercy and God's justice, they dismiss me in disgust

— She came out like your husband's folk doesn't have anything from our side

they lived on the plaza before I did, knew the same neighbors, the same stores, the same noises in the building except the furniture was brand new then, the drains worked, the pipes were intact, the same mailman delivered their postcards, copies of old prints, evenings punctuated by the kitchen clock that doesn't work anymore, random warped record albums, random incurable diseases, the commander would shove my godfather away

— No time for prayers

the driver's wife, who'd help serve at table whenever the ambassador came to talk to us, would go in and out of the garage with the wash basin, the ambassador disappeared, the Spanish military men disappeared, the ex-policemen left for France, Morocco, Venezuela and changed their names, got jobs in cafés, as hotel messenger boys, telephoned telling us to leave, the general

— Cowards

looking for my mother, I'd knock on the door, sit down, there may be space on the sofa, or in my father's chair, on the window bench, take my place at the table, like I used to, facing the Last Supper, the napkin ring with my name in relief, Fátima

why Fátima?

before Mercês Church blends me into the night, what's to become of the deaf woman when the army gets here, her orange wig, her illness, her smile, maybe they'll take the others and leave her in peace with her teacup, approving of her bureaus

— But of course

if I tried to talk to her, show some concern, ask her

— Are you better?

the gardener's clippers in the yard would cut my words, make them fall from my mouth in limp slices, pink syllables scattered over the carpet and she, arranging the blanket around her knees

— Excuse me?

no

— But of course

arranging the blanket around her knees

— Excuse me?

still, she wasn't talking to me, or to her husband, or to Celina, or to the general, it was to someone we couldn't see, whom I didn't see at first but then, paying more attention, I found a picture frame, an old lady with a white braid and pitcher of soda water, sugar and coffee who was calling out

— Mimi

why Mimi, why Fátima, why Mimi?

so I couldn't tell her, everything seems different to me today but I don't know why, the trees, the retirees in the garden, the lake where leaves are making black patches of what's left of the sun, the people on the esplanade and around the statue, martyrs' gestures blessing me in silence, something in all of this reminding me of separations, farewells, a lack of intimacy between us and everything, tell her I'm moving around at a loss among strange objects, this stove could be mine, this clothes washer, this iron, the harlequin perched on top of the fan encourages me, I couldn't count on the cruet set with its two porcelain countrywomen whose hats are the stoppers and whose arms carrying the little baskets are the handles, you can always tell which one's the olive oil because her apron's cracked, tell her that between me and my husband, between me and my godfather, that it's not out of love, it's not that I love them, tell her that I'm afraid, that the Spanish military men, the ex-policemen, and the American ambassador have all left, that if we look around

and in no time at all, when we understand better, we'll look around

the only person left here with us is my mother, standing up in the corner of the room embarrassed in her Sunday dress, wearing the shoes she'd been saving for her coffin, the only person left is my mother looking for her glasses in her purse the better to see the pantomime cow being chased among the planters by government soldiers, and which ends up in a heap against the wall with the two of us, listen, with the two of us, you and me, with the two of us, listen carefully, inside.

23

Of course I go to the hairdresser so I'll be pretty tonight when my uncle lifts me up in the living room higher than everyone else

— Fly Celina fly

discovering what's living on top of the armoires, things they don't want me to touch, the oil stove, medicine, fishing rods, the gun missing its trigger that they didn't use to keep up there till one day my grandmother ran toward me, dropping her scaling knife, her mouth and eyes looking like I'd never seen before, hitting my hand as hard as she could

— Don't touch that Celina

and after she hit me, she held me, sobbing, pressing her cheek to mine and giving me candies, the way grown-ups do to say they're sorry

— Promise me you'll never do that again Celina

(later I found out that years before I was born my grandfather went out to the yard and within a couple of seconds the lemon trees started shaking and the blackbirds didn't come back for a week, the gun dropped into a rain puddle, they said after the shot the silence was so profound that)

I had to pick the candy out with my fingernail so I could answer her with my mouth full

— I promise

wrapped in silvery red with another layer of cellophane, I'd smooth out the silvery pieces carefully so they wouldn't tear, I'd take them to school inside a book, my envious schoolmates

— If you give me the striped one I'll ask my father if you can come to the beach with us on Sunday

old broken down automobiles between the dunes and the road, we, in the back seat, bored to death, under umbrellas, big bottles, towels, picnic baskets, if we sang, adults holding screwdrivers covered in oil stains from head to toe would appear at the window furiously telling us to be quiet, if we laughed at their blotched noses, they'd look at us out of the corner of their eyes wanting to strangle us, if my friends' mothers opened their mouth, their fathers would get behind the wheel so vigorously the springs would dance, furiously scraping at a faulty horn with their thumbs as the ocean and pine trees protested right back

— If you know so much about it you do it

so Sundays at the beach were fumes, gasoline vapors, a line of rubber rings and metallic parts dripping black drops, mothers' pleas reduced to uncombed, fearful whispers releasing handles, passing around sandwiches consisting mainly of bread so we'd be quiet

— For the love of God watch out for the children

get back home almost nighttime, brought by a tow truck, the car hanging on the hook behind us, at one point there were no headlights or even a road, or walls, or trees, not even dark red animal eyes jumping out onto the pavement, we'd only come back to life at our front door, when they'd grab me mercilessly from the depths of my sleep, my uncle's voice way off in the distance, from a world I refused to enter

— Help

my body jerking up the staircase dropping tatters of sleep they'd tried to cover me with along the way

— This little girl's like lead

one knee asleep, someone unbuttoning my tufts

because my clothes were part of me

the blouse from my back, Mickey Mouse's colors blended into the shelf, the brightness cut through my eyelids like an acid knife, they tossed my ankles into the sheets, squishing them with tourniquets or fingers

tourniquets

stealing even more sleep

— Quiet

I'm certain there were several of me since one wanted to cry and couldn't, another tried to escape and they held her back, the brightness disappeared, Mickey Mouse disappeared, the elbows pressing down on my chest moved away

— Okay

I pushed my nose up against the wall, covered my head with my pillow, felt some warmth and went back to being just one of me, the ocean shone for a minute and evaporated immediately, taken away by the tow truck heading down the road and after that, everything was liquid and warm, then nothing, if I pulled the candy from the roof of my mouth and showed my grandmother, she'd back away frightened, looking at me as if I were some kind of lizard

— Go wash your hands Celina hurry up or you'll spread sugar all over the house

my finger, funnily enough, my silly little finger terrorized the adults, I'd run around the house pointing it in the air and they'd shoo me away

— What're you doing?

leaning back to avoid me, my mother, my uncle, even my father escaping silently into his newspaper and so, of course, I wash my hands and go to the hairdresser so I'll be pretty in the evening, I ask Elisabete to do highlights and hide the grey, I refuse to leave till my forty-year-old lines, which she calls expression lines, fade into the lotions, I wear my black blouse, dangling earrings, dark stockings to hide my cellulite, varicose veins and stretch marks Elisabete swears I don't have

— But what stretch marks dona Celina?

I see well enough I've got them, just take a look, I contract my muscles, squeeze my skin a bit

not even very much

if Mickey Mouse were here, and thank God he's not, he'd immediately yell, the idiot

— Aren't you a sassy gal

shaking in fun, the gardener straightening the nards, the driver, his hands in his pockets standing in front of the garage, the limestone lions, their throats to the sky, as ugly as can be decorating the stairs, the deaf woman under her orange wig

— But of course

the general, the commander and the bishop offering me a chair with that friendly male dispatch, filled with hidden nips and swear words, if I'd brought my grandfather's revolver, even without the trigger, I'd shut their greetings up in an instant

— Madame

Mickey Mouse agreeing with me in falsetto giggles, pointing at them with his little rag paw

— Morons

my husband's partner hugged my waist under the pretext of leading me to the bar, the orange wig followed us with indulgent kindness entirely lacking in interest, jealousy or bitterness

— Why don't you answer the telephone Celina?

so many people, but no one there to pick me up and lift me way up above everyone else till I reach the ceiling and discover what's kept on top of the armoires, dried insects, pieces of glass, a broken alarm clock, everything

candlesticks ashtrays cups glasses

which my maid breaks and rushes to hide just like the way she sweeps trash under the rugs, no one to pick me up and help me fly, it's true Elisabete tries, the waxing girl tries, the pedicurist tries

— I swear on my own good health you look younger than me dona Celina

hands like a child's, smooth necks, supple napes, peach fuzzy cheeks, back when I looked like them every single day someone would send me a bouquet at the insurance company, you couldn't even see the doorman behind it as he brought it to me, my mother's envy when I'd get home

(— Who gave that to you young lady?)

she'd try on my clothes in secret in the hope that they'd fit her and her hips would burst my skirts, my only bottle of perfume, empty, lipstick, gone, all I had to do was look at her and she'd start screaming as if possessed over the cruelty of passing years

— It wasn't me

she'd slam her bedroom door and my father would look up from the newspaper, if I could have peeked in I'd have seen her shiny with lotions, stretching her face with her hands, replacing her eyebrows with ever thinner eyebrow pencil lines, augmenting her bosom with cotton from the pharmacy that showed through her button holes, throwing my bouquets in the garbage can, hiding her missing teeth with her lips

— Collards

even the one in front that kept her from smiling, she'd sit at the table
covering her mouth with her hand, pointing at my bouquet

— Might as well not have sent you flowers as this lousy bouquet

sitting at the mirror, her back to me, we'd meet in the mirror above
brushes and tweezers, a picture of me as a baby with a little gold chain
around my neck and below the photo Our little Celina at six months,
my eyes just like her eyes, same shape, same color, when we went out
shopping she'd tell me

— Don't call me mother

if I got mixed up and said mother she'd right away say

— Oh kids

we, looking at ourselves in the mirror above brushes and tweezers, she
was suddenly so afraid of dying, behind the silence

— Pick me up

it wasn't her age that frightened her, it was death, being alone at
night with that horrible wind among the poplars, bodies disappear from
cemeteries who knows where they end up, her tired chin, drooping like
an animal's

— Don't let me die I'm so peaked aren't I

maybe we both wanted to

— Go away

hold each other in the cramped little room where my perfume was
dancing

— Go away, get out of here the doctor assured me this thing in my eye isn't cataracts seriously think about it of course it's not cataracts old people's disease folks with one foot in the grave what're they going to say next cataracts I'm always like this in the spring with the change in temperature as soon as I mentioned pollen he agreed and prescribed ten drops morning and night

my husband's partner holding me by the waist under the pretext of leading me to the bar

— Why don't you answer the telephone Celina?

the blind woman following us with indulgent kindness entirely lacking in interest, jealousy or bitterness, it was the orange wig calling me

— Tart

it wasn't the sick woman who said it, hugging my mother in the little cramped room, talking to the mirror, expression lines, stretch marks, cellulite, varicose veins, talking to me even though her back's to me in the now enormous room, with spotless curtains, starched and clean, stretching the skin on my face, blinking, moving my mouth, trying out a smile, picking up another mirror to check my profile, my turkey waddle thickening my throat, tendons, the moles I discovered months ago spreading over my hands, someone must know of some sort of cream, an elixir, a lotion, some kind of soap to wash them off, I take a sleeping pill, I lie down and the morning goes by, if I ever got hurt, my uncle would look for invisible powders in his pocket with big theatrical gestures, take them out with enormous care so they wouldn't fall, he'd open and close his fingers over the spot where I'd gotten hurt making a sizzling sound with his tongue, announcing

— It doesn't hurt any more

and it really didn't hurt, I mean, it may have hurt just a tiny bit, just enough for him to take the invisible powder from his pocket and prepare the sizzling sound, which was the best part of the miracle, compress his gums and suck in his cheeks

— Tsssss

turn to me

— Tsssssss

all over the place, opening and closing his fingers easing the whole
world's pain, my uncle would constrain me, sitting me on his other knee
and applying an extra dose of consolation, reinforcing the cure, he'd say
the treatment was made from ground angel feathers which, in addition
to being difficult to acquire, were also very expensive, you can't imagine
the endless effort it takes to convince an angel to pull out a feather, and
if a person doesn't know how to handle it in the right way, if falls apart
in the air, a complete waste

— When you're big I'll let you

if I had the powder now I'd treat my mother

— You're all better

I'd take care of the deaf woman, watch her hair grow back in a flash
and not just her hair, her color too, all the death accessories thrown out,
the oxygen tank sent back to the medical center, the hospital bed, down
to the cellar, get close to the general whom the ambassador, the Spanish
military men and the ex-policemen were abandoning, asking the commander to hold his coat for him, with no pistols, machineguns, bombs,
changing house every day to elude the army

— Now what?

startled every time the doorbell or the telephone rang, all of sudden
I saw my father's eyes in his, the animal fear, the shortness of breath, the
cough, I opened my handbag looking for the invisible powders thinking
I'd help him

— It doesn't hurt

each day a bouquet prettier than the day before, and more expensive on account of the cellophane, an elderly gentleman, a friend of the
director, standing opposite me, my officemate polishing her nails, a white

teardrop oscillating, the accountant adjusted his glasses with his middle finger, instead of answering the elderly gentleman, I couldn't stop thinking about that drop, getting thicker, sticking out my arm to keep it from falling, putting a paper napkin underneath it, to prevent

— Rita

but if I said Rita she'd be startled and the drop

(my life, I'm not sure why, clearly depended on that drop)

would splash into a star on the table, get that bottle away from her, screw the brush back in, save myself, as soon as I stood up there was another bouquet of flowers, bigger than the others, a shinier, starched bow, crackling petals loomed between me and the elderly gentleman, preventing me from keeping track of the drop, the accountant's glasses, his middle finger pushing them all the way up his nose to his forehead

—Would you like to have lunch with me tomorrow young lady?

getting lost in his hair, floating off his ears, sliding back on his head and falling onto his back with the quiet insect sound of light things on the floor, many years from now

not many

I won't be able to make out the names of magazines, I'll hesitate crossing the street, the dizzying distance between the sidewalk and the pavement, my shoe feeling its way blindly in midair, many years from now, if I'm not careful, I'll end up living alone in a basement, Mickey Mouse transformed into a dirty rag, warped windows, broken kitchen bulb, gusts of wind fighting my shawl, the next week a dress, then another dress, a calling card, a line crossing out his profession, With compliments from, my mother would shut herself up in her room

—I'll be right there

trying them on before me, her face, her frozen smile in the doorway made me feel sorry for her

— What do you think?

she'd wear them to the grocery store, to the butcher's, talk too loudly in the café hoping someone would notice, but none of the men at the counter were my uncle, if only she'd known Elizabete

— Cellulite no chance Ma'am I'd give anything for a body like yours

restaurants with French menus, dishes they'd take a match to without leaving any cracklings, I'd wait for him to start so I'd know which fork to use, the manager would order the trays around by lifting his right eyebrow, hiding my pants under the tablecloth, as I handed over my checkered coat at the cloakroom, I'd notice the other coats, the fabric, cut, colors and I'd be ashamed of mine, I'd answer questions with silence, my mouth full, at one dinner when he put his palm over my hand I didn't dare move it I sensed the weight, his pinky up and down between my ring and my wrist, as soon as the hand gave up to sign the check, I put mine in my lap, the partner was mocking him behind his napkin on the other side of the table, get the revolver without the trigger, get rid of my grandmother and, if they don't hit me and the revolver doesn't fall in a rain puddle

— Don't touch that Celina

see his mouth open, the surprise, the shaking lemon trees, the black-birds taking a week to come back, they say that after the shots the silence is so profound you can hear the lemons on the ground, the general asking the commander

— Now what?

everyone wearing an orange wig just like the deaf woman, so many messages on the answering machine

—Why don't you answer the telephone Celina?

everyone wearing an orange wig, the general, the commander, the bishop and the bishop's niece *something like a goodbye today*

the deaf woman alert in the pine woods, you don't sense the bats or the branches, but the wind, yes, my grandfather putting the barrel inside his mouth, buried with neither mass nor cross in the plot where they'd pile up the unpardonable sinners the priest refused to bless, not even a date, not even a name, just a pile of dirt, tomorrow if they find us in whatever's left of the house, whatever will they do with us, my black blouse, my jewels, you don't sense the bats or the branches, or the driver, the cleaning lady will find three months' salary on top of the microwave, I'd thought of leaving her a message on the notepad

(the pad of paper and pen were also on top of the microwave and the money on top of the pad of paper, if anything needs cooking, no matter what, it gets left on the counter between the microwave and the grill, sometimes it's as if we're a couple with our codes, messages and signs that outsiders won't recognize, for Christmas she gives me embarrassing gifts, usually some awful knick-knack, gazelles, nymphs, a squatting Mexican, two girls in bathing suits holding up a plastic clock that I have to put in the display cabinet in the living room so she won't take offense, wishing they'd break sooner rather than later, but they never do, it's always the things I like that get broken, the bother of having to hide all that stuff in the kitchen when I have guests, the bother of not forgetting to put it all back as soon as the guests leave, if by any chance I don't remember, she'll do it for me, screaming her offense at the top of her lungs, turning on the lights, the living room in the dark and the display cabinet hurling glitters from the altar where the gazelles, the nymphs, the squatting Mexicans and the girls in bathing suits, enormous and tyrannical, annulling my crystal, accuse me of ignoring them, sulking ostentatiously, showing off the artistic detailing I hadn't noticed, for example, the gazelles have blue eyes, for example, on the nymphs' bosom, there's a suggestion of milk, for example, each of the girls holding the clock has a gold tooth, symmetrical, smiling, terrifying)

I thought of leaving her a note on the pad, I bit the top of the pen and started writing

Dona Alice

I crossed that out and started writing

Dona Alice I wanted to thank you

I crossed that out too thinking if my cleaning lady were to show the note to the army they'd figure out it was me who'd

Dona Alice I wanted to thank you for your work for me all these years

then I tore it up, burned it in the sink, turned on the faucet so the ashes would disappear, whirling down the drain clockwise, I cleaned the smoke stains with the coarse side of the sponge, lined up the little gifts in their place of honor in the display cabinet, in the middle, pushing the crystal to the back and turned on the light, as a substitute for the message

it wasn't age that frightened her it was death

and I kept the light on as I left so in the darkened room the gazelles, the nymphs, the squatting Mexicans and the girls in bathing suits were all that was left living in a cavernous desert with a plastic clock

each number with a different tone, it's true

stuck at six o'clock, with the unshakable and final authority of stopped clocks forcing us to abide by them, praise be if dona Alice, in comparing her watch to the clock and holding them both up against her ear as if the future and time itself were a mere question of winding, doesn't decide to smack it a few times to get it started, she might not care about dust or stains, or greasy cutlery, but the arbitrary maintenance of minor mechanisms verged on the papal, divine axioms, the strength of dogma, she'd arrive at three and if she happened to stay till after seven she'd warn me on the little note pad, I stayed forty-three minutes overtime Ma'am adding up all the minutes till she'd earn a day

Tomorrow I have a doctor's appointment and I'm not coming because you owe me a day

underlining that last phrase, a crooked pile of minutes next to the appropriate week, an entire page of miniscule eternities on top of the microwave, I'd never understood the inconsistency of time, sometimes so fast, sometimes painfully long, expression lines, cellulite, stretch marks, varicose veins, not counting years, instead counting trips to the dentist, sporadic menstruation, how to stay attractive after fifty, women's true fulfillment in maturity, in attachment twelve simple effective exercises to rejuvenate the arteries, Aphrodite, the gadget that comes apart, set on top of the bed, eleven thousand five hundred *escudos* plus shipping, eliminates undesirable fat, money-back guarantee, Venus the well-known Italian institute divulges at no cost the secret of firm breasts, it would be seven o'clock when my uncle arrived, sometimes I tell them to use the linen tablecloth, the candlesticks, champagne, two places at the table because my uncle will be here in no time at all, my mother happy, Mickey Mouse happy, the apartment, hard to explain, but somehow changed, my grandmother peeking out from the stove worried about my father, the smell of cologne that I discovered only years later was cheap, he'd set down his briefcase and newspaper on the chest and before greeting anyone, no matter whom

— Fly Celina fly

my grandfather's body wasn't in the yard, just lemon trees and blackbirds, whimpering hens dreading nightfall, sometimes I keep lighting the candles till the wicks die into the silverwork of the candlesticks, I bring out the cold dinner from the kitchen, peek under the tablecloth and don't see even one knee touching another, not one child with a bow on her head

today I'm going to the hairdresser's so I'll be pretty, not one line, not one split end, much younger than Elisabete Sandra Carla

not one girl looks at me clutching her box of silkworms close to her chest, the one aiming the revolver without a trigger at me and the silence is so profound that

Dona Alice I wanted to thank you for

no

Dona Alice I'm saying

no

the general, the commander, my husband's partner, the bishop and the bishop's niece, dona Alice I'm not writing this but I'm so afraid, the wind through the pine trees and at nine o'clock

not at seven like on the plastic clock, at nine o'clock I'm certain the deaf woman approves, accepts me, agrees with me, there aren't any Spanish military men or ex-policemen guarding the road, my uncle would leave his briefcase and newspaper on the chest before greeting anyone, no matter whom, he'd pick me up by the waist and lift me up way higher than everyone else, the furniture down below, and school, and pumpkin soup

that word fills a mouth right up, pumpkin pumpkin

I had to eat it so I wouldn't offend the poor who don't have anything

— Poor things don't have any soup such a pity and you won't eat Celina

if I ever reached out for the fruit bowl, my grandmother would grab my arm

— If you're not hungry for soup, you're not hungry for peaches

by the tilt of the bodies I was sure it was my mother's shoe and my uncle's shoe, my father put down his napkin, pushed back his chair to reach for the bottle of wine, my grandmother stopped looking funny, my father poured the wine into a glass, propped up his newspaper and went on reading, if I went out on the porch to peer out at the pine woods, I'd notice the wind, the flashlight among the trees, the fat woman walking behind the driver, she'd take three steps, stop to rest, then set off again, I'm sure the deaf woman knew about the detonator just as I'm sure my father knew about my mother and my uncle

— You bastard

I left the display cabinet light on as I left, the gazelles, the nymphs,

the squatting Mexicans and the girls in bathing suits in the living room,
I pushed down so hard on the notepad that even though I'd torn out the
page you could still see the words indented on the one beneath

Dona Alice I wanted to tha-

clearer and easier to read than if they'd been in ink, I still considered
going back to the house, tearing out that page and burning it in the sink,
scrubbing the sink with the coarse side of the sponge, that page and the
next to make sure my message was completely hidden, going back into
the dark apartment, empty except for the gazelles, the nymphs, the squatting Mexicans and the girls in bathing suits holding the plastic clock stuck
at seven, slowly putting the key in the lock, tiptoeing down the hallway
and warning Mickey Mouse

—Don't tell anyone

finding my uncle's briefcase and newspaper on the chest, the smell of
cologne, his shadow looking for my bed

— Celina

his fingers trying to find me under the sheets

— Celina

his eyes trying to make me out on the pillow

— Celina

surprised at the luxuriousness of the armoires, the bureau, the curtains
the absence of my bears and rabbits on the shelf, the giraffe, the gorilla,
going from room to room looking for me

— Celina

seeing me with my hair done, wearing my black blouse, not recognizing me, more beautiful than ever and not paying me any attention,
busy looking for an entirely dull child, missing her baby front teeth,

scratched knees, afraid of the dark, and wanting to go bike riding with her in Campo Grande park, the two of them heading off toward the lake as if I didn't exist, ignoring me, chatting with each other till they were out of sight.

24

WHEN MY FATHER had his stroke he split into two different people and neither of them was he: his shoulders shifted in two opposite directions, the fingers on his right hand were like a child's, resting on his knees, sleepily peaceful under his gigantic, old left hand, half of his face, oblivious withdrew without seeing me, while the other half would lose control in a fury, half of his mouth stretched completely open, the wrinkles on his cheek veering away from his teeth in egotistical anger, his enormous, round pupils staring at me shouting I have no idea what, unfocused concentric films, onion-like domes, not disgusted but startled, his shoes banging the floor, fearful castanets, one side would win over his lips and he'd manage a word

— Daughter

that his shoes would accompany in a sort of disjointed Morse code as I'd look around trying to figure out whom he was talking to, since that fellow, aside from the hair and wedding band, wasn't my father, the bones were falling out of his suit, his legs were like mannequin legs in store windows, when they lose their varnish and the plaster starts flaking, his days-old beard covered him with a mossy glaze, his round metal watch, similar to his but way too big for his wrist, pretending to tell the time accurately, trying to convince me

it didn't convince me

that my father was that desperate sluggish man, his gums hidden behind his lips

— Daughter

my mother, fooled by the clock's trickery, approached with his soup

— Move over Simone

around his neck she'd tie the towel normally used to cover the window, the gigantic hand would tremble, one of his shoes would dangle in the air, the second hand would jerk its way around the clock, my mother would hold the spoon to the peaceful half, the angry half would struggle against the soup which was dripping from his chin getting his collar dirty

— Daughter

as if uttering

— Daughter

were a nervous tic, rather than him talking to me, as if it were something his mouth knew by heart unaware of what it knew, my father consisted of a group of disconnected parcels at odds with each other, canceling each other out, alien to each other and the term

— Daughter

was no more than the result of accidental combustion, every once in a while, his Adam's apple would pop out after a spoonful of soup, then contract unexpectedly, his round pupil would soften for a few seconds then expand, my mother glowing in joyous victory

— He swallowed

she'd hurry, persist with the broth believing she was obtaining my father's consent bit by bit

(the thing is, it wasn't my father but strange parts that someone had gathered randomly, it couldn't have been my father since my father never said

— Daughter

he said

— Huh

he said

— Hey you

he said

— Simone

whenever he wanted to borrow money or whenever I caught him rummaging through my drawers and even then the

— Simone

didn't mean

— Simone

it meant

— What are you doing here leave get out of my sight

as he dropped the coins in his pocket unconcerned about me, or once, my earrings, another time my confirmation medallion, right before Christmas, the necklace my aunt had given me, I scoured every pawn-broker's hoping to find it in the window, little tourmalines I adored, with a silver-plated clasp)

so my mother hurried, persisted with the broth believing she was obtaining the consent of the parts of which my father was supposedly made up, but the Adam's apple was stuck, the carrot going down between his collar and his neck, the absent-minded pupil elated, the rounded pupil angrily popping out as if on a spring, the spoon came up against a curtain of teeth, parrot feathers shaking, jostling out

— Daughter

and going back to bed in instinctive pride since

— Daughter

didn't mean anything, had never meant anything, he walked by me
with my confirmation medallion, which I could sell today or tomorrow
to help buy the café in Espinho, adjusting his hat and bossing me

— Shut up

when I hadn't so much as complained, my mother acted as if she
didn't notice, a friend of hers had come over to crochet together, her nose
buried in the needles, the door slammed shut shaking the windows then
opened back up since the latch didn't work, small buses rumbled through
the room till my mother did away with them, banging the hinges and
turning the key and now, not even

— Huh

or

— Hey you

or

— Shut up

just the little child's hand resting in the crib of his knees, just halves of
a stranger fighting to gain control of his tongue, the losing half recoiled,
the winning half unable to dominate his lips, escaping his cheeks in a
murmuring wrinkle, groaning folds that crystalized into

— Daughter

unexpected, I wanted to answer not my father but the parts held
together by precarious wires

— I'm not your daughter

becoming aware of the garage, the smell of gasoline, the mattress on
the cement, the coarse smoky sheets, aware of the oil reflecting a square
of heavy dark sky, not at all like the outside sky, aware of my boyfriend
transporting bags and suitcases to the van, had I introduced him to my
father, his peaceful eye wouldn't have paid any attention, lost in distracted pondering, but his ferocious eye would have expanded toward
me, swallowing me up with the approval of the shoes vibrating on the
floorboards, my mother closed the living room door and talked to us in
the kitchen, the three of us cramped between the ironing board and the
stove, four or five tangerines and parsley growing in a cookie tin on the
kitchen shelf, tiny drops of oil, cold meat and grease, a butterfly rubbing
its antennae in the sink, my mother peeking out into the hall, afraid all
the dislocated parts would join together and get us in trouble

— Huh

the doorknob turning, uneven steps, the shoes banging the floorboards one after the other, the asymmetrical scarecrow limping toward
us, threatening to collapse in his empty suit

— Hey you

grim silence interrupted by a plunging cough, the butterfly moved
its little legs, pushing up invisible sleeves, when you touch their wings
a fine silky dust stains your fingers, in May dozens and dozens of them
would crawl out from the black sewer rocks, I found my father more than
once kneeling by the gutter, smoking and counting the coins he'd stolen
from me, the parsley in the cookie tin needed watering, the tangerines on
the shelf were shriveling up, the nozzle of the kitchen sink faucet was a
cracked rubber tube, my mother to my boyfriend, whispering, in a panic
that the living room might hear

(a cubicle with a veranda facing the Alcântara train station, they
covered the sewer, constructed buildings and the trains disappeared, I
remember the boats on the river and that they'd let me smear red on my
cheeks during carnival, watching the drunks masquerading as women,
blowing kisses at each other at the tavern, enormous bosoms, exaggerated

thighs, scarves around their heads, the police shoving away the laughter, fervor, embraces

— Move along move along

the only luxury was the tea cart, but it was missing a wheel, we'd inserted a piece of folded cardboard so it wouldn't wobble)

my mother walked on tiptoes to the door, leaned in to see if she could figure out the syllables tossed out at random, how many groans did it take to produce

— Daughter

she'd return to the kitchen, looking back, at high tide the Tagus would grumble complaints up through the drain, my mother as quietly as she could, arranging the tangerines

— What do you want with my Simone?

(at carnival the drunks masquerading as women would wave at me out on the street

— Bye-bye fatty

not that it was true, maybe just strong, but not fat, just envious since they didn't have a tea cart like ours, so perfect it was a shame we kept so many knick-knacks on it, simple folk, dock workers, factory workers, far less important than my father kneeling on the rocks, who was a courier at City Hall before he retired, not fat, strong, the doctor explained with arrows

— The glands

before the new buildings, the veranda facing the Alcântara train station, boats, boats, my father's brother died of a fever in Macau)

my boyfriend, not understanding the mysteries of the living room, the shoes, the lungs, my mother, I hadn't remembered to clean up the

kitchen, polish the stove, put the dishes back in the cupboard, I prayed
no cockroach would trot across the baseboard, never dreaming my future
would be old tires, carburetors, batteries, serving at table and getting the
trays mixed up when the ambassador had dinner there, I, who'd never
been anyone's servant, seeing the deaf woman sitting on the terrace,
getting up and smiling as she smelled the nards like a saint in ecstasy,
the communists waiting for the van between the garage and the wall,
fewer and fewer Americans, fewer ex-policemen, my boyfriend working
with the alarm clocks and wires for fewer and fewer hours, almost never
any automobiles arriving at night, or headlights shining on the oak tree
through the little window, I'd wake up in the middle of a dream thinking I'd run away, not to my mother, of course, but to someplace where
no one knew who I was and where my father wouldn't steal my money,
rummaging through my drawers

— Huh

get a job in a boarding house, a store, a factory, a bar in Madrid, I'd
remember the café in Espinho and calm down, the general

— Now what?

my boyfriend trying to understand the muffled sounds, the shoes on
the floor, the intervals of silence when

the shoes on the floor, the intervals of silence when

— Did he die?

my mother leaning out and by way of an answer

— Daughter

the evil eye threatening me, pulling his belt from his trouser loops,
the crippled leg of the tea cart, if at least my boyfriend had seen one of
the other three, with the wheels, the child's hand lit by sunshine, the old
hand trembling next to it, the bishop finding me in the pantry fetching
the dessert plates

— Come here cutie

the general having disappeared behind his arm in a pigeon-like movement, my boyfriend's boss ordering us to be quiet as he turned out two
thirds of the light bulbs, using a handkerchief as he unscrewed them,
the furniture and dishes fading, the gleaming of the glassware, vanished,
while the smirks on everyone's face got bigger, the blinds were lowered
but not even then did the smirks lessen, blemishes sticking to blemishes,
the commander with his machine gun on the porch, checking out the
road to Lisbon, the pine trees, the road, beetles deserting the flashlight
and spreading out all over the garden, the oak tree and the garage a
blended mass shivering in the wind

— The army won't get here for sure before tomorrow morning we
have all night break camp

the orange hair fluttering like the nards, the widow's cigarette moving
from her mouth to the ashtray, her little ceremonial blouse, bracelets, the
perfume ever heavier now that she had no facial expression, just cleavage,
her shoulders hunched in wait and some sort of silent agreement between
her and the deaf woman, the owls fled the oak tree, heading toward the
hill, on the slope, a tractor's low beams paused briefly on the tureens,
turned away in boredom before discovering the profile of the general
who was gripped by panic

— The army

at the same time the widow and the deaf woman, charmed at the
thought of the troops, became very cheerful, although the widow's joy
evaporated in cigarette smoke and the deaf woman hid inside her fake
hair, they saw me, my boyfriend called me from the patio

— Simone

not with his lips, but moving his chin, calling me back home in
Alcântara holding my suitcase on the doormat

— Simone

to reach the river you passed by abandoned houses behind stacks of bottles and hay, sheds filled with broken glass, tents like church mangers with dozens of Christs, Saviors, born in straw to spread beauty and wisdom in drug-infested neighborhoods

this is My Body this is My Blood

pills, needles, little bags of powder, blessed be the Lamb, my mother worried in the living room where the ferocious half was battling its mouth trying to control it like a live trout

— Where do you think you're going Simone?

she opened the door looking for help, my father on the sofa, a towel around his neck, turning his asymmetric shoulders to us, crooked as if someone had broken them and fixed them in a hurry, the pupil recoiling from stuck eyelids, the larger one devouring his face, my mother shaking the suit, which at the very most was filled with reed skeleton

— Just look what your daughter is doing to us Hélder

his cheek puffing in and out at us before finally releasing a

— Huh

that withered, sighing with exhaustion, for a second the two halves joined and I found my father again, till I realized it wasn't my father, it was a clay doll breaking into dead pieces like the deaf woman, the commander, my boyfriend's boss, the widow and the bishop in the pantry

— Come here Simone

the general

— Now what?

the deaf woman fooling around with the soda water and coffee, smiling at the daisies, my father in Alcântara struggling to say

— Daughter

among baby Jesus mangers, I only went back to that part of the city once and when we went by the building I saw light through the curtains, something tiny and short

my mother?

moving around without making a noise, I found myself thinking about what might have happened to the tea cart, I saw the tangerines and the parsley that needed watering and I'm pretty sure I don't remember the cookie tin ever having cookies inside, something tiny and short feeding soup to something useless and protesting

— Huh

I never sent them money, never wrote them, never called the neighbor next to their basement who'd give them messages, there she is climbing the stairs clutching her rosary, first the right foot then the complicated maneuvers of her left foot, encased in an orthopedic boot, joining the right foot with bang, the ceiling was decorated with stucco roses surrounded by a pyramid of leaves, the doorbell pull above the sign please keep the door closed was practically falling off, the only time I went back to that part of the city was the night when we went to pick up arms from the Spanish Civil Guard at a storeroom near the mangers where the Christs were born, Miserere Nobis, adored by the three wise men, eyes closed in prayer, as they searched for the vein they climbed the hill slipping on boulders, went around the remaining mulberry trees frightening the cats, my boyfriend approached a pick-up truck, flashing signal lights and while they were piling up crates my mother's window went out, the curtains gave way to a grey square among other grey squares, I was sure they'd said

— Hey you

and it wasn't one of the Spaniards or my boyfriend or the newborn Jesuses trying out parables on non-believers

the kingdom of God is like a mustard seed man has sown in his field

it was someone inside the pick-up

— Hey you

I'd wake up at two or three in the morning, turn on the light and there he'd be, wearing his hat rummaging through my drawers, pulling out socks, slips, pullovers, my secret notebook announced on the cover This Diary Belongs to Simone Ramalho, my gland medicine pill bottles

— It's her glands

and the basement neighbor eyeing me, afraid and respectful, I bet she was climbing the stairs clutching her rosary, first the right foot then the complicated maneuvers of her left foot, encased in her orthopedic boot, joining the right foot with bang, my father rummaging through my drawers looking for money, without thinking about my glands at all

— Hey you

I grabbed the machinegun near the Spaniard's van where the guy in the hat was arranging the last crates with tiny child's hands, if it had been daytime I'd have seen the towel around his neck, half of his face drawn, the enormous pupil, the hopeless feebleness with no gums

— Daughter

pink stucco roses, pyramids of leaves, the veranda shutters we could never get to close, I smacked the guy in the hat or the drunk masquerading as a woman who was insulting me at the tavern, a crooked scarecrow collapsed on the slope in his empty suit while his plunging cough, while his mouth

— Huh

while the bishop, while the commander, while the general

— Huh

in the room where they were dismantling the fair before the army got there, if I don't go to Espinho, if they don't give me the café, if we don't make it out of this house on time, hide the car on the bramble trail, set off the detonator in the pine woods, the guy in the hat sitting in the willows staring at me, the Spanish Civil Guards holding my arms, taking me away from my father, pushing me, my boyfriend grabbing the machine gun from me

— Are you crazy?

faces appearing and disappearing inside the storeroom, the widow's cigarette between the table and her lips, the Lamb's mangers lit up, the deaf woman blessing me with a smile, the bishop's goddaughter staring at them both and then at me as if she suddenly understood

— Hey you guys

my mother tied the towel around my neck, brought the carrot soup and the spoon closer to me, I tried to explain to my boyfriend that I wasn't sick, wasn't an invalid and he could talk to me like everyone else, I never stole money from anyone, never went down to the sewer to smoke and count my money, but my mouth wouldn't cooperate, the sounds were paralyzed, I couldn't feel my gums, I didn't feel myself, thank God a complete sentence slowly formed, echoing syllables, the whole eye flew into orbit trying to save the sentence, make it clear, better, helping to keep it from drowning in leftover words, shards of memories, stiff gestures, maybe mine, floating around randomly, very old faces, familiar and strange

no, familiar

no, strange

no, familiar

I don't know if they were familiar or strange because something was changing without completely changing, some parts strange and some parts familiar, although the familiar part was strange and I couldn't really make it out and they were watching me, boleros, paper lanterns, the starlets at the dances getting out of the taxi, yes, the starlets since the child-like hand started shaking when he saw them, it could have stayed still, but I felt it trembling, I swear it lifted itself happily and trembled, the Spanish Civil Guards locked me in the van and kept on piling up the crates, talking about me, the headlights reached the Savior of the World Lambs, Father Introibo ad altare Dei, I'm not sick I didn't have a stroke, and the answer was Et Deo quid etc., here's the proof that I'm normal, I just don't feel like carrying on, the Lambs, Ecce Homo, okay, that's it, Ecce Homo Ecce Homo, they kept being born in the mangers, the sentence got bigger letter by letter in the living part of my head, the other part would brighten every once in a while, bringing my mother along with him and getting confused, not just my mother, stucco roses and pyramids of decorative leaves, tangerines on a shelf, a boot struggling upstairs, Gisélia, I think it was Gisélia holding her skirt in the wind on the wall by the river, the guy in the hat got up from the slope feeling his neck to check for blood, walked toward me dressed like a woman, sorry, dressed like a man, pants, sweater, his wrists hidden in the sleeves, pads sliding off the shoulders, he tripped on the machine gun, kicked it with the tip of his shoe toward a ball of broom shrub that my dead half couldn't see

(brambles, bushes, the tea cart, a crest of dirt)

I was seeing my mother, Gisélia, the bishop's ring in the pantry, my boyfriend and the guy in the hat staring at me in the pick-up, the Spanish Civil Guards piling on the last crate and pointing at me, I remember words sort of running together, tumbling one after the other, although they seemed to be in the right order they didn't make any sense, I under-stood each one individually but not when grouped together, since they were leaping over each other, getting mixed up, cancelling each other out when my sentence was all set and ready to go, obvious, glorified, clear, putting the entire world in order, I brought it out slowly, my tongue to the roof of my mouth without anything out of place, steady diphthongs, correct vowels, perfectly coherent, the best, the most beautiful, the fullest sentence I've managed to this day, no doubts, secrets, mysteries everything so profound and at once so simple, the parts of my body that weren't mine belonged to me again, I don't need anyone to feed me, get me up, lay me down, change my clothes on Tuesdays, watch me sleep, afraid I'll die, you can all rest assured, I'm not going to die, they wipe a sponge over my face in the morning, my symmetrical shoulders, my matching eyes, my hands the same age, I, exactly the same as the me in the pick-up truck in Alcântara, I turned to the window, having made up my mind to explain the reason, the motive, the real explanation, I leaned my nose, my forehead, it was my forehead, on the crate so they'd hear me better, my forehead saying

— Listen everyone

recommending them

— Listen everyone

confidently warning them

— You're finally going to find out

no drooling to embarrass me, no muscles to betray me, no tooth to forbid me, the Spanish Civil Guards and my boyfriend waiting reverently, I had the impression that someone

(the guy in the hat still feeling his neck?)

was commenting

— She's crazy

but it wasn't the guy in the hat, it was the wind fooling around with the houses, the wind's obsession with messing up walls, so I cleared my throat, stuck out my neck, pushed my tongue against my gums, I felt as if a part of a part were slowing down and wilting, nothing important, just a part of a part, the whole, complete sentence, flawless explaining the world, moving beyond my lips and the wilted part, when they rolled down the window

— Huh

exactly what I'd intended to tell them, what I'd intended to clarify

— Huh

only God knows how hard if it was for me to get all that out, to be
so generous with them, so useful

— Huh

and then I could reward myself by stretching out on the seat, taking
off my bones, putting one of my unequal hands on top of the other while
everything quieted down inside me, and my wife and my daughter left
the room and all that was left was the tea cart.

25

ON THE BUREAU in my room, next to the photograph of my grandmother, there was a photograph of me as a child, about five or six years old

(they must have written the date on the back)

dressed up like an angel for the procession in Coimbra: my feet were in earthly sandals, bought two sizes too big

(my mother stuffed the gap at the toes with cotton

— Hush Mimi

— My toes hurt I don't want to

— No they don't be quiet)

but my shoulders reached out into canvas goose-feathered wings that my feet prevented from flying meanwhile my face, although frozen in time by the camera, was always messed up with my embarrassed tears. From the time I got sick, I noticed my eyes didn't blink anymore in the picture: they weren't child's eyes or any other kind of eyes, they belonged to someone in bed, timeless, ageless, asking in a voice not my own

— Why?

not angry, not spiteful, surprised

— Why?

and with this my eyes would go back to blinking, my face took up its complaint

— My toes hurt I don't want to

the wings wobbled, dead feathers fell off, they'd painted my eyebrows and made ringlets in my hair like they do in heaven, they'd cut a halo out of tin, pinned it to my tunic, my grandmother, who was having her braid done, watched me from the top of the stairs from her invalid's throne, my cousins, their hands also held in prayer, were lined up waiting for me in the yard, ready to rise up in incense-infused levitation in spite of the cotton stuffed into their sandals and the lambs the servants had strangled hanging from ropes over by the kitchen, my mother and aunts emerged from the restaurant dressed in black, with candles in paper cups, the waxy flames hollowed their bones, their lips disappeared and their noses grew longer, turning them into ghosts, vague mourning made up of flickering prayers quieted the hens and strengthened the trees, my family were replaced by a procession of ghosts smelling like clothes just out of storage, my father took off his cap out of respect for the moving platform and to me he looked naked without it, my grandmother crossed herself, spreading her smells, the bells brought vast quantities of mystery into the room, the innards were slithering down the rock, brains stuck on hooks, dangling jaws, a long drop drooling from the chin

— Now what?

the general, the bishop, the commander, Fátima, Celina and my husband all stuck on the kitchen hooks, I, with my two-sizes-too-big sandals and fake wings, the army about to enter the living room any minute, and the innards were still trickling, if they take off my orange wig and the blanket from my knees I'll be naked too like when I was getting my infusion at the hospital and the doctor would check my fish bubble breathing

— Tired dona Mimi?

wanting to surround my stretcher with the screen, finish me off, kill me, the countryman's daughter's empty wheelchair stopped on the ramp and he, apologizing to everyone, talking to the wheelchair, holding his beret in his hands, the doorman pointed to his broken-down car there blocking access for the ambulances and fire trucks

— You gotta leave my friend

the cylinders working agitatedly in smoky commotion, the blanket waiting for me in the back seat of the car, I remember the smile, the wave as she left, her fear whe-

— I'm not going to die right?

when the elderly woman's rosary dropped, brains stuck on hooks, dangling jaws, a long drop drooling from the chin, my grandmother crossed herself wafting perfumes, the broken-down car teetering on the ramp, the part attached by ropes dragging a few meters behind finally fell off, they took me into the doctor's office, the doctor opening windows, people lying down, equipment, machines, screens where lines following indecisive routes would appear, creatures in pajamas with bandages and tubes sitting at backgammon boards that no one was using, X-ray cameras, emaciated men, a sick woman with yellow arms that would stick to things

— I don't have cancer I don't have cancer

fire extinguishers on windowsills

in case of

a woman whose swabs were falling apart, heading towards the stairs, a hospital worker catching her by the ankle

— Dona Laura

and she, unable to move, but still trying in stubborn lethargy, through the closed windows, hazel trees, buildings, innards slithering down a rock, a long drop drooling from a chin, I noticed my eyes had stopped blinking, not my eyes, not even one pair of eyes, in the doctor's office something sort of timeless, ageless

— Let's take a few weeks' rest from the treatment dona Mimi

pictures in frames but not my grandmother and not one angel wearing sandals two sizes too big, my husband tormenting his key ring, the
doctor using his cheeks as if they were fingers molding syllables out of
plaster and it wasn't

— Let's take a few weeks rest from the treatment dona Mimi

what he was really saying, was

using his magnifying glass for his tongue to make his syllables
enormous

each vowel, red, each consonant, lilac, forcing me to listen with my
eyes, not both eyes, with a single eye that didn't blink any more, was

— It's not worth keeping up the treatment dona Mimi

but it didn't matter because his son was smiling at him approvingly,
I could tell my husband was talking by the way his shoulders moved
upwards and also that the doctor was whispering something behind his
hand, his cheeks molded more syllables, had I been able to understand
him, I'd also have understood the trees in the intervals between his sentences, not the hospital hazel trees, but the laurels in Coimbra, I'd understand what's going on now in the pine woods and what those lights are
on the trees after the driver's van crosses the patio, my cousins would
wake up at night, whispering in my ear

— Did you hear that?

and I didn't hear anything, not even the clock, only the intimate
sounds from inside my bodily cave, the commander turned the veranda
doorknob and shot out at the nards, we climbed the stairs very slowly,
opened the curtains and my parents and aunts and uncles were seated
along the wall, each of them with their handkerchief, my grandmother's
thrown off in a corner, the casket on the table, one of the kitchen servants kneeled down and started singing, the lights in the pine woods
were circling, searching for something, neighbors also seated along the
wall, whispering, murmuring, sighing conversations, fanning themselves,
the commander came back into the room and left his rifle leaning on

the arm of the sofa, every time a van shook the house the bishop would pray, when the light went on again in the pine woods Celina's expression changed, I don't know why but it seemed as if she were telling me above the others' heads

— Leave

the voice of a second servant over the voice of the first

these masses of swarming flies

my cousins would wake up in the middle of the night whispering in my ear

— I saw Mama Alicia in the hallway don't move

the floorboards would creak and it was my father with his cigar back from the café, he'd try to hang his overcoat on the coat hanger and the coat hanger would elude his grasp, he'd move his overcoat away and the coat hanger would follow, my mother went to the entryway and the coat hanger panicked and stopped fooling around, my father taking advantage of the truce calculated the distances

— You can't even show us any respect on the day of her funeral

I'd get out of bed and peek and there wouldn't be anyone walking up and down the hallway, no one on the throne moistening her braid in brandy and giving household orders, as soon as the servants quieted down, the chained dogs, their muzzles pointed up at a patch of a moon would start barking, my parents, aunts and uncles went down to the restaurant with the neighbors for the funeral supper, I took the angel out of the trunk, replaced Mama Alicia's shoes with my own sandals, tucked the halo between the pillow and the nape of her neck, tied the wings onto the shoulder pads of her wedding dress, opened the bedroom door, pleaded with her, tangled up in laurel leaves

— Get out of here quickly before they get back

hoping to vanish in the direction of Galicia, fly above the rooftops shedding geese feathers, one of my uncles came out into the yard with a pot of leftovers to calm the dogs down

— Quiet

the dogs crouched next to the bowls and started howling again, if we had a dog in the garden how many nights would he have howled at death on account of me, at first they were immobile, sniffing out the mysteries and then, arching anxiously as if before rain, we call them and they don't come, they avoid us, recoil, the chickens and goats do the same thing, a flurry of turtledoves, they must realize our bodies are inside out, notice the seams, the patches, the threads, the places where the sawdust or old rope stuffing is rotting

— Let's have a few weeks rest from the treatment dona Mimi

the dog that was playing with the lady in the photograph in the doctor's office staring at me halted, having suddenly lost interest in her, settling in on its hind legs in a corner of the frame, elongating himself into a howl, the doctor to me although I hadn't said anything

— Pardon?

my grandmother quiet in the urn, although I'd pulled up her sleeve so she noticed the wings, I bet no one in Galicia would take her to the cemetery and shut her inside the earth along with the moles, they'd give her a throne bigger than ours and she'd boss everyone around and watch the roses sprout from the ocean, Mama Alicia had obeyed my parents for the first time ever, resigned, submissive, with the orange flowers from her wedding, not real petals but little wax buds dissolving on her forehead, I managed to lift her body from the casket, show her the lid engraved with Christ, the box of screws and the hammer on the table, the halo slid off the nape of her neck, her wedding dress tore and underneath the dress there was something cold, not my grandmother, something cold, they'd put someone there in her place just like they'll put someone in my place, Mama Alicia escaped from my hands, fell onto the pillow in crooked inertia and started laughing, the bishop was furious, the oak tree pulled away from the garage roof, the bright flashlight in the pine woods, the commander

— You ratted you turned us in?

aiming the rifle at him, the bishop's goddaughter

— My God

the general without paying any attention to the commander clapping his hands and laughing trying to stop him by buttoning his jacket

— We're by ourselves right we're by ourselves?

astonished and happy at once, happy no, he made it seem as if he were happy, watching his face, though, you could tell, he was definitely not happy, flattened out in the chair, afraid of the communists, of the army, afraid they'd put a carnival mask on him with glasses and a moustache, force him to dance, hang him in the basement and pour gasoline all over him, the light in the pine woods turned on and off, when the wind changed direction it brought the smell of the wild cane plantation and of the river slime, maybe the frogs, I can't hear, maybe water, sometimes I wish I were normal so I could listen to the water in the summer, how the stones move in circles, the talking bubbles emerging, my reflection is never clear, always muddy, when I thought I was seeing myself as I really was, not like the lying photographs, a sigh of slime or the laughter of the general who was falling off the chair onto the carpet, buttoning and unbuttoning himself in an awkward rush

— We're by ourselves right we're by ourselves?

staring at the bishop, the bishop's goddaughter, the commander, my husband, looking for the Spanish Civil Guards, the American ambassador, the ex-policemen and not finding them, elbowing Celina away, who was trying to help him

— Don't you dare touch me

taking her for a communist, a soldier, someone who'd come to arrest him, humiliate him, belittle him, lock him up in some prison, the shifting wind brought the canes and those big leaves that dissolve in the river, sometimes fig leaves, sometimes poplars, take him off to some bull ring, ravine, cellar, basement and then electric wires, lit cigarettes, broken bottles scratching his skin

— Don't any of you dare touch me

looking at us like the prisoners held between the garage and the wall looked at me, I remember a woman the secretary led to the storeroom and then brought from the flowerbeds shaking seeds from her clothing, now missing an earring and hairband, rubbing her handkerchief on her lips and looking at the blood on it like I remember the first time my husband and I, barely two seconds alone in the hotel bedroom and I started crying not because I had any regrets or fears or was missing my family but because of something I didn't know how to say, there was a print over the bed that I've never forgotten, a windmill, cows, ducks, a boy in a wagon, a waterwheel, I was terrified of that print, held my purse tight to my chest without feeling like anything, without wanting anything, without thinking anything, believing that as long as I held my purse against my chest I wouldn't feel dirty, I can't explain it any better but I still felt like I was dirty, my body changed when I was thirteen and I didn't tell anyone, I hid the stains that came out of me in the part of the yard where they'd bury animals, little stains, hairs, a smell that almost didn't smell but it smelled like

like ever since I got sick

a body, misery, I hid my death in the dirt in the yard till I ended up facing it in that print over the bed, a windmill, cows, ducks, a boy in a wagon, a waterwheel, a tiny bar of soap wrapped in paper in the bathroom, a tiny tube of shampoo, a toothbrush cup wrapped in cellophane, a narrow closet with two or three hangers and an extra pillow, my death was a hotel room with pentagonal walls and faded flowers, when you turned on the light switch only one of the two pink lamps made itself known, lit from inside like oranges in May, I buried myself crouching down there in the yard, my mother in the kitchen

— Mimi what's going on?

stomp the dirt quickly, stand up straight, flee, lock myself in the bath-room with the tiny tube of shampoo and little bar of soap, turn on the shower and get clean again, just me and my skin with no traces of any-one, when I was small and I couldn't get to sleep Mama Alicia would lay me down on a pillow way too big for me and would fall asleep with her face close to mine and one day out on the street, buildings and fountains

no

not buildings and not fountains, a windmill, cows, ducks, a boy in a wagon, a waterwheel, my husband or the secretary shaking seeds from clothing and I, pressing a handkerchief to my lips, the earring hook that tore my earlobe didn't hurt, it tore but didn't hurt, he was the one who took me away from the others into the pine woods and shot at me, I mean ordered me to open my mouth and I didn't, I never opened my mouth in the storeroom except when my blouse opened and he tried to kiss me, in the pine woods when my blou-

— I told you to open your mouth didn't I?

my other ear tore, get the tiny shampoo and little bar of soap, turn on the shower and get clean again, if I were normal I'd hear the water running down my arms, just me and my skin with no signs of anyone else, something, I don't know what's hurting my back, I don't know his name and he separated my legs, it didn't hurt because I couldn't relax and they laid me down on a pillow much too big for me, a face near my face, I mean the pine branches talking to me, two or three jays on the thistle branches, my mother calling me from the kitchen, the blonde woman in the picture frame, the doctor sculpting syllables

— I told you to open your mouth didn't I I told you to open your mouth

everything so far below, belonging to no one, too far away for me to be concerned, to be upset, I'm not scared that it's not worth continuing my treatment, the machineguns don't scare me, the shots, opening my mouth, if you want me to open my mouth I will, I feel bad about the earrings, by now I don't feel bad about the earrings, they gave them to me the year I graduated from high school, I got home, a little blue box under my napkin, gold circles with a ruby in the middle, little screws in back, eight days after my wedding

there was no yard where I could bury my shame while everyone else was asleep

I saw the print in the living room, the windmill, cows, ducks, the boy in the wagon, the waterwheel except far bigger and in a more expensive frame, I wonder where the pillow is that Mama Alicia would lay me down on next to my brother's crib in the attic, from the day my father broke his hip he'd concentrate on how his bones felt and predict rain, my husband pointing at the picture

— Since you were so amazed with it I bought one just like it for you

when Celina or the bishop's daughter looked at it I was sure they saw the shameful stain that came out of me, they'd complain to my mother who was calling from the kitchen

— Mimi what's going on?

looking for her glasses, if she'd seen me hooked up to the tubes in the hospital bed or with the doctor making those huge syllables, so many red vowels, so many lilac consonants

— It's not worth continuing it's not worth perseve-

she'd have grabbed a rabbit right there in front of the nurses, doctors, the orderlies that transported the dead bodies down to the cellar and would have started to undress it, so disappointed in me

— I never expected much from you

staring at me in irritated resignation, signaling to a helper to season the sauce

— On account of her manner it seemed likely gentlemen

tasting the sauce, putting it back in the pan, angry because there wasn't enough salt or cumin

— How many times did I tell you, scold you warn you to change your
behavior when there was still time you didn't pay any attention couldn't
even do that what did I tell you

my cousins warmed up dinners made of ants, pebbles, and I'd be in
trouble, off in a corner, my nose pressed against the wall among all the
noise of aluminum platters and quartered animals till my mother tired
of me, hanging around along with the lamb skulls stuck on hooks, and
I, my skull equally filled with gray innards slithering down the rock

— Are you still here?

not her daughter, a nuisance the servants had forgotten to pour into
the bucket and take from the kitchen just like they'd have done with my
grandmother if I hadn't

my cousins

— *Did you hear me?*

*and there was nothing not even the clock on the stairs, just the sounds from
the cave of my body like wind blowing in a sort of silence that's nearly music
and like fear saying our name over and over, we go upstairs, open the curtain,
my parents and my aunts and uncles sitting along the wall without talking
each of them holding a handkerchief, the casket on the table, one of the serva-*

taken from the kitchen if I hadn't

*one of the servants kneeled down and started singing, murmured conversa-
tions, sighs, fanning, the voice of a second servant over the voice of the first one*

those masses of swarming flies

*no one on the throne moistening their braid in brandy and giving the
household orders, the dogs my uncle tried to calm down with pots of leftovers,
crouching in the dark with drawn-out howls, my parents in the restaurant
for the funeral supper, the top of the urn with the sculpted Christ, the box of*

screws, the welding nozzle, hammer, hide her in the earth like I hid my stain

dump it into a bucket, carry it off to the kitchen and throw it in the trash like they'd have done with my grandmother if I hadn't opened the bedroom window, taken the angel from the chest, replaced her shoes with my sandals, tucked the halo behind her neck, tied the wings to her wedding dress shoulder pads, and helped her up to

my grandmother looked around, told me to check the hallway, the office, close the door and not make any noise

— Don't make any noise

she'd approach me, smiling mysteriously for once not tired and not wrinkled

— I'm going to teach you how to make Coca-Cola, it's a secret, get some soda water and coffee and don't tell anyone

helped her up to the windowsill where we'd see laurels, the night and fields, we'd fly above the dogs and lamb skulls, the picture of the windmills, cows, ducks, the boy in the wagon, the waterwheel, the stains and hairs, the smell that almost didn't smell, but it smelled

the same as ever since I got sick

my body, my misery, the two of us would fly away, clean, to

— I'm going to teach you how to make coca cola, it's a secret Mimi

we'd fly away, clean, to Galicia so far away from my husband, where beneath the rain, roses sprout from the ocean.

26

SOMETIMES JUST AS I was falling asleep, I'd feel an electric shock through my legs and I'd wake up thinking I had to stop existing in order for there to be a tomorrow since, if I didn't stop existing then today would never end, not the today of daytime, when I was me, but the today of night-time, when I don't know who I was, the church lying across the house, squashing the canary, footsteps and voices, I'd ask

— What am I?

and the answer would be a sort of frightened loneliness, I'd ask my mother

— What am I?

my mother would check to see if I had a fever, putting her mouth to my forehead, then tell me to go out and play

— Go play

Naturally if I brushed my teeth and I didn't have a fever there was no reason to worry about me, how many times did I swear I had a fever just to feel her mouth on my skin, I'd check the lipstick mark

— She kissed me

I'd touch it lightly so as not to ruin it and everything seemed simple, easy, no loneliness at all, I'm her daughter, my cousin wanted to wipe it off with her handkerchief

— Come here Fátima, you've got something on you

I'd run to the kitchen or to my room since as long as my mother was on me I felt free from all that stuff they'd tell me under the weight of the church, warnings from someone or another, the plane trees would warn me, stores would warn me, clothes hanging outside on the verandas would warn me, I didn't dare argue

— What?

because I was afraid they'd explain what I dreaded and wasn't

how should I put it

death although it seemed like death

(it's hard to write this because when you turn it into words it doesn't make sense any more)

a kind of anxiety, dread, uncertainty over myself, when I told my mother about the electric shocks in my legs she answered looking very sure of herself

— It's because you're growing

that's why, on my birthday, when I was a year older going from one day to the next on the calendar in March, on the twentieth I was five and right after that on the twenty-first

(another mystery, one date on the calendar you're one age then all of sudden, bingo, you're a year older)

I was six, I'd run

no I didn't run, I'd go and stand next to the pencil lines on the door jamb, trying to figure out how much bigger I'd gotten now that I was grown, I thought it was a trick, that God was lying

I think I probably found out before a lot of other people about God lying

the person that killed the general wasn't the commander it was

my clothes fit me exactly the same way as the night before, neither too tight nor too short nor faded, they tied my hair with the same ribbon, still gave me orders and advice that you give kids, I'd gone up just the tiniest bit you couldn't even see since the last pencil line, my godfather offended me bringing a box of candies he left on the sofa forgetting to give it to me, I kept hoping someone would sit on it, but they kept pushing it out of the way, they'd get uncomfortable, searching around, twiddling their rings, sadly they gave it to me undamaged

— Your godfather's present Fátima did you happen to thank him?

the canary waddled across its perch, a big tease

(— I'll tell you in a minute)

my godfather's smile would flutter in his cassock, and I was ridiculous in my little girl dress, humiliated by God's trickery

if the army interrogates me, I'll stick to my story, the commander didn't kill the general and it wasn't Mimi either, who I called dona Mimi, also, it wasn't dona Celina, but in her case dona was my way of insulting her because she always gave me such superior looks, each of her eyes an attacking rabid dog, barking as if she thought she were superior to everyone else, sitting there behind her cigarette, prettier and more elegant than any of us, younger, richer, and then there was that black blouse that made all the men bark just like she did with her eyes, throwing themselves at her, their teeth bared, up against the bars of her eyebrows, and she, indifferent to it all as if nothing else existed besides her cigarette and boredom with everything, I don't remember her ever taking any interest in anything or anyone besides herself, her hairstyle, her perfume, her jewelry, all the men's eyes on her, they'd approach her and chicken out, barking even louder as they recoiled, Celina would be staring at the ashes from her cigarette, taking in the compliments as if they were her due or not even taking them in, not believing them till the dogs would finally quiet down, defeated, coming back to us, curling up lazily at our feet in resignation, the person who killed the commander wasn't Mimi, or Celina it was

my mother would bring glasses of good wine and a cake with six candles which was really just one candle

stuck to a saucer we used when the power went out

cut into six pieces, which at first wouldn't light, as soon as the match
made contact, the wax and whipped cream would blend into a mess, one
of the candles leaped from the paper plate to the tablecloth and from
there to the floor, my mother stuck it back in so firmly it disappeared
flickering into the cake, giving off pretty bad-smelling smoke rings, spitting sugar and ashes out from candied cherries, exactly what I should
have done with the canary that kept mocking me

— You're never going to become a woman Fátima

what I should have done to all of them if I hadn't been so stupid and
starting blowing out the candles, which wouldn't give up, it seemed as
if they were about to go out, then they'd change their mind with a burst
of energy, if my cousin hadn't killed them with two fingers slathered in
whipped cream, all the while looking as if she were about to throw up,
and if my mother hadn't taken the knife to the cake which by then no
one except her dared taste, my cousin and I were putting our slices on
the windowsill in view of the pigeons, pretty sure the pigeons would be
interested in the almond filling then it'd be goodbye whipped cream, my
father thinking no one was watching hid his piece, discreetly feeding the
ants, shoving it under the console with his ankle, my godfather kept his
as far away from himself as possible without losing sight of it, apparently
afraid the piece of cake would jump out at him, swallowing him up like
a frog, and my heroic mother, on the verge of disappointed tears over
the feigned appetites, seemed so desolate that I had to repossess a few
crumbs from the pigeons, chewing them out of pity, just like I'd chew
the pieces of toast the deaf women used to pass around with that little
smile of hers, which didn't seem like a smile at all, more like

I'd have sworn

she wanted to pardon us all for some sort of sin or another, more like
shyly begging forgiveness, her facial expressions disappearing at a signal
from her timid antennae, except when she'd turned to

so skinny my God, nothing but her translucent nose, and the little bone in her chin beginning to tremble

look at the pine woods as if their trunks, the blackbirds, the breeze were bringing her a promise of recovery, as soon as she turned back to us Celina would pick up her cigarette and then it was her eyes that were like dog eyes except not barking, begging the way dogs do, almost human, humble

— Don't say anything

I, studying the two of them forgetting about the toast, the tea

— Don't say anything about what?

then, the same smile, same cigarette, my godfather and the deaf woman's husband in unison, the general drowning in his own laughter, his teeth covered in slobber

— We're alone aren't we isn't it true we're alone?

after my father dies, no, after this is all over and done with whether or not my father's still alive I swear I'm going to take my mother on an outing to Montijo, hopefully she won't sit in the mud and I or the commander with his shotgun, the tip of his shoe, knee

— *Get up you coward be a man*

every time a van headed off to Lisbon, its headlights shining on the ceiling and the highest pictures, the general's laugh would die down, his legs would shrink as he tried to get up, his fingers grasping at the commander's, my godfather's, the deaf woman's husband's ankles

— It's them isn't it I bet it's them

the picture over the fireplace was of a windmill, cows, ducks, a boy on a wagon, a waterwheel, and even though everything in the picture was just like it is in real life, the colors, the design, the details of the little flowers, I was sure the deaf woman tried not to look at it, if I happened to be near I'd be able to tell she'd get antsy in her chair, as if looking at that picture would make her discover something secret about herself, as if a picture had ever spoken, when the lights moved onto the animals, the waterwheel and the wagon didn't exist anymore, the orange wig would go back to sparkling in the faded light among the porcelain cups and the tea pot, Celina's eyes would hide behind her cigarette, almost human, humble

— Don't say anything

and I, studying the two of them

— Don't say anything about what?

thinking about what could happen in the pine woods beyond the treetops, the pine needles, the wind, I never came across gypsy tents or anyone stealing wood or blackberries or anything else, I never saw acrylic sap mugs drinking from the trees but even so Celina kept insisting

— Don't say anything

as if there really were something more than the treetops and the needles and the wind, something only the two of them knew about or which Celina knew and the deaf woman had discovered later with her look of death and her smile like out of an old photograph

(where the damask background and violet stains make everyone look sweeter)

she normally had on her face when she was lying on the terrace looking out over the world, a blanket over her legs, almost unreal near the wisteria, waving just like it, noticing Celina

— Don't say anything

the person who killed the commander wasn't Mimi, or Celina, it wasn't my godfather, it was

the deaf woman agreeing without moving her lips or her expression, the living room and the hall in bitter faded light, the perfume of the nards, which the gardener had stopped taking care of, flowing with the anguishing dew through the open veranda and maybe that's the reason the deaf woman smelled like nards, Celina

dona Celina

(calling her dona Celina was my way of insulting her because of her superior way of looking at me, hidden behind her cigarette, prettier and more elegant than any of us, younger, richer, and then there was that back blouse making all the men's faces bark, throwing themselves at her, surrounding her, getting closer and closer growling off in corner of the carpet)

Celina to the

the person that killed the general was

Celina to the miserable deaf woman embalmed in the nard dew smell of her own death, wearing the smile they say dead people wear in the casket and it's not a smile dear God, it's a terrified grimace, for example, the photograph of my grandfather on the cross at the cemetery above the little vase of flowers screamed out fear

Mimi dona Mimi

Celina not an order, request, a worried plea

— Don't say anything

and the deaf woman without moving her lips

— I won't say anything don't worry

looking through the pine trees, almost invisible blending into the night, all traces were gone except for the wind rustling the treetops and the general asking in a whiny flat voice

— We're alone aren't we isn't it true we're alone?

abandoned by the American ambassador, the Spanish Civil Guards, the South African secret policemen who'd given us weapons, the papal nuncio who'd receive the communists and accompany them to the stairs, the general on the floor laughing hysterically

— We're alone aren't we isn't it true we're alone?

maybe knowing what Mimi and Celina both knew, possibly, the army surrounding

the house waiting for us, murmured warnings, the canons, the bazookas, I've got to take my mother to Montijo, the commander to the general, forcing him to get up when he heard steps in the entry hall, which weren't ev-

— Are you gonna confess you turned us in?

weren't even steps it was the Virginia-creeper scraping what was left of the nards because the deaf woman's house was also dying, she didn't notice the maids were wearing her earrings, the crystals on the sideboard were increasingly sparse, plates were missing from the cupboard, belts or slacks were dangling out of drawers, I tried to tell her

— Dona Mimi

as if she could hear me, as if, even if she could hear me, she did when all she heard was her grandmother's image or the person she called her grandmother or maybe she was, it's always hard to understand family relations among the poor, the divvying up of their miserable lot is stronger than blood, some kind of countrywoman on a throne, the owner

taught her granddaughter
the owner of a restaurant in Coimbra
I take to mean
of a tavern in the countryside with living space upstairs
(it was so easy for me to imagine the kitchen, the yard, the chicken coop, the kinships, the bickering, stingy suspicions, small vanities, small hatred, Sunday best stored in a camphor chest, a sick uncle coughing into the platters)

all she heard was the image of
let's agree
her grandmother, placed on the marble top of the bureau next to the
image of an angel, a little girl, her hands held in prayer, wearing sandals
that were too big for her, wire wings attached to her shoulders, poor dona
Mimi with no wings at all to save her from the army, from the communists wearing cardboard glasses and paper noses coming at us from a
burning cellar, dona Mimi surrounded by her locked suitcases

— But of course

that's how I'd always imagined the communists, not creatures like us,
talking like us, not men, not people, not demons or sent from the devil
like my godfather would claim, simply masked clowns, cardboard glasses,
paper noses, fake beards, torn capes waltzing around in a cellar, obeying
the secretary who'd encourage them with his pistol

— Oh joy oh joy

the general, terrified of those sad clowns whose only hope was we'd
shoot them between the garage and the wall, transport them to Cabo
Ruivo bridge and throw them into the Tagus, I don't remember their
features or gestures, I remember the masks, the straw mustaches, the
domino masks, the deaf woman watching us leave and going out on the
veranda, still able to walk, making her way down the stairs, disappearing
into the kitchen to tell the maids what to do, her husband talking to
Celina behind us or using us to make Celina listen to him as her angry
eyes barked, rabid dog growling, I didn't choose a woman, I chose a
housekeeper, passion is nothing, love is nothing, I bet the deaf woman
could understood his words, I could tell by the way she'd be there and be
absent at the same time, fluffing her hair, rubbing her hands together, as
if cleaning herself away, afraid we'd notice her and discover something I
don't know why or how, if I could only tear away the parts of my body
my godfather would touch

I think that was it
the only thing I could think of was to ask my husband

— Take me away

because we're alone aren't we isn't it true we're alone, we sit in Torel gardens in the morning, playing cards, watching the pigeons, from our window we look out at other windows where people like us are also looking out, the judge's daughter trotting off on her errands with her velvet purse she'd fill with cardboard pretending to be rich, my father holding out my Sunday coat

— Tell me don't I smell like an old man

the canary wobbling from perch to perch, unable to sing, also smelling old, one of these days there'll be a little pile of disheveled feathers at the bottom of the cage, not yellow, grey, my mother couldn't bring herself to touch it

— No

my cousin wrapped it up inside a cloth and threw it in the garbage, my father came in and saw the empty cage

— The bird?

on Sundays they'd go to the cemetery to refresh the water in the vases, from the trails of tombstones you could see the river off in the distance, the districts Amora, Seixal and Alcochete, the little cup of lemon tea in the tiny bakery, the tables tattooed with cup rings and I

— You don't smell at all daddy

as the general tried to grab the deaf woman's ankle in the hope that her ankle could save him from dying

on Sundays at the cemetery, refreshing the water in the vases, we didn't see anything beyond the trails through fields and the river way off in the distance except for angels praying like the image on top of the bureau with stone wings that looked as if they were made of canvas and goose feathers

grabbing the deaf woman's ankle, my godfather's, the commander's, mine

— We're alone aren't we isn't it true we're alone?

the smell of the nards, the wind through the pines, the picture of the windmill, cows, ducks, the boy in the wagon, the waterwheel, that Mimi

dona Mimi

refused to look at when the van headlights shone on it for a second on the shadowy wall, the person who killed the general, who fired the shot wasn't the commander, wasn't the deaf woman, wasn't Celina

dona Celina

it wasn't my godfather, it wasn't the deaf woman's husband, it wasn't the army that didn't get there or find us in the living room in a flurry of handcuffs, uniforms, and yelling

— Quiet

or

(wait just a minute and I'll tell you)

the communists waiting on the hillside, four or nine or thirteen people on the crest of the ravine and a tractor below, cliff grasses, a piece of a fence, when I say communists I mean the man wearing a tie, the red-headed teenage boy, one or two women whose ages I couldn't guess, maybe my mother cutting my birthday cake, my cousin wrapping the canary in a piece of cloth, my father kept putting birdseed in the empty cage for months afterwards, he'd fret staring at the perches in bewildered disappointment

— I don't hear any singing

the general finally got up

(Celina to the deaf woman

wait, that's not how you write it,

dona Celina to dona Mimi after she'd been staring at the pine woods, rather, at the tree tops, the darkness, the wind

— Don't say anything

dona Mimi in her orange wig, her baggy clothing now pinned to fit her shrunken frame

— I won't say anything don't worry

ignoring my questioning like a child interrupting an adult conversation, tugging at their sleeves

— Don't say anything about what?)

the general finally got up, not the general, my godfather looking at me with that slimy expression enveloped in tenderness

— Fatinha

he crossed the dark room, opened the veranda door onto the rose bushes and beds of nards, there was no big shadow from Mercês Church, no plaza, only the chairs the neighbors would bring outside on summer evenings, sometimes a light goes off in me and I remember every single one of their names, and their professions

senhora Irene, sergeant Gomes, doctor Mateus who wasn't a medical doctor but had a government job

the general became serious once more, authoritarian, rigid, slapping his crop against his thigh, calling the commander, my godfather, the deaf woman's husband

— Pack up your cases gentlemen we're heading to Vigo within the hour

and Celina, once again

dona Celina

pleading

— Don't say anything

prettier and more elegant than any of us, richer, each of her angry eyes a rabid dog growling, now there was a flashlight among the tree trunks and that was what she didn't want the deaf woman to tell, the army and the communists waiting for us out on the road beyond the house, at the garage gate, the oak tree, the vegetable garden, the pine trees, soldiers, a ghost clown wearing cardboard glasses and a paper nose, obedient, sub-missive, just waiting for us to douse them in gasoline before we hanged them, not one car, no one, just the flashlight between the branches look-ing for something in the pine needles, Celina insisting

— Don't say anything

the deaf woman's smile, grimacing like an angel in wire goose-feather wings

— I won't say anything don't worry

so that was it after all, the army, the communists our death that those women, I mean Celina and Mimi

dona Celina dona Mimi

shared in secret, our death precisely today, on my birthday, Mercês Church placing its enormous hand over the rooftops, no threats, no anger, more like warnings than anything else, the mulberry trees were warning me, the store windows were warning me, the laundry out on the verandas was warning me, the canary wouldn't stop teasing me, gig-gle trills

— You're never going to become a woman Fatinha

my mother taking the knife to the cake

fine wine glasses, the six candles that were really one candle which we'd stick on a saucer when the electricity went out

cut into six pieces with the fish scissors, one of them jumped from the plate to the tablecloth and from there to the floor, the general came back inside from the veranda and before he repeated my name, touched me, asked me to smell his coat, I grabbed my mother's knife, no, the machinegun, no, the knife, I picked up my mother's knife as the deaf woman had agreed

— I won't say anything don't worry

and now I'll tell you about the pigeons that fly from the cornices on the plaza and spread out soaring above the river.

27

AFTER MY UNCLE left the house that day my father would still take me fishing on Sundays: he'd open the car door, his eyes angry, without saying a word, wait till I got settled into the back seat along with the fishing poles, hooks, and bait, then he'd put a straw hat on my head with a pat, as if bunging a cork into a bottle, he'd tell me to put the elastic under my chin and to be quiet when I'd already put the elastic under my chin and was already quiet, furious at him, hoping that none of my school friends would see me with that awful elastic, he never said I was pretty, never smiled at me, never took my hand, never talked with me, if I leaned forward trying to see myself in the rearview mirror, in the hope that I wouldn't look as ridiculous as I thought, instead of seeing my face I'd see his wrinkled eyebrows

— Sit back right this minute Celina

I'd think without daring to say out loud

— I hate you

I'd never been so cheeky with him in my entire life, I was thinking as I wished he'd die

— How come you weren't the one to go away and leave us in peace?

our neighborhood would disappear behind us before my grandmother or my mother could help me, keep my father from leaving me alone and scared by the river in Oeiras, then instead of the eyebrows in the rear-view mirror his mouth was there making me put my hands down and sit back in my seat

— Damn it all can't you sit still for one second?

so with nothing better to do I focused on the cans of bait, there was a swordfish on the labels, I tried to unscrew the top without making it squeak so my father wouldn't notice, but his eyebrows appeared in the rearview mirror again, quivering angrily, his hand came back towards me but he couldn't reach

— You're not going to be still till you get a slap is that it?

the car veered to the right, over the sidewalk, a wall with a bullfight poster grew large in front of us, a woman coming out of a pharmacy jumped out of our way, the car straightened out with a choleric jolt, the woman calmed herself down by placing her fingers on her chest, the mouth and eyebrows appeared in the rearview mirror parted in shock, coming together again little by little in a suffocated threat

— As soon as we get to the fishing wall you'll see

I kept hating him for another minute or so, wrinkling my new sweater on purpose, tearing off a button so I could blame him later, helping my mother rail against him

— It was Father's fault

my mother shoving the sweater in his face

— Nice right nice?

she'd bring out her sewing box and, as she mended, she'd lift her nose sniffing murderously

— Nice right nice?

till I'd forget and turn around in my seat, my back to him, making faces at other drivers, vans, motorized bicycles, invalids' tricycles filled with crutches and exhaust pipes every last one of them waving back, nicer than my father, I'd show them the fishing poles, hooks, the basket for the sea bass with seaweed at the bottom, I'd stretch out my mouth with my fingers, lift my eyebrows, pull my ears out just like an elephant or some other terrible beast, hold up my middle finger like I'd seen a man do one time in an argument on the tram, I did that to a jeep that honked back outraged, my father at the wheel

— What does that fool want Celina?

first I'd wave, then I'd stick my middle finger up, then the waves back at me would change into threats, index fingers wagging back and forth, I lay down on the upholstery, feeling a sort of resistance against my body, then the snapping of a fishing pole, I rested my head on my elbow, drifting away into a marshy sense of well-being, even better with the soft seat and the proximity of the river when my father

— Wake up

then I noticed the waves, not really waves but piles of debris bumping up against the Tagus wall, I scorned the ungrateful can of bait I found so offensive, a reel handle hit one of my legs maliciously, with the typical feigned indifference of things, for a second, I thought my uncle was there having decided to save me from the cruel world, I stood on tiptoes for him to pick me up

— Uncle

my father in his baseball cap, which along with his rubber pants and boots made him look like a child who'd grown up for no particular reason and was covered in wrinkles, buildings with windowless verandas, dunes and dry bushes next to dirt, three or four palm trees gesticulating hysterically, storks' nests inside cement deposits, so paralyzed and artificial they must have been fake and, on the opposite side, fishermen on tarpaulin stools imitating the storks, drifting animals, lengths of algae exciting the birds, smelling exactly like the cans of bait, although less dense and more rotten, my father was assembling his fishing pole, checking the reel, the float, sticking a piece of swordfish that wasn't real swordfish onto the hook, the belt on my dress was squeezing my kidneys, the socks they made me wear bent my toenails, the elastic from the hat hurt my throat,

if we'd at least brought along a comic book, my metal stove, one of the
rabbits from my bedroom shelf, my father gritting his teeth, saying from
the side of his mouth, so as not to disturb the grey mullets

— Not one peep out of you

unlike my uncle who liked me to talk, answered my questions, sang
along with me, once he let me have a little puff of his cigarette but instead
of smoke hot mist filled my mouth and I got the entire filter wet with
my tongue, my mother grabbed the cigarette away, angry at my uncle

— That was it never again

although her anger would disappear in the same instant replaced by a
little sway, a wave of her fan, a little pat on his cheek, just like a young girl
my age as soon as my uncle handed her the cigarette, all dark and broken

— You're so crazy

the fan fluttering around the house in little giggling hops, when it
opened, ladies in low cut dresses danced with men wearing wigs, when
she closed it you could see it was torn, her skirt came above her knees,
her heels trotted down the hallway in happy little squeals

— You can't catch me

my grandmother put the key in the door holding a bag of groceries
and she stopped right there on the doormat, even if we didn't see anything, we still saw my uncle and my mother chasing each other right in
front of her, then my mother locked herself in the bathroom, my uncle
trying the doorknob

— Hey, that's not fair

from my grandmother's expression you could practically hear my
mother's laughter, the faucet running, her hair combs, perfume bottles clinking against the enamel, my mother's sing-song voice, my uncle
noticing the grocery bag, and backing away from the doorknob looking
oblivious and mumbling some sort of warning, reinforcing it with a

cough, my mother fiddling with the bottles even more

— Did you choke?

my uncle's voice, a muffled curse, his cough insistent and explaining

— It's the old lady

more perfume bottle noises, more running water, romantic boleros, her high heels pecking at the tiles, the bathroom door lock gave way, and my mother emerged overflowing in fragrance, a paper carnation stuck behind her ear, and bumped into my grandmother who made the sign of the cross without dropping the groceries, the passionate verses died right down, the paper carnation wilted in her fingers, my uncle, who'd picked up a newspaper and was reading upside down, silently repeated his curse words, although the carnation was wilted it managed to fill the entire apartment revealing some kind of sin to my grandmother far too complicated for me to understand but which seemingly affected my uncle in a confusing way, and my mother and father, by then my uncle had stopped coughing and was winding the wall clock with excessive care, he'd certainly never done that before, checking the time on his wristwatch then adjusting the hands, my mother released a nauseating whiff of perfume, her hair covering one of her eyes, my absent father represented by his glasses case, full of life there on top of the radio as if the glasses case

actually looking a bit like a victim

were my father there suffering, my grandmother was watching the radio fearfully as if the case were about to get up indignantly

— What's going on?

she grabbed the paper carnation and threw it out the window

— Scoundrels

the house without the carnation seemed like a second-hand store, the ladies in their low cut dresses and the gentlemen wearing wigs stopped dancing, the furniture and curtains aged in boredom by a few centuries,

the wall clock issued contradictory chimes, hesitated a bit over some difficult calculations, then become confused, and just to make sure, it chimed
again, got stutteringly stuck searching for clarification in its memory,
my uncle advanced the hands and the grateful mechanism, resumed its
peaceful digestive rhythm, my grandmother put the groceries away in
the cupboard, shaking off my uncle who was trying to help, my mother,
overtaken with sudden domesticity, was furiously attacking stains on the
tablecloth that no one else could see, as well as on the windows, the arm
of the chair, I peeked out the window but couldn't see the carnation in
the yard down below, my grandmother flared her nostrils to meet the
aroma in an attempt to determine just how big the offense was based on
the amount of perfume

    — To make matters worse right in front of the child the scoundrels

my father, one fishing pole to his right and another to his left sat on
the stool, his legs up on the wall, the seagulls going crazy over the can of
bait, the river had barely calmed down when the palm trees caught my
father's attention with breezy diphthongs

    — The scoundrels

a trawler looking like a coal stove rolled out towards Estoril
admonishing

    — The scoundrels

the buildings fired off tiny bird eggs that grew wings instead of falling,
the body of a run-over cat, like a package of fur, examined me from the
edge of the road and I couldn't help it by taking it home to be with my
gorillas, my mother

(just a second before you go back to your mother: some of the roof
tiles at Carcavelos beach were decorated with clay nymphs, some of them
missing heads, others with broken fingers, that's all for now, sorry, go on)

I was saying that my mother was washing her hands in the kitchen
trying to help with lunch she hated helping, my uncle winked at me
hiding the telephone receiver behind his hand, sighing

— Of course I only love you my little turtledove I don't understand
your worry

my mother raised the vegetable knife suddenly, my grandmother who
in the meantime had calmed down, screamed from next to the pot of
spaghetti

— Isn't it enough you've disgraced one woman you rat hand over that
telephone so I can tell her who she's talking to

my uncle hung up with one last sigh

— Sorry my little turtledove but I can't right now

he spread his sleeves out to the Sacred Heart of Jesus recruiting
accomplices

— Can't a man take a work call from a department colleague anymore people?

he tried to kiss my grandmother, who was swiping him away with a
spoon, he was smiling at my mother and the vegetable knife relented,
he was imitating Mickey Mouse at nighttime, he was almost exactly like
him, which made me think he must have been spying on us, he'd pick
me up by my waist, lift me up to the ceiling

— Fly Celina fly

he'd head out to the café without his jacket, clicking his heels like in
the movies, my mother, worried

— Mind it's cold out there

clinging to the door in a glow of tears, when she noticed me her entire
face disappeared into her handkerchief, for the first time and noticed a
little aluminum pot on the stove shelf which as far as I knew we'd had
forever, I wanted to caress her bowed head and her neck

— No

a chunky little pot, I shook it and the metallic knick-knacks went into a frenzy, a rusty key, a nail, an old coin covered in verdigris, my grandmother put it back on the shelf while the key and the nail argued clankingly

— You just can't rest till you've broken something can you?

her eyes grew moist, looking at me from behind the spaghetti as if she wanted to hug me but instead of hugging me she cut into the margarine violently, angry at my mother, all kerchief and shoulder blades, blowing her nose in an enormous anguished rumble

— You've always been so foolish

my father reeled in the hook and baited it again, a bus ran over the dead cat who stopped studying me, now pleading with the storks for help, the debris from the river was getting stuck on the walls waiting for a tentacle of foam to drag it back out, the echo of the palm trees opposite the river

— You've always been so silly

the little aluminum pot begging from the shelf

— Grab me

they might take the old coin at the store in exchange for a tortoiseshell hair clip, or pewter charm, I went to get my giraffe, my most reliable stuffed animal should there be any unpleasantness, and handed it to my mother so she'd stop crying, I only had to cover the hole on his back so no sawdust would leak out

— Here, take him

the giraffe dangling in the air, disoriented in the kitchen, my grandmother seasoning the spaghetti pretending not to pay any attention, the apartment wasn't ours, it was hers, she'd inherited it from her husband who was in the police, one time I found a pair of handcuffs behind jars of marmalade and strawberry jam that must have been used on some thief, who knows, maybe my grandmother also arrested robbers and safecrackers, there was a policeman in her wallet next to my baby photo, a fellow seemingly without a single drop of ferocity running through his veins, drowning in disappointed hesitation, my grandmother clarified the situation explaining that his job was to copy out parking tickets in a ledger and I lost interest in the policeman, shocked at having a grandfather that didn't scale walls like Spiderman or share a cave with tamed wolves, but then I started imagining the parking tickets might have been a ruse and got excited again, it was still possible that he had a cave and wolves in a more discreet neighborhood, I checked out the chances of a Spiderman with my grandmother who buried them with two shoveled words

— Poor fellow

sometime later the photograph vanished from the wallet and I no longer shared the space with that sad chucklehead, lacking both nightstick and uniform, registering tickets in old ink, after the seventh or eighth bus the cat's body was reduced to a little rag of blood getting smaller by the minute, the giraffe flew off in a little cloud of sawdust, bending its ears toward my mother

— Here take him

something was sniffing in a melancholy way, then inhaling noisily, her nose emerged from the handkerchief, caught off guard by the giraffe she recoiled suddenly, she realized I was handing it to her, hiding the leaking sawdust with my shoe, she drew both of us, the giraffe and me, into her tears and I wished it had just been the animal because my mother's nose scared me, the fishing rod bent into an arch on account of something weighing on the hook, my father's cap sprung up from the stool enthusiastically

— Daughter

he'd never called me

— Daughter

I wanted so badly for him to say it again

— Daughter

and leave the reel handle alone, had he lifted me up, I would have liked him better than my uncle, he didn't even have to

— Fly Celina fly

all he would have had to do was pick me up or hug me or something, I didn't need any Mickey Mouse, money for my baby teeth, bicycle rides or the circus or anything like that, if he'd just tousle my hair saying

— Daughter

that would have been enough for me in order to tell him I'd hate for him to die or leave us, I was just mad at you, I didn't mean it, stay with us even though you don't talk much, or dance, or do imitations, you can read the newspaper all the time, don't come to tell me goodnight, frightening away the night with little cartoon squeals, first the float came up, then the sinker, after the sinker the dripping sludge, not one grey mullet, not one sea bass not one

not even

one of those tiny disgusting eels you can't even eat, that you take off the line and throw in the gutter because the fish don't like them either, I tried to help my father get the mud off the hook and my father, spiteful

— Get out

little birds' eggs that turned into sparrows in the bushes, buildings, a gust of wind made slanted pleats on a sand dune, the palm trees

— Get out

stick my thumb in my mouth quickly, bite it and my fingernails down to the bone, I had to keep it from drowning me, whatever it was in my stomach, disappointment, anger, the desire to do I don't know what rising up inside me, just like my mother was drowning in her handkerchief, the giraffe flattened without his stuffing, maybe my grandmother would sit at the sewing machine, make him fat again, sew up his tummy, the giraffe

— Help me

and I, like the cat, unable to do anything, watching a stuffed animal die is worse than a real one, the giraffe turned into another handkerchief my mother was blowing into, the real handkerchief inside one of her sleeves and the giraffe in the other, from next to the boiling spaghetti I managed to complain

— You don't wipe your nose on a giraffe

I shut myself inside my bedroom, talking to my hippopotamus, getting away from that quivering grief, my grandmother keeping herself busy with random drawers of shuddering cutlery

— You're always so silly

my father settling back on to his stool, his eyes staring beyond the lighthouse, eyes so much like the giraffe's that for a second, I thought he was leaking away through his bellybutton just like the giraffe, I'd plug it with my little finger, stop him turning into a shabby little hide

— Don't spill any sawdust father

his neck drooping, his legs drooping, his torso getting narrower and narrower, hollower, I take his hand, try to convince him to not drain away into a cat corpse and to stay with me

— Don't spill any sawdust father

promising we still had time together, to go to the circus, Campo Grande park, talk with each other, my uncle wasn't the only one, he could too, promising him he could, but how could I talk to him, promise him, show him, when we weren't used to it, he didn't care about me

— Daughter

by chance, excited at the grey mullet, I couldn't do anything else except grab his shirt, the fabric gave way and underneath, his elbow, arm, I'd take that old coin with the queen's profile and buy him a little present, a plastic bag of mints, a triple-bladed pocket knife, a little plastic ring, my mother noticed the giraffe in irritated surprise

— What's this?

as I started to answer her my father said

— What's this?

refusing to be helped, the giraffe fell silently to the kitchen floor, my mother and father looked at me as if I'd broken a vase or bent a spoon, my mother, my father and the bishop's niece who finally understood, nevertheless they didn't scare me because they weren't going to hit me, they couldn't because the flashlight in the pine woods went on and off three times just like I'd ordered, the daisies were bending in the darkness, the oak tree by the garage was saying

— Goodbye

tomorrow dona Alice will find an empty house, the display cabinet lit up, the bed made, not one speck of dust to be found, the clothes in the washer, the sun through the curtains, such a nice day one feels like singing.

28

I'M SURE THERE'LL never be a café in Espinho because to this day, in my whole life no one has ever done what they promised me: once we're past the entry gate he stops the van any old place, the side of the road, a bridge, a restaurant, some small town with not a single light on, he leans over my knees without bothering to explain, opening the door on my side, then straightens up again, his hands back on the steering wheel, the stupid little doll hanging from the rearview mirror bobbing back and forth, the headlights shining on bushes, grasses, maybe some old fountain or estate wall, sandbags and road workers' tools waiting for tomorrow morning, and he, without looking at me

— Get out

he waits for a second, his hands still on the wheel, turns out the small light in the van roof so his face can't be seen, with his finger he traces a red line that runs all the way to the edge of the map, finds the continuation on the next section making that awful noise maps make when they're folded and unfolded at night, like forest fires or wooden bullfight bleachers, the calls, the tension, the yelling

— What are you waiting for get out

the side of the road, the double arched bridge, a plantation wall still decorated with the broken remains of a painted tile scene, men in tunics, hogs, dogs, servants on horseback, the finger following the red line to where I won't be going with him, I'll stay here in this village trotting from doorstep to doorstep knocking on every single locked door, one of those tiny provincial cemeteries where at day's end they shoo the hens away and padlock the tombstones, an oil lamp flickering in a corral, the pocket flashlight following his finger shows railroad tracks, hostels, the names of rivers, he leans over my knees again and my bag of clothes tumbles down in front of me, Our Lady and my sewing box probably all messed up

— What are you waiting for get out

or else some truck stop, a shed out in front, jaws and shoulders at the counter, shoes snuffing out matches among peels and husks, the waitress brings bowls of soup out from the kitchen, dizzy from exhaustion and collard steam, cows cramped in cargo beds lowing not with their mouths but with their sunken eyes, the wind blowing back and forth among the beech trees, everything else calm, the hills, the clouds, and the wind blustering among the beech trees, my bag of clothes set down at the entrance next to the peanut dispenser and the cigarette vending machine, my Our Lady definitely unharmed, heads turning to stare at me wearily, slowly, looking like cow snouts, my boyfriend straightening up at the steering wheel

— You've never seen me you don't know me

the van tires spinning in the gravel, a broken blinker light patched with plastic and black masking tape, the van stopped at what looked like a flowerbed, actually a triangle of roots torn apart by cats, and I, running

like hell I was, me and my eighty-three kilos running

I, walking towards him with my bag of clothes

— I made a mistake he's sorry let's go the two of us to Espinho

thinking about curtains, I want blue and white curtains in my café, a counter made to look old, printed menus, a stuffed wild boar, thinking about Saturdays and Sundays, we could hire performers, they'd use our bedroom to change in and when they left their smell would linger on the furniture

Miss Celeste Miss Lucy

silver hairclips, little tulle roses decorating shoulder straps, the wind among the beech trees died away, the broken-tile scene vanished, there aren't any locked doors, there's no restaurant, setting my bag down on the car seat, peaceful calm world, years ahead of us

— What a fright

you've no idea how panicked I was, what I was thinking, the nonsense that crossed my mind, my boyfriend way up there pushing my bag out and then the sound of breaking pottery, Our Lady, poor thing, definitely beyond repair, the van hurtled from the village to the road jerking like a turkey

— You say anything to anyone about me you'll regret it

the wind started up again among the beech trees, the cows' boulder eyes deeply sad, the way those eye-lashed rocks followed me, as if I were on the verge of sticking a nail into their backs and hanging them up in chains, they don't get angry, they don't beg or sob, it seems to me everything's lifeless tonight, except fear, the figures in the old decorative tiles, men in tunics, hogs, servants on horseback, blue in a landscape of blue orange trees, surprised by me entering the restaurant, untying my bag talking to myself

— I knew it I knew it

looking for pieces of my saint among the towels and pillowcases, every single piece accusing

— You did it

the waitress cleaning her arms on a dishcloth, envying me my luggage, a paralyzed guy in mute ecstasy, the truck drivers, their spoons lifted, suspended, one two three five ten oblivious cows with thick copper rings holding bread, the continuous clanking from the cigarette vending machine, delivery boys playing cards, still wearing their motor-bicycle helmets, something appears in the vending machine tray and I don't want to see it, everything is hounding me, threatening me, circling me, it's not the pine needles hurting my legs, it's a sort of bramble, my boyfriend's flashlight is looking for a marking on a tree trunk, tracing ovals in the pine needles, you can see the terrace and the roof of the house beyond the oak tree, you don't notice the nards or the people in the living room

— I can't find the detonator Simone

since the deaf woman's husband unscrewed the light bulbs, scraps of windows, vaguely pale, figures I think must be them, the bishop and the general, the women who hate me, the commander on the porch firing at the roses, the waitress finds the cracked plastic soap container or my hairbrush, hides them in her apron or slips away to the counter combing her hair, the paralyzed man's gums are getting bigger under his cap, just leave the bag behind, run, hide inside the shaking boulders, the worn flanks, the fear in those eyes and still the jaws and shoulders are all lined up at the counter, the cook submerged in steam and, along with the cook, my father and his two unequal halves, the right side choosing his letters working them out slowly like in a puzzle

— Daughter

as my mother tied a towel around his neck, if I told them

— I can't find the detonator

if I said

— Help me

the brambles and the pine needles would stop hurting my legs, the flashlight would stop tracing ovals in the pine needles, if I paid careful attention I'd hear the oak tree branches scraping against the garage, the obsessions that things have the same as people have but they don't have feelings and whims like people do, who knows maybe furniture is like us and, if furniture is, why not tangerines, parsley, who can really tell me that that's not how things are, my boyfriend looking for the marking on the tree

— I can't find the detonator Simone

the tea cart missing a wheel, the little child's hand on top of the giant hand, the dreamy half and the cruel half fighting for control of his mouth, my father recognizing me without knowing me in mechanical exhaustion

— Daughter

if I'd arrived home and asked them

— Help me

or asked them here at the restaurant, since they're taking my soap container, my hairbrush, the only necklace I own, the mirror with the silver handle, I mean the handle and the silver circle that's missing the mirror, my satin dress with the lace trimming, the one that makes me look thinner and which I never got the chance to wear, if I'd asked them, hanging around the peanut dispenser and cigarette vending machine

— Help me

would the little child's hand have prevented the commander from shooting me and would my mother have readjusted the sofa I used for a bed and taken me back again without being embarrassed on account of the neighbors, the scandalized whispers as we went past, if she took me back, I'd never complain about sleeping on the sofa any more, I'd try to save electricity, maybe get a job at the variety store or the bakery, and I'd give her all my wages instead of blindly stumbling around the pine woods listening to the wind

— Simone

through the snails and shells in the dirt

— I can't remember if it was that rock over there is one of our signs

everything looks so different at night, the trail that used to lead to Lisbon now goes north toward Sintra, you could sense the ferns and the smell of the ocean, my boyfriend studying the rock, blowing off the dirt and tossing it away

— It doesn't have the marble vein I was wrong

if one of the truck drivers would take pity and give me a ride back to Lisbon in the cargo bed surrounded by low moaning cows even if they dug a nail into my back and crucified me in chains I'd say

— Mother

and my mother wouldn't allow it, she'd stop that hammer just like she'd swipe her umbrella through the air at the boys who'd tease me out in the street

— Good-for-nothings

and she'd help us find the detonator, shuffling through pebbles, the end of a wire, the wooden box buried in the pine needles

— Is this it?

my mother and father looking at me from the painted tile scene, dressed like the men wearing tunics among the hogs, dogs, servants on horseback, frozen for centuries on the plantation wall near the arched bridge, I wonder what the deaf woman would do now, her knees covered with her blanket, not even hearing us, but still making out our words as we left today

— I'm leaving Ma'am

she didn't reprimand us, didn't give me away to the others, only answered

— Of course

consenting, her orange wig bobbing, her rings shivering, she'd have me serve at table along with her maids, raise her brow when I got the platters mixed up, speak to me as if I were just some tramp

— Leave that one take it away not like that hurry

just like the general, the bishop and the widow, noticing me only to boss me around or tease me, the number of times I thought, if I only weren't afraid, telephone the army, ask one of the communists even with the cardboard glasses and paper nose

— Help me

one afternoon a woman

a man

no, a woman, really, a girl, I remember her freckles, her tiny bones like a starling's, I remember something wrong with her tooth, it was chipped, I didn't tie her wrists, I left the rope loose, I'm certain of it

I think

no, excuse me, I'm really sure I told her

(an owl, I noticed an owl in the treetops or maybe not a real owl but an owl my terrified imagination came up with from some knotty twigs in the branches, pinecones, gathered shadows, something we'd think up as children afraid of

forget about that, I've already talked about myself so much, whenever I get the chance I go on for hours and hours, when we get to Espinho)

going back to what I was saying, I'm sure I said

— Help me

and the communist was quiet, hadn't noticed the loose rope, hadn't understood my words, the chipped tooth with the filling

really, a filling, a brown one

serving no purpose, stupid, hiding in her lips, get rid of it, goad it, tear it out

— Help me

the commander was talking to my boyfriend's boss, the secretary was having one of his fits, putting his cigar out on one of the prisoners at the other end of the line, I never thought I'd see him cry

— Oh joy oh joy

all the communist had to do

(I remember the freckles)

was to run from the gate toward the hillside and up about hundred meters at most to reach the Belgian neighbor's house, the engineer with the Dobermans, his wife, her chest exposed, and the round swimming pool, beyond the engineer's the coast was clear, just the town, people shopping, the school, his bare-bosomed wife shiny with cold creams, the engineer in his swimming trunks, completely oblivious, taking care of his camellias and scolding the dogs, black skinny beasts with blond eyebrows, they never barked, they panted, squashed up against the railings, I came across them one day tearing a rabbit apart

I was going to write packet how strange a slip of the hand, a slip

without making any noise till there was nothing left but fur, like the little fuzz off those seeds coming from nowhere, going nowhere, and the Belgian's wife nearby, lying on her stomach reading magazines, the prisoner on the girl's right seemed to understand, or was about to, but he had no time to get it fully because the shot made him forget, lying down slowly into a little cone shape, the communist imitating him with her brown chipped tooth, the Spanish Civil Guards and the ex-police-men brought long bags, people inside those bags really seemed more like objects in that strange way of something being alive when it already isn't, for months I kept thinking about that tooth, for example I'd be starching some ironing or making dinner and just thinking about the clothes or dinner and not thinking about anything else at all, drifting then

all of a sudden

that tooth would take the place of whatever I'd been thinking about or not thinking about, when I'm not thinking about anything I feel like things are taking me over and I exist through them like dead people exist through

let's suppose

a tea cart, sometimes I miss the tea cart, it wasn't my parents or I who put it there, maybe some old uncle, my grandparents, some other person but who and how and when, a friend, a neighbor, a gift, a favor and no way, no one owes favors to poor people whose only reason for existing is precisely to owe favors, so I'd starch the ironing or make dinner and that tooth would stare at me, a tooth with something wrong, a chip

a filling

behind cardboard glasses and a paper nose, after the shot the nose fell over her mouth, the tooth disappeared under the fake nose, the bullet spared the real nose, seventeen years old at most, no eighteen or nineteen, a child's cheeks, a child's eyes, the ex-policemen put her in a bag before I said

— Wait

here today, tonight, it's the tooth looking at me through the pine trees in the dark, not the wind through the snails and shells in the dirt, not the humble halo of lights from the village, but the tooth and the carnival nose hiding the tooth, as they were closing the bag, I felt free, all she had to do was to run from the gate toward the hill and from there to the engineer's house about a hundred meters farther, if that, the town was just on the other side of his wall, then just step inside one of the two identical cafés, Café Ideal and Café Palace, on either side of the butcher's and always so empty, you never even saw the owners, four of five tables, a vase of flowers on the counter, a stone sink and faucet to wash glasses, the same long neon light constantly flickering and above all, what matters most to me, the telephone between the window and the garbage can, call the army, tell them to come, describe the route, at the chapel turn onto the dirt road, not the paved road, the dirt road, where there's a pile of sand and a gentle pine tree, go over the wooden planks to cross what we call a river but what's really just a trail of mud and some sorry looking reeds, and in July, frogs, in November they're quiet and by the end of the planks you'll see the garage and if you don't see it, Sergeant sir, you'll see the oak tree, it's impossible to miss the oak tree it's so big the gardener's found roots all the way to the nard bed, even as far as the terrace, even as far as the house they've shown up, then, sir, what you'll see is a sort of hunchbacked house, three stories, green shutters, chimney covered in metal, the ex-policemen patrolling the box trees, people wearing cardboard glasses and carnival noses at the garage door, maybe Spanish Civil Guard, maybe communists, maybe the bishop

— Cutie

chasing the maids with a slimy quiver, if you go into the living room and find them inside sunk in their armchairs in frightened defeat, you'll know it's the living room by the picture over the fireplace, a landscape that gives you the creeps, not really the creeps, but makes you feel guilty for no reason, a windmill, cows, ducks, a boy on wagon, a waterwheel, take one look at that and you just want to go home and forget, lie down, and have someone bring a mug of hot chocolate to your bed, tuck you in, tell you

— Goodnight

tip toe out and leave you alone looking out the window, the night through the windowsill and happy memories, and if you don't have any happy memories think about bicycles and slides, kids on roller-skates on a cement hallway, piped music in a bright apartment, thinking about music helps, how many times have I thought about the songs those starlets sang at the dancehalls, I know entire verses about heartache, fallen women or, even further back, my father whistling in the mirror, some rigmarole that made no sense, as he shaved his foamy cheeks, he'd always leave a flake of soap on his earlobe or cut his chin, the flake would get smaller as it dried and the cut would turn dark, by the time he got home from work, you wouldn't even be able to see it among his wrinkles or else it had become a wrinkle itself, so if the communist in the clown mask, not exactly a woman, more like a girl, not fully developed, with a filling in her chipped tooth, a little brown square in her upper front tooth, if she calls you, sir, from the Café Ideal or the Café Palace, and her voice sounds hesitant as it comes through to the noisy barracks, maybe that sound of breaking glass when someone holds the receiver too close to their mouth, afraid they'd discover us on the plaza and jump her, drag her back to the garage and the wall, when you make it to the house, pay attention to the picture of the windmill, the cows, the ducks, the boy on the wagon and the waterwheel, before you deal with us, take it down from above the fireplace and slash it with your pocket knife, turn it to face the other way before you start wanting to go home and forget everything, think about bicycles, slides, happy memories, when I was a little girl they gave me toy binoculars that looked like real ones, you'd squint through the tiny hole and instead of seeing the world bigger, I mean the misery I experienced when I got bigger, you'd see a lady dressed in white in a wave of poppies, nothing special, you know what I mean, nothing to pay particular attention to, a lady dressed in white in a poppy field, you couldn't make out her face, but even so, you have no idea how well I remember her, sometimes I think she's the widow, or the deaf woman or the bishop's goddaughter, sometimes I think she's me, who I'd like to be, who I ought to have been, if my glands had allowed me, sometimes I think she's my mother when she was younger, before she became a cleaning lady, before her rheumatism and kidney problems, if I had those toy binoculars now, I'd have found that detonator ages ago, near the lady in white or the pink fingers holding the stem drawn in microscopic detail

(they spent more time on the stem than the rest)

the middle and ring fingers crooked, the little finger rounded like someone holding a tea cup when there's fancy company, I always pick up my cup as if there's something missing, forget-me-nots, maybe a feather, or the rather vaporous and airy something that she was made of, then I give up on the waving poppy fields and I just grab the cup with all my fingers because I'm afraid I'll break it, I hold it so tight my skin marks the cup, even using detergent it takes forever to get it off

with all this talk of the binoculars, sorry, I got over enthusiastic, lost my train of thought, where was I

oh, right, when you get to the house, sir, before you deal with them, take the picture down from above the fireplace, turn it around to face the other way, without looking at it, and then, yes, then you can tie their hands behind their backs, make them line up on the sofa, first the general, then my boyfriend's boss, then the bishop, then the commander

I almost forgot the commander

then the three women, don't let the sick one's skinniness make you feel sorry for her, the blanket over her knees, and the wig, the smile that isn't really a smile, more like a nervous tick

— Of course

line her up with the others, shove her if you have to and talk loudly, maybe carry her if necessary, order one of the soldiers to bring you a can of gasoline from the cellar

one is enough, it's not worth wasting more than that on them

order another soldier to pour the gasoline all over their clothes, and force them to be happy, to sing along with you, to dance using their feet, legs, shoulders and heads disguised with straw mustaches

— Such joy such joy

and that's that, whatever you feel like and spare me the trouble of spending all night searching for a rock with marble veins among the pines, afraid of the swaying trunks and of my boyfriend, don't tell anyone but I'm afraid of owls, I'm afraid of the wind, a pine cone falling off a branch makes me jump in fright, I'm not sure if my heart can take it, if I can take it, can stay here very much longer, it's up to you now, depends on how you like your fun, on how many minutes you have, on your patience, imagination, whatever you want, you could set a match to them, hang ropes from the wooden beams, use one of the machineguns at the house so you don't have to use your own, whatever you feel like, I really don't care so long as you get it right, put an end to this, there are plenty of cardboard glasses and carnival noses for you and the others you'll bring with you, just look in the second drawer down from the top in the mahogany dresser, the one with the pieces of string, reusable wrapping paper, thimbles, needles, buckles, household trash, for you it'll be pure delight, excitement, a party, and for me dear God I don't ask for anything more

than to catch the van to the peaceful, safe café in Espinho, and not to look through the back window for one single second at the cluster of black trees not seeing us crying.

29

AND ALL OF a sudden, let's just imagine, Coimbra. Walking out onto the porch and seeing the moon through the plane trees, or my grandmother's office, endless boxes filled with bills, a calendar with a picture of a plaza in Santiago or Vigo, photographs of country folks, eyebrows hidden under their hat brims, the pitcher of soda water, the sugar and the coffee within reach: my cousins and I would play till dinner time near the chicken coop, torturing the ants, if we went further out, to the cherry trees and the corncob doll with the torn vest that terrified the sparrows, we'd look back to see the two restaurant lights with their polished spiral scrolls widening into bowls where the bulbs were screwed in: if they burned out, my mother's assistant would climb up the step ladder, put the old bulb in her apron pocket, use two fingers to twist the new bulb in and the room would brighten, prolonging the shadows on the sideboard, creating mysteries, strange hollows, illuminating the wallpaper, the dispensary jar with the dried plane-tree branch, the Moroccan plates on either side of the console, thankfully my cousins were busy making obstacles for a file of ants

(little pebbles, pointless branches, maybe even big ones, a furrow indented with a cane stick)

leaning over to watch their detours, the confused trotting, deliberations, conversing antennae, they don't notice the room isn't the restaurant, with its tables, tablecloths, the menu set vertically between the mustard and salt shaker, napkins folded inside glasses waiting for customers, cheap prints, stained around the edges, of friars feasting on ham and gentlemen with rifles in tricorn hats chopping turkeys, the little hatch in the wall through which my mother

her cap and sweat are in plain sight

is handing out laden platters and getting them back empty, thank goodness, I'd say, my cousins are busy with the ants and don't notice that the room is bigger than the restaurant, furnished with Chinese sideboards, armchairs, sofas, niches displaying expensive decorative pieces made of bronze and crystal, just the same lamps

(not really the same of course, it's unimaginable how many antique stores I had to scan to find them, in Lisbon, in tacky stores in the provinces, in private homes where they'd look at me askance, eyeing my money with deep distrust)

the same lamps with the scrolled cups

five

where they'd screw in the bulbs and instead of the busy tables, conversation, coat hanger, overcoats slung over each other, jackets, umbrellas, my uncles serving, their pencils behind their ears, my grandmother presiding from upstairs wielding her cane

thank goodness my cousins, busy driving the ants crazy over by the chicken coop, don't realize that we aren't in Coimbra, thank goodness they've tired of teasing me because I'm deaf and throwing lizards and dirt clods at me, they aren't peering through the lit windows and don't notice it's not the restaurant, aren't surprised looking at each other, first in disbelief, then afraid, then their chins quivering, faces deformed, about to start crying, undecided, wanting to escape, but where to, how to escape if they don't know where they are, to get help from their parents who aren't there since instead of the house in Coimbra, the plane trees, servants quarters, basin, shed, all of a sudden they discover a three storied house with a swimming pool and a garage next to pine woods they don't recognize, something like a slope between the city and the ocean, a city bigger than anything an eight-year-old could imagine, bigger than Coimbra, where people don't greet you, streets leading to unknown places, plazas and lakes spiraling like shells, a horizon of churches and an ocean, different than at Figueira da Foz, with train tracks along the beach leading out to the bay, the hills, not plane trees, not poplars, bronze Neptunes draining water from their empty eyes, circular walls running into each other dizzyingly, echoing tiles, thank goodness my cousins are having fun sticking pieces of paper and burning matches into a new ant hole, under the hyacinth roots so there's no danger they'll peek through the lit windows, now curious, not in a panic, stepping all over my pansies, my carnations, my nards, stepping backwards to crush them again

— Good

elbowing each other, laughing, seeing me there in my orange wig in my invalid's chair, alerting my mother at the kitchen door

— Auntie, Mimi's in there dressed up like an old woman

studying me like they do the ants, with a cruel thrill, the general and the bishop, the bishop's goddaughter, Celina, all of them quiet, waiting, holding their teacups, except for the commander machine-gunning the flowerbeds, a light in the pine woods first white then blue making circles in the wind, my cousins leaning their chins on the windowsill

I bet they're on tiptoe, scratching my walls with their shoes, trampling the creeper vine I've just had planted, three noses up against the window, the youngest wearing glasses with one lens covered, if she took them off, the defective eye would be still for a second then wander, I always wanted to grab it and bring it back before it could disappear through a crack in the wall, countless fingers gripping the windowsill dirtying it, hair ribbons coming untied on their own, buns, bangs, sliding platters lost on the floor

(what's the army going to say tomorrow when they find them here, what absurd speculations will they come up with on the radio, in the newspapers, I wonder if the firemen will look for children's corpses in the ashes, tiny earrings shining among the broken tiles, in the burnt wood, the roof tiles, the picture of the windmill that will, of course, survive)

tiny earrings

(Mama Alicia's present for First Communion)

three mouths still missing teeth, braces straightening out the new ones, the braces in chorus to my mother who was leaving the kitchen, intrigued, wiping her hands on her apron

— Who told Mimi she could be inside there dressed up like an old woman?

my mother adjusting her cap as she asked, animals in a flurry, escaping the patio, the alarmed judicial grandeur of the turkey in his stiffly starched black coat, Mama Alicia, maybe having heard the ruckus, told them to move her chair over to the veranda, my father leaving the cash register, buttoning his vest, my family looking through the windowpanes into the lit living room, the expensive objects, the bishop's ring, Celina's cleavage, I, dressed like an adult wearing lipstick, face powder, long stockings, hiding behind the teapot in nervous embarrassment, don't get me in trouble, don't beat me, don't get mad at me, don't say I can't go to the movies on Sunday, my mother came away from the window without recognizing me, the servants returned Mama Alicia's throne to the top of the stairs, my father went back to the cash register, loosening his vest, his hand on the keys like a dead fish, any minute now it would drop into his lap, one last quiver of finger scales before finally holding still, the chickens clucking and squabbling around the washbasin, the turkey judge, with awe-inspiring statutory wisdom, was seemingly reading out wills, if, making up some sort of excuse, I leave this room and walk past the garage, I'll be back home, the driver kneeling in the pine needles examining stones has nothing to do with me, the bishop's worries, his taking his ring on and off over and over again, my husband counting the suitcases in the entryway, pausing to think, going upstairs to bring down a bag, none of them have anything to do with me and I don't care about Celina and her constant cigarette

— Leave

pointing at the gate and beyond the gate, the road to Lisbon, the cigarette insisting

— Leave

stubborn, fake, the bishop's goddaughter hovering, an interrogative kite, I have nothing to do with the flashlight that finally recognized the rock, the second rock with the enormous marble vein, the bump in the pine needles, the carving in the tree trunk, the fingers combing through the needles, separating wires, winding them around dowels, the battery cone pointing at the clock, the fat girl's mouth counting along with the driver's ten minutes, eight, seven, six, five, hopefully the firemen never see the picture, never find out about the nights at the hotel and my anxiety, turning on the shower as fast as I could, sliding the plastic shower curtain rings, washing myself

washing myself

my cousins understanding showing each other the windmill, the wagon, the waterwheel

— Auntie

entertain them, take them swimming, take them to my bedroom, let them put on my French spray cologne, its hidden tears floating through the air, smudge themselves with my blushers and eye shadows, blending colors, red, green, brown, black, try on my fancy hat, mantilla, fur coat, shoes, trail around rolled up carpets and marble stairs in my high heels, feel the lights flickering beneath shivering sequins and the whiff of a silver fox's forest smell, Celina surprised, the general, his nose in the air, the commander putting down the machinegun to load the pistol, threatening the door, the entry hall, the garden

— The communists

leave with my cousins till Mama Alicia's cane protests with furious thrusts

— Is there no rest for the weary in this hellhole ladies and gentlemen?

my aunts and my mother emerging all at once from all the doors, shooing us into the bedroom with huge, silent gestures, pointing at the throne warning us to be quiet, the cane kept torturing the floor boards, emphasizing her grumbles, when they switched off the lights I became aware of the plane trees, which weren't there in the glow, the reflection of the furniture was there in a black square and, superimposed on the reflection of the furniture, a ghost looking like me, transparent, passing through everything with no hair ribbon, wearing a long blouse, a speck of toothpaste on my nose, the black square transformed into a brown square with branches waving slow goodbyes, you could make out the form of the chicken coop, the pharmacy sign between the rooftops, the flashlight in the pine woods now still, steady, two minutes, the fat girl counting with the clock, the driver readying the lever, get my cousins out into the yard quickly, tell them about a new ant hill packed with galleries and chambers in the cement well, Mama Alicia would never forgive me, there'd be no more sharing Coca-Cola secrets, no more Galicia, the only thing left would be the cane upstairs complaining, what would my mother say when she heard the explosion, if I could get up from my chair, walk, the Sunday quails, bells, my brother's crib in the attic and no baby in the sheets, the commander assuring himself the army had not surrounded the garden, the bishop's goddaughter was gathering looks, smiles and cigarette pirouettes between Celina and me, setting them about in various combinations, turning them inside out, changing their order, trying to make them fit as she tried to understand, the wind would bring the nards into the living room, the figurehead at the swimming pool gushed silent waters, I didn't notice the roses because nighttime devours them or else there never were any roses and I thought there were, my husband looked at the picture, looked at me, I locked myself in the bathtub sobbing in regret, one minute, and now, one second following the next, the hand moving in a circle on the way to an instantaneous ghost, so easy to imagine the driver and the fat girl protected by tree trunks and sandbags, so easy to imagine the explosion the flames, the scarlet walls, the gables crumbling, my cousins

forty-one seconds

disappearing from the mirror in one last trace of lipstick along with the low-cut blouses, slaves from India, their skirts at their ankles, their high heels broken tripping down the hall with the first hissing of a fuse and the first bang, their palms out, facing the restaurant as the furniture shook, the bishop's goddaughter who finally understood, insulting us

— Bitches

the commander pointing the machinegun at the slabs of stucco falling from the ceiling, at the spurt of steam from a suddenly exposed pipe, a harsh whistling of gas, the mother-of-pearl inlaid armoires toppling and trembling, Celina's cigarette escaping her fingers, escaping the ashtray

— Leave

rolling underneath the sofa and burning the fabric, she pleaded

— Leave

looking sorry, an expression of

thirty seconds

pity, the lamps with the spiral scrolls went out, I couldn't see the plane trees in Coimbra anymore, the chicken coop, the pharmacy, the shiny sand, the dirty slime of the Mondego river in August, I no longer saw the picture

I was glad not to see the picture any more

the windmill, the cows, the ducks, the boy on the wagon, the water-wheel, I never got married, I was never at a hotel, I never spent hours in the shower scrubbing myself with a pumice stone and soap, cleansing myself of myself, I'm still sitting next to the anthill on a Saturday afternoon, measuring how deep it is, calculating the galleries, the tunnels, where they laid their eggs, my brother's crib upstairs in the attic, with the first breeze the gauze decorations waver a bit, sometimes I think a measly little cry, a plea, a barely audible wail shuddering

twenty-six seconds and the driver's body laid flat on the dirt

throughout the loquat tree, I'm near the anthill or making afternoon tea in toy pots with torn leaves, insects and pebbles, there may be an old woman wearing an orange wig in some big room but she's too far away for me to make her out, looks like she has a blanket over her knees and a teacup or sugar bowl or teapot, an old woman among other old people, suitcases, pistols, smiling at the woman in the low-cut blouse

— But of course

and telling her no, it looks like another woman is grabbing her by the neck

— Murderer

among falling objects and the smell of nards, it seems like my cousins are running toward me wearing mantillas, silk scarves, tiaras, shawls, charcoal eyeshadow and eyeliner, my grandmother was calling me waving her cane

— Mimi

and I can't see the house anymore, demolished, engulfed in smoke, flames, the van driving off from the pine woods, northward, a picture over the fireplace that I didn't care about at all, crumbling to cinders, one of those vulgar landscapes in beach hotels, the turkey approaches dilating his wattle, hiccupping facts and figures, the cherries rotting on the ground, it's bathing day, they'll call me in a few minutes for my turn, they put the basin in the pantry, along with the onions, collards, corn, rice, my mother brings the pitcher and the sewing scissors to trim my nails and it always hurt, someone was saying

— Five seconds

not here, on the other side, or they weren't saying it and I was just thinking it and later I didn't have time to figure out anything else since they were scrubbing my chest and my back, pouring scalding water over my shoulders, ordering me to

— Be quiet

and as they wrapped me in a towel, I think I saw Celina, at least I saw a pretty woman with her hair done, looking at me with a sort of pity, her face little by little blending into the sound of the bells, the toppling, explosions, shots, and over the peaceful tolling a uniformed military officer, or a man wearing cardboard glasses and a carnival nose bowing toward us vowing I've died.

30

WHEN I FINALLY understood the gestures and looks exchanged between
the widow and the deaf woman, the first thing that came to mind was
to get rid of them, this time I'd use the pistol, calling the commander
or explaining to everyone else what was going on in the pine woods, it
wasn't just branches and crows, there was the circling light and the footsteps in the dry pine needles, another pair of shadows besides the shadow
already searching, questioning, hesitating, digging through the earth, but
I realized right away it was all for the best and I lost interest in them just
like my father realized it was best to lose interest in us, the canary would
still hop from perch to perch, spill his bird seed, beat against the cage,
my mother still complained about the blood on the rug, ashamed when
we had guests at Easter, if only we were at home, she'd cover the wood
floor and the chairs with torn sheets, and check our shoes as we came in
from outdoors, making us show her our soles

— Wipe those little feet on the doormat for me you're dragging in
mud

so we ended up living in a sort of tomb filled with shrouded figures
silently at peace, in the shadow of the church façade, my mother desperate about the blood stains

— Now what?

and my father quiet, except for his eyes bobbing around the room,
indifferent to my mother, my cousin, me, the light in the pine woods, you
could hear the downstairs neighbors' faucet, a drawer, someone turning a
radio on and off, the strokes of a broom, the major's niece battling with

the rheumatic man in the stairwell, if we hadn't closed the window maybe his eyes would stop roving between the curtains and the windowpane, tired of my mother who was approaching with a bottle of bleach, of the driver checking out the connections and coils, tired of me, holding a useless glass of water

— Father

tired of the widow behind her cigarette, the wires screwed down with nuts, the lever all set, and in the priest's case the explosion lasted ages within the space of just a few seconds, I felt like screaming and now I couldn't care less, totally indifferent, I was watching Celina

— Leave

and not only the deaf woman, everyone should get out of there and leave me alone to take care of my father in peace, he and I and Mercês Church, the telephone rang and went silent, the general was holding the receiver hoping it was a call from Spain

it's too late for them to call us, general, sir, the driver's setting off the mechanism right now, at this precise instant it's all over, my mother and cousin will undoubtedly read about it in the newspaper or hear about it from neighbors without realizing it's me

the commander tripped over a suitcase as he was firing his machine-gun at the nards, not the plants, just the aroma, a sort of stubble of wavering petals and stems beyond the swimming pool, as soon as they fired the gardener, the insect ridden, cancerous nards succumbed, bowing down in pale defeat, the roses crumbled on their wire trellis, the oak leaves made the terrace even more filthy, empty little hands, the granite discus thrower had dived into the grass between the garden and the garage, a hose around his neck, judging from the sound of spongy soles on August afternoons, there were most likely frogs all along the wall, round animals resting on their own parapets sprouting foam, when we went to Setúbal, I'd help my grandfather find them in the streams, we'd chase down their goiters, their tired leaping, their stern eyebrows serving as customs officers, we'd prod them with cane poles, they'd drip moss and keep squeaking, my grandfather in his breeches and tie would settle himself next to the trellis laughing at the vines, or else there were no customs frogs, no goiters, no spongy soles, I'm sure my grandfather and Setúbal are not part of my life, there's no way they could be, I made it all up, I'm sure the general and the commander, the deaf woman's husband and my godfather aren't part of my life either, I made them all up, gathered around the telephone, their heads together, I invented the worry, the hurry, the fear, vainly tapping it to get it going, looking at it in disbelief

— Now what?

the general lifted the receiver thinking it might be broken, the commander pointing his machinegun, hating the nards, the deaf woman's husband pushing the general out of the way and putting the receiver back on the telephone

— If you don't leave it alone how do you expect it to ring?

not a single instruction from Spain, no indication of which route to take, no automobiles waiting for us on one of the gravel side roads

(I can clearly see laurels weighed down by the rain, a roofless abandoned ruin, a fox in some kind of bush, all bark and teeth)

no automobiles waiting for us, headlights turned off, no colonel from the Civil Guard coming toward us smiling, I made him up, I'm eight years old, if that, when my father wakes me up

— Do you want to be late for mass?

I'm rid of the house, the night, the widow furious at me

(you could tell by the cigarette's frenzy and the fingers of her free hand tapping the ashtray like a piano)

because I thought about second-class beach hotels when I looked at the picture, a badly designed landscape, cheap, really vulgar, from a charity bazaar, too many colors and uneven paint, disproportionate, the wagon further away than the windmill but bigger, the duckbills as big as the cows, the boy with the whip leaning back in an impossible position, the horse's neck too long as if it were a giraffe, one of the horseshoes was gigantic and the rest were tiny, ever since the first day I haven't understood a picture like that in rich peoples' house, walnut furniture along with that print, gentlemen, so now it's obvious I'm eight years old, only a child would dream like that, children like horses, wagons, windmills, waterwheels, nards, horrible pictures, I used to adore the lids of candy boxes and tea tins, loving couples, cats playing with balls of yarn, little boys holding teddy bears with two giant tears running down their cheeks, the happy promises I made to the teddy bear and the little boy, the stories I'd tell them, how I suffered along with them, promises of friendship, plans to save them, that's how it's so obvious I'm making this up, it makes no sense, Celina would know what I think, unless Celina doesn't exist either, it makes no sense for those men to gather around the telephone, my father vomiting blood and my mother squatting down with a soapy sponge, it makes no sense to go and die, I simply cannot understand why they don't tug at my knee and warn me

— Wake up

since Mercês church is that shadow over there, the creatures in my dream seem to be with the blackbirds and the trees and what they call pine woods, and since they think there's a garden, a pool and a garage where we live, all you have to do is pay careful attention to the buildings, the neighbors, the butcher, our door over there, notice the pigeons, why don't they get mad

— Do you want to be late for mass?

and instead, the driver I've invented is searching through the dry pine needles

(not dry pine needles, it's the dust left by sandals on the church steps, the usual trash, papers, cigarettes, rags, tumbling down the stairs)

the driver finding the lever

(how stupid, that's a lie, there's no lever, don't let me get upset, don't believe it, keep this heart from, keep this sweat from, there's no lever, one of the beggars, who leaned down to pick up a match or a lost coin, hiding them in his pocket and heading down one of the side streets off São Bento avenue, dragging a worn-out slipper from his right ankle, a beggar, of course, you can tell by the dirty hair, the hat, the drunkard's bows, it might be the retired man from the general store, the man whose wife left him for a traveling salesman, exactly, I recognize him now, the nose, how skinny he is, the same dog, her ribs sticking out, attached to a string)

the driver looking through the dry pine needles, finding the lever, checking the connections, the battery and wires, lifting them up a little, testing the contact, the fat girl holding the flashlight, the car about thirty meters down the hill, the tacky little seaside café in Espinho, the awning over the café terrace, the indifferent waves

(just as I'd thought, no more, no less, if there were any further need, here you have the final proof of how dreams make no sense, Espinho, never in my entire life have I ever been to Espinho, I must have come across the name in one of those vacation pamphlets, on offer at the supermarket

fifteen unforgettable marvelous days in July, entirely free, on the pleasant Espinho coast for you and your wife

in a magazine at the dentist's, why not Algarve or the south of France or Venice, the images we collect without realizing it, illogical connections, the absurd make-believe of a sleeping child)

meanwhile the general

(of course a little girl's never content with a captain or count, it's always generals, always kings and princesses)

my godfather, that is, the bishop

(what else, I'm starting to have fun now that I'm getting the hang of how this works, never a verger or a priest, at the very least, a bishop)

the commander

(all that's missing here is the inevitable seafarer, the corsair, the pirate, heroic navigator, how everything becomes so childish, predictable, the caravel driver and on and on)

the deaf woman's husband

(the unexpected element bringing it all together or maybe not unexpected, let me think about it, consider the situation more carefully, the geography teacher, the son of the woman on the second floor who one Sunday as he was leaving tousled my hair, the colleague from my father's work who fixed the stove for us, answering my mother

— No, no it's nothing

and accepting a liqueur, his embarrassed buttocks perched on the edge of a chair, I remember he was called Adelino, I never forgot that name, you can't scare me, little one, from the time I understood how things work, I was never frightened again)

therefore

(let's laugh a bit at your expense, okay, at the expense of your dream, don't get me wrong)

so here we have the general, isn't that right, the bishop, right, the commander, right, my father's work colleague

sorry

the so-called deaf woman's husband, isn't that right, the four of them, right, hovering over the telephone that's not ringing

(if I'm saying something wrong don't be shy, don't hesitate, please correct me)

outside in what

(because it's not the pine woods for God's sake, now I'm the one saying we need to see this out)

out there, in the pine woods, the driver

(so I wasn't wrong, see, thankfully I wasn't wrong, it really is the driver)

out there in the pine woods the driver and the fat girl are waiting four three two one seconds

four three two one zero

they pull the lever, and if my father hadn't had the sad idea of tugging at my knee

— So?

I'd do what you want and die, I know how to die beautifully, I'm quiet and everything, I'd fall forward, theatrically, very solemn, with my hand on my chest and my eyes closed, I'd die a little, holding my breath, my leg asleep, the tickling under my chin, feeling like laughing, I'd die a little just for the pleasure

look how nice I am

just for the pleasure, you understand, of making you happy.

31

To TELL YOU the truth, I'm absolutely positive I've never looked as beautiful as I do today. Before I left the house, I saw a young girl, eighteen years old, if that, smiling back at me from the mirror

— See you later Celina

wearing a black blouse the same as I am, except really young, with that aroma of cool shadow beneath an old stone arch that young people have even when they wear perfume, picking up my keys, putting my cigarettes in her purse, turning back to fix her eye make-up, without a trace of wakeful nights, nary a wrinkle or any sign of aging

(oh to be eighteen, my God, when the gentle hand of two hours of sleep smooths out every crease in our skin)

a young girl switching on the living room display case lights, frowning like a little rabbit at the cleaning lady's gifts, moving around my apartment as if she owned it, glancing at a photograph of me at her age and looking displeased, maybe even thinking she's ugly, poorly coiffed, decrepit, just like how I bet Elizabeth thinks of me, in spite of her protests, she glances over the furniture as if it were a sort of goodbye, lingering at the chest that had belonged to my uncle, knitting her eyebrows as if she were about to cry, whenever I made that face my mother, wagging her finger,

— You're not going to start crying are you?

she looks at herself full face, in profile, from the back, glancing over her shoulder strap and blowing herself little kisses, knowing she's never been as beautiful as she is today, for once

(and frankly, it's about time)

Elizabete and the manicurist aren't lying, both of their mouths agape, silenced, they had to have meant it, a couple of teenagers envious of a woman of the world, without realizing the woman of the world envies them even more

(that saying about the gentle hand of two hours sleep able to smooth creases both inside and out, glassy lake water after the skipping stones of alcohol, tobacco and insomnia)

the other clients nodding parakeet secrets, they too, amazed, making up lovers, ill-gotten riches, lesbian inclinations, the shrill trace of curved beaks knitting lies in my wake, the girl at the cash register, without my having left a tip

— I hope you won't take offence dona Celina if I say how beautiful you are?

a bitter woman, burdened with debts and illness, her pancreas, kidneys

and the bitter are hard-pressed to dish out compliments

spend eleven months saving up money for a week at the spa to take the waters, and by the end of the bicarbonate treatments, juice for lunch, juice for dinner, her kidneys are worse off, climb three flights of stairs, no elevator, lugging the Saturday groceries, resting her bags and lungs on every landing, turn the stairwell light back on, keeps going out, count how many floors to go, pick up the bags that are digging into her fingers, takes a breath, continues climbing, inside the apartment's covered in crypt dust, submerged in mortgages, a threadbare carpet, a gas bill demanding to be paid, double her tip

— I hope you won't take offence dona Celina if I say how beautiful you are?

frowning at the outrageous bill, biting back angry words in silence, if she'd cut her bangs maybe her kidneys would swallow a little stone or two and her features would sweeten, strike up a conversation, invite her for a cup of coffee downtown, owned by a lady with an expensive name and rings, somehow reconciling impatience and need, addressing her clients in rude haste, homemade cakes, croquettes, disgusting food, the girl at the cash register holding a bill, no, an insect, a nauseating creature, if we were to go to the café the lady with the fancy name, accustomed to clients who were cousins of cousins, would judge our background according to our manners and how we dressed, immediately recovering grandparents, country estates, palaces, her lips showing us the available tables, accompanied by a friend with a gold wristwatch barely liberated from the pawnbroker's.

— Ladies, if you could please wait outside we haven't opened yet

we, reduced to nothings, while they went on about their vacations in Switzerland using affected terms of endearment, they'd lived in Brazil after the communists, selling encyclopedias in São Paulo, and upon their return they exchanged their houses for little exile apartments, where their unemployed, depressed husbands drank away their depression on the rocks, foisting their golf clubs onto more fortunate relatives, the salon cashier pocketed her tip inside her apron, tied with hatred, the parakeets held out their nails to the manicurist, their little curved beaks chirping nastiness at me

— It's obvious how that fox figured out her life

I, as beautiful as I've ever been, eighteen years old if a day, steady on my feet, victorious, shoulders aligned, as slender at the waist as a young girl, a cool shadow underneath a stone arch even wearing my perfume, my mother among the parakeets with equal fury, comparing her one pair of shoes with the collection in my closet, I got my keys, put my cigarettes in my purse, turned back thinking I'd fix my eye make-up, batting my lashes to make my irises dilate, the hazy mysterious look that lends the nearsighted the aura of sleepwalkers, the lit display cases showed off the cleaning lady's gifts, turning them into antiques, with those prices, I waved to the furniture, seemingly content, I lingered over the chest that had belonged to my uncle with an itch I prefer not to go into, a secret little cry, he'd keep postcards in the top drawer

(fado singers, sea doves in the eaves, Austrian peasants)

and also letters with lipstick marks, lips shaped like hearts pierced by arrows in permanent ink, Carmencita, Armandina, Lucrécia, maybe the elderly ladies in Campo Grande park, a bracelet engraved With Love, my mother wagging her finger

— You're not going to cry are you?

when my mother was the one doing the crying, her still features, drops running down the wrinkles in her cheeks, all I missed was some-one to take care of me in the dark, whereas she missed hidden caresses, conversations, laughter, I looked at myself face on, in profile, from the back, glancing back over my shoulder strap knowing I've never been as beautiful as I am today, don't worry I won't cry, I'm happy, it's been ages since I've felt so light, not even the stain on the entryway ceiling, I'm not sure whether it's a leak or smoke, just like Corsica on the map, it made me just the tiniest bit sad to think there'd be life beyond this night

and don't bother me because there's no way, I'm gorgeous

I'd ask dona Alice to call the plumber or mason, men on ladders, pencil behind their ears, messing up my house, rubble all over the place, enamel on the rug, a boot with no laces pounding the stucco at my eye level, empty beer bottles along with cans of plaster, a motorized bicycle, a bundle of trash instead of a gas cap, blocking the landing, close the door for the last time, leave, for the past week the doorknob has been sticking every single time I try to lock it, you can hear the metal parts rubbing against each other, steel grating steel, finally obeying against its will with a click, I'd ask myself as I went through my purse, tissues, dark glasses

(with my dark glasses and a headscarf looking like an actress trying to get away from autograph hounds)

if I could get it open, the way I used to remind myself that I should jot down the firemen's telephone number under the letter F in my agenda so I could avoid having to sleep on one of my friends' sofas, in unfamiliar

rooms that smelled of tobacco and fertilizer, my sleep interrupted by a
hostess's concerns, attentive questions

— Would you like another blanket Celina?

and ever present, my mother's little finger, warning me, angry

— You're not going to cry are you?

my feet over the edge, strange pillow, a hotel logo would billow in
the curtains and bring me back, the smell of tobacco again, the plants in
vases, the taxis dropping off guests, the doorman's bowing and scraping
in English, my peeking at the window with just one eye

(curtains in this color make it seem like it's raining misty chrysanthemums even in August)

surprised at how people exist, the smallest, most timid bit of loneliness peeking out from every object, that ridiculous basket still wrapped
in cellophane, the picture of what looks like a married man

(the necktie, the moustache)

maybe owns a business, maybe the friend of a friend, somewhat con-
cealed by the strategic camouflage of photographs of nieces and nephews
and Christmas cards, encircled with pink ribbon, making the isolation
so much more apparent and bitter, fighting colds with soluble aspirin
with no help whatsoever to stir it, blouses and skirts peeping through
overnight bags, hurried visits, from six to six twenty, from the necktie
and moustache careful with his rear end

— Don't squeeze me too much, don't leave any marks

the collar carefully examined up against the light afterwards, the coat,
each accusatory strand removed, end up with no one and nothing more
than an aura of aftershave, a clod of mud on the carpet and that stuff
on the sheets

— You're not going to cry are you?

don't clean the mud clod, don't clean that stuff, caress it, imagine, keep something of yours with me, don't worry because I'm not going to complain, I'm not going to compromise you, I won't talk, every once in a while a bouquet of carnations, a quick telephone call in a neutral voice on account of your colleagues, the hotel logo

Hotel Con inental Hotel Con inental Hotel Con inental

that won't stop calling me, a gigantic black butterfly, probably poisonous, on the plants in the vases, make myself as small as possible under the blankets, peek out at the butterfly, fail to see it, panic, discover it on the parchment lampshade, maybe with antennae, pincers, ask the tie and moustache to have dinner with me at the drop-leaf table, the sofas will consent, wear the outfit with the slanted low-cut that excites you, warm the wine, put the lit match to the candle, melting us into each other in sensual intimacy, and later the irritated saliva on the wick

— Don't worry mother I'm not going to cry

a drop of wax on the lace tablecloth, wait for him to leave to scratch it off with my fingernail, the hand with the wedding band reaching for the platter of steak and mushrooms still untouched, the irritated explanation

— If I could eat twice I promise I would don't be offended

and in the morning the poisonous butterfly, no, the friend, the poisonous butterfly that metamorphosed into a friend in a large cloak, barefoot, her big toe bent over the toe next to it

(if she didn't wear silver nail polish you wouldn't notice so much)

touching my back with tender concern, her forehead anxious under her moisturizer, some kind of green lotion around her eyes

— Did you sleep well Celina?

the cellophane-wrapped basket infinitely melancholic, ceramic swans I hadn't noticed before lined up on the shelf, a newly bound encyclopedia, a gardening book, a culinary dictionary, colored photographs of the recipes on the page opposite the ingredients, chopped onion, half cup flour, six eggs, grey and white oriental platters fastened by little hooks hung on the wall, get back home wearing clothes from the day before, without having brushed my teeth or taken a shower, flee the butterfly, the moisturizer, the crooked toes, the basket, the swans, find a gas delivery truck out in the street blocking my way, honk forever before anyone shows up, feeling desperate about the unfinished outside walls, a faded awning outside a grocery store, a woman with a feather duster getting irritated with me from a ground-floor apartment riddled with parrots, three of them twisting and turning, a basset hound staring fixedly, his expression devoid of suffering love, the truck driver emerges from around a corner adjusting his cap, taking his time under the grocery store awning, ignoring me, chatting and scratching his ear with someone I can't see, someone the woman with the feather duster recognizes, as do the parrots prancing as a threesome, ruffled, perplexed on their perch

(ah to be a sorceress or a witch, to cast an evil spell and all that would be left of him would be a little smoke over a sweaty cap on the ground)

the discomfort of being dressed without having showered, my make-up in a shambles, hardened patches cracking on my face, the sticky fabric making me itch, feeling as if every inch of my body were a burden, the uneven sofa has left my bones in disarray, my friend above me in her Turkish bathrobe, multiplying her goodbyes, one of her thin wrists

(the left, the right?)

holding a pot, the truck engine starts and the gas canisters jolt and collide, the miserable façades jolt and collide, the parrots lift their bunion claws assailing the pot, why not take a trip, change jobs, get a bigger apartment in a less depressing neighborhood, stop taking pills that don't make the future any better, the truck finally pulls away, the trees waver, the doorman at the Hotel Continental butters up the English tourists in, the rosy atmosphere, bowing in his belly-button jackknife bows, the gas cylinders pile up, clinking out fears, it's my turn to pull away and, in the rearview mirror, I see the cap teasing me, change my clothes as soon as I walk through the door, my coat, shoes, plug the tub, bath salts, bubbles, as I enter the bedroom my uncas I enter the bedroom my husband tossing my open purse on the bed, startled, my hairbrush, dental floss, lipstick, eyeliner pencil, half pencil, half top, credit cards, checks, his trembling fingers altering his voice

— Don't you have any cigarettes?

now that my grandmother's not here, to walk slowly toward the door, down the hall, treading like a thief, like Mickey Mouse, skipping over scuffed floorboards, pass the alcove we used as a pantry, the window leading out to a well of dark walls

(trash at the end, carnivorous wall lizards, stinky, the stockings I didn't like and threw out there)

separating me from the neighboring building, the sound of cracked pipes coming from I don't know where, maybe the kitchen, could be there, wrap my hand around the porcelain doorknob with the inlaid frieze, the latch gave way and suddenly, the coatrack with my father's Sunday slacks, the terracotta pharaoh, the haloed Virgin on the side in a little cloud of plastic, the small bottle of yellow liquor, the dead scorpion swimming inside, my uncle's shirt next to the scorpion, waving his sleeves as if he had any

(what a stupid memory)

thrown from the bed, the bedspread on the floor, the high-heeled shoe with the nail on top of the bedspread, on its side, reminding me of a dead rabbit and, along with it, all of a sudden, a succession of scattered confused images from a damaged film, the breeze from the veranda blowing a bus ticket around the floor, the alarm clock from the bedside table ticking, Mickey Mouse preventing

— Close your eyes don't look

the alarm clock on the bedside table ticking, tin arteries, my uncle's cigarette holder in the ashtray, the film spooling faster, an elbow, the back of a neck, someone struggling and giving in, jerking and panting, the high heel without the nail dancing on the bed, a chin appearing and disappearing in a drowning whirl, because of the jolts

— You're not going to cry are you?

given the streaks across the film it was impossible to make out who the people were, apart from the security guard, absolutely certain I didn't know who they were, a couple, strangers whom I don't feel like talking about, who took advantage of my father being at work and my grand-mother at the doctor's to take over the bedroom, Mickey Mouse tried to make a case, with idiotic reasoning, the kind of nonsense stuffed animals come up with, which only a fool would believe and which I refused to listen to, as I pulled the doorknob with exacting care, with those thief-like gestures, the pharaoh and the scorpion would never torment me again, I forgot the coat rack, the alarm clock fell silent, I answered her wagging finger, shifting into a sulk

— And what would I have to cry about?

I thought about going back in case the bus ticket were a palindrome

(I'd put it away in the bag with the others)

but I gave up without really understanding why maybe because I felt like

why not?

being alone in the dark, maybe because I felt like

why not?

studying, I made Mickey Mouse be quiet, threatening to throw him down the building well, where the carnivorous wall lizards would gobble him up, I dangled him by a paw and showed him the May mud, he was extremely nervous and he looked down and said he was sorry

— Forgive me

I almost decided to throw him down since the last thing I wanted was to see my uncle that night with his feigned caresses by the gorilla's and teddy bears' shelf

— You're so pretty Celina

my uncle, Elisabeth and the manicurist, the receptionist with her
bitter pancreas and kidneys frowning at the bill, the entry hall mirror
normally so cruel and today as I left

— See you never again mirror

more indulgent, enthusiastic, it was on the mirror's rather than my
own account that I looked again, full face, in profile

(really, no tummy at all, well, almost no tummy)

from behind, one last glance, looking back over my shoulder strap, a
kiss of thanks, I called the elevator and felt like singing and, as I pulled
the grille shut, the elevator smiled at me, I placed my hand on that happy
smile and the elevator suddenly grew serious, hiding its happiness, when
it reached the second floor

(after a long scary delay and hissing cables)

I hunched up against the buttons to make space for the judge's daughter-in-law to squeeze in with me, her entire fat self along with the little
dog she was carrying, the judge's daughter-in-law found me serious there
against the aluminum plate and hugged her dog even more closely

wearing a winter coat and a collar with its blood type and the owners'
address

to her ample bosom, the building manager hated the dog because it
would pee on the decorative ferns in the lobby, as a result of the animal's
liberties the ferns took on a brownish tone, shed their leaves and died,
within a month, accompanied in their demise by the devastated manager,
I'd come across him on Sundays, following the progressive collapse with
nursery-school vigilance, looking disgustedly at the criminal drops that
would evaporate, smelling like ammonia, I left Mickey Mouse in the
corner, his arms and legs tangled, and settled into the living room with
my grammar book open to irregular verbs, after burying my mother's
crochet in the bucket of remnants, I memorized two whole pages, I, who

couldn't even memorize the words to a bolero, my grandmother got back from her outing at exactly the moment my uncle came down the hallway, tucking his shirttails into his slacks

(I got the impression that it was from the windowsill that Mickey Mouse, so opinionated, offered his theories on shirttails, but I wasn't interested in false insinuations)

my grandmother, noticing the animal upside down, noticing me studying my irregular verbs and my uncle smoothing out his hair without a drop of blood in his face, leaned over to pick up Mickey Mouse and put him down between the sofa pillow and me, my mother's high heel without the nail appeared with fake naturalness

(bitter comment from the stuffed animal, not mine)

one of her eyelids blue, the other with no make-up, my grandmother, swayed by Mickey Mouse's intrigue, seemed to be snarling through pursed lips for no reason whatsoever

— What a sorry sight

and for the first time since I could remember she started rearranging random objects and offered me stevia to sweeten the sulfur taste of the tension dripping through the atmosphere and, after the wordless anger directed at my mother and uncle, who were simply not at fault, my uncle having pulled himself together and my mother screwing her earring back on, my grandmother suggested I exchange my irregular verbs

(she tended to worry greatly over my teacher's predictions for my future, restricted to a long career as a cleaning lady, relegated to poverty tempered with scouring pads and handouts)

for my gorilla and giraffe, the sugar down my throat making me cough, my grandmother, convinced I didn't feel well for some obscure reason having to do with the strangers in the bedroom

— You two won't rest till you've killed the girl

although

(in spite of Mickey Mouse's confused speculations)

I was certain no one in my family, much less my mother and my uncle, had occupied the bed while my father was at work, and to back me up, the scorpion in the yellow liquor didn't say anything, the terra-cotta pharaoh didn't complain, as soon as my grandmother appeared the strangers hopped over the veranda railing and disappeared down the alley and I bet by now they're way far away, just a couple like any other at the metro station or some café in Santos, the animal had discovered a semblance of guilt in my mother and uncle, like my husband throwing my purse, his fingers trembling, making up excuses, and I thought those fingers were normal

really normal

my husband putting my brush back, the dental floss, lipstick, half an eyeliner pencil, half a pencil whose end I'd bitten and dented, credit cards, checks, the foolish excuse

— Don't you have any cigarettes?

from someone who hasn't even smoked in ten years, Mickey Mouse, meddlesome, no one having asked him to chime in

— The sorry fellow thinks you have a lover Celina

Mickey Mouse through my mouth before I'd had the chance to shut him up given that my tongue was pushing against my gums so I was too late closing my mouth

— You think I've got a lover?

not my voice, a little cotton felt whisper, a downy murmur, damp sentences coming from something falling apart inside the dark well between the buildings, torn apart by wall lizards and covered in mud, none of us could figure out how he'd fallen although my grandmother stared at me in silence without getting me in trouble

(grown-ups have such strange principles)

she happened to find him the following week blubbering in the trash
can, as she was looking out the window to clear her conscience, after
combing through the entire apartment looking for her knitting which
she was actually holding, my uncle went down from the third floor using
a borrowed ladder, we watched him descend like a brave miner, holding the flashlight in his mouth, my mother wringing her hands afraid
he'd die or scrape his knee, delicate little confused sounds like paws, the
flashlight moving right and left revealing the crochet my mother didn't
see, covering her eyes with anguished sleeves, bricks, rocks, rusty pots, an
enamel faucet, a pigeon corpse, thank God, luckily not even one ghost,
the flashlight pointing at us, getting closer and closer, balancing on the
rungs of the ladder, my uncle's face, dirt on his ears, filling the window,
something that looked like a cockroach leaping off his neck, soot on his
lapels, a shirt button caught on a hook, my grandmother turned to me
again silently before she started to tend to Mickey Mouse, brushing off
the leaves, insects and dirt, sewing up his injured back, replacing his sick
eyes with old coins, handing him back to me, her head nodding toward
the window

— Don't even think of it

I thought I'd keep her from adding to my criminal record, consisting
of one or two lies on page one, also I'd aimed a kick at a cat once but
didn't even make contact, and ate a third of a bag of vanilla cookies with
strawberry filling, I wanted to convince her it wasn't true, climb onto her
lap, talk to her about what I didn't want to talk about without needing
sentences, fall asleep on her lap that night, for example, when I'd never
been so beautiful, Elizabeth bowled over, the manicurist bowled over, the
mirrors bowled over, my new blouse, my authentic pearls, my underwire
brassiere, a young girl of eighteen, if that, never did she see even a hint of
a wrinkle, not one sign of aging, ease the tension her medicine couldn't
ward off, protect her from the sulfurous-tasting drips, from the white
blood cells, from sitting alone at the kitchen table in the middle of the
night, her breathing troubled as she stared at the little hole between the
tiles into which the ants scurried and, before getting us out of bed again,
the exaggerated silence of feigned sleep, the purplish circles under her
eyes, her weight loss, weak stomach muscles creating an apron of skin

under her apron, after a few months, the heat, flies, handkerchief covering her face, a clean body's smell of starch and vinegar, no difficulty in breathing, no complications with her white blood cells, my sister-in-

— You're not going to cry are you?

sister-in-law lifting a corner of the handkerchief with the cautiousness of someone lifting the lid off a pan to check on the stew

— So peaceful gentlemen

men, their cigarettes hidden behind their fingers, taking guilt-ridden drags, my uncle, who didn't live with us anymore, knowing nothing about it, my father, wearing two different-colored socks, all over the living room sniffing out fear, surprise, my gorilla leaned its head on mine in moldy-smelling consolation, I went into my parents' bedroom, now that there was no one to look after me, to play with the pharaoh and my husband accidentally putting the scorpion bottle down between my hairbrush and checks, closing the purse on his second try in an embarrassed hurry that made me feel sorry for him and for me

no, just for him because I'm so beautiful tonight

— I thought you might have some cigarettes Celina

sorry only for him since I feel like singing, I left the display cases lit, I'm not entirely sure but I think I left lights on throughout the apartment so that tomorrow dona Alice will understand how happy I am, I left a tray with a bottle and glass on the dining room table so she'll drink to me, although unfortunately I doubt she'll do that, she'll think I drew a line on the label to trick her, a test, her employer trying to find out whether or not she's honest like when I forget money on top of the copper plate or leave letters unopened on the mail table, feeling sorry for my husband, for my cleaning lady, sorry my grandmother and my uncle can't see me today, in no time at all the deaf woman's house, the hopes from Madrid, the driver in the pine woods, Elizabeth's and the manicurist's mouths far too round, quiet, for them not to be telling the truth, the receptionist at the cash register forgetting her bitterness and kidneys

— Dona Alice you won't take offense if I say how pretty you are?

the dead gorilla, the dead bears, dead Mickey Mouse, the terracotta pharaoh ended up breaking and we threw it in the trash

(now I'm remembering a plaster walrus, and less clearly, further back in time, a tulip frozen inside a glass sphere)

the well between the buildings containing my past, climb down to the second floor on a borrowed ladder and get it, the bicycles in Campo Grande park, fishing on Sundays, acrobats at the circus, those blonde strands my mother hated so much, thread the needle

(I can still do it without glasses, it takes me longer, I miss once or twice, but on the third try I get the thread through)

sewing up the tears that meanness and old age go through, rainy afternoons, the chin trembling on its own, no one's done anything

I'm not going to cry, don't worry, I'm not going to cry, I'm feeling so good now, if you don't believe me then ask the men in the street, we'd go out together, I came up to your thigh, I'd hold on tight to your hand, afraid of the boys constantly talking to you, green animals secreting birdlime, soles chasing us, suddenly stopping, an old man on a bench staring at us over the knob of his cane and now

sorry

I have to find a taxi because they're expecting me at the house between Lisbon and Sintra, the general and the commander, the bishop and his goddaughter, the deaf woman's husband, people you don't know, don't know who they are, I didn't get the chance to introduce them to you, I'm the only one missing to start the gathering, a supper, colleagues getting together, not including the two out in the pine woods helping me out with a favor I asked of them, if you want to have a better look at the blouse, I can face you, or stand in profile, turning my back, I'll go down the hall and back so you can see my walk, my pearls, make-up, loose hairstyle, my purse with the little silver chain to go with my coat, this aroma of cool shadow beneath a stone arch that young people have even when they don't wear perfume, go ahead, tell me if you can spot a single wrinkle, a bad night's sleep, any sign of aging, just look how light we are when we're happy, you didn't notice Mickey Mouse

— You're so pretty Celina

for once in his life sincere, just imagine, the stuffed animal didn't like you, you have no idea how many tales he made up about you, the incredible lies he'd whisper to me, for example that one afternoon in your room, when father was at work and grandmother was at the doctor's to see to the white blood cells that ended up seeing to her, it wasn't two strangers in that film that played so quickly, in the streaks, the scratches, it was my mother and uncle, think how awful, it was my mother and uncle and now, if you don't mind, instead of a kiss, just smile at me like I smile on the stairs on the way to catch a taxi, not a shabby smile, not a wavering grimace, not a cheek muscle sagging, sagging, come to the window say goodbye and smile, don't stop smiling till you get in the taxi, till the automobile has rounded the corner, till there's nothing more left of me than

(let's say)

a bus ticket, maybe a palindrome, that a breeze from the veranda sends away, out and about, with no destination.

32

Dear Gisélia,

it turns out it'll be five or six months before we make it to Espinho: the colonel from the Spanish Civil Guard suggested we stick around here till they prove the ordeal at the house

(I don't know if you remember the house between Sintra and Lisbon that blew up a while ago, it was all over the newspapers, it's all the radio reported for days on end)

till they prove the ordeal at the house was just a bad accident, maybe the owner stored bombs there, no one knows why, and during a get-to-gether with friends someone was careless with a match either that or, to my way of thinking, there weren't any bombs at all, except in the newspapers' imagination, in order to get more readers, in order for radio stations to get more advertising, it was probably a gas cylinder, those newfangled things, the kind that don't smell so you don't notice when they're defective and make tragedies easy to happen, all you've got to do is turn on the stove burner innocently and there you have it, bang, a burst of flames and the entire neighborhood burns down, I heard there were half a dozen corpses inside, as one tabloid said

(to think just how bad gossip can get)

they'd been part of a group trying to bring back the dictatorship, a group that went after democrats and other good people

(democrats!)

with machineguns, gasoline, homemade bombs, photographs of the criminals on the first page of the newspapers, an army officer, a navy officer, a hotel owner, and women too, a socialist daily hinted there was also a bishop, the church denied it right off, furious at the outrage, listing previous horrible atheist slanders against God and family, the Catholics, indignant at Sunday mass, and they're right, provincial newspapers demanded apologies, the socialist daily backed down with some vague article praising the Pope's anti-capitalist attitude and then

(and this hurts)

my boyfriend's photograph was also on the first page where they called him

(this is completely nuts)

the presumed perpetrator of the crime, I had to read it twice before I even understood the words, they claimed the minister's airplane, the bullfight ring, the priest's automobile, you of all people, since you know him so well, must have died laughing, a shrimp, a timid guy who was even afraid of my parents, who wouldn't hurt a fly, who never even uttered a word around you guys, his little hands in his pocket, looking down, never talked, never argued, never picked a fight, your fiancé was always messing with him and the poor guy would keep quiet, they'd put wasps in his beer and he'd just take them out, they'd ram into him and he'd say sorry, Benilde pretending she had a crush on him, running her hand over his face

(I don't know if you remember)

and he, lost and scared, even with me he was always careful, respectful, gentle, never getting too close, that kind of shyness poor people have, for him to be presumed perpetrator is, at the very least, funny, the colonel of the Spanish Civil Guard, a kind-hearted man, out of charity got us a room near the ocean in A Coruña, it rains all day long, grey seagulls, people just like us on old run-down streets, and now, just like he himself said, truth and olive oil always rise to the surface, be patient, wait for things to calm down, as he himself says, although I'm not sure, as he himself used to say, because we never saw him again, he left us a few pesetas

(wherever they've gone)

and went back to Madrid without ever sending a letter, or calling, not even the slightest sign of any interest, we cook in our room, almost never go downstairs, you can never tell with the communists, you never know if someone's out there in the rain, the seagulls, they told me the army in Lisbon were bothering my parents with questions, they searched their apartment for detonators, pistols, letters, a sergeant found a clown nose in a drawer, one of those carnival accessories we used to play with, showed it to the lieutenant and the lieutenant

— We've got it

they ripped open the mattresses with scissors and knives, sliced through the pillows, messed up the pantry, my father with his napkin around his neck on account of his stroke, one child's hand, one gigantic hand, my mother got really agitated and forgot his medicine and chicken soup, the soldiers' jeeps blocked the traffic, a bunch of curious neighbors were dumbstruck, the tangerines on the windowsill, the tea cart, I keep thinking that if only I'd followed your advice and forget about passion

(— Have you noticed what he's like Simone?)

I'd be with you all now instead of here in this endless winter, my face pressed against the window all afternoon, every afternoon longing for the balls, watching you all dancing, sitting down next to me massaging your ankles, glowing, happy, your hairdos in a shambles

— You're so lucky to be sitting here resting

getting up again for a paso doble or a tango, the streamers, paper balloons, the club's founders framed on the walls, the starlets' feathers dropping on the platform, fluttering, leaving a vague smell, fur stoles trotting around in a rush, with the envelope of cash, off to another stage, another ball where more feathers, legs, more vague perfumes, the presumed perpetrator standing all the way at the end of the bar, not drinking his brandy, shoes with upturned toes, the awful combination of a checked jacket and striped pants, Fernanda

— Do you know that clown Simone?

a clown for sure, about to light the filter end of his cigarette, an unexpected flame, his expression changing, the cigarette tossed away, as horrified as if it'd been a live insect in a drink, the sorry looking eyes staring into the brandy, Benilde's smile as she pointed him out over a bouncing shoulder, you, checking your insoles for a pebble or a piece of leather that was hurting your heel and keeping you from the waltz, you showed me a tear in the sole of your really expensive stockings, when you saw the checked jacket leaning over his drink trying to get the cigarette out using his thumb and forefinger as tweezers

(rain on the windowsills, the lurching wind, the sheets always damp, the towels never dry, the tap water giving me diarrhea, I hate A Coruña)

holding your shoe, your hand inside, not finding the stone, or a piece of leather, whatever it was that was spoiling your waltz

— I don't see how they let losers like that in

the loser whom the radio and the newspapers had, on account of their readers and sponsors, suddenly turned into the presumed perpetrator, who would think an idiot who lights the wrong end of a cigarette could blow up houses, the deaf woman's and the Belgian engineer's, I think he was Belgian, also blown up, the dogs with the blonde eyebrows floating in the pool, some hidden shacks now missing their walls, piles of ashes and sobbing survivors, firemen's lanterns circling rooftops, a shaken minister taking in votes and tears, dark interiors, basins, holes, refrigerators torn apart, stretchers and IV balloons on their way to Sintra, the Belgian engineer interviewed in an exclusive, direct broadcast from Brussels, speaking Portuguese like dented wheels running over each other, the presumed perpetrator

(or clown, if you prefer)

lying on the mattress in the garage, empty tires, soot, the oak branch still scratching against the little window, in A Coruña, waves blending into the rain, blurry through the mist and cold, never any letters, not one postcard, no voice over the telephone, the fellow two doors down who

works in a restaurant, scolding his son, the clown started coming with
us on outings to the esplanade at Belém on Sundays, we'd get there and
he'd be on the other side of the lawn waiting for us, cloudy shadows up
in the sky, not like Lisbon where people don't walk, they float, the clown
like a lost sheep, thinking he was being spied on, windows and balconies,
so at the mercy of strangers and the helps' contempt

(presumed perpetrator can you believe it Gisélia?)

humbly waiting for the bosses' orders, meaning you guys, left out of
conversations, adventures he wasn't part of, dinners he wouldn't be invited
to, people he didn't know, not only at the mercy of the orders and the
teasing, but thankful, accepting, laughing at jokes he didn't understand,
thinking we were all so interesting, agreeing to everything, quiet, malleable, loyal, easy, imitating the way your boyfriend would cross his legs,
the way Fernanda's fiancé would lean back in his chair, the way the two
of them would make fun of women at other tables, even though he knew
his lowly position kept him from making fun of anyone, embarrassedly
scratching his cheek, slowly, hesitating, you could almost already see his
future, rented hiding place, his suitcase on the bed, two shirts, dispos-
able razors, the weekly bath, the caretaker job at some useless office you'd
barely notice between a pawnbroker's and a closed-down hairdresser's,
one of those offices where slow pointless papers pass from one rubber
stamp to the next, you could picture his family, granite rooms above
some animal pen, in the provinces or on the outskirts of north Lisbon,
unfinished buildings, children with bottles in the fountain at city hall,
a bunch of boring jobs, cash in a metal box hidden in the sheets, and
that night at the ball, I was sitting in the chair that was too small for me
just as lonely as he was, my purse on my knees, my dress sewn from one
of my mother's, missing the satin and, with that, the poor fellow's arm
trembling at my back, legs unable to find the music, the other couples
angry we kept bumping into them, our hands, clammy and limp, damper
and damper the more we tried to come up with some sentence, anything
at all, our way too serious faces, looking like we were drowning, the
clarinets and trumpets playing in unison, my huge body knocking him
over, our cheeks rubbing against each other, quickly separating, Fernanda
scandalized and her mouth

— What's going on?

Benilda scandalized and her mouth

— Simone

it was impossible, my little silver ring wasn't digging into him as he gripped my hand, mute clarinets, mute trumpets, only the two of us left on the dance floor swaying ridiculously, the open window was moving the streamers back and forth, it was already very late, suddenly so late, windy outside, our thin coats, the clown's steps twenty meters away from us, your boyfriend

dear Gisélia

— What do you want?

and the clown's steps thirty meters away from us, his checked coat and striped pants staying out of the street lights, Benilde

—Look at the bat Simone

my mother checking him out, bitter and harsh, half of my father bristling, angry, the presumed perpetrator fading into an alcove, wishing he didn't even exist, the café in Espinho, future riches, my mother and father, they could come live with us, the giant's wrist shaking harder and, even so, there were still five or six months to go before we'd get to Espinho, that's what the Spanish Civil Guard officer said, but he never came back to visit us, the time it would take to prove the explosion was a really gas accident, one of these modern products, meanwhile this rain, this room, last week I called my mother and no one answered, the ringing was choking in the empty apartment, you could tell by the echo there wasn't any furniture, the army took it all or else my father had died and my mother had gone to Tomar get over it, to a cousin's, all I remember about Tomar is a river but I can't remember the name, a slanted room, I fell asleep, so bored, lulled by a couple of voices retelling memories, the day my grandfather was in the hospital, the previous day, the day when we, memories following one after the other tumbling onto the floor, lightness like disoriented dead butterflies, lunches salty with underlying grief and withered years, the rain in Galicia and the clown in the checkered coat and striped pants setting up an alarm clock and tubes on the little table he won't let me touch in our room, making who knows what and talking about the pine woods between Sintra and Lisbon

(the van waiting on the mulberry trail)

from where you could see a roof, an oak tree, flowerbeds thick with nards, the bodies in the newspaper reports wandering behind the curtains, one of the women

(the newspapers described the women)

searching through the dry pine needles for the presumed perpetrator's flashlight, among tree trunks and disturbed owls, maybe it was the widow, later the radio ended up completely absorbed in details about her, everything her maid said, the lighted display cases, the opened bottles mixing perfumes, a stack of formal dresses piled on her bedspread, the farewell note written on the pad left on top of the microwave usually used for messages and three months' salary on the plate where she'd always left money, Dona Alice, thank God, I don't need anything, leave everything as it is and drink a little whiskey to my health, one of the women who, from what the station said, was our accomplice

(our

Gisélia

I, in the pine woods in the middle of the night, as afraid as I am of insects and snakes, can you believe it?)

they spent nearly an hour of the sponsor's time on stupid craziness having to do with stuffed animals, fishing on riverbanks, bicycle rides in Campo Grande park with some missing uncle, my boyfriend, excuse me, the clown, making who knows what, attaching yellow and blue wires to the hands of the alarm clock, joining them to tubes I'm not supposed to touch, he'd carry them from the brief case to the table so slowly and carefully, when he hid the briefcase he wrapped it in towels, then it was the television's turn, challenging the radio, saying the deaf woman, a friend of the other woman with the stuffed animals, who lived at the house and was probably the leader of the group, disguised in an orange wig to fool the army, the man in the denim outfit who called himself the gardener and claimed he worked for her

(on the screen his face was blacked out to prevent the presumed perpetrator from taking revenge)

swore she spent the afternoons in a chair on the terrace guarded by the ex-policemen, on Thursdays she'd go out, on the pretext she was sick, to choose targets, victims, or to buy weapons from the former secret service or from the Americans or Persians, no one ever saw her family, no one ever visited, one of the maids had told him that she'd shut herself in her room concocting poisons from coffee and sugar, the day after the dance the clown planted himself opposite my window, when I lifted the blinds he didn't even smile, he hadn't changed clothes, he hadn't changed his tie, his eyes were that purplish tone so you could tell he hadn't slept, even though he didn't want to, your boyfriend said he could spend time with us at the Belém esplanade, his obedient, thankful, bland manners, he always agreed to sit on the dirtiest bench in the windiest spot, he'd offer cigarettes, dig through his wallet to pay the bill, it would come and he'd grab it, wanting to be liked, not just a clown, a harmless fellow, didn't make one move on me, not a single compliment, kiss, or invitation whispered in my ear, maybe because by then he was already working on the alarm clocks and tubes, then one Saturday out of the blue, April twentieth

— Tomorrow you're coming with me

you suspected something

— What did he say Simone?

I, heading to over to the van

— Nothing

my mother, seeing us with the bag

— Where do you think you're going?

my father searching for words inside the napkin tied around his neck,

his shoes nervous, his knees awkward, the two sides of his mouth fighting spit trying to put a speech together, something that made sense, an
order, a firm sentence that I'd hear, near the tea cart in obedient silence,
my mother, triumphant, the clown sent off with one monstrous finger
showing him to the stairs, my father's lips twisting over his spoon of
chicken soup, his round right eye, reached out to me, wavered, drew
back, losing interest in me, turning back inside, wondering, I suppose
there were voices down there, scraps from when I was a kid, clouds over
shoulders, my grandmother calling him, didn't seem at all like a request,
an order, the usual

— Daughter

his lips tight over his soup spoon, the complex movements of his
Adam's apple, him trying to swallow, a little drool with grains of rice
running down his neck, my bag jumping down the stairs

(the presumed perpetrator couldn't lift it)

my mother caught between the letters the lazy mailman had left on
the doormat and the van waiting in the street, you who lived almost right
next door, in your curlers, holding your hairdryer

(the price tag dragging on the sidewalk)

— Simone

and now A Coruña, this room, seagulls and waves, you should have
called me more loudly

— Simone

and not let me go, made your boyfriend scare the clown off

— What do you want?

turning back with me and the bag toward the house where my mother
was picking the envelopes up off the doormat, her arm reaching out so
she could read them, the van going down the hill alone, heading toward

a future I couldn't know anything about, the mattress in the garage, the bullring, the priest's automobile, waiting in the bushes for the widow's husband, gas poured all over cellars, the piles, bones on the hillside, the weekly's speculations that had no basis whatsoever, to be back home and go to all the dances with you, massage your ankles during the breaks

— You're so lucky to be here resting

glowing, happy, your hairdos in a shambles, fanning away your exhaustion with the entrance ticket that sent waves of cologne in my direction, then I'd be perfumed too, not as strong as the cologne the starlets wore, which made me want to lie right down in it, but a sweet absence that helped me dream of aluminum window frames, seamstress jobs, boating vacations to Morocco, going with you all to the movies standing by myself at the end of the line with no partner, always sitting furthest off to the edge so the actors and actresses seemed to overlap each other and it was hard to read the subtitles, the curtain over the exit let cold seep down my neck and the loudspeaker yelled mushy dialogues into my ear that kept me from sleeping, Fernanda would ask her fiancé for his handkerchief, easier for her to work up the tears, Benilde would console herself buried in some collar, a new one every month, you'd always ask me

— Didn't you cry Simone?

drying yourself off on your sleeve, you'd come back to us from happy sorrow, from some far-off place where you felt good being scared, worried, suffering, you thought I was strange with my dry eyes, unchanged mood, and that I didn't care about the future of the poor countess whom the millionaire, injured in the war, had taken as his nurse, and in spite of that

(people are so foolish)

was about to get married

(his blind friend, overflowing with kindness, who never let him make one false move, brought him back to reason with the authority of his illness) and in spite of that, the fellow with the war injury was about to marry the twisted tricky blonde garbed in leopard print, sugary sweet in front of him and horrible behind his back she only wanted his money and his tobacco plantations, when the rich man, even though he was still young, was getting around in a wheelchair and the doctor didn't know whether or not he'd ever walk again, the blonde to the countess

— All I want is his money

the countess couldn't answer and meanwhile the blind friend, who was entering the room right at that moment luckily heard everything, Fernanda kept clutching her fiancé's handkerchief till she finally found a lipstick mark

(she didn't wear lipstick)

was explaining that playing hard to get will whet men's interest, the millionaire by now cured in spite of the terrible doctor, was seeking out the countess in a humble garret, no bell, just two velvety notes

(plim plim)

and no sign of the countess, Benilda, hiding her eyes leaning into the current collar, stayed there with the encouragement of fingers unfastening hooks, heading towards her lace

— I can't even watch you all tell me later how it ends

the countess lying face down on the bed murmuring

— Leave me alone

and blowing little kisses toward the door, the countess's white cat, very intelligent, recognizing the millionaire with its feline instinct, lifted his little snout

(substantial applause from the audience)

lowered it

(the frowning audience sighed in collective pain)

raised it again and trotted over to the door

(the audience was divided between hope and fear, Fernanda, her hands held in prayer, on the edge of her seat

— Oh dear God

people in the first rows on their feet waving their arms)

the cat, his tail like raised like an antenna, was rubbing up against the door jamb trying to get the countess's attention, close-up of the blue-eyed millionaire madly in love, close-up of the countess listening for advice from her blind friend, who'd died in the meantime of something unknown and incurable, encouraging her, still wearing his dark glasses, from the celestial zones where he now lived, still in his immaculate suit and echoing murmurs, close-up of the millionaire giving up on the door-bell, heading, disappointed, back down the stairs leading out to the street, close-up of the countess, first in a crazed inner struggle and finally

(Benilde emerging from the collar in near cardiac arrest

— I'm going to have an attack I bet I'm having an attack)

agreeing with her blind friend who

(mission accomplished)

had dissolved into smoke, reuniting with the angels, she was fanning the bed, which by the way was huge and, although modest, was decorated with a golden headboard, she then nearly knocked over the crystal lamp with the family crest, dashing toward the velvety notes with so much enthusiasm that her skirt hiked up over her waist

(the panting audience didn't even notice her legs, an insensitive clod tried to whistle from way in back with most of the audience wheeling toward him about to tear him apart for his lack of respect) she appeared on the landing lit by wall lamps with silk shades, firm, her nostrils flaring and her red hair still perfectly coiffed, the cat jumped onto the millionaire, half way down the stairs wearing a suit that showed off his weightlifter's body, close up of the millionaire caressing the cat and looking up, close-up of the smile with perfect teeth

(Fernanda pushing her fiancé away, caught up in the smile

— There should be a law against men like that)

close-up of the countess opening her arms, encased in elbow-length gloves, the camera panning back, one of them descending the stairs as other ascended, still holding the cat, the long gloves around the actor's neck

(it wasn't an actor it was life)

close-up of the crystal lamp, including the family crest, its crown gradually lit red and getting bigger and bigger until it filled the screen along with the words The End, the lights came up, tiny normal faces, ugly, emotional, the same size as mine, theater lights, some of them burned out, wrinkling our skin, the ticket lady slathering mosquito repellent on her forehead, the lady selling cakes and cold drinks next to the posters advertising future movies, coughing into her apron, floorboards showing through the threadbare carpet, a bird fallen from a tree like an eye meeting another eye, rusty enclosed verandas off buildings, bare mulberry trees, badly dressed men taking pickaxes to the streets, an alarming blind man, earthbound, entirely lacking in kindness, gropingly storing his guitar back in its case, everything old, gloomy, dull, you whispering in my ear, drying your cheeks

— Didn't you cry Simone?

even more grey and worn

(sorry)

than I'd imagined, the vast world of movies narrowed down into a reality of mended linens and clothes that take forever to dry just like this

endless rain, these five or six months between me and Espinho, just like
I'm taking forever to finish this letter, just like the clown

(isn't that what you call him, called him, call him?)

if he takes too long working at the little table in the bedroom with the
alarm clock, the tubes, adjusting the hands to some random time, two
thirteen, six twenty, five nineteen, it doesn't matter, one screw after the
next and now first the yellow wire, next the green wire, the top sealed,
the box in the closet, writing your name

(dear Gisélia)

on paper till I don't know if it's you, if it's me, I can't tell which of us
is talking to the other, which of the two of us we are, who's looking out
the window at night, who's setting off the detonator in the pine woods,
the scary owls, the scary silence afterwards, and the van headlights rum-
bling down the hill

(a bush, a veranda, an intersection, a hint of lights)

on the road to Spain, you're so lucky you can rest, so far away from
the seagulls, waves, the fear of falling asleep, the widow's eyes waiting
there telling me yes, you should have called me sooner

— Simone

for me to massage your ankles between dances, you should have kept
me away from the oak tree and the garage, the lonely pillow like a great
big teardrop, you'd talk with me, help me, invite me to the Belém esplanade on Sundays, my mother never questions me when I go out with
you, my father doesn't push his sentences out one side of his mouth,
which finally give up, fall silent, his shoes stop moving, his knees rest,
there aren't any grains of rice dribbling down his neck, I even managed to
hide a photograph of the two of us in my bag, but it got lost or else the
presumed perpetrator, who never liked you, tore it up behind my back,
we're friends aren't we never mind all that stuff the radio and newspapers
made up, that magazine where I'm in a picture between the general and
the deaf woman in the wig

(a general and a deaf woman they claim, don't believe it)

the ex-policemen, the widow, the commander, lies working away, complicated scheming, just like in a novel, the radio broadcasting news, ploys to attract more sponsors, keeping me away from my café, Friday variety shows, the starlets changing their outfits in my room and me finding sequins on the rug the next day, a garter hook, a pink feather resting on my pillow, why do I have to put up with the newspapers being against me, all the anger, the resentment, if I could only explain who I am, that I have to take medicine for my glands, make them understand how unimportant I am except for massaging your ankles at the balls, that I sit at the very edge of the row when we go to the movies, always at an angle from the screen so it seems like the actors overlap with each other, and it's impossible to read the subtitles, the exit curtain letting cold seep down my neck, the loud speakers blasting out sappy dialogues that kept me awake, in A Coruña if there's ever even a sliver of sunshine it immediately hides deep in the trees like some nervous Eskimo, you can tell the leaves rustling, filled with doubt and worry, among the branches you see a glimmer of fearful light and then it rains again, since we don't have lights we use a flashlight and we see furniture propped up with pieces of cardboard, carvings in the coat tree and on the back of the chair, piano music making the world even sadder

(tell me honestly if you think there's anything sadder than piano music on a rainy afternoon, it always makes me think of a little girl in braids among stopped clocks, an aunt in mourning, silk-embroidered pillows on a wobbly little sofa)

piano scales coming from somewhere in the building, a child's fingers hitting the wrong keys, a little girl in braids and woolen stockings, no, a little nearsighted boy in shorts wearing glasses, the aunt in mourning, the smell of lemon verbena, a relative in a hospital bed, the sun arching out from behind a tree, giving up, disappearing, beyond the corner a ribbon of ocean hidden behind houses, fishing ships, invisible trawlers, a locomotive or liner shivering, drowning, I'm at the bottom of the page

dear Gisélia

and I'm finishing this letter, the point of the pencil has gone blunt again so I can't write long goodbyes, wishing you good health, sending hugs, another couple of paragraphs about the esplanade at Belém, greetings to Benilde and Fernanda who'll listen without paying much attention, sucking on orange slices from their soft drinks, thinking about you all back home, your boyfriends, kisses, the phone call a little later, Catita waiting for you outside, you scaring away his enthusiasm with your shoe, getting your knees away from him in roughhousing panic

— Let me go let me go

the vertical piano where your sister in braids, between stopped clocks, no, your near-sighted brother wearing shorts hitting the wrong keys, the aunt in mourning, silk-embroidered pillows on a wobbly sofa, the flower patterned lampshade blinking at each note fluttering reflections, I'm asking you to believe me when I promise there were no generals, no commanders, no deaf women or widows peeking out at the pine woods, no house, no bombs and no presumed perpetrator, I'm begging you to ignore the newspapers and the radio

(the readers the sponsors)

and we're still friends, you've known me since school, we're neighbors, I stole money from my mother so you could buy the coral earrings, just like I'm begging you

(don't get offended)

to tell your brother to stop playing the piano, lay the felt cloth over the keys, close the lid, and keep himself busy with a picture book on the little wobbly sofa because even just now the clown

(as you call him)

or the presumed perpetrator

(the newspapers' choice)

just got the box out of the closet, took off the top, examined the tubes, the screws, wires, the little detonator handle the presses the coils, looked out at the waves, shook his head at the miserable room, the furniture propped up with cardboard wedges, the sad music coming from somewhere in the building, please understand it has nothing to do with you, it's not at all personal, I didn't mean to hurt your feelings, I would never have let twenty years together end up like this, it's the piano, you understand, and that we're already out of money, that we've lost the café, there's no more Espinho, it's the world of sadness and so

(what choice do we have right tell me what choice do we have)

if the piano doesn't stop we'll move the lever finally connecting the coils and you won't even notice the bang, you'll notice the silence, I promise, all you'll notice is the silence, it doesn't hurt, you won't suffer at all or maybe not even silence, you'll notice

(before you notice anything at all, before everything stops bothering you, irritating you)

the branches waving, the wind through the branches and maybe

(I'll do whatever I can, whatever's possible, I can't promise)

a van heading down the hillside toward Galicia and in your mailbox, among the ashes, rubble, flares, bricks, pieces of roof tiles, this loving letter addressed to you.

MICHAL AJVAZ, *The Golden Age*.
The Other City.

PIERRE ALBERT-BIROT, *Grabinoulor*.

YUZ ALESHKOVSKY, *Kangaroo*.

FELIPE ALFAU, *Chromos*.
Locos.

JOE AMATO, *Samuel Taylor's Last Night*.

IVAN ÂNGELO, *The Celebration*.
The Tower of Glass.

ANTÓNIO LOBO ANTUNES, *Knowledge of Hell*.
The Splendor of Portugal.

ALAIN ARIAS-MISSON, *Theatre of Incest*.

JOHN ASHBERY & JAMES SCHUYLER, *A Nest of Ninnies*.

ROBERT ASHLEY, *Perfect Lives*.

GABRIELA AVIGUR-ROTEM, *Heatwave and Crazy Birds*.

DJUNA BARNES, *Ladies Almanack*.
Ryder.

JOHN BARTH, *Letters*.
Sabbatical.

DONALD BARTHELME, *The King*.
Paradise.

SVETISLAV BASARA, *Chinese Letter*.

MIQUEL BAUÇÀ, *The Siege in the Room*.

RENÉ BELLETTO, *Dying*.

MAREK BIENCZYK, *Transparency*.

ANDREI BITOV, *Pushkin House*.

ANDREJ BLATNIK, *You Do Understand*.
Law of Desire.

LOUIS PAUL BOON, *Chapel Road*.
My Little War.
Summer in Termuren.

ROGER BOYLAN, *Killoyle*.

IGNÁCIO DE LOYOLA BRANDÃO, *Anonymous Celebrity*.
Zero.

BONNIE BREMSER, *Troia: Mexican Memoirs*.

CHRISTINE BROOKE-ROSE, *Amalgamemnon*.

BRIGID BROPHY, *In Transit*.
The Prancing Novelist.

GERALD L. BRUNS, *Modern Poetry and the Idea of Language*.

GABRIELLE BURTON, *Heartbreak Hotel*.

MICHEL BUTOR, *Degrees*.
Mobile.

G. CABRERA INFANTE, *Infante's Inferno*.
Three Trapped Tigers.

JULIETA CAMPOS, *The Fear of Losing Eurydice*.

ANNE CARSON, *Eros the Bittersweet*.

ORLY CASTEL-BLOOM, *Dolly City*.

LOUIS-FERDINAND CÉLINE, *North*.
Conversations with Professor Y.
London Bridge.

MARIE CHAIX, *The Laurels of Lake Constance*.

HUGO CHARTERIS, *The Tide Is Right*.

ERIC CHEVILLARD, *Demolishing Nisard*.
The Author and Me.

MARC CHOLODENKO, *Mordechai Schamz*.

JOSHUA COHEN, *Witz*.

EMILY HOLMES COLEMAN, *The Shutter of Snow*.

ERIC CHEVILLARD, *The Author and Me*.

ROBERT COOVER, *A Night at the Movies*.

STANLEY CRAWFORD, *Log of the S.S. The Mrs Unguentine*.
Some Instructions to My Wife.

RENÉ CREVEL, *Putting My Foot in It*.

RALPH CUSACK, *Cadenza*.

NICHOLAS DELBANCO, *Sherbrookes*.
The Count of Concord.

NIGEL DENNIS, *Cards of Identity*.

PETER DIMOCK, *A Short Rhetoric for Leaving the Family*.

ARIEL DORFMAN, *Konfidenz*.

COLEMAN DOWELL, *Island People*.
Too Much Flesh and Jabez.

ARKADII DRAGOMOSHCHENKO, *Dust*.

RIKKI DUCORNET, *Phosphor in Dreamland*.
The Complete Butcher's Tales.

RIKKI DUCORNET (cont.), *The Jade Cabinet.*
The Fountains of Neptune.

WILLIAM EASTLAKE, *The Bamboo Bed.*
Castle Keep.
Lyric of the Circle Heart.

JEAN ECHENOZ, *Chopin's Move.*

STANLEY ELKIN, *A Bad Man.*
Criers and Kibitzers, Kibitzers and Criers.
The Dick Gibson Show.
The Franchiser.
The Living End.
Mrs. Ted Bliss.

FRANÇOIS EMMANUEL, *Invitation to a Voyage.*

PAUL EMOND, *The Dance of a Sham.*

SALVADOR ESPRIU, *Ariadne in the Grotesque Labyrinth.*

LESLIE A. FIEDLER, *Love and Death in the American Novel.*

JUAN FILLOY, *Op Oloop.*

ANDY FITCH, *Pop Poetics.*

GUSTAVE FLAUBERT, *Bouvard and Pécuchet.*

KASS FLEISHER, *Talking out of School.*

JON FOSSE, *Aliss at the Fire.*
Melancholy.

FORD MADOX FORD, *The March of Literature.*

MAX FRISCH, *I'm Not Stiller.*
Man in the Holocene.

CARLOS FUENTES, *Christopher Unborn.*
Distant Relations.
Terra Nostra.
Where the Air Is Clear.

TAKEHIKO FUKUNAGA, *Flowers of Grass.*

WILLIAM GADDIS, JR., *The Recognitions.*

JANICE GALLOWAY, *Foreign Parts.*
The Trick Is to Keep Breathing.

WILLIAM H. GASS, *Life Sentences.*
The Tunnel.
The World Within the Word.
Willie Masters' Lonesome Wife.

GÉRARD GAVARRY, *Hoppla! 1 2 3.*

ETIENNE GILSON, *The Arts of the Beautiful.*
Forms and Substances in the Arts.

C. S. GISCOMBE, *Giscome Road.*
Here.

DOUGLAS GLOVER, *Bad News of the Heart.*

WITOLD GOMBROWICZ, *A Kind of Testament.*

PAULO EMÍLIO SALES GOMES, *P's Three Women.*

GEORGI GOSPODINOV, *Natural Novel.*

JUAN GOYTISOLO, *Count Julian.*
Juan the Landless.
Makbara.
Marks of Identity.

HENRY GREEN, *Blindness.*
Concluding.
Doting.
Nothing.

JACK GREEN, *Fire the Bastards!*

JIŘÍ GRUŠA, *The Questionnaire.*

MELA HARTWIG, *Am I a Redundant Human Being?*

JOHN HAWKES, *The Passion Artist.*
Whistlejacket.

ELIZABETH HEIGHWAY, ED., *Contemporary Georgian Fiction.*

AIDAN HIGGINS, *Balcony of Europe.*
Blind Man's Bluff.
Bornholm Night-Ferry.
Langrishe, Go Down.
Scenes from a Receding Past.

KEIZO HINO, *Isle of Dreams.*

KAZUSHI HOSAKA, *Plainsong.*

ALDOUS HUXLEY, *Antic Hay.*
Point Counter Point.
Those Barren Leaves.
Time Must Have a Stop.

NAOYUKI II, *The Shadow of a Blue Cat.*

DRAGO JANČAR, *The Tree with No Name.*

MIKHEIL JAVAKHISHVILI, *Kvachi.*

GERT JONKE, *The Distant Sound.*
Homage to Czerny.
The System of Vienna.

JACQUES JOUET, *Mountain R.*
  Savage.
  Upstaged.
MIEKO KANAI, *The Word Book.*
YORAM KANIUK, *Life on Sandpaper.*
ZURAB KARUMIDZE, *Dagny.*
JOHN KELLY, *From Out of the City.*
HUGH KENNER, *Flaubert, Joyce
  and Beckett: The Stoic Comedians.*
  Joyce's Voices.
DANILO KIŠ, *The Attic.*
  The Lute and the Scars.
  Psalm 44.
  A Tomb for Boris Davidovich.
ANITA KONKKA, *A Fool's Paradise.*
GEORGE KONRÁD, *The City Builder.*
TADEUSZ KONWICKI, *A Minor
  Apocalypse.*
  The Polish Complex.
ANNA KORDZAIA-SAMADASHVILI,
  Me, Margarita.
MENIS KOUMANDAREAS, *Koula.*
ELAINE KRAF, *The Princess of 72nd Street.*
JIM KRUSOE, *Iceland.*
AYSE KULIN, *Farewell: A Mansion in
  Occupied Istanbul.*
EMILIO LASCANO TEGUI, *On Elegance
  While Sleeping.*
ERIC LAURRENT, *Do Not Touch.*
VIOLETTE LEDUC, *La Bâtarde.*
EDOUARD LEVÉ, *Autoportrait.*
  Newspaper.
  Suicide.
  Works.
MARIO LEVI, *Istanbul Was a Fairy Tale.*
DEBORAH LEVY, *Billy and Girl.*
JOSÉ LEZAMA LIMA, *Paradiso.*
ROSA LIKSOM, *Dark Paradise.*
OSMAN LINS, *Avalovara.*
  The Queen of the Prisons of Greece.
FLORIAN LIPUŠ, *The Errors of Young Tjaž.*
GORDON LISH, *Peru.*
ALF MACLOCHLAINN, *Out of Focus.*
  Past Habitual.

The Corpus in the Library.
RON LOEWINSOHN, *Magnetic Field(s).*
YURI LOTMAN, *Non-Memoirs.*
D. KEITH MANO, *Take Five.*
MINA LOY, *Stories and Essays of Mina Loy.*
MICHELINE AHARONIAN MARCOM,
  A Brief History of Yes.
  The Mirror in the Well.
BEN MARCUS, *The Age of Wire and String.*
WALLACE MARKFIELD, *Teitlebaum's
  Window.*
DAVID MARKSON, *Reader's Block.*
  Wittgenstein's Mistress.
CAROLE MASO, *AVA.*
HISAKI MATSUURA, *Triangle.*
  LADISLAV MATEJKA & KRYSTYNA
  POMORSKA, EDS., *Readings in Russian
  Poetics: Formalist & Structuralist Views.*
HARRY MATHEWS, *Cigarettes.*
  The Conversions.
  The Human Country.
  The Journalist.
  My Life in CIA.
  Singular Pleasures.
  The Sinking of the Odradek.
  Stadium.
  Tlooth.
HISAKI MATSUURA, *Triangle.*
DONAL MCLAUGHLIN, *beheading the
  virgin mary, and other stories.*
JOSEPH MCELROY, *Night Soul and
  Other Stories.*
ABDELWAHAB MEDDEB, *Talismano.*
GERHARD MEIER, *Isle of the Dead.*
HERMAN MELVILLE, *The Confidence-
  Man.*
AMANDA MICHALOPOULOU, *I'd Like.*
STEVEN MILLHAUSER, *The Barnum
  Museum.*
  In the Penny Arcade.
RALPH J. MILLS, JR., *Essays on Poetry.*
MOMUS, *The Book of Jokes.*
CHRISTINE MONTALBETTI, *The Origin
  of Man.*
  Western.

NICHOLAS MOSLEY, *Accident.*
Assassins.
Catastrophe Practice.
A Garden of Trees.
Hopeful Monsters.
Imago Bird.
Inventing God.
Look at the Dark.
Metamorphosis.
Natalie Natalia.
Serpent.

WARREN MOTTE, *Fables of the Novel:*
French Fiction since 1990.
Fiction Now: The French Novel in the
21st Century.
Mirror Gazing.
Oulipo: A Primer of Potential Literature.

GERALD MURNANE, *Barley Patch.*
Inland.

YVES NAVARRE, *Our Share of Time.*
Sweet Tooth.

DOROTHY NELSON, *In Night's City.*
Tar and Feathers.

ESHKOL NEVO, *Homesick.*

WILFRIDO D. NOLLEDO, *But for*
the Lovers.

BORIS A. NOVAK, *The Master of*
Insomnia.

FLANN O'BRIEN, *At Swim-Two-Birds.*
The Best of Myles.
The Dalkey Archive.
The Hard Life.
The Poor Mouth.
The Third Policeman.

CLAUDE OLLIER, *The Mise-en-Scène.*
Wert and the Life Without End.

PATRIK OUŘEDNÍK, *Europeana.*
The Opportune Moment, 1855.

BORIS PAHOR, *Necropolis.*

FERNANDO DEL PASO, *News from*
the Empire.
Palinuro of Mexico.

ROBERT PINGET, *The Inquisitory.*
Mahu or The Material.
Trio.

MANUEL PUIG, *Betrayed by Rita*
Hayworth.

The Buenos Aires Affair.
Heartbreak Tango.

RAYMOND QUENEAU, *The Last Days.*
Odile.
Pierrot Mon Ami.
Saint Glinglin.

ANN QUIN, *Berg.*
Passages.
Three.
Tripticks.

ISHMAEL REED, *The Free-Lance*
Pallbearers.
The Last Days of Louisiana Red.
Ishmael Reed: The Plays.
Juice!
The Terrible Threes.
The Terrible Twos.
Yellow Back Radio Broke-Down.

JASIA REICHARDT, *15 Journeys Warsaw*
to London.

JOÃO UBALDO RIBEIRO, *House of the*
Fortunate Buddhas.

JEAN RICARDOU, *Place Names.*

RAINER MARIA RILKE,
The Notebooks of Malte Laurids Brigge.

JULIÁN RÍOS, *The House of Ulysses.*
Larva: A Midsummer Night's Babel.
Poundemonium.

ALAIN ROBBE-GRILLET, *Project for a*
Revolution in New York.
A Sentimental Novel.

AUGUSTO ROA BASTOS, *I the Supreme.*

DANIËL ROBBERECHTS, *Arriving in*
Avignon.

JEAN ROLIN, *The Explosion of the*
Radiator Hose.

OLIVIER ROLIN, *Hotel Crystal.*

ALIX CLEO ROUBAUD, *Alix's Journal.*

JACQUES ROUBAUD, *The Form of*
a City Changes Faster, Alas, Than the
Human Heart.
The Great Fire of London.
Hortense in Exile.
Hortense Is Abducted.
Mathematics: The Plurality of Worlds of
Lewis.
Some Thing Black.

RAYMOND ROUSSEL, *Impressions of Africa.*

VEDRANA RUDAN, *Night.*

PABLO M. RUIZ, *Four Cold Chapters on the Possibility of Literature.*

GERMAN SADULAEV, *The Maya Pill.*

TOMAŽ ŠALAMUN, *Soy Realidad.*

LYDIE SALVAYRE, *The Company of Ghosts.*
The Lecture.
The Power of Flies.

LUIS RAFAEL SÁNCHEZ, *Macho Camacho's Beat.*

SEVERO SARDUY, *Cobra & Maitreya.*

NATHALIE SARRAUTE, *Do You Hear Them?*
Martereau.
The Planetarium.

STIG SÆTERBAKKEN, *Siamese.*
Self-Control.
Through the Night.

ARNO SCHMIDT, *Collected Novellas.*
Collected Stories.
Nobodaddy's Children.
Two Novels.

ASAF SCHURR, *Motti.*

GAIL SCOTT, *My Paris.*

DAMION SEARLS, *What We Were Doing and Where We Were Going.*

JUNE AKERS SEESE,
Is This What Other Women Feel Too?

BERNARD SHARE, *Inish.*
Transit.

VIKTOR SHKLOVSKY, *Bowstring.*
Literature and Cinematography.
Theory of Prose.
Third Factory.
Zoo, or Letters Not about Love.

PIERRE SINIAC, *The Collaborators.*

KJERSTI A. SKOMSVOLD,
The Faster I Walk, the Smaller I Am.

JOSEF ŠKVORECKÝ, *The Engineer of Human Souls.*

GILBERT SORRENTINO, *Aberration of Starlight.*
Blue Pastoral.
Crystal Vision.

Imaginative Qualities of Actual Things.
Mulligan Stew. Red the Fiend.
Steelwork.
Under the Shadow.

MARKO SOSIČ, *Ballerina, Ballerina.*

ANDRZEJ STASIUK, *Dukla.*
Fado.

GERTRUDE STEIN, *The Making of Americans.*
A Novel of Thank You.

LARS SVENDSEN, *A Philosophy of Evil.*

PIOTR SZEWC, *Annihilation.*

GONÇALO M. TAVARES, *A Man: Klaus Klump.*
Jerusalem.
Learning to Pray in the Age of Technique.

LUCIAN DAN TEODOROVICI,
Our Circus Presents…

NIKANOR TERATOLOGEN, *Assisted Living.*

STEFAN THEMERSON, *Hobson's Island.*
The Mystery of the Sardine.
Tom Harris.

TAEKO TOMIOKA, *Building Waves.*

JOHN TOOMEY, *Sleepwalker.*

DUMITRU TSEPENEAG, *Hotel Europa.*
The Necessary Marriage.
Pigeon Post.
Vain Art of the Fugue.

ESTHER TUSQUETS, *Stranded.*

DUBRAVKA UGRESIC, *Lend Me Your Character.*
Thank You for Not Reading.

TOR ULVEN, *Replacement.*

MATI UNT, *Brecht at Night.*
Diary of a Blood Donor.
Things in the Night.

ÁLVARO URIBE & OLIVIA SEARS, EDS.,
Best of Contemporary Mexican Fiction.

ELOY URROZ, *Friction.*
The Obstacles.

LUISA VALENZUELA, *Dark Desires and the Others.*
He Who Searches.

PAUL VERHAEGHEN, *Omega Minor.*

BORIS VIAN, *Heartsnatcher.*

LLORENÇ VILLALONGA, *The Dolls'
Room.*

TOOMAS VINT, *An Unending Landscape.*

ORNELA VORPSI, *The Country Where No
One Ever Dies.*

AUSTRYN WAINHOUSE, *Hedyphagetica.*

CURTIS WHITE, *America's Magic
Mountain.*
The Idea of Home.
Memories of My Father Watching TV.
Requiem.

DIANE WILLIAMS,
Excitability: Selected Stories.
Romancer Erector.

DOUGLAS WOOLF, *Wall to Wall.*
Ya! & John-Juan.

JAY WRIGHT, *Polynomials and Pollen.*
The Presentable Art of Reading Absence.

PHILIP WYLIE, *Generation of Vipers.*

MARGUERITE YOUNG, *Angel in the
Forest.*
Miss MacIntosh, My Darling.

REYOUNG, *Unbabbling.*

VLADO ŽABOT, *The Succubus.*

ZORAN ŽIVKOVIĆ , *Hidden Camera.*

LOUIS ZUKOFSKY, *Collected Fiction.*

VITOMIL ZUPAN, *Minuet for Guitar.*

SCOTT ZWIREN, *God Head.*

AND MORE . . .